Kept Safe

by

Catherine Grove

Instagram: @catherinegrove_author

Twitter: @CGrove_author

Web site: catherinegroveauthor.ca

Catherine Grove, PO Box 499, Carp, Ontario K0A 1L0

Title: Kept Safe

Format: Perfect bound book

ISBN: 978-1-9992393-4-3

Description: Entitled woman and duty-bound British officer must adapt to marriage and culture, while navigating political intrigue, post-war of 1812, frontier, Upper Canada.

Publisher/Author: Catherine Grove

Coverpainting: Guy Burland Roberts (1896-1969), used with permission of Hillary family

Cover design: Samuelle Grove (Instagram: @samuellephotography)

Design and Production: Catherine Grove, Craig Macartney

Editor: Craig Macartney, Dynamic Writing, Saint Martins, New Brunswick

Printed in United States of America

Thank you, dear readers,

for travelling with me back in time

to meet these courageous women

who bravely accompanied men to war,

fought for freedom,

eked out farms in deep forest,

and rebuilt a war-torn Canada.

Thank you to Craig Macartney,

Mary K. McNeill,

my understanding family, and my supportive husband,

for patiently working with me.

This book is dedicated to

country wives and camp followers

whose names

are lost in time.

Significant participants:

Captain Wesley Bryson-officer of the British army, stationed in Canada for four years (since 1811), age 25.

Lady Olivia Fairworth (Libby)—ended an understanding with Captain Bryson five years earlier (1810), age 28.

Charles Eldenmont—brother-in-law of Lady Olivia Fairworth, husband of **Lady Charlotte Fairworth Eldenmont.**

Jane Blythe (nee Devon Montbriar)—**niece of Charles Eldenmont,** adopted daughter of Canadian Missionary **George Blythe.**

Daniel Fremont—heir to Eldenmont-Hurstmere Estate, arranged fiance of Lady Olivia Fairworth.

Leo Voisin—French trader, former voyageur. Husband of **Marie-Jeanne (**Kahnawake-Mohawk).

Jean Le Grand, Pierre Le Vieux—master freight voyageur, cook

Meg McGuire—owner of McGuire House Inn, Kingston, Ontario. Widow with five children, ages 5-14.

Lizzie McGuire—eldest daughter of Meg McGuire, age 14.

Rosetta George—African refugee from Virginia, age unknown (between 17 and 20).

Jenny Cowlie—washer woman and garrison midwife.

Major McTavish—garrison commander at Kingston, husband of **Mrs. McTavish.**

Mrs. Norton—Methodist missionary in Kingston.

Pierre Sabin—Montreal entrepreneur, age 30

Lieutenant Stephen Reed, Mrs. Violet Reed—British Officer, age 26, and wife.

Catherine Bayard—daughter of **Alfred Bayard**, American Loyalist entrepreneur

Sally and Ian Douglas—settler family, neighbours of Wesley Bryson. Oldest son, **Jamie**, age 13.

Annie/Anwaatin Nyaweh—daughter of an Anishinaabe elder, sister of **Joseph Nyaweh**

John Oneida—Six Nations warrior, British scout and translator, second husband of Anwaatin/Annie.

Private Ernest MacLaren—red-haired Presbyterian, Scot recruit, age 16.

Miss Isabelle Maxwell—sister of **Lieutenant Maxwell** and resident of York.

Mrs. Carter—landlady, wife of **Joshua Carter**, mother of **Samuel Smith Carter**.

Maggie Stewart—widow, approximate age 65, daughter of Scot trader and Anishinaabe woman.

Meena—Haudenosaunee healer from Quinte.

Busy—Wesley Bryson's cow. **Gizzy**—Wesley Bryson's wolf-dog.

Historical Characters referenced in this work of fiction:

Granny (Mary) Hoople—learned healing practices as a captive of Delawares, considered first 'doctor' of Stormont District, caring for both British and American wounded during war.

Mrs. John Stuart—elderly widow of **Reverend John Stuart**, mother of **Reverend George Stuart**.

Richard Cartwright—businessman, member of Provincial Executive Council, husband of **Magdalen Secord Cartwright**.

Laura Secord—Loyalist heroine of the War of 1812, walked 20 miles to warn the British military of impending American attack, wife of **James Secord**, sister-in-law of **Magdalen Secord Cartwright**.

General 'Red' George McDonnell—commander of Cornwall and Stormont District Fencibles.

Private Robert (Robbie) Harris—Barbadian recruit, 100th Regiment of the British Army, age 15.

Major Sir Francis Gore—Lieutenant Governor of Upper Canada (1806-11, 1815-17), on leave in England 1811-15.

General Sir Gordon Drummond—Canadian-born provisional Lieutenant Governor of Upper Canada (1813-14), Governor General of the British North America (1815-16).

Maria Hill—"Daughter of the Regiment", heroine of the War of 1812, battlefieldsurgeon's assistant, disregarded orders and followed husband's regiment (100th) through 2 campaigns at Niagara.

Catharine Adonwentishon Brant—Clan Matron of the Turtle Clan of the Mohawks, widowed third wife of Mohawk military and political leader **Joseph Brant**.

Reverend John Strachan—Conservative religious leader, educator, politician of Upper Canada.

Samuel Jarvis—age 23, son of Executive Council Member **William Jarvis**.

Levius Sherwood—elected legislative representative of Johnstown District, age 39.

Historical places—present day naming:

Newark—Niagara-on-the-Lake, Ontario.

York—Toronto, Ontario.

Billidore Rifts—submerged under the River Styx of the Rideau Canal Waterway.

Terms:

Anishinaabe—culturally and linguistically related indigenous people of eastern and northern Ontario, including: Ojibwe, Odawa, Potawatomi, Mississaugas, Nipissing, and Algonquin peoples.

Haudenosaunee—Iroquoian confederation of indigenous people of northeast North America, including the Six Nations: Mohawk, Oneida, Onondaga, Cayuga, Seneca, and Tuscarora. Other Iroquoian related nations include Creek, Cherokee, and Delaware peoples.

Sovereignty—The recognized authority of a nation or people to self-govern.

Kept Safe

Part I—Hope, Chapter 1

Hertfordshire, England (November, 1814)

Part II—Reunited, Chapters 2 to 20

Montreal Island, Lower Canada (late spring, 1815)

Part III—Awakened, Chapters 21 to 45

Cataraqui River, Upper Canada (early autumn, 1815)

Part IV—Unceded Strength, Chapters 46 to 74

York, Upper Canada (winter, 1816)

Part I—Hope

Hertfordshire, England (November, 1814)

—1—

"Why must you continue to repel Mr. Fremont's attentions?" Charlotte Eldenmont emitted an exasperated exhale. "The man has recently returned from the Indies, and is in want of settling down to wife and hearth. Your disinterest will drive his quest to other pastures."

Olivia looked past her sister's shoulder, through the window. Her brother-in-law, Charles Eldenmont, insisted his grounds be well manicured. All for show, she recognized, like the cold décor of this room, and their marriage.

"I hold no affection for the man. Neither he of me." She returned attention to Charlotte. "You desire I marry your husband's appointed heir simply because you failed to birth a son, and do not wish your home to be taken from you should you find yourself a widow."

Charlotte smoothed an imaginary crease in her skirt with a swift sweep of hand. "Insulting me changes nothing." She looked up, chin quivering, as the comb of a hen about to squawk. "Daniel Fremont is amiable and respectful of you." Her breath deepened. "Remember, dear sister, any endowment you had was spent ridding you of that tutor."

It was a familiar thrust, her older sister reminding her of an infatuation, more than four years past. Olivia tensed, anticipating her final twist.

"It took no convincing for that man to trade affection for the military commission we offered. That's how little you understand of these matters."

Olivia dipped her quill in the writing desk inkwell with practiced poise. "To whom else am I to write?" she answered.

1

"Reverent Haynes...and make mention of a donation to his Mariner's Mission." Charlotte sniffed. "Mrs. Haynes, poor dear, married beneath her station. She understands the situation and will dutifully chaperone to ensure no implication of impropriety."

The hallway door opened and their newly arrived Canadian cousin entered. Olivia set down her pen. Jane Blythe slowly walked the length of the sunny Morning Room. Born Devon Montbriar, Jane was the product of a scandalous elopement, a quarter of a century ago. Yet, she carried herself with confidence and a firm gaze, unashamed. Her movement had a strength Olivia had long ago suppressed.

Though the woman's wool dress was of out-dated style and her appearance unadorned, envy bubbled up within Olivia. How long would it take before Charlotte crushed this naïve Canadian's proud bearing?

"Pray, forgive my intruding," Jane Blythe curtsied. Her straight back revealed the apology merely form.

"I finally gain acquaintance of my dear niece." Charlotte smiled, with uncharacteristic affection. "Is your room satisfactory?"

"The room is most agreeable," she returned. "Thank you for welcoming me into your home, dear aunt."

Charlotte returned to dictating plans for a hunting party, to take place at her step-brother's estate of Albyn Abbey. Jane sat, hands folded in lap, giving occasional attentive nods to the discourse.

Was the woman aware she'd already been put forward to Charles Eldenmont's business partner, William Garnett, as a potential replacement for his recently deceased wife?

"I need no introduction to society, dear aunt," Jane amicably supplied, at the conclusion. "I only desire to be with family."

Was she so obtuse to think living under Charlotte's roof would come without cost? Jane glanced at her, a mere flinch of smile escaping, as though she had heard Olivia's thoughts.

In the presence of this Canadian, longing stirred. Dare she ask Jane if she had any acquaintance of a Lieutenant Bryson, posted somewhere in Canada? The colony was not so populous; surely Jane might have come across him. No, she must bide her time and glean what she could before making such an attempt. If hope lingered for another chance, she would abandon all and go to him.

"I fear I still carry an odour of the ship." Jane interrupted Olivia's thoughts, eyes twinkling. "Might I have a bath arranged?"

Charlotte tittered with condescension; Olivia immediately recognized Jane Blythe was no fool. The woman had taken inventory and was prepared to define her position in this house.

Envy eroded to fear. Jane would be a competitor for both sister and marital arrangements. She heaved a defeated sigh. Under God's good sun was it possible for women to stand together in goodwill?

Part II—Reunited

Montreal Island, Lower Canada (late spring, 1815)

—2—

Olivia Fairworth slipped off sabots, hiked up her skirts, and waded into the river until water reached above her knees. Small pebbles pressed into the soles of her feet. She ignored the pain. Her mind was on the river upstream.

On this hot July afternoon, without privacy and means to dry herself, she settled for splashing water about her face and neck. Scooping water up into her hand, she flicked a trickle down her back. Like a giddy girl, she shivered with pleasure.

At 28 years of age, she never thought such freedom would be possible.

Three weeks she had been waiting at *Notre Dame de Vieux Moulin*, on the shores of the Saint Lawrence—a month since writing the Kingston Garrison to inquire of him. This was time enough to consider the wisdom of her flight to Canada. The words of Wesley's cryptic message—*I have kept safe*—no longer seemed an invitation, but an accusation. She almost hoped he would not come for her; she almost feared it, too.

The great silence at *Notre Dame* was just as much comfort as the chants of Compline. Both brought order and stability to her troubled thoughts.

"Your concerns, I understand," Sister Superior soothed, assuming she was simply nervous about marriage. "You are like a King's Daughter and 'ave crossed the ocean for your 'usband."

"A princess?" Libby asked, curious at such a reference.

"*Non, ma fille.*" The matriarch tilted her head, revealing a smile within her wimple. "'Zee first men in New France tamed the land, but 'ad no wives to tame 'zem. So, our king sent a call for good Christian women to come from France, promising a dowry. 'Undreds

4

responded. My foremother came from the city of Rouen and knew nothing of—"

"Her family allowed this?" Olivia gasped.

Sister Superior patiently shook her head at the interruption—this Protestant knew no better. "She was an orphan, raised in a convent. All my grandfather's grandfather wanted in a wife was kindness, 'onesty, and affection."

"And they were happy?"

"Ten children speak for 'appiness," Sister Superior nodded. "Now go out and enjoy sunshine, my daughter, and don't worry. God will take care of you."

Doubt eroded Olivia's confidence; waiting has a way of doing that. She would not force marriage on him, as her family had sought to force on her. Perhaps Wessie could find her a position as governess with a prominent Montreal family. Her French was passable, her musical accomplishments middling, yet her stitchery was excellent. Even the sisters at the convent praised her work, lamenting that, as a Protestant, she was not permitted to work on their altar cloths.

"*Oy! Mademoiselle!*" a man shouted from out on the river.

She looked up at the silhouette of a large canoe on the shimmering water. Three men sat, paddles resting across the gunwales; two other canoes followed, farther out, traveling together for safety.

"*Oui, monsieur,*" she shouted back.

"*Est-ce que la couvent Vieux Moulin est 'ci proche?*"

Her heart leapt; she recognized his voice, and he was looking for the convent.

"Don't you know me, Wesley Bryson?"

He jumped into the waist-deep water and reached into the canoe for pack and boots. Swinging them over his shoulder, he bid '*Adieu*' to the canoe's occupants and approached her in silence. Water swirled around him in larger and larger eddies, until his movement caught

them both. It was good his voice was still familiar, for he looked a stranger wearing homespun and buckskin clothes, and with a full black beard.

"Libby?" He studied her with quick intensity. Reflected sunbeams danced across her face. Her youthful glow revealed a health he'd never seen in her before.

She let down her skirts, suddenly conscious. "I'm here, Wessie," she laughed nervously and turned back to the shore. He followed, distracted by wet skirts clinging to her pale legs. Fumbling for words, he found none.

At the beach, she offered her hand with a formal curtsy. He let his pack fall to the ground. Then he remembered, he was not here of his own choosing, but had been summoned to marry her. Anger infused his awkwardness. With a bow, he brushed lips across her hand, as would be expected.

Libby released his hand to shake out her wet skirts. His features hardened in the five years since she'd last seen him. War had changed him.

"Pray be honest, as a friend should." She went straight to the crux. "Is my coming to Canada of your desire?"

"You have rejected both our love and friendship, Libby," he honestly returned. "I gave my word to your family. Why did you come?"

"I've run from a marriage Charles forced on me."

"How am I to run from this one?" Wesley raised his hand to shield his eyes from the sun.

"You sent assurance of constancy through Devon Montbriar!" she shot back in proud defence.

"I should have kept my cursed mouth shut. I was paid to leave you alone."

"But you didn't," she groaned, with another brisk shake of her damp skirts. Turning away, she slipped on her sabots.

He looked downriver, where the canoes had gone. Then, sitting on a nearby boulder, he put on socks and boots.

"Pray forgive me for not respecting that I was paid to leave you alone." He breeched their silence. "You know I can sometimes be a loose cannon."

"Your shot landed." Her voice trembled. "I took hope with your message, Wesley." Inhaling deeply, she clenched her fists. Five years had passed since he had invaded her lonely world. When her family threatened his ruination, she'd no choice but to reject him.

"Hope?" Wesley picked up his sack and turned to her. "That I still might hold affection after you humiliated me?"

"If I mean nothing to you, then why are you here?" Her jaw jutted in challenge.

He'd forgotten her pride. Yet life had changed. He was now an ambitious entrepreneur and soldier; no longer their family tutor, nor subject to the will of her guardian, Charles Eldenmont. She would have to conform to his expectations.

"You've had banns published at Christ Church, in Montreal, and my commanding officer expects me to return with a wife," he declared, offering his arm. "I can't afford scandal, Olivia. You leave me no choice but to proceed into marriage."

"I've made a fine muddle, haven't I?"

"You'll have to live with it." He replied with quiet finality. "We'll both have to."

"Then I'll do my best to be a good wife," she soothed, gingerly slipping her hand within his arm. Despite his disposition, he treated her as a lady. Slowly they walked up the path to the convent.

"At seven bells, I'll come for you. Pray make necessary arrangements to be ready." Briefly touching lips to hand, he left her at the convent's large oak door.

Her heart quickened with hope and anticipation. "He's bitter towards me," she mused, stepping across the convent threshold, "because he's not indifferent."

—3—

Ten days had passed since her letter found Wesley Bryson. This should have been ample time to prepare for today. Never had he expected to see her again. And never had he anticipated the depth of her audacity.

I was a fool to think any affiance possible with you! It seemed only yesterday she'd hurled these words at him, in the garden at Hurstmere. Yet, five years later, after all had been decided, she'd followed him to Canada.

His trained military eye caught movement in a window of the convent's upper floor. Resisting giving her satisfaction, he did not glance back. He hadn't realized the depth of anger he still held. Had he lingered longer, he risked losing composure and incurring further regret. How easily Olivia Fairworth could unravel him!

He spat on the ground. Long-buried shame erupted as he remembered his naïve presumption of love between tutor and an earl's daughter. A military commission in the Canadian Colonies, paid by her brother-in-law, Charles Eldenmont, secured his riddance.

It had been nine months since he recognized the Niagara woman who had nursed and fed his men after the campaign at the Forty. He had offered her his berth, on a Kingston-bound ship, for she seemed desperate to flee Canada before winter fell. War had prepared him for unanticipated encounters—Americans cleverly disregarded European rules of engagement and civility. Yet, when he noted the Eldenmont seal on a letter she'd presented as argument, uncensored passion flared.

Sarcastically, he asked the woman to carry a message for him: "Tell Libby that I have kept safe that which she entrusted to me."

He'd given no specifics with this message. Yet, somehow, his intemperate quip had reached Olivia and she had instead construed it as invitation for marriage. Guilt flushed through him. Any implication of constancy was a sham.

In his Canadian exile he'd pursued fulfillment with new-found independence, confident that Olivia had been swiftly married off to further Eldenmont wealth and connections.

Meanwhile, he had been mentioned in dispatches, decorated, and had purchased a captaincy from fur-trade dabbling profits. He now aspired to a government appointment, hoping to recover from a naïve speculation in iron ore deposits.

Charles Eldenmont may have laid the threshold to success, but he'd walked through into opportunity, and gained wisdom. He'd be jiggered to allow that man further interference in his life, yet he had no choice but to marry her. She'd made that certain.

"She'll be Mrs. Bryson—a humble English bride," he pronounced aloud, regaining a measure of control.

Up the dusty road he strode, to the home of his sympathetic friend, Leo Voisin. Tonight, he would catch up on Montreal gossip, talk a little business, and glean of Leo's wisdom.

Fifteen years ago, *Le Vieux Lion*—the Old Lion—broke his leg portaging the Long Sault rapids of the *Grand Rivière*. Forced from a voyageur life of transporting furs and trade goods, Leo had married

Marie-Jeanne of the *Kahnawake* Mohawk people, and expanded into trading.

The *Kahnawake* openly traded with the Americans throughout the war, avoiding both North West Trading and Hudson's Bay monopolies. Now prosperous, Leo Voisin remained deceptively humble. Through their friendship, Wesley made good profits selling furs.

A warm greeting met him, as he entered the doorway. Children gathered and Marie-Jeanne kept bustling in the kitchen. A sixth child slept contentedly within a hammock, swung by Leo's occasional tug of a cord. In a corner rocking chair, an aged native woman snored, unlit clay pipe drooping from her lips.

"*La mère de ma belle-mère*—Marie-Jeanne's grandmother," Leo offered with an affectionate smile. "She was the healer who set my leg."

Marie-Jeanne placed platters of baked fish, roasted vegetables, and potatoes on the table. The old woman roused with a sharp snort, and they all gathered to eat. Chatter filled the air, seamlessly blending English, French, and Mohawk. Wesley ate heartily. At the conclusion of the feast, Marie-Jeanne set a large sugar pie before him. The children fell silent, anticipating his response.

"*Ma tarte favorie!*" His exclamation prompted a flood of giggles from the children, as he fulfilled an honoured role, portioning out the treat.

While the old woman cleared away the dishes and Marie-Jeanne replaced the baby's swaddling, Leo raced their children through Chaplet prayer.

"*Notre Père qui est aux cieux, que Votre nom soit sanctifié...*"

The old woman returned from the kitchen and pronounced a Mohawk blessing, before Leo shooed the children up to bed. A crucifix watched over the room; aromatic herbs smoldered in the fire, a reflection of Leo's earlier, simple life. The contrast with Olivia's palatial home of Hurstmere loomed. Life on his clearing would be difficult for her.

He heaved a deep sigh. Life with Olivia would be difficult for him.

Returning from upstairs, Leo lit his pipe and asked, "You're early for Christmas, *mon ami*. For what reason do I owe 'dis welcome visit?"

Wesley declined the offer of a pipe. The saga of his upcoming marriage spilled out, encouraged by Leo's occasional "Go on, my friend."

"She's robbed me of choice, Leo. What am I to do with her?" he concluded.

"Aha! The mystery of 'dat attractive h'English woman at the convent, is solved." Drawing deep from his pipe, Leo nodded at his wife. "What say ye, woman?"

In the tradition of the *Kahnawake*, Leo welcomed her voice. Marie-Jeanne rose to fill three goblets with brandy.

"We wait, *ma choix*," he prompted.

"She's bought thread from me and her stitch work is praised by the Good Sisters." She passed a goblet to her grandmother and another to Wesley. Pausing, she sipped from her husband's goblet, before handing it to him. "Her French is passable," her lips turned up mischievously.

"You made her speak French?" Wesley gulped.

"I speak whatever I want." She laughed lightly with a swish of her skirt. "From what I understand, a beautiful older woman has crossed an ocean for a crazy man."

"Crazy?" Wesley sat forward.

Leo snorted with a slap of his thigh. "*Mon Dieu*, Wesley—if you 'ave to ask what to do with a beautiful woman—*t'est vraiment fou*."

11

The old woman cackled, "Crazy Englisher asks what to do with a beautiful wife!"

Wesley's face warmed and he looked down, rubbing his forehead with his hand. "I mean...how should I...never mind." Waving his hand, he joined in their mirth.

"The Good Lord 'as sent 'er to you, Wesley. Make 'er your wife!" Leo affirmed, with a flare of his pipe and a nod at Marie-Jeanne. She sat on her husband's knee playfully roughing his hair. Their ease together, Wesley admired.

"And thank the Good Lord your previous arrangement has been resolved." She wagged a finger at Wesley. "Hearts will be broken in Montreal."

"Montreal has officers aplenty—I'll not be pined for." He set his empty goblet on the table. "I've arranged for Major Reverend Whitley to meet us half-way from Montreal, at Lachine. With war so recent, I must promptly return to Kingston. The additional nine miles to the city would be an unnecessary delay. And I know that Padre appreciates any excuse to get away fishing on the Lake. A chaplain's service is respectfully Christian enough for an earl's daughter."

"An earl's daughter? *Bien fait* and good night!" Marie-Jeanne helped her grandmother to her feet, then picked up the baby by the cradle board handle and they retreated up the stairs.

Leo leaned forward intently. "Talk is, your partner, Sabin, was busy at cards while in Montreal. I'm not sure 'e—"

"I know, I know..." Wesley acknowledged, biting his lower lip. "Pierre Sabin's willingness to gamble was why he agreed to my venture with Stephen Reed," he defended. "But our arrangement has ended and I'm the wiser. Iron ore is not easy money."

"*En-tout-cas...prends-garde, mon ami.* A man with debt can forget loyalties." Leo leaned back in his chair. "But I always remember mine. Tomorrow, I'll sail you to Lachine. After all, you've brought me much business." He chuckled, "You know...an influential wife, once tamed, might be your making."

"Or my breaking," Wesley grunted.

—

That night, Leo's curt "Make her your wife!" kept him from sleep. Muskets and military strategy he understood. He was renowned for preparing British recruits to withstand the rigors of a Canadian military campaign. He'd even gentled a wolf-dog. Yet, forging a lifelong union with someone he didn't trust was beyond his experience. He needed to remain guarded; not coddle, yet be kind.

He knew nothing of the blighter arranged to marry Olivia. But he could be sure, with an Eldenmont hand on it, no consideration had been given to her wants. As for his desires? Whether this was a gift of providence, or divine redress, he would accept responsibility for his situation.

Intemperate words, thoughtlessly flung on a Burlington wharf, had recruited her to Canada. Marriage awaited them. With a strong sense of duty, forged through war, he would prepare her for the harsh world to which he'd called her.

—4—

Olivia pulled the thin woolen blanket up to her neck. Canadian spring was unexpectedly colder to that of England. "I should have insisted on warmer bedding," she shivered. "I've taken no vow of poverty."

Soft footsteps pattered outside her door; the nuns were on their way to sing early morning Matins at the church across the lane. Hints of dawn showed clear skies over *Lac Saint Louis*, bordering Montreal Island's southern shore. Her wedding day promised fair weather and a pleasant return to the city.

Upon first arrival, she'd stayed at the Grey Nuns convent, in Montreal. After a few days, not knowing how long the wait, Mother Superior encouraged her to travel 17 miles west of the city to the smaller *Vieux Moulin* convent, to wait for her fiancé. "Accommodation cost is more reasonable than 'ere and tranquil without brewery workers, voyageurs or soldiers."

Neither was there proper society in the village, she soon found out. Three weeks slowly passed with church, stitchery, and brief forays to rustic shops, where only French was spoken. Bored, she craved the diversion of teas, socials, and dancing. This was the fifth month since she had left England and her funds were nearly depleted.

Fortunately, Wesley had come before she had to part with any of her jewellery. She had written five Montreal jewellers for an estimate of their value, should that need arise. For safekeeping, she stored them within the small casket that held her choicest silken undergarments. They were the only mementos her older sister allowed, of their mother who had died at Olivia's birth: a pearl brooch, three heavy gold chains, a ruby ring, and a sentimental pendant of two nested hearts.

Where had Wesley spent the night? She knew that war could harden a man, perhaps also unforgiveness. Hopefully, surprise of her arrival was the reason for his coldness. But she was confident she'd soon thaw his heart, for he was honourable and she'd be a good wife.

Bathing in the side basin, she swept and tied up her hair, away from her face. Since leaving England she'd learned to tighten her corset without help. Proudly she donned her wedding ensemble: a favourite cream silk gown with matching jacket, bonnet, and slippers.

Kingston held promise of shops, church, assemblies, and proper society. If Wesley's clearing on the Cataraqui River was in a tidy hamlet, like those along the Saint Lawrence, she would be content. Surely it would only be a short carriage ride to the Barracks, for he certainly would not expect her to live in officer's quarters. Only camp followers, wives of the lower ranks, lived there. Perhaps he had already procured servants, from among these women, to keep house and cook.

Canada was surprisingly civilized. Even the Native wife of the shop-owner attended church, garbed in European style. "And she speaks passable French—might even understand a few words of English," Olivia chuckled, remembering those few times when she'd bought thread at the well-stocked shop.

A gentle rap at the door announced two stout postulants. "It's easier going down than up," she offered, unapologetic for having her large trunk packed. With a stoic groan, they lifted and steered it down the narrow stairway, depositing it on the convent porch.

Wesley stood at the bottom porch step; his scarlet uniform enhanced by the early morning sun. To her delight, the beard remained, covering his scar. Beside him, the trader and his dark-skinned native son waited, both in deerskin and red woollens. They must rent out rooms, she concluded, for Wesley would never associate with such people.

Sister Superior came out on the porch and silently formed a prayerful cross over them. Olivia returned a hint of curtsy, and Wesley presented his arm to guide her down the stairs.

"*Monsieur* Leo Voisin has graciously offered to ferry us to Lachine." He released her arm, to grasp the strap at one end of the trunk. The trader took the other. With a loud "Ouff!" and a quick heave, they marched down the path to the village wharf.

The lad turned to Olivia, white teeth flashing, and cheekily held out his arm for her. She strode by him, following her trunk to the wharf, where a *bateau* waited.

"You're going to have to replace this monstrosity with two smaller cases," Wesley huffed, gingerly balancing in the rocking boat to ease the trunk down in the centre. "It's too awkward for portage and will never survive the trip." He held out a hand to guide her aboard.

Muddy water rippled over the boat's flat keel. Hesitating, she put aside thoughts of her slippers, accepted his hand, and perched on a bench, behind the trunk. Wesley and the boy, sat at the front, hands on the sail boom. The trader was behind her, at the tiller.

Catching a sharp gust, the sail took them away from shore. Olivia cast a final glance at the convent. On open waters, piercing wind chased off any warmth of the morning sun. Shivering, she clasped her silk jacket tightly about her.

"The Padre...Quebec Gate Garrison...meet us in Lachine," Wesley shouted cheerily, his words scattering in the wind. "...always looking for excuse to fish *Lac Saint Louis*."

"How nice," Olivia supplied, distracted by water sloshing at her feet. She tried to lift her feet away, but it was too late; her slippers were now wet. Sabots would have been a better choice, but she'd left them behind. Discreetly she lifted her skirt, hoping to protect her dress.

Wesley again shouted back at her, and she struggled to listen. "Can't be long from duty...been charged to investigate war claims...Niagara."

Olivia nodded. Niagara was where the Canadian cousin, Jane Blythe, hailed from. Her thoughts shifted to the promise of shops in Montreal. Perhaps she could replace the ruined slippers before her wedding.

Leo and his son began to sing, *"M'en revenant, de la jolie rochelle..."*

Wesley joined in. This was the first time Olivia had heard him sing. In her enjoyment of his robust voice she forgot her slippers. Soon she would be his wife.

They sang for over an hour, then abruptly stopped. Leo Voisin lit his pipe, enveloping her in sweet tobacco aroma. He pointed his pipe stem toward a creek outlet on the shore. Nearby, a church steeple stood out among a cluster of stone buildings.

"*Ça pue ici—la Rive Saint Pierre* is Montreal's sewer."

"It stinks...well, we shan't tarry so I won't mind," she replied brightly through tightly pursed lips.

"Hopefully." Wesley affirmed, as they pulled up to the Lachine landing. "We'll take rooms at the Lakeshore tavern to freshen up should there be a delay." Nimbly, he stepped across the watery gap and tied up the *bateau*. Near the wharf, in front of a large stone building, a rowdy group gathered about a smoky campfire. Striding purposely to them, he returned with two men who helped unload Olivia's trunk.

With a courtly bow to Olivia, Leo Voisin gave Wesley a small sack. "Jesuit's Bark for your bride," he declared. And with a wish for happiness and a bid of '*Adieu*', the Voisins sailed away.

"Medicine," Wesley offered in brief explanation, stuffing the sack within his pack, "from one of the finest families I know."

"My trunk! It holds all I own." she gasped, pointing down the road. "Those ruffians have taken it out of sight, Wessie."

"I've hired voyageurs of the Hudson's Bay Company, my dear, not thieves." He tucked her hand within his arm. "Those gents are God-fearing adventurers, a remnant of the noble people who opened up our Canadian wilderness. Soon they will be no more, replaced by steam power." A few steps further, he paused to face her. "Lady Olivia must also be no more, my dear, for I insist that you be known as Mrs. Bryson."

"Mrs. Bryson?" Pulling hand away, she stepped back. "Am I to be denied birthright and status?"

"I refuse to be known as Lady Olivia Fairworth's husband," he tersely replied, restoring her hand within his arm. "You will be welcomed as my wife—a Captain's wife."

The edge in his voice shocked her. She looked ahead at the stone building where her trunk had disappeared. "I understand," she demurely replied. Better to appease, than entrench.

"We follow your trunk." He gently squeezed her gloved hand. "And pray indulge the inn owner. He's a gruff old Brit but keeps a surprisingly clean establishment."

Up the dusty road, they hastened and entered a crowded, smoke-filled front hall. Sallow eyes followed them to the base of the narrow staircase where a sour-faced man, the two voyageurs, and Olivia's trunk waited.

"I've 'jacent rooms fer the night," the curmudgeon grunted, "if 'ya pay up front."

Wesley retrieved the funds from his purse and they followed her trunk up to the rooms. Olivia's simple, furnished chamber had a small window overlooking the river. The bedding was clean; it would have to do.

Wesley turned to her, eyes softening. "Your shoes and dress are an unfortunate casualty of the journey. Pray change, then we'll lunch, and kit you out with something more practical."

—5—

A message waited at the inn: the chaplain had been delayed. Wesley tossed the note into the flames of the tavern fireplace and went upstairs to inform Olivia there would be no wedding today. He changed into civilian attire of trousers, a homespun linen shirt, and his well-worn deer skin coat.

Olivia came down garbed in a plain brown linen dress, carrying a small matching reticule purse. Her humble choice surprised him. Yet, with hair tucked within a straw bonnet, her appearance remained pleasing. Olivia Fairworth was stylish, in whatever she wore.

His stomach growled impatiently as he led her to an empty table by the window. Without the slightest ceremony, the tavern keeper set plates before them: pickles, ham, thick slices of bread, and two mugs of ale.

"Might I have a glass of wine?" Olivia pushed her mug away.

"Bah!" The tavern keeper flashed his toothless smile. "T'is a brewery town—wine's been claimed by Hudson's Bay 'ficials."

They ate in silence, swallowed up by thick tobacco smoke and the indecipherable drone of pub talk. When the food was gone, Wesley rose and offered Olivia his arm. Together, they set off west, toward the village shops. Stealing a sideways glance at her, he squared his shoulders.

Pulling skirts close, Olivia frowned. "Dusty roads and tobacco, both are disagreeable," she muttered.

"We're on the main portage between Lachine and Montreal," he defended. "Carts take this Lakeshore road to avoid paying toll."

The afternoon sun was no match for the glare she dealt, passing those congregating about the smoky Hudson Bay campfire. "Did those lazy loafs buy our wine?" she huffed. "My stomach roils from ale."

Wesley inhaled deeply. "They're voyageurs, Olivia. They wait for freight from Montreal, and if we're lucky, they might wait for us."

Stopping before a shop, he drew her attention to a crowded window display. "Looks promising," he encouraged.

"Mish-mash!" She shook her head with a delicate flick of her hand. "What could we possibly find here?"

"It's not finery we seek, Libby." He opened the door for her. "You need mosquito veiling, sturdy boots, and a pair of woolen trousers for the trip inland."

"Trousers?" she gasped.

"Aye. Skirts and undergarments won't protect your legs."

A rosy blush lit her cheeks. "Do we not travel by coach?"

He patted her gloved hand. She had much to learn on the trip ahead. "Once we leave Montreal Island, roads are abysmal, and inns filthy with vermin." With a light press to the small of her back, he guided her in. She leaned away.

The plump matron looked up, beckoning them to navigate the labyrinth of crates and barrels that separated them from her counter. Crammed shelves displayed bolts of cloth, ceramic canisters, and wooden boxes.

"I need slippers, and a laundress to clean a stained silk garment," Olivia declared to the matron.

"I 'ave no shoes, *ma chou*, but 'de cobbler, down the way, works fast," she cheerily replied. "Maybe soak 'de skirt in white vinegar, rinse in cold water and see if—"

"Mosquito veiling is what we seek," Wesley curtly interrupted, "and trousers for the lady."

"Trousers, eh?" She winked at Wesley. "I 'ave a boy's pair most suitable. Sadly, machine veils are all sold, *monsieur*, but cheese cloth is h'almost as good." She leaned forward. "Your lady will need somet'ing to save 'er finery for better days." She freed a bolt from beneath a tower of brightly coloured plaids. Bold stripes of red bled through the brownish wool fabric. "Woven 'ere in Montreal," she boasted. "A good weave, perfect for 'ouse dressing. She won't fret about stains on 'dis."

"A bit of staining might improve it," Olivia grumbled.

"Two bolts for 'de price of one." The shopkeeper freed a second bolt, setting both to the side, with a firm nod.

"You've enough finery for a captain's wife." Wesley smiled at Olivia. She looked away. "I also need to replace a large trunk with two smaller ones," he continued.

"I'll sweeten 'da price if you h'agree to trade your trunk," she returned. With a quick scratch under her cap, she retrieved a bolt of cheese cloth and set it atop the bolts of fabric.

"Excellent!" Wesley affirmed and arranged delivery. Restoring Olivia's hand within his arm, they strode out into the bright sun.

An abyss of quiet opened between them.

"Not what you hoped for, aye?" His words fell flat. He then attempted to console her, promising, "In Kingston, you'll enjoy a few days' rest at the respectful establishment owned by my good friend, Mrs. McGuire, when I report in at the garrison. You're marrying a soldier, still on duty, pray remember. War is just over and the border is—"

"How can I forget?" she snipped, cheeks flushed. "Hideous house clothes, denied my rightful heritage, are you also to abandon me on your little farm?"

Startled, Wesley recognized fear. He'd seen the same in his mother's eyes. Stoic defiance of her family may have forged tenacity, but Olivia had spent her life completely dependent on the good will of others.

"It is our farm." He returned, gently lifting her chin, fingers tentatively lingering on her soft skin. "Work with me, Libby. Every officer's wife will seek you out in Kingston, hungry for news of England. I must rely on your discretion."

"Mrs. Bryson, aye." Her eyes narrowed. "Is Mrs. McGuire a lady of repute?"

"She's a Loyalist widow with five children and is completely trustworthy," he submitted.

"And what of your ventures outside of soldiering?" she pressed, her voice sharpening.

"My money is tied up in mining, fur trade, and some property investments, all respectful endeavours. Unfortunately, we will have to live on my clearing for a few years, for they have yet to yield a desirable profit."

"I must have at least one servant," she declared and walked off, down the road.

Sucking air through clenched teeth, he appealed for heavenly patience.

"Mrs. McGuire has arranged for Mrs. George to be your companion and help you." He caught up with her at a cobbler's shop window.

"This Mrs. McGuire seems to have great influence over my life," she asserted, adding, "Perhaps I can replace my slippers here."

"Perhaps you can wear boots." He parried. Guiding her in, his fingers pressed into the stiff corset, beneath her linen dress. For her safety, he would have to convince her to abandon the restrictive garment.

The cobbler looked up from his work table. Wesley nodded. "Have you any military surplus? Perhaps blucher boots?"

"None to be 'ad, sir." He returned a sympathetic smile. "But business is slow, so I can fit you up a pair of sturdy boots in a matter of hours."

"They're for the lady." Wesley directed Olivia to sit on the bench and remove her shoes. Apologizing profusely for the need to measure her feet, the cobbler promised delivery later that evening.

As they strolled back to the inn, church bells tolled, summoning villagers to evening Angelus prayer. Only one grizzly voyageur remained by the smoky fire at the Hudson's Bay Office. Musket in hand, he watched over the pile of kegs and crates.

"They've gone off to drink our wine," Olivia scoffed.

"They've gone to mass," Wesley corrected. "Please understand that Canadian ways are different, Olivia. Mrs. George, your companion, will not be a servant. Had I even the funds, servants are difficult to retain when they can easily have their own home. And I do not abide with slavery or indenturing. Fortunately, Mrs. George is agreeable to stay with you, for she's a refugee in need of board."

"A woman alone?"

He resisted reminding her she had also come to Canada, alone. "There's been much upheaval, with this war," he instead replied.

At the tavern, roasted chicken, carrots, and potatoes waited on the communal table, along with a pitcher of ale. Wesley filled her plate with a generous assortment. Upon release from church, others joined them. Olivia picked at her food, distracted.

"Eat up," he cajoled. "Enjoy what you can, for there'll be only beans and pork on the journey to Kingston."

"I detest beans." She held her head high. "That's all we ate on that horrid sea voyage."

"Eat, Olivia!" His voice sharpened with frustration. "Others at the table will resent your waste of food."

"I need to rest," she pushed her plate away.

He emptied his plate, then ate hers. She gazed out the window; whether in pout or hurt, he couldn't fathom. Had he been too insistent about her need of a house dress? Or maybe it was the boots? Tomorrow would be better, he resolved, and led her up to their rooms.

She pushed by when he opened the door. "Choose practical clothes, for tomorrow's travel," he managed, before she slammed the door.

—6—

Two trunks waited along with the bolts of fabric, trousers, and other purchases. Olivia slipped the trousers on and groaned. They fit.

After redistributing possessions between the smaller trunks, she splashed the few remaining drops of rose water on her handkerchief, and kept it out. Tomorrow it would shield her from the town's permeating stench. In Montreal she would buy more scent.

Her light-blue silk and ivory laced dress, worn at her step-brother's December shooting party, would be perfect for her wedding. She packed it in the smaller of the two trunks, for easy retrieval.

Best to not ruin any other clothes on the dusty ride to Montreal. Re-wearing the brown linen dress, with a fresh cotton undershirt, would be good for travel. With those horrid trousers beneath her dress, and the tan cardigan she had knit on the ocean crossing, she would not be chilled by the lake wind.

"He'll not complain about my practical choice," she chuckled, confident she had enough time to change before they wed at Saint James church, in Montreal.

Sharp rapping at the door quickened her heart. It was only the cobbler delivering her sturdy boots.

From the window of her darkening room, a golden sun was visible, sinking into the lake's shimmering waters. Far off, in the distance, came agitated shouting.

"Drunken rabble," she muttered, looking down onto the street. She recognized Wesley's tall silhouette. He was talking to two men, their conversation too low to discern, but she heard his laugh as he strode off in the direction of the Hudson's Bay Office.

Jane Blythe's vivid descriptions had implied Canada to be an idyllic forest garden, inhabited by noble heroes. Yet, Olivia found the want of Canadian etiquette revolting. Even worse, Wesley's polite remoteness resembled the cold courtesy she'd observed in her sister's marriage.

Tears trickled down her cheeks. She brushed them away with the back of her hand. "I mustn't give in to this," she sighed. "Not everything is dire."

His brief caress, when he touched her cheek, revealed promise. She regretted not kissing his hand. Yet she was rankled by his presumption to purchase ugly fabric for her to wear as a house dress. More so, he'd purchased two bolts of it! Did he want her to be mistaken for a housemaid? Canada may have broadened his shoulders, but it certainly numbed his sensibilities.

—

Olivia looked down the stair to where Wesley waited. To her delight, he'd worn his scarlet uniform for the journey to Montreal. A tall man stood beside him, dressed in woolen trousers and a deerskin jacket. A priest was on his other side, robed in a surplice, with a sacramental stole draped over shoulders. Wesley took her hand, introducing them as Major Reverend Whitley and his companion, Major Brewster.

Behind them, the tavern keeper growled at a nearby waiter, "Go fetch the lady's trunks!" Olivia winced.

"You're my third wedding this week," Reverend Major Whitley jovially announced, oblivious to the tavern keeper's demeanor. Clasping hands excitedly, he tottered back on his heels. "And Major Brewster," he nodded at the tall companion, "has generously agreed to serve as your witness."

With a pronounced sniff, he beckoned Olivia and Wesley to stand before him. "Shall we get the deed done?"

Olivia grasped Wesley's arm, confused. "Aren't we to Montreal— that's why I dressed as I am."

"We stand before a chaplain, Olivia." Wesley's hand rested firmly over hers. "This tavern must do, my dear, for there is no protestant church in Lachine."

Curious patrons crowded around them, subdued to silence by yet another of the tavern owner's bellows. All attention centered on her. Her wedding was indeed taking place. Exhaling, with a defiant jut of her chin, she turned to the Chaplain.

"Proceed, Reverend," she submitted, her voice barely a whisper. Coaxed through prayers, she offered her vow and signed the required documents.

Tavern patrons erupted in a rowdy cheer. "A kiss!" they demanded. Wesley attempted a chaste brush of lips to her cheek. She turned away, her bonnet meeting his nose.

Without further hesitation, Reverend Major Whitley pulled off his vestments, revealing deerskin clothing and his readiness to embark.

"A gift, Padre, to compensate for journeying up from the Montreal Garrison." Wesley dug out a small purse from his inner pocket.

"No inconvenience at all," he cheerily replied, accepting the coin. "Major Brewster and I are always up to get out the city for spot of fishing." With one final blessing and a merry "God speed!" they departed. Wesley guided her to a chair by an open window, next to her trunks.

"I'll fetch my sack," he blithely declared, giving coin to the tavern owner for use of the hall, before hastening away.

Reality set in. She was now Mrs. Bryson.

"A drink on the 'ouse!" barked the owner, ordering two patrons to carry her trunks to the landing. Pressing a cheese clothed package into her hands, he winked, "Meat pie for 'yer bridal breakfast."

She stuffed the pie in her dress pocket, her eyes clouding with disappointment. Wesley had not lied to her. He'd simply withheld truth, allowing her to naively assume their return to Montreal for a proper ceremony. Might more deception be possible?

Wesley returned wearing a red woolen shirt, trousers tucked within moccasin boots and his deer skin coat. "I'm travelling as a civilian, not a soldier," he explained, his chipper manner deepening her annoyance.

"And I'm travelling as a peasant," she shot back, "forced to marry in this frightful ensemble."

"Your choice of clothing, my dear, not mine." Grasping her hand, he led her outside and they hurried along to the Hudson's Bay landing.

Two cargo canoes waited, loaded and ready to depart. Her trunks were already lodged between oil-cloth sealed packs. Each craft was manned by diverse crew of Natives, Europeans, and even a few Africans, all dressed in deerskin, colourful shirts, and woolen tuques. At their approach, the group greeted them with a robust *"Félicitations!"* A pungent mixture of sweat and tobacco rose up, catching her breath.

"This is humiliating," she coughed, pulling her rose-scented handkerchief from her sleeve and clasping it to her nose. Gingerly, Wesley guided her to the vacant midsection bench and squeezed in beside her.

Jean Le Grand, the *Maitre,* stood and removed his red woolen tuque. Motioning the crew to quiet, he bowed his head, as did they.

"Pray!" Wesley quietly urged, slipping his sack beneath their bench. "Or at least pretend." He saluted the steeple of the stone church, with a brief head bow. "Voyageurs don't take life lightly, Olivia. Neither should we."

After a minute of silence, the men launched the canoes into the river. Stroke, stroke, stroke, they dipped paddles in with rhythmic beat.

Then, without warning, the *Maitre* began to sing a silly song about plucking a bird, his voice robust and deep. The crew joined in, as did Wesley, seemingly oblivious to her ire. Though they stayed near the shore, the wind was brisk. Her loosely knitted cardigan offered poor protection and a chill soon overcame her.

Within the hour they passed the Convent of *Notre Dame de Vieux Moulin*. Sister Superior's words of advice returned: "All my grandfather's grandfather wanted in a wife was kindness, 'onesty, and affection." This was also what Olivia desired from Wesley. She trembled, but not from the chill. She'd seen little of this from him in their two days together.

Wesley slipped off his coat. Draping it about her shoulders, his arm tentatively lingered, resting against her back. "Not quite the Atlantic, but it does bite," he offered, adding, "Tell me of your crossing."

She looked up into his brown eyes, her vexation fading. He'd always listened to her, attentive and empathetic. That's what first drew her to him. That's why she'd come. Loosening bonnet straps, she set aside her hurt and began her account of the voyage to Canada.

"My cousin, Will Marston, is a merchant marine and provided passage on his trading vessel. He's recently married and asked that I tutor his young wife, who sails with him, in her new station in life."

"Tutor?"

"Married a bar maid from Glasgow." She raised her voice over the wind. "Did my best, to make a silk purse out of a sow's ear."

Wesley looked away.

"I wasn't a complete failure in my duty," she leaned against him. "She's a kind, willing soul, and she did teach me to knit."

"Knitting is a useful skill." He returned attention. "Did your cousin treat you well?"

The wind picked up, rendering conversation difficult, yet she persevered. "He is a gentleman. We were only ashore, once, in Jamaica."

"Does he also trade in humankind?" he smiled tersely.

She pulled away. "Unlike most Fairworths, he's a repentant abolitionist. He made sure we witnessed slavery's cruelty. I saw a man branded—his cheek disfigured—a horrid Jamaican punishment for attempted escape."

"A man presuming dignity, aye?" He stroked his beard. "Sounds familiar."

"The beard hides your scar." Her voice had grown hoarse, fighting to be heard above the wind. "That Cambridge fencing match intentionally marked you for presumption. It belongs in the past." She looked ahead.

"I hold it as a mark of wisdom," he claimed, barely audible.

Traversing the open waters of *Lac Saint Louis,* they were now fully exposed to wind and turbulent waves. Their small craft began to rock up and down, water splashing over gunwales, spraying their faces. The voyageur's humorous song changed to chanted entreats for *"Beau vent, jolie vent, souffle, souffle, doucement"*—Good wind, pretty wind, blow, blow, gently blow.

Oars slashed through angry waters. They pressed on toward a windmill on the far western shore. Caught within the lake's fury, Olivia gripped both hands on a gunwale, praying repeatedly, *"doucement, doucement."* A sudden gust ripped the bonnet from her head. Wesley's arm shot out, attempting to seize it, his elbow finding her forehead.

"Good Lord!" He hollered over the din, pulling her into his arms, protectively cupping the back of her head. A wave broadsided their canoe, drenching them.

Olivia laughed, shaking her head gleefully; Charlotte would be mortified.

The canoes pressed on. Beyond *Ile-Perrot*, the course narrowed and wind died back. Watery mist rose on the horizon, forewarning of turbulence ahead.

"*Pointe-aux-Cascades.*" Wesley declared, pointing out a cluster of boats, anchored north of the falls. "We'll not take the canal but portage—our first of many." Approaching the shore, a few voyageurs stepped into the knee-deep water. So did Wesley, and he held out his arms for her.

"We unload away from shore to protect canoes from damage, should they touch bottom. I'll carry you ashore."

She grasped onto his neck as he lifted her. "Why do we not take that canal?" she challenged.

"Canal fees would eat up the trip's profits, Mrs. Bryson. Our first portage should take about 2 hours, after which we'll reload and paddle another 8 miles. Tonight, we camp at *Coteau-du-Lac.*" Setting her down, he waded back toward the canoe to help unload.

"You've paid passage, Captain Bryson," she bristled. "Leave the work for porters."

"I agreed to pull my load to travel at a good price." He bowed with an exaggerated doff of an imaginary hat.

Hobbling up the bank, she sat on a boulder to ease her cramped legs. Stomach growling, she retrieved the meat pastry from her pocket, picked off a piece of lint, and took a bite. "Gristle pie," she muttered, tossing it into the water.

Wesley and three other crewmen hoisted the first emptied canoe, on their shoulders. Carefully climbing the muddy path, they continued past her, into the misty forest.

The larger of her trunks was strapped to the back of a burly African man, its weight distributed over a forehead band. "Pray, take care," she ordered. He shot her an impatient frown and continued on.

Ignored for over an hour, piece by piece she watched their progression. Would she eventually be hoisted up like freight and carried along the muddy trail? Finally, Wesley returned.

"Last trip," he announced, introducing her to Pierre Le Vieux—Old Pierre.

"*Viens, madame.*" The grizzly, toothless man motioned her to follow. He had Wesley's sack draped over his shoulder.

Spray chilled the air, and the roar of the nearby rushing water made conversation difficult. She'd done enough shouting for today. "Not that I have anything to say to an old geezer," she huffed. To the north, between trees, she could see a *bateau* on the canal, being towed by horse. Her muddy skirts hampered movement and her boot caught on a tree root. Down she fell, banging knee against a rock.

Old Pierre turned, with an offer of his hand. "*Prends-garde, Madame Bryson.*"

"Doing best as I can..." she fumed, scrambling to her feet and struggling behind him.

As she reached the end of the trail, smoke from the crew's pipes added to the mist. One canoe was already reloaded, and the sun lowering in a fiery sky. Behind her, the moon glowed through light cloud cover.

Wesley turned, smiling proudly. "You've done well on your first portage, Mrs. Bryson. We mustn't dawdle, for they've nearly finished their pipes." He held out his arms.

She limped toward him. He returned a questioning frown.

"Naught to worry, Captain. 'Tis but a knock to my knee," she curtly supplied, noting the fiery sky, ahead. "Is that a forest fire?"

"Not a fire, Mrs. Bryson, but a peculiar sunset," he assured her, and gently set her in the canoe.

—7—

Wesley heard nary a complaining word of her limp, muddy clothes, or red mark that foreshadowed an ugly bruise on her mid-forehead. Thankfully her trousers offered some leg protection. Yet he wished he could free her of that corset. If she ended up in the water, he needed her free to move.

Eight miles of paddling remained between *Les Cascades* and *Coteau-du-Lac*. The sun was well past its peak, as they took to the water. They paddled until the sun had vanished, beneath the horizon, a faint twilight glow hailing night. Following the pale moon, the boat crew sang to hasten their travel.

"C'est l'aviron que nous mène en haut..."

"What's this *'aviron'* the crewmen keep singing about?" Wincing, Olivia pulled his coat about her. "And where is the 'high' place?"

"It's the oars that lead us to the far north," he translated. "Oars draw voyageurs in their wandering life."

"I'm thirsty," she returned.

"You're surrounded by clean water, my dear. Cup your hand in the river and partake."

"Like an animal?" She managed a few mouthfuls, water dripping down her chin, wetting her dress front.

Stroke by stroke, they pressed on, until a roaring mist announced rapids ahead, and another portage. Nearing shore, Wesley pointed out cannons, aimed in their direction A wooden blockhouse loomed, mid-field, with two musket-armed sentries silhouetted in the moonlight. To the right, a narrow canal ran the length of the field,

32

parallel to the river. Several campfires glowed on its far side, in front of the low stone garrison.

Wesley would not visit the garrison. Identifying as civilian bettered his reconnaissance of the Saint Lawrence River. Stepping into the water, he held out his arms, thankful for her light weight. Portaging, lack of sleep, and consideration of Olivia's well-being had depleted him.

"Do they know we're not savages?" She clung tightly to his neck.

"Indigenous people are our trusted allies, my dear. Jean Le Grand is well known at *Coteau-du-Lac*." Aware of her corset's stiffness, he again pondered how to rid her of the garment without prompting insult. Leaving her with Old Pierre, he returned to help unload. A raindrop splashed his cheek. Another, swiftly followed.

"*Madame* Bryson!" Old Pierre handed her a wooden bucket, motioning to the water. "You fill," he ordered, walking away.

Wesley watched her fill the vessel, amazed by her compliance. Scrambling across the open field after the old voyageur, she carried the bucket to the campsite. Setting it down, she gazed about, attention caught by some commotion. Following the direction in which she looked, Wesley noted a woman crying out on the far side of the canal, waving arms about; Olivia appeared to be in her sights.

"Get over here, girl!" the woman screamed, unladylike with effort.

"Jingles!" Wesley put down his load. "As if today hasn't made enough demand of Libby."

"Hurry over!" the woman shrieked.

Olivia hastened across the dark field towards the canal. "What's your problem, dear woman?" she asked, stopping before the lock bridge.

"Come across, you miserable wench!" The woman thrashed about, attempting to hurry her. "My boots encase my feet. My clothes rob me of breath!"

"Where is your servant?" Olivia set hands on waist. She leaned back, appearing to assess the situation.

"I've none and my brother has gone to the ruddy garrison," she rasped, shaking a threatening fist at Olivia. "Make yourself useful!"

Wesley was about to join Olivia to help the woman, then stopped. He recognized the lady from last year's Christmas *fête* in Montreal. They had shared but one dance, enough for him to find her company unpleasant. He remained in the shadows.

"What can I do 'fer you?" Olivia asked, sauntering across the lock bridge, with a crude swagger. Standing before the woman, she folded her arms.

"Insolent camp follower!" the woman stormed. "Remove my boots! Blasted buckles and clasps are beyond my reach."

"I've no blade ta scrape off 'dat muck and end 'yer misery," Olivia taunted. "And you should 'ave dressed sensibly, milady."

"My brother, the lieutenant, will take a switch to you for such insolence!" The woman tore off her bonnet, dashing it into the mud.

"Bosh! Now you've ruined a fine bonnet, as well as 'yer boots." Olivia tossed her head back with a shoulder shimmy. Wesley chuckled. He'd not thought her capable of such mannerism. "I hope 'dat brudder comes back a'fore 'yer feet rot off. You should 'ave dressed sensibly, milady!" she repeated, slowly ambling back toward the bridge.

"Strumpet!" The woman screeched after her.

"Besom," Olivia retorted, crossing over.

Wesley stepped out from behind a tree as she passed. "Bravo," he whispered.

"Her precious feet will survive," she muttered, her pleased grin blending with his mirth.

"As will you, dear woman," he returned with kindled pride.

Insects buzzed and frogs croaked in evening song, as they tramped back to the camp. The raindrops swiftly increased in intensity, developing into a downpour.

"*Madame Bryson!*" Old Pierre greeted her warmly, pipe drooping from lips. "*Viens manger! On a pleins des beaux fèves.*"

Olivia's smile vanished along with her humour. Plenty of beautiful beans bubbled over the fire.

Fortunately, a tantalizing aroma of biscuits escaped from a cast iron oven. A chorus of pipe-smoking voyageurs invited them under the oil cloth, draped between the two canoes. At the edge of the crude shelter, the crew had set up a small tent.

Olivia accepted a steaming bowl and mug of ale, and sat beside him on the smaller of her trunks. He wiped his bowl clean. She poked at the floating chunk of fat with her biscuit.

"Finish mine, Wesley." She handed him the bowl.

He ate quickly, returning their empty bowls to Pierre. "Time for bed, Olivia. Tomorrow will soon come."

"Is there not a local inn? I'm quite drenched and need a hot bath." She drained the mug of ale. Her suppression of a burp, with dainty touch of a finger, strangely charmed him.

"The small tent has been provided for your privacy," he lifted the tarp, allowing her to rise. "You'll be covered and dry."

"I don't feel well." Her brow creased with another delicate press to her lips.

"Slip inside, and remove your outer clothes and corset." He guided her towards the tent. "Inside is a dry woolen blanket to keep you warm."

Her eyes flew open, darting at the men around the campfire. "Not here!" she glared at him.

"Good Lord, Olivia!" he whispered through clenched teeth. "I've no desire for...'er..." Noting her glistening eyes, he paused and, instead, prompted, "You need to get out of those wet clothes and rest, Mrs. Bryson. I'll watch over you."

"I won't," she hissed, wiping nose on her sweater sleeve.

"Heed your own advice, dear woman, and dress sensibly."

With a sombre nod, she slipped within. The tent's movement evidenced her wrestling with wet garments. An alert voyageur looked over and dealt an elbow nudge to his neighbour. Wesley didn't know how to tell her, that she wouldn't be sleeping alone, among these men, so near a military camp.

To his relief, she poked her head between the tent flaps, and looked up at him. "If you stay out in the rain, you'll take ill and die. That would leave me in a fine fix."

"Under those terms, I presume you are inviting me inside." He crawled between the flaps. The woolen blanket was wrapped tightly about her, like a coat of armor. She lay facing away. He hung her wet garments on the tent cord.

"How can any woman move in this wretched garment?" He asked, stuffing the corset into his sack.

—8—

Olivia dared not answer; but his slumbering rasps soon settled the matter of what was expected.

She wasn't naïve. She'd learned more than desired from her gossiping maid. Yet this was her wedding night and she was unsure how to proceed with the whole business. A kiss would have sufficed, to confirm the care she'd felt in his arms when he carried her to dry land.

Sleep came in dribs and drabs. Face tingling, her back ached and she was very aware of the manly chorus of grunts, snores, and other noises outside the tent. Her gut churned with hunger. She thought of the scorned meat pie, regretting she had not, at least, eaten the crust. Then she mused that these disgusting conditions might be divine retribution for abusing Jane Blythe's trust. She had overlooked the woman's coarse hands, tanned complexion, and boyish gait, but this was not license to falsely implicate her in her flight to Canada.

"I was such a fool," she sighed, as pale light slowly trickled through the tent.

"*Levez! Levez!*" shouted Old Pierre, outside.

"Wake up, Mrs. Bryson, if you wish to eat today." Wesley gentle squeezed her shoulder before crawling out. His legs remained visible between the tent flaps. She dressed un-corseted, brushing dried mud off her dress, and tied her hair in two side braids. Her combs had vanished along with the corset.

"You've stolen my corset." she hissed, scrambling out between tent flaps. "How dare you!" Insects buzzed in greeting. Wesley picked something out of her hair.

"*Dépêchez-vous, Madame* Bryson," Old Pierre beckoned, unlit pipe drooping from his lips. "*On va manger.*"

"One is going to eat?" She inhaled deeply. "He dares presume I am one of them!"

"Bushes await you as privy, Mrs. Bryson. I'll stand guard." Wesley tersely replied. "We've a long day ahead."

"*Tiens!* You 'ave been kissed by the sun." Old Pierre handed her a mug of hot coffee with a blueberry scone, upon her return.

The biscuit was warm, the coffee strangely invigorating. She ate enthusiastically, while the crew packed canoes, then paused to smoke their pipes. Sentries shouted from the blockhouse, the guard changing. There was little activity across the field, beyond the canal, and no sign of the muddy wailing woman. Her brother must have returned.

Wesley picked her up, waded into the water, and gently set her in the canoe. "Old Pierre brews a bit of tobacco in his coffee," he whispered. "Remember to drink from the river when you thirst. I'll be in the lead canoe, to allow you more room."

The sun rose and the moon faded along with the morning mist. Continuing west, they entered a broadened reach of the Saint Lawrence River, known as *Lac Saint François.*

"Beau vent, jolie vent, souffle, souffle, doucement..."

The voyageurs struck up yesterday's chant, this time on calm waters. Olivia drifted into a drowsy state. The song had no end. Neither did the lake. That gentle breeze, of which they sang, began to hurt her cheeks and neck. Splashing water on face, she attempted relief. Her itching skin felt rough, and she began to wonder if she'd caught lice off the crew.

A splash startled her. Fish were jumping out from the water's smooth surface, hunting insects. In the front canoe, Old Pierre threw a line in the water, dragging it back to his canoe. Shouting "Hoot!" he pulled out a wiggling fish. Slashing it open, he washed it in the water, threw it in a bucket, and tossed his line back out. Fish entrails floated by, jumped at by other fish. Bile rose in Olivia's throat.

Squinting in the water's glare, she fumbled through her pockets, unable to find her rose-scented handkerchief. Lost! It was her last whiff of civilization. Fortunately, the crew's stench was not as strong today, and did not add to her nausea. Heaving a sigh, she wondered how easily she'd grown accustomed to their odour. Then she gasped. Could it be that she, too, reeked?

Since childhood she'd been kept pristine, anticipating her father's rare summons. His heir, a year younger than she, born of her step-mother, received all the attention. By 11 years of age, she was living in the home of her elder sister, Charlotte, serving as playmate to her young nieces.

Midday, with sun high in the sky, Olivia was parched. Yet she dared not drink from the lake. Where could she relieve herself? Her skin's prickling convinced her that she had, indeed, caught lice. Miserable, she looked across to farms along the shore. Gone were the charming slope-roofed stone cottages she'd admired in Quebec. In their place were squalid log cabins with crops planted around charred tree stumps.

"We're stopping for a pipe," Wesley shouted from the lead canoe.

Pulling up to a landing, he stepped into the shallows and held out his arms.

"Loyalists are a slovenly lot," she remarked, clutching his neck. Miserable itching heightened her irritation, yet she refused to complain.

"We've come through a war, Olivia," he curtly returned.

"Is it too much imposition for you to find me something to eat?" she murmured through cracked lips. Their eyes met as he set her on the landing.

"I'll see what I can do," he conceded, exchanging a nod with Le Grand.

Up the hill, a heavy-set woman waited on the threshold of her log cottage. She held a musket firmly in hand

"I'll 'ave none of you thievin' bunch of 'alf breeds on my land!" she raised the muzzle.

Wesley stepped in front of Olivia. Beside them, Jean Le Grand folded his arms with a shout of, "Captain Bryson's wife is in need of rest."

"I don't see no Capt'n," she bellowed.

Wesley stepped forward. "The less said, Mrs. Swallow, the less I report."

"How do you know my name?" She lowered the musket.

"I served with your husband at Chrysler's field—God rest his soul." Grasping Olivia's hand, he stepped forward.

Mrs. Swallow drew from her pipe, emitting a shroud of smoke. "Frenchies stay down there; Mrs. Bryson can come up," she shrugged, pointing her pipe stem beyond the house. "Privy's out back. I'll get a bit 'o something for 'yer missus."

Opening the privy's slotted door, Olivia pressed through the swarm of flies. Mrs. Swallow waited at the cabin's back door. "You've seen a bit 'o wear," she remarked, leading her in.

A plate of biscuits and cup of tea waited. The teacup was chipped on the rim, and flies hovered above the table. Wesley whisked them away with a sweep of his hand and handed Olivia the top biscuit. "Take one, Mrs. Bryson, with some spruce tea," he prompted.

Mrs. Swallow lifted her waddling chin and frowned; Wesley nodded encouragingly at Olivia's hesitation.

She bit into the dry biscuit, then quickly took another bite, before returning it to Wesley. "Finish mine, love. It's delicious." Only a few drops of bitter beverage crossed her lips, enough to wash the morsels down.

Wesley complimented Mrs. Swallow on the savoury aroma of stew bubbling in the kettle. With a quick glance about, he handed the woman coin, and motioned Olivia to the open door.

"A bit 'o advice, woman." Mrs. Swallow held her back, with a sharp tug of her sleeve. "At your age, I know your eyes are open, but learn to duck if you don't want his fist to land."

Stepping under the beating sun, Olivia touched her head where Mrs. Swallow had gestured, and winced with pain. Hastening after Wesley, she demanded, "What's on my face?"

"Americans!" He turned, scowling. "One would never guess who won the battle."

"She's not a Loyalist?"

"Her husband was, but families span both sides of the river. Before the war, cross-river courting was easier that going upriver."

They reached the water's edge.

"Am I well-worn?" She flung arms about his neck.

Taking her in his arms, he whispered, "Other than a slight bruise on your forehead, you look fine, Mrs. Bryson."

—9—

Running fingers through his hair, Wesley bit his lower lip. The purplish-yellow bruise on her forehead and her delicate complexion mottled with sunburn did not bode well. Fortunately, her limp was gone. Why didn't she share her discomfort with him?

Yesterday's taunting of the snobbish shrew had briefly drawn them together. It was the first time they'd shared a laugh in a long time. Yet today she pushed him away, angry at matters beyond his control. He had little patience for her proud fortitude. What was he to do with such a frustrating woman? Any effort to comfort seemed to draw insult. He felt it best to return to the lead canoe and allow her space.

Jean Le Grand said they would not stop in Cornwall, to make up for time. Perhaps, at Long Sault, Granny Hoople might provide a remedy for her sunburn.

By dusk, they pulled up on shore. Old Pierre set up camp, and prepared to boil beans and roast fish on a stick, while the others unloaded the canoes.

"I believe you are slightly burned by the sun," Wesley broached. "There is a woman nearby—a healer—who was invaluable in the Chrysler campaign."

"A woman on the battlefield?"

"One only had to step out their door to be on a battle field, Mrs. Bryson." He led her to a well-kept stone cottage.

An older woman opened to his rap, releasing a tantalizing aroma of freshly baked bread. She wore a plain green dress, of an earlier style, her grey hair braided down her back. Sharp grey eyes surveyed them.

"A mite late for calling," she challenged.

"Pray forgive the hour, Mrs. Hoople." He bowed. "My wife needs care."

Her hand alighted on Olivia's cheek and she invited them in to sit by the fire. "You're sunburnt and mosquito bitten, poor girl. I have something for that...and..." she paused, eyes opening as if in recognition. "Within you are embers that refuse to die." She nodded. "Don't waste them on the past. They're meant to start a new fire."

A new fire. The healer's words caught Wesley with insight. Olivia's tenacity was a strength, to be redirected.

From a pantry cupboard the old woman retrieved two small crocks. Dipping fingers in one, she slathered brown greasy ointment over Olivia's cheeks and neck.

"Better, aye?" Granny Hoople's face crinkled in smile. Olivia looked up with a pitiful sigh. "Now, where's your bonnet?"

"It blew off on the lake," she sniffed, "and Captain Bryson knocked my forehead trying to catch it."

The matron shot him a hard look. "You were at Chrysler's field, aye?" Without waiting for reply, she returned attention to Olivia. "Probably not used to a diet of beans, poor girl."

Olivia nodded.

"In the other crock is somethin' to scare away mosquitos, gnats, and your husband." Her scowl returned to Wesley. "Too late for her bites, Captain. I don't abide swamp fever comes from bad air. I hope you have some bark."

"I do, ma'am," he replied

"I'll get your woman somethin' decent to eat." At her side table, she sliced off half a loaf of bread.

Sniffing the contents of the second crock, Olivia erupted in a fit of choking. "I can't possibly wear this," she gasped.

Granny Hoople shrugged. "You'll learn to wear what you must—it's bear's fat and skunk oil." She put the bread in a small cotton sack, along with a pickle and two thick slices of roasted meat. "Venison," she remarked. "Save the bag to set cheese and wear this hat." She handed Olivia a battered straw hat, from a wall hook.

Refusing Wesley's offer of coin, she sent them down the darkened path towards their camp, with a wish for happiness.

"She's a witch," Olivia blurted out.

His arms slipped protectively about her. "She's a survivor, Olivia. Delawares massacred her parents when she was a child, and took her to replace one of their murdered children. As a young woman, she chose to return to her people. Blessed, we are, that she had been trained in native healing arts. She saved many from sepsis on the battle field."

"I did not think savages had a heart."

"You'll soon learn there's been much savagery done by Europeans, in this blasted war," he tersely replied, his neck muscles tightening.

"I believe you've forgotten civilized living, Wesley Bryson." She marched ahead and accepted a bowl of beans and mug of ale from Old Pierre, but no fish. Their entrails remained vivid in her mind. On a boulder away from Wesley, she ate alone, Granny Hoople's gift seemingly forgotten.

That night, in the privacy of the tent, she demanded a change of clothes.

"You'll only stink them up with skunk oil," he grunted, and lay with his back to her.

—10—

Beyond the Long Sault rapids, the voyageurs fought the current of a narrowing Saint Lawrence. Charred cabins, tumbled fences, and shattered trees along both shores evidenced recent war.

"*En roulant, ma boule roulante, en roulant ma boule.*"

"A silly song, for such a dreary country." Olivia dipped a hand in the river, flicking water at her face.

"Our good fortune was that the Americans were over confident." Wesley huffed, adjusting his sack under their bench. "Have you enough room, Mrs. Bryson?"

"Do I annoy you, Captain Bryson?"

"Not everything is about you, Mrs. Bryson," he returned, stabbing his finger toward the Canadian shore. "On that field, 135 men died and 400 were wounded. If not for the Mohawk and Algonquin warriors by our side, we would have been defeated. The odour of carbine yet haunts me."

Her Canadian relation, Jane Blythe, had implied a certain madness living near a battlefield. Had Wesley retained some instability?

"War is over, Wes," she soothed, slipping a hand within his arm. "You must make effort to dispel the gloom."

"I still live with it, Olivia." He turned to her, eyes ablaze. "Native allies were forced to choose degradation over annihilation. We now reduce them to dependency, appropriating their land and freedom, and I am charged to ensure this to completion."

"Our benevolence serves Natives."

"I investigate war compensation claims, on behalf of European settlers who live on unceded or falsely obtained Native land. Complete hypocrisy, worsened..." He stopped and drew a deep breath. "My name has been proposed for a position with the Office for Grants and Sales, where I will be tasked to assign more native land to settlers."

"Settlers need land." She stroked his arm to calm his passion.

"Stolen land?" he challenged, his voice sharp. "Back in 1763, the King declared western Canada as Native hunting ground, unless they chose to cede it. Ten years later, Native sovereignty was revoked to appease French colonists. As a result, French rights to law, religion, and language are protected at the expense of First Peoples, who are now reduced to fauna of the forest, Olivia. British surveyors divvy up their land."

"Do you honestly think you can make a difference, Wessie?"

"What worth is my life if I don't?"

"Come, share Granny Hoople's food with me." She withdrew her hand and retrieved the food sack from under the bench.

"I'm content, Olivia." Their eyes met. "Please eat before we approach *Le Saut du Plat*."

"Flat Rapids?"

"Smooth Rapids," he corrected. "Deceptively smooth waters that hide sharp rocks."

The image seemed to fit him, as well, she thought.

Near shore, he stepped into the water and held out his arms. "Mmmm—Granny Hoople's skunk oil," he whispered, setting her on the beach. "Spread it generously, Libby, for mosquitos crave soft skin." Her face warmed.

Old Pierre approached with a half-full bucket of water for her to carry. "*Fais ça vite*, before rain," he ordered. Wind had begun to pick up. The old man lit a campfire with coals from his sand bucket and soon had beans boiling.

"Tomorrow is our last portage at *Les Gallottes*. The day after, you'll be in Kingston." Wesley announced. He set up their tent, then returned to help unload the canoes.

Following a quickly eaten plate of beans, Olivia crawled into the tent and wrapped the woolen blanket about her.

Blinding lightening tore open the sky, releasing a deluge that continued throughout the night. "Sleep, sleep," Wesley murmured beside her. Olivia pulled his arm about her waist.

She awoke in a soggy tent, woolen blanket wet, his deer skin coat covering her. In the grey dawn, with no possibility of a fire, they quickly loaded the canoes. Only one man boarded each craft to help steer. The rest of the crew, Wesley included, tied ropes around their waists and hauled the canoes through *Les Gallottes* rapids. Holding skirt above trousered knees, Olivia struggled to follow over the slippery trail.

The African voyageur began to sing of a fox, wolf, and rabbit. Others joined him, adding choruses that grew sillier with each round. Even Wesley added a stanza about a fish, prompting guffaws of laughter.

Olivia went silent. Seeing Wesley labouring left her feeling ill. Only horses and the lowest of people pulled barges through canals.

Beyond the rapids, the rain ceased abruptly, leaving a cold mist hovering above the river. They boarded their crafts. Olivia didn't need Wesley to carry her to the canoe, she was already soaked to the core, yet she held out her arms, if only for reassurance of his embrace.

Oars dug into the waters, as the voyageurs pressed on. To the north a block house appeared in the fog. The single sentry waved. Le Grand waved his red tuque in return.

"Fort Wellington," Wesley offered, as they continued on.

"Are we not stopping?" she shivered.

"We keep to Le Grand's schedule."

The crew began to sing about bathing in a clear fountain and a woman they would never forget. Later, they paused for a pipe smoke, but remained in canoes, out on the river. Hungry and cold, Olivia clutched Wesley's arm. "When do we rest?"

He pulled her into his arms, his body felt cold as ice.

Entering the Lake of a Thousand Islands, the canoes deftly wove between countless shores; some islands large with small farms, others mere rocks piercing through the water. The sky dimmed as the sun set behind grey clouds.

"We camp for tonight," Le Grand motioned ahead to the beach of a forested isle.

Olivia stumbled onto the sand, legs heavy, head light. Wesley caught her in his arms.

"A bath and soft bed will make everything go away," she moaned, wondering if such would ever again be possible.

"Soon, Libby, soon," he quietly reassured, arms remaining about her.

With canoes emptied and set on their sides, cargo neatly packed on the bank, the voyageurs draped a tarp between the crafts. The ground was soggy. Old Pierre coaxed enough of a fire to bake a pan of biscuits. Maitre Le Grand passed around a keg of '*médicament*' while they lit their pipes.

"Medicine?" Olivia asked, keg in hand.

"Drink up," Wesley encouraged, "A hearty swig will warm you."

The fiery liquid seared her throat, its vapours filling her nose, leaving her gasping for breath. Wesley stroked her back to calm her

"You're a brave one, my dear. Try again, slower this time," he coaxed.

"*Doucement, Madame*," Old Pierre echoed.

Carefully she sipped the liquid, feeling it slowly flow down her throat. Her chest warmed and head lightened. After a third swallow, she passed the keg back to Old Pierre.

"Put Granny Hoople's ointment on," Wesley directed. "Midges and gnats will be vicious, tonight."

"Am I *repulshiv*?" she asked, tongue loosened and thick.

"A mite drunk as a skunk," he replied, "with charming braids and peeling nose."

Her swirling head stilled against his shoulder. "The tent is too wet to set up," he whispered, guiding her under the tarp. She fell into a deep sleep, among the snorting, snoring voyageurs, his arm protectively about her.

Beans, biscuits, and coffee greeted the dawn. Oars dug into smooth still waters, swiftly travelling the last reach of the Saint Lawrence River.

"*J'entends le Moulin...Tique, Tique, Toque...*" came today's song. "I hear the windmill...Ticka-Ticka-Tock."

"Today we arrive in Kingston," she hummed along, "A ticka-ticka-tock."

—11—

By mid-afternoon, the Point Henry sentry of the Royal Dockyard permitted them passage between Cedar Island and outer Hamilton Cove. Ahead lay Point Frederick and the British Fort Frontenac. Wesley pointed out a frigate, to the north, anchored in Navy Bay. A sailor balanced within the rigging of one of three furled masts.

"How is it possible to portage a ship of that size?" She sat forward; hands clasped. "Is there another inland passage?"

"It was built here, at this ship yard," Wesley laughed, relieved by her renewed curiosity. Yesterday's hardship now seemed far off. "Rumour is a canal is planned to enable sail directly from England."

"Never again to portage would be a mercy." She leaned against him. "Are you acquainted with a Captain Lord James Cliveton who served here during the war? I was briefly acquainted with him, at my brother's hunting party upon his return to England."

Wesley hesitated. He did remember the man; they'd even shared an evening of respite last summer, in York. Facilitated by much port and war fatigue, Captain Cliveton confessed a deep admiration for a Canadian woman with whom alliance was doomed by family responsibility. In turn, Wesley shared his humiliating pursuit of Olivia, and his subsequent banishment to Canada. In camaraderie, they'd toasted to a better future.

"Captain Cliveton is a fine fellow," he offered. "Do you know the lady his family selected?"

"Aye." She looked away. "Sylvia Pinney was intended for his late older brother. My step-brother is married to her sister."

"Poor fellow," Wesley pronounced. Olivia nodded in agreement.

49

Navigating by anchored ships in Cataraqui Harbour, they pulled up to the Cartwright wharf, north of Kingston's Fort Frontenac barracks. Wesley quickly secured a cart and left instructions for delivery of her trunks.

Streets were deserted and pubs full at that hour, leaving them little risk of being seen. Olivia was visibly bedraggled from the voyage. With a firm grip of her hand, he marched up Barracks Street, away from the harbour.

"Pray slow down," she panted. "My limbs are asleep." She stopped to lean against the stone fence of a burial ground, at the top of the road. "I almost believe you are hiding me?"

"You can rest at McGuire House. I prefer..." He paused, choosing the best possible words. "I wish for you to be at your finest, when introduced. This town is a cesspool of gossip."

"Am I not fit to be seen?" Hand glancing over hair, she quickly tugged at her dress and cardigan, attempting to set her appearance aright.

"You look charming, Mrs. Bryson." Taking her arm, he guided her across the road to a large white clapboard house. Their hired cart had just pulled away, empty. Rapping sharply on the courtyard door, they entered a kitchen.

"Capt'n Wes!" A sandy-haired boy ran to him, arms out for a hug.

Behind him, rosy-cheeked Mrs. Meg McGuire curtsied with a welcome smile. Wiping hands on apron, she reached out to Olivia. "Mrs. Bryson," she greeted warmly. "Your trunks are up in your room, and water already warming for a bath." She led them up the narrow back stairs.

Wesley was pleased. Overlooking the courtyard, the gaily papered room had a colourful patchwork quilt on the bed, bright rag rug on the floor and a knitted cotton towel laid out for bathing. Mrs. McGuire had prepared her best chamber for Olivia.

"You are indeed thoughtful, Mrs. McGuire," he praised.

"The scullery will soon be ready for Mrs. Bryson." She nodded proudly and left.

"Scullery?" Olivia's hand flew to her throat, eyes widening. "Am I to bathe in the kitchen?"

"The scullery." He repeated. "It's too much to ask for water to be carried up here." He looked about the room and clicked his heals. "I'll look in on you after I report in at the garrison." Down the stair he fled, without waiting for her reply.

In the quiet of his quarters, he stripped down, washed in a basin, then lay on his narrow cot. His mind needed setting before meeting with his commander, Major McTavish. The attending batman returned with his only uniform cleaned, and Wesley declined a shave. He was enjoying the beard's ease of care.

The Major did not seem disappointed with his surveillance, though he had little to report, aside from observations made at the Swallow house. No firm evidence brought into question the woman's loyalty. However, Wesley recommended her removal from the property compensation list, for her house appeared undamaged by war and her filthy offspring were well-fed.

"Progress!" Major McTavish affirmed, with pleasure.

"The Padre had little to pass on—his mind given to fishing," Wesley added, making no mention of his conversation with Leo Voisin. That was his business and had nothing to do with border security or war compensation.

The Major stood. "I'll grant you a week's leave to settle your bride." With a throat-clearing cough, he added, "Mrs. McTavish anticipates Mrs. Bryson's attendance at afternoon tea, tomorrow, to meet our ladies. At that time, I'll expect you and Lieutenant Reed to report on arrangements for Niagara."

Wesley thanked him for his consideration and went out into the night. With the onset of twilight, Barracks Street was now bustling. Two shadows wrestled outside Thiboud's Inn, urged on by taunts from a gathering crowd. Ignoring duty to restore discipline, he crossed over to Grave Street and on to McGuire House.

"Mrs. Bryson has taken supper in her room," Mrs. McGuire greeted upon his arrival. "Have you eaten, Wes?"

"I've not had time," he sat at the kitchen table. She set down a mug of ale and slice of savoury meat pie.

"She's waiting for you," she prompted.

He pushed the empty plate away, finished off his ale and slowly climbed the stairs. With a gentle knock, he opened the door. Olivia sat by the window, dressed in a delicate night dress, hair tumbled loose about her shoulders.

"I've been watching for you." Her voice was barely audible, untouched food remained on the table. "You abandoned me."

Inhaling deeply, he stepped into the room and closed the door. "I told you I had to report in at the Garrison. Hasn't Mrs. McGuire welcomed you?"

"She's a common innkeeper, Wesley!" she huffed. "It's her duty."

"We are her guests, Olivia," he returned, firmly. "Try your best to forgive my neglect of only a few hours, having been your constant companion for the past six days. I had to report to my commanding officer."

She stood to face him, eyes piercing. He knew at once he should have waited to see her settled before leaving. Gingerly he stepped forward, reaching for her hand. "I've come to ensure your comfort," quickly adding, "before I return to my quarters." Immediately he recognized his error.

She sprang by him, blocking his escape, hand gripping the door knob. "Don't you dare leave me, Wesley Bryson! I've endured my sister's shame from her husband's tart—I'll not have you do that to me."

Throwing hands up, he groaned, "Do you think I'm off to see a woman?" Her mistrust, coupled with a sympathetic nod to the sister who'd separated them, was beyond tolerance. She needed to have her eyes opened.

He folded his arms. "Perhaps it's time you learn that I am the result of such a union," he returned, calm and measured.

She gasped, face visibly paling. Wesley waited for acknowledgement of his confession. "I thought you a tenant's orphan," she finally conceded, hand remaining on the door knob.

He took a step towards her. "I've had to live many lies as a natural son—a bastard of the manor."

Her eyes widened. "What else have you lied about?"

"My truth is that French is my mother tongue, not a language acquired at Cambridge," he took another step forward. "As an *émigré* from a country at war with England, my mother thought it best to change her name from Brisson to Bryson."

"And your father's name?"

"Not important—I am not acknowledged." He noted the quiver of her lip. "He simply provided schooling and sponsored my attendance at Cambridge upon my mother's death—hence my being a tutor." He reached his hand toward her. "The only good from tutoring your ignorant nieces was meeting you."

"Your name and status are false." Her hand slipped from the door knob. "What can I trust?"

Though close enough to take her in his arms, he held back. "Expect me to honour my marriage vow and never treat you as my mother was."

"A village ladybird?" she sniped, with a jut of her chin. "I should hope not!"

"Pray, give my mother respect—she was a kind, generous woman." He could not take offense, for he recognised a fear he'd seen in his mother's eyes. Never had he wanted to cause such to someone in his care. "I have pledged before God to respect and honour you above all others."

"Others?" She shrouded her face within her hands. "Yet you shame me by leaving, after all I've submitted to over the past week?"

Gently lifting her chin, he looked into her glistening eyes. "Pray rest, Libby." His senses filled with the lingering scent of her bath. "We've much to resolve."

She pressed his hand to her lips.

"We need time to properly reacquaint," he tendered in weak protest.

"Do we?" Her other hand slipped within his coat. "I accept you, Wesley."

Daring not leave, he took her in his arms.

—12—

Olivia awoke to his whispered promise to return that night. Laughter travelled up to her window from the sunny courtyard. She flung on her night chemise and looked out.

In front of a chicken coop of clucking brown hens, Mrs. McGuire pegged laundry on a line. A tall female African servant sat on a nearby bench, folding clothes her mistress had removed from the line. Their indistinguishable exchange prompted hearty laughter from both women, and Olivia's curiosity about such familiarity between servant and mistress.

The sky was clear and Olivia needed to purchase scent. Shimmying into a corset, she selected a lace-trimmed muslin dress and found her parasol. With a quick glance in the looking glass she assured herself that the bruise on her forehead had mostly faded and the skin of her nose had cleared.

Small reticule bag in hand, she descended the main stairs, to the front parlour. Four small tables and chairs, set out along the wall, defined this as an assembly room for guests. She sat at a table, awaiting attendance. Several minutes passed and none came. Crossing the room, she slammed the front door to summon Mrs. McGuire. Behind her a door creaked.

"Mrs. Bryson?" Mrs. McGuire poked her head out. "I've a meal waiting in the kitchen." With an impatient hand wave, she directed her in, to sit at the large kitchen table.

At the far end, a plump pipe-smoking matron was ironing sheets. "Mornin'," she greeted, glancing up, smoke rushing from between her lips.

"Mrs. Jenny Cowlie," Mrs. McGuire introduced, and placed a generous plate of eggs, fried potatoes, and onions before her. "She's both laundress and garrison midwife, so we must attend to her busy schedule. Your travel clothes are already out on the line."

"In my trunk, I've a mud-stained silk dress that needs—"

"Out on the line, along with your underthings," Mrs. Cowlie grunted. "Thanks to 'yer Capt'n."

Through the window, she saw her silk garment fluttering next to the brown travel dress, missing corset, and underclothes. Her heart warmed at Wesley's thoughtful contribution to her day.

Mrs. McGuire sniffed with hint of a twitter. "There's nary a bean on the plate—I didn't dare after your inland journey. So, eat up, a'fore your walk." She returned to darning a sock, snipped off a thread, then further disclosed, "The Captain says you're expected at the McTavish home for a gathering of officer's wives, this afternoon."

Walk and an afternoon gathering? The woman's presumption piqued Olivia, yet hunger overcame insult and she ate heartily. "Is there a shop where I might purchase scent?" she pushed away her empty plate.

"Cartwright's shop 'as fine goods. You can set that in the sink." Mrs. McGuire nodded at her dish. "Mrs. George will accompany, for t'would be good to make acquaintance."

"Will she attend the afternoon's gathering?" Olivia asked.

Mrs. Cowlie snorted. "When 'ell freezes over."

The courtyard door opened and the tall African servant entered, head uncovered, without tignon. Setting a basket of greens on the table, her dark eyes fixed on Olivia.

Whether from the young woman's assertive bearing or the sight of her cropped tight black curls, Olivia was appalled. The thin beaded braid at the woman's nape only added to her discomfort. She rose from the table, intent on leaving.

"Mrs. Bryson," Mrs. McGuire set down her darning. "I present Mrs. George."

Olivia's breath caught; this woman was her companion. Clutching reticule, she turned to Mrs. McGuire. "I was not expecting Mrs. George to be a Negro. I'm profoundly disappointed you think this acceptable."

Mrs. Cowlie set the iron on a grate and crossed her arms. Mrs. McGuire quietly disappeared into the pantry.

"This shall be grand fun, Mrs. Bryson." Mrs. George flashed perfectly formed teeth, high cheekbones accentuating her proud stance and set hands on hips. Olivia looked toward the pantry, foot tapping beneath her dress.

"Where is this shop, Mrs. McGuire?" she asked, upon her return.

Mrs. McGuire held out a cloth-covered basked. "Take this," she answered. "Mrs. George will accompany you. And pray inquire after Mr. Richard Cartwright's health, for I've heard he's doing poorly. Afterward, you—" her eyes fixed on Olivia, "—and Mrs. George will take this to Mrs. Violet Reed."

"Mr. Richard Cartwright? Mrs. Violet Reed?" Olivia accepted the basket. "What have they to do with me?"

"Mr. Cartwright is a politician and businessman—it would be well for you to follow his affairs. Mrs. George looks in on Lieutenant Reed's wife several times a week, as does Mrs. Cowlie." She opened the courtyard door, stepping aside to allow them by. "Enjoy the morning, ladies."

Briskly stepping out, Olivia opened her parasol.

"Cartwright's shop is on Grave Street," Mrs. George touched her elbow, gently guiding her away from the cemetery. Soldiers mulled around the barracks beyond the burial ground. "Shall we share your parasol?"

"Lead on!" Olivia thrust the parasol in her hands. Stepping back, she made space between them. Forced to follow the woman, she waited, impatiently looking about, while Mrs. George paused to converse with a grey-haired African man.

"How's the old gent faring, Mr. Gutches?" she finally inquired.

"Won't be long a'fore he's passed," he returned with a shoulder shrug, and continued on.

Olivia entered Cartwright's well-stocked shop. Quietly stepping in behind her, Mrs. George waited just inside the closed door. Although the shop had no rose water, a pleasing lavender scent was available. As instructed by Mrs. McGuire, upon completion of purchase Olivia inquired of Mr. Richmond Cartwright's health.

"He's getting stronger, every day," the shop clerk supplied with a polite smile.

Returning outside, Olivia could feel the bright sun shining overhead; the risk of sunburn was great. "Make room for me, under my parasol," she conceded, quickening her step to keep up with the woman's confident stride.

Mrs. George smiled patiently, and lowered the parasol. "I forgot how fast I can walk," she offered. They continued from Quarry Street, to a row of small stone cottages, sharing a courtyard, off Brewery Street. With a playful shrug, she rapped on the door and looked back at Olivia as if they were conspirators, then entered without waiting. Olivia followed her in.

The dank cottage's interior odour hinted of urine and fried meat. Retrieving her silk handkerchief, Olivia sprinkled a few drops of lavender water on it and held it to her nose.

Drawing apart thick curtains, Mrs. George lifted the sash of the street window, flooding the room with air and light. Beneath the window, a woman reclined on a day cot. Her thin muslin shift revealed a belly swollen with life.

"Mrs. Bryson has come to visit, Mrs. Reed," she announced, "and brings news of England."

"The disarray...pray forgive...servants are so difficult to keep in Canada," Violet Reed fretted quietly. Matted hair fell over her gaunt face, yet traces of beauty remained in her fine features.

She offered a hand to Olivia, her fingers claw-like and cold to the touch. Then she grasped Olivia's hankie, wrestling it loose, sniffing of it deeply. "Lavender reminds me of home," she exhaled, eyes closing, and repeated, "Servants are so difficult, these days, so I am without refreshment to serve."

Olivia was frozen, dumbfounded, still staring at her hankie when Mrs. George mercifully cut in.

"No need for concern, Mrs. Reed. We've come with tea, scones, and even cups, compliments of Mrs. McGuire." She arranged the simple repast on a low table.

Opening her eyes, Mrs. Reed raised her head and motioned Olivia to sit on a wooden chair, next to the cold hearth. Mrs. George draped a sheet over the woman, pulled a comb from her pocket and began to disentangle the woman's hair.

"Tell me of England," she demanded during these ministrations, Olivia's hankie clutched to her bosom. "I miss my Hertfordshire."

"My family also resides in Hertfordshire." Olivia feigned enthusiasm. Mrs. Reed's eyes widened.

With a satisfied nod, Mrs. George tied her hair in a ribbon. She then disappeared out the rear courtyard door, releasing a stream of sunlight from the courtyard. Dust particles danced to the pump's squeaking song.

"Tell me of your people," she ordered, head returning to the pillow. "Perhaps our families are acquainted. My Father was headmaster at a school near Cheshunt—such a bastion of civility compared to..." Eyes closing, her voice faded.

"My father is land steward at Hurstmere," Olivia supplied and poured three cups of tea. Cheshunt was far enough away that there was little chance of any encounter. Behind them, Mrs. George arranged the bed, then swept the floor with quiet efficiency.

"You must be relieved to escape such a godless house." Mrs. Reed coughed into the handkerchief and wiped her lips.

"You have intimate knowledge of the family?" Olivia searched her face, without recognition.

"My aunt supplies me with local news, for she resides near Albyne Abbey. As you know, that estate is aligned to Hurstmere, through marriage." She again sat up, face alight. "Tell me of life within that great house?"

"You are probably more informed than I," Olivia returned curtly.

Mrs. Reed's eyes narrowed. "At your age, and being a steward's daughter, you've little marriage opportunity—" Her attention shifted to the scones; Olivia passed her the plate "—and a willingness to overlook Captain Bryson's..." She bit into a scone; her words lost in muffle.

"I'm done." Mrs. George pulled up a stool, with a pleased exhale.

"So am I," Olivia rose, with a brisk curtsy. "I insist you not stir from your rest, Mrs. Reed. Good-day." Abandoning both hankie and Mrs. George, she grasped her parasol and fled outside. Mrs. Reed's pathetic condition had completely unraveled her poise.

"Don't feign camaraderie, Mrs. George," she huffed when the woman eventually came out. "I am beyond endurance and face another trial this afternoon, with more officers' wives."

"Mrs. Reed is not right in the head."

"Abandoned in such squalid conditions and in the family way—is there any wonder?" Olivia clenched her reticule.

"None of us get what we deserve. She knew duty came first when she chose to marry her Lieutenant."

"Is your husband as cruel?" Olivia glanced up at the gathering clouds and collapsed the parasol with a sharp snap.

"There is no Mr. George." Her eyes fixed on Olivia. "I took the King's name when I chose the Crown's protection."

"Like those Quebec brides of long ago, presuming to be a king's daughter?" Olivia sniffed, "Well, don't presume my company is yours to choose."

"I'm with child and have little choice. You're ill-prepared for this world, so neither have you." She walked away, leaving Olivia to return to McGuire Inn, alone.

The kitchen was deserted. Voices travelled from the front room, where Mrs. McGuire engaged in animated discussion with at least two men. "It's no wonder there are no guests at this inn," Olivia scoffed, escaping up the back stairs.

—13—

A full ewer of water waited on the bed stand; the room had been tidied and bed made. Olivia pulled off her dress, bathed, and lay on the bed.

The morning's frustrations clung to her and she tried to blot them away with a cold damp cloth pressed to her forehead. The woman's pathetic claim to her scented handkerchief disgusted her. What manner of a man was Lieutenant Reed to reduce his wife to such condition?

Restless for distraction, fingers lightly danced over the side, where Wesley had slept. Eyes closing, she longed to return to the pleasure of their intimacy. Last night he'd possessed both her heart and body with such tender passion that she knew he would never treat her as Violet Reed had been.

The front door slammed, jarring her back to practicality. She must rouse for this afternoon's gathering.

With a gentle rap to her door, Mrs. McGuire entered. "Cider and cheese, a'fore you dress," she announced, setting a tray on the window table.

Olivia rose and swilled the cider to quench her thirst. Then she poured herself another glass. Extending a nod to her hostess, she motioned to the flowered muslin frock atop her trunk.

"If you please," she muttered, turning her back to the woman, with assumed compliance. "My corset needs tightening. I had such difficulty doing it up, this morning. And the high back buttons of my dress are a nuisance. I've not been able to dress properly since leaving England."

Mrs. McGuire deftly tightened the laces, with a sharp tug. "You'll need to get a shorter corset stay to allow you to hew and draw." She shook out the dress with a sharp flick of the wrists. "Lovely choice— arms up."

"Hew and draw?" Olivia lifted her arms. "Whatever does that involve?"

"Hewing firewood and drawing water." She slid the garment on, arranging it over her slight frame. "Pray, appreciate Mrs. Reed was woefully unprepared for Canada and could not adjust to—" she paused, shifting her feet. "She's never recovered from the Ague. Her husband does his best."

"Does he?" Olivia faced away for the buttons to be fastened. "Abandoned in a filthy cottage, heavy with child?"

"He's taken lesser duty in town, to care for her. Mrs. Cowlie and Mrs. George do what they can to help."

"Mrs. George? An unwed woman with child?" Olivia turned to face her. "It's appalling that you are party to such scandal."

"You don't know her story." She folded her arms and stepped back. "I'll accompany you to McTavish House—the air will do us both good."

Mrs. McGuire left her on the steps of an imposing stone residence. The well-tended front garden hinted of discipline within. A young maid swiftly responded to Olivia's bell pull. With a cheeky prance, she led her through richly furnished rooms and out to the back garden.

Mrs. McTavish, the hostess, was easily recognizable; confidently seated by a tea trolley. Hawkish eyes quickly assessed her entrance with an approving nod. She stood and, with a curtsy, guided her into a circle of 10 seated ladies. "I'm pleased you have come to our little gathering," she whispered with implied confidence.

A flurry of curtsies and polite exchanges followed, with Olivia struggling to retain names. Most were about her age, except for Mrs. McTavish, Mrs. Stuart, and a dour matron who remained seated beside her. She thought of a gaggle of geese, preening for place in line. The matron's prominent, beak-like nose added to Olivia's amusement. She stifled a giggle. Mrs. McGuire's cider may have sated her thirst, but the effect lingered far stronger than any such beverage in England. Seated, hands folded in lap, she skirted and flirted a barrage of questions, posturing the manner of a land steward's daughter.

The circle hushed when Mrs. Stuart, inquired if she knew of Viscount Captain Lord James Cliveton, who had departed for England that previous autumn. Olivia's senses heightened.

"An earl's son here?" Olivia managed. The ladies tittered, except for Mrs. Stuart, who fixed a studied gaze on her.

"We keep good company in this community," Mrs. Stuart asserted, exchanging a subtle nod with the matron.

"I understand he has now succeeded to the earldom," the matron amended, touching a gloved finger to the side of her nose. "Opportunity skirted our ladies, for he kept his family connections private until departure."

Succeeded to the earldom. Olivia sobered. Life, death, and ambition continued on in her absence. The Pinney sisters were now both countesses, with Elspeth married to her brother Nicolas and Sylvia securing James Cliveton. The family was finally elevated from the sordid origins of their wealth. Perhaps the Eldenmonts had even foisted Jane Blythe on Daniel Fremont. But what did that matter? She was Wesley's wife.

"That trollop in Niagara certainly tried," Mrs. Stokes punctured the gathering's gaiety, with an arrogant sniff. "Tragic how low George's Blythe's daughter fell." Quiet 'tsk-tsks' resonated among the ladies.

George Blythe. Olivia piqued at the mention of Jane Blythe's step-father. Had Jane and James Cliveton been intimately connected? She'd seen no evidence of this last December, at the Albyne hunting party. Jane (known there by her birthname, Devon Montbriar) disavowed any possibility of their acquaintance while in Canada. Even Mrs. Haynes, the chaperone, vouched for her. Yet these women gossiped as if this was a known scandal.

"Who is George Blythe?" Olivia pressed.

Mrs. Stuart dealt her a sharp look, setting cup on the side tray. "He was a peculiar missionary on the Niagara frontier. An abolitionist and advocate of Native and Black fugitives."

"That is good," Olivia returned.

The garden hushed. Mrs. Stuart raised her chin. "He rejected civilized Christian society, shared his medical work with his daughter, and even permitted her to keep intimate company with savages." Every word seemed to pierce. "Of course, she lost respectable association. When George Blythe was murdered during the American occupation..." Her face pained in grimace. "...his daughter was left without Christian censor and threw herself after Captain Cliveton. Fortunately, he was called back to England for an advantageous match with a fine lady."

Olivia's stomach tightened. She had assumed Jane's awkwardness upon encountering James, stemmed from a deprived upbringing. That poor woman had been forced to observe her lover court another, under Charlotte's cruel judgment. James Cliveton had even dared lift a toast, in Jane's presence, to "those fine wenches left behind". Yet, she had done no better to the woman, implicating her in eloping to Canada.

"What became of this daughter?" she ventured.

"She chased him as far as Montreal." Mrs. McTavish concluded. "And that's where our knowledge ends. She is now lost to all decency."

Olivia's face warmed, wondering how she must be now spoken of. Surely Charlotte would provide some proper excuse to prevent scandal from falling upon her daughters.

—14—

Stoic, at attention for over an hour, Wesley endured dressing down from Lieutenant Colonel Red George McDonnell, Commander of Cornwall District and the Stormont Glengarry Fencibles. In the presence of Major McTavish and Lieutenant Stephen Reed, the red-bearded commander paced the cramped office, revisiting many grievances. Few had to do with Wesley.

"Explain yourself, Bryson!" Red McDonnell spat out, cheeks ruddy. He leaned in, so close that Wesley could taste the rum on his breath. "You passed by the Cornwall Garrison, yet did not trouble to report in. How do you expect to serve in the Canadian Fencibles if you think us so low?"

"I was travelling as a civilian with my new bride—sir!" Wesley promptly answered.

"Our Cornwall ladies are beneath her consideration?" he scoffed.

"My bride is shy—sir!" he defended. Best to keep his answers simple.

"I hope you've chosen well." Red McDonnell shot a glare at Stephen Reed. "I wouldn't want another English rose to wilt on us." Attention shifted to Major McTavish. "And Gore better choose well, with this blasted canal. I've already established Rideau Lakes as the best portage to the Grand Ottawa. Yet, now, I hear that Gananoque to Irish Creek is being proposed, to avoid American threat." He turned to Stephen Reed. "You have a clearing up there, Lieutenant?"

"Sold my land to Captain Bryson—sir!" Stephen Reed shot back.

The heat of the Commander's eyes returned to Wesley. "You've settled on the Gananoque River, Captain?"

"Cataraqui River, sir, near Billidore Rifts," Wesley corrected.

"With marriage, I hope you've given up a penchant for wild life." His lips turned up in a sneer and he spun to face McTavish. "Ensure proper surveillance of Cataraqui's upper reaches, Major. Too damn many Americans in the bush—Colonel McLean presumes too mighty of himself at Brewers Mills." He left with a slam of the door.

"At ease," Major McTavish immediately ordered. "The Commander had outlived Lieutenant Governor Gore's patience and will not long be in Canada. But while up the Cataraqui, Captain, follow up on the situation at Brewers Mills. It will remind Colonel McLean he is still under British rule."

Curtly dismissed, they exited the garrison.

"Pierre Sabin is back in Kingston." Stephen breached their silence as they slowly walked up Barracks Street. "He reports no evidence of iron at Lyndhurst. I doubt if he even got that far."

Wesley emitted a frustrated oath. "We were naïve in funding his venture. Leo Voisin heard that he's run up gambling debts in Montreal."

"With our investment?"

Wesley turned to his companion, "Best to consider it wisdom gained. I don't trust him."

"I never have, Wesley." Stephen returned a patient smile. "Supplies are arranged for your trip to Billidore. I'll have them waiting on the Cartwright wharf and Private Harris will accompany you." He paused, as if weighing his words. "I've also sent word to Quinte for John Oneida to accompany you to Niagara and serve as your guide."

Wesley sucked through his teeth as if in pain. "I need no guide."

"He's invaluable, Wes. And you will need a translator," Stephen pressed. "Whatever has passed between you, it cannot be denied that he will bridge both worlds."

Wesley looked up at the overcast sky. He could not fault Stephen Reed's initiative.

"I trust your judgement, Stephen." He rested a hand on his comrade's shoulder. Rank did not matter when in private; their friendship had been firmly forged through the credence of war. They stopped before Thibault's Tavern.

"Are you comfortable with Mrs. Bryson going to your Billidore clearing?" he asked. "Will she be satisfied living under such rustic conditions?"

"Thank you for your concern." Wesley stroked his beard with a throat clearing cough. "To be honest, I'm no longer sure I am satisfied farming under rustic conditions." He paused, hesitant to say something that might grieve Stephen. "Mrs. Bryson chose to follow me to Canada and understands I'm a soldier and duty must come first."

"I'm sure Mrs. George will help her adjust to the clearing."

"I hope so," Wesley laughed. "My wife has little experience with homemaking, but our trip inland showed her willingness to rise to the challenge."

Stephen Reed ran a hand through his hair, and Wesley knew he'd chosen his words poorly.

"Allow me privilege to purchase a hearty meat pie, for you and Mrs. Reed," he offered immediately. "It's the least I can do to compensate for Mrs. George's departure."

"She'll be sorely missed, but Mrs. Cowlie has agreed to care for Violet."

"You're doing your best, Reed." Wesley opened the tavern door. "It's hard to keep black dogs at bay."

"My best never seems enough." They stepped inside. "I hope Mrs. Bryson will fare better."

—15—

Olivia dismissed the McTavish maid at the front door of McGuire Inn with a curt nod. The chit had walked so quickly; she'd become breathless trying to keep pace. Even if the girl were needed to prepare dinner, there was no excuse for rudeness in a servant.

The door's bell announced her entrance. Mrs. McGuire was deep in converse with a tall, well-dressed gentleman. He turned and Olivia's breath caught: Thick back hair complemented tanned skin and remarkable blue eyes.

"Ah...*La Madame Bryson...très charmant.*" He bowed, pressing lips to her hand.

She returned a curtsy. Behind him, Mrs. McGuire frowned, wiping hands on her apron.

"I am Pierre Sabin, a comrade of your husband, the *capitane.*" He released her hand, eyes twinkling. "I am enchanted to meet 'is choice."

"We'll talk later, Pierre." Mrs. McGuire opened the front door. Her rude interruption vexed Olivia.

"Never you mind about that gent." She chided, closing the door behind him. "Come out back for a wee bite." Laughter travelled from the kitchen.

Mrs. George and Mrs. Cowlie looked up, from the table. Five children sat with them ranging in age from toddler to an attractive, light-haired girl approaching womanhood.

"And?" Mrs. Cowlie asked.

"Told 'im to take 'is dreamin' and schemin' elsewhere," Mrs. McGuire answered.

"Scootch over, Lizzie. Give 'yer chair to Mrs. Bryson and fetch a stool," she directed the eldest girl and set a heaping bowl of stew before Olivia. This was the first time, since leaving the nursery, Olivia had eaten with children. Mrs. Cowlie passed her a basket of bread rolls. Her unanticipated smile revealed a prominent gap in her teeth, where her pipe had propped this morning.

Upon tasting, Olivia dealt an affirming nod to Mrs. McGuire, and bit into the soft roll.

"Always put a bit 'o beer in it to bring out the flavour of the meat," she returned proudly.

Conversation resumed, allowing Olivia to eat uninterrupted. They spoke of people and events that held no interest to her. A lad of about 10 years of age gathered dishes, and put them in the stone sink. Lizzie filled a tea kettle, set a platter of sliced cranberry loaf, and pot of butter on the table.

Dining at Hurstmere followed strict etiquette, she had eaten convent meals in silence, and the campfire beans were a fading nightmare. Olivia nibbled at buttered bread, amused by their rudimentary exchange.

Though somewhat inappropriate for young ears, the children attended their conversation with polite deference. Mrs. Cowlie described a woman's childbirth at the nearby village of Picardville. A recent shanty fire, prompted discussion of the evils of drunkenness, suspected as cause of the fire. Mrs. McGuire then committed to finding shelter for the homeless family, and Mrs. George said she would ask around for donations of clothing and furniture. Then the topic of Richard Cartwright's health came up.

"The shopkeeper said he's getting stronger every day," Olivia volunteered, eager to participate.

"Mr. Gutches says he doesn't have much longer on this earth," Mrs. George corrected.

"Mr. Gutches would know best," Mrs. McGuire surmised. Lizzie sat down and drank a sip of her mother's tea.

"That lovely cream dress is laid out on your bed, Mrs. Bryson," Mrs. Cowlie broached, "I 'spect you'll not be wearing it in the near future, but it's ready for Christmas season, should the good Captain take you to Montreal."

Barely suppressing indignation at such presumption, Olivia mustered, "I doubt my husband will repeat that horrid journey to Montreal any time soon."

"He goes every year." Lizzie gushed. "It's much easier by dog sled."

"Sadly, the shoes 'ave shrunk," Mrs. Cowlie persevered. "Young Lizzie would 'preciate some dancing shoes."

"I'll have no officers around my girl," Mrs. McGuire flicked her hand, motioning her daughter to the stone sink. "Manage the crew, Liz, while we go out front for a wee glass of port." She led them through to the front room, filled four crystal glasses at the sideboard and they sat around a table. "To Mrs. Bryson, and her new life." She lifted her glass in toast.

Finely cut crystal sparkled in the candlelight. Olivia's implicit inclusion within their familiarity surprised her. More so, how could she take offense when they drank from such expensive glasses? The liquid slipped easily down, warming her throat and dissolving irritations. "Does anyone ever stay at your Inn?" she ventured.

Mrs. McGuire chuckled, "Only those I choose." She refilled Olivia's glass.

"I'll 'ave another." Mrs. Cowlie slid her glass forward.

With a toss of her beaded braid, Mrs. George declined more port. Setting down her empty glass, she folded her hands in her lap. Her alert eyes showed engagement, yet she did not seem inclined to talk. Perhaps she shared Olivia's growing apprehension of the move to the clearing.

"I've 'erd yer Captn's got a fine place and Mrs. Douglas is just a stone's throw away," Mrs. Cowlie supplied, as if reading her thoughts.

"Another Scot?" Olivia sipped again, wondering why Mrs. McGuire served such a rich beverage to servants, rather than saving it for guests.

"English—from Camden. She come a few years back, on my ship, and we shared quarters in Montreal." She paused to thumb a wad of tobacco into her pipe and light it.

"Mrs. Douglas is a soldier's wife?" Olivia rubbed the back of her neck; a headache loomed. She glanced at Mrs. George, noting her calm expression.

"She were, until 'angfire brought 'is end." Mrs. Cowlie's hard squint turned on Olivia. "Garrison blaggards secretly cast lots to court her, a'fore he was cold in the grave."

"Hang fire," Mrs. McGuire quietly corrected her pronunciation.

"Soldiers violated her?" Olivia rubbed her left temple.

"None of that sort." Mrs. McGuire put down her empty glass. "Perhaps you're not aware that widows of the lower ranks must marry within weeks of their husband's death. That's how morality is maintained with families living in close quarters. Only one in six of the enlisted is allow privilege of a wife and in a common garrison dormitory—"

"Common dormitory!" Olivia exclaimed, "Where's decency in that...and what of daughters?"

"Marriage, servitude, or their own devices, when they come of age," Mrs. George quietly supplied.

Mrs. Cowlie cleared her throat. "As I were saying...Ian Douglas come along, a settler with four motherless. He courted her right proper, and even took her babe as 'is own." She paused, with an affirming puff of smoke. "Of course, being treated so fine, she soon gave him another. Your capt'n arranged the match, and Leo Voisin brought her up the Saint Lawrence."

"This Leo Voisin must be more than a trader," Olivia surmised. "He would do a chaperon proud."

"Aye. An 'umble man, who wants 'appiness planted in the world," Jenny Cowlie looked up at the ceiling, as if in prayer.

"Aye, Sally Douglas has done better than most," Mrs. McGuire, confirmed, retreating to the kitchen.

"What of your story, Mrs. Cowlie?" Olivia asked, her temple easing upon hearing good.

"I seen two 'usbands die—that were enough for me. They gave me four children—only my Willie lives. 'E serves in the tropics—where Robbie 'Arris is from." She shrugged, "Funny how that be."

Mrs. McGuire returned with a covered basket. "Here's cranberry loaf, some cheese, and a dozen boiled eggs for the girls at Picardville." With a shared nod, the laundress and Mrs. George went out into the twilight.

"Does Mrs. George live at Picardville?" Olivia asked, returning to a tidy, empty kitchen.

"Goodness, no!" Meg McGuire chuckled. "She boards with Methodist missionaries—the Nortons—on Bagot Street. Picardville is for women who must rely on their own devices. Mrs. Cowlie has a cottage at the end of Brewery Road."

"She's not bothered by rowdies, a woman alone?"

"They wouldn't dare," Mrs. McGuire shook her head, eyes crinkling in amusement.

The courtyard door opened. Wesley came in; Olivia's heart softened. After all these years, he still bit his lower lip when deep in thought.

"Is there any cranberry bread left, Mrs. McGuire," Olivia pulled out a chair for him at the table, her hand briefly lighting on his back. Only after he'd buttered his bread, did she ask "What is hang fire?"

He bit into the bread and washed it down with a generous swallow of tea. "Are you acquiring knowledge of weaponry, Mrs. Bryson?" His tired smile rested on her and he took her hand.

"Hang fire is the bane of a new recruit," he began. "With gunpowder of questionable quality, there can be a delay between pressing the trigger and firing the weapon. Sometimes this delay is mistaken for misfire—complete failure to fire. The unfortunate soldier checks his weapon, meets a fiery explosion, and...." His thumb caressed her fingers. "A few good men have been burnt, blinded, some even killed

73

by hang fire. But this is something you need never trouble over, my dear."

A shiver crept up Olivia's spine.

"Church, tomorrow, and afternoon tea at the vicarage." He rose, bowing to Mrs. McGuire.

"Then you must to bed early," Mrs. McGuire replied with an understanding smile.

—16—

Leather prayer book in hand, Olivia slipped her arm within Wesley's. Walking to morning service was a new ritual for her.

"An important ritual," Wesley reminded her. "For if one doesn't attend a place of worship, one is in danger of being thought a free thinker, or even worse, a republican."

Outside the church, people mingled about, exchanging greetings. In England, her family carriage would pull up and they would proceed to a prominently positioned pew with minimal interaction.

Remaining at her side, he helped with name recollection of the ladies from the McTavish tea. She enjoyed how his scarlet uniform handsomely complemented her lace-trimmed light blue silk dress. His participation in the exchange of pleasantries on the weather, places of origin, and praise of fashion amused her.

Suddenly, the general merriment hushed. The crowd parted, as though Moses had divided it, himself. Mrs. Stuart's dour companion of yesterday's Tea strode through, her sharp nose pointing ahead, with Mr. Gutches in her wake.

"That old crone was at the McTavish hen gathering," Olivia whispered in her husband's ear.

"I hope you met her approval," he murmured. "Mrs. Cartwright is one of the kingmakers of Upper Canada."

Olivia offered a curtsy and polite, "Good day, Mrs. Cartwright." The matron passed by, eyes remaining firmly ahead.

"I believe I have made an impression," she huffed. "That besom froze me out."

"She's bereft, with her husband's illness." Wesley released her hand, to return the salute of a young African soldier. "I present to you, Private Robbie Harris, a trusted assistant and the best shot in Upper Canada. He will be accompanying us to the clearing."

Tolling of the church bell interrupted her return of acknowledgement. They stepped back to allow Mrs. Stuart to pass. She returned a curt nod to Olivia's curtsy.

"The Widow Stuart, acknowledges you," he encouraged with a proud nod. "Her son is a widower, as well, and those are her grandsons."

An elderly African woman followed the former reverend's widow, clasping two well-dressed boys each by the hand.

Wesley and Olivia were among the last to enter the chapel. He led her behind the packed public back pew, to stand at the back with a group of soldiers. The elderly Black woman accompanying Mrs. Stuart was also at the back, seated on a stool, in a far corner.

A slight lake breeze, entering through a door propped open with a brick, was Olivia's only relief from the stench of sweat.

"Saints preserve me!" she huffed, retrieving her scented handkerchief. "Don't you rent a pew, Wes?"

"I stand with my men." He squeezed her hand. "I embrace no privilege in the House of God. Would our Lord demand payment?"

Young Reverend Stuart opened with a rousing hymn, prompting enthusiastic harmony from the soldiers, and Olivia's headache. After five verses, the congregation sat and began liturgical prayers. Olivia followed along from her prayer book. Beside her, the wiry African soldier distracted her with faultless liturgy recitation, without aid of a prayer book. Then her aching back quickly diverted attention, and she lamented wearing heeled shoes.

A dog scampered through the door. Snout held high, it ventured half-way down the aisle. Muffled laughter stirred at its energetic sniffing. With a firm kick to the beast a soldier dispatched it, slamming the chapel door shut.

The air grew thick and her head light. Shifting from foot to foot, she sighed. Wesley glanced at her, eyes questioning.

"Therefore...with angels and archangels and all the company of heaven, we laud and magnify thy Holy Name, evermore praising thee and saying..." Reverend Stuart enunciated.

The African soldier looked up at the ceiling and formed a cross in the air with his hand. Olivia swayed, clutching Wesley's sleeve. Quicker than the dog's expulsion, his arm slipped about her waist, and he hustled her out into fresh air.

"Good Lord!" She collapsed on a market square bench, inhaling deep. "You must rent a pew if you ever expect me to return."

"I stand with my men," Wesley quietly reaffirmed. "They have fought by my side, remain obedient to my command, and I am accountable for them." Their eyes firmly locked.

"Then I shall become a republican," she retorted.

Wesley shifted attention to the Lake and suggested a promenade along the shore. "We shall catch some lake breeze and then indulge in a Ploughman's lunch and cider, at Picard's Tavern."

She felt their stroll too short, for sun and breeze had barely cleared her head when they turned back to town. "Pray forgive my expectation of your endurance," he quietly offered.

"Be patient with me, Wes," she returned.

He patted her hand, tucked it within his arm fold. "Tomorrow we leave for the clearing, my dear, and soon I must leave you." He guided her up the steps, into a well-maintained tavern. An attendant set a platter of buttered bread, pickles, boiled eggs, and cheese before them, along with a jug of cider.

"I must take care with cider." Olivia sipped slowly. "We have a vicarage tea, this afternoon."

"It would not be good to be both a republican and drunkard." His eyes twinkled. Glancing at the door, his grin dissolved. Curious, Olivia turned.

Impeccably dressed, Pierre Sabin sauntered over to their table. "*Madame* Bryson, again! How enchanting," he declared, pulling up the chair beside Wesley.

"Pierre," Wesley acknowledged brusquely, his frostiness vexing Olivia.

"Are you also a republican, *Monsieur* Sabin?" she teased, in attempt to dispel the tension.

Pierre Sabin's eyes widened. "Pardon? I do not understand."

"You do not attend church?" she restated.

"Ahh...*je comprend*." He flashed well-shaped teeth. "I attend mass."

His teeth immediately reminded her of Daniel Fremont; her former fiancé also had distinguishing ivories.

"We must be off to tea at the vicarage," Wesley stood, and Olivia rose in acceptance.

"Why do you not like him?" she probed, as they strode down Johnson Street. "Is he not your business partner?"

"Was my business partner," he abruptly corrected. "But trust was misplaced and I have yet to…" Pausing, their eyes met. "Hopefully, I am the wiser." She did not probe.

Tea at the Stuart's was a rigid affair. The old widow hosted a selection of officers and their wives, her grandsons banished to the back garden. Olivia recognized several ladies from the McTavish garden party and the church service.

Mrs. McTavish discreetly mentioned her early departure from church, expressing concern for her health. "I would have offered you place in my pew, had I known you had none." Her hard gaze landed on Wesley, across the room from them. He had just finished conversation with an elderly gentleman.

Olivia thanked her for her consideration, assuring her that Wesley would soon acquire a pew. Mrs. McTavish's attention shifted to a nearby group of officers and inquired of their recent fishing expedition.

In want of who or what to talk about, this being her third gathering with these same people in two days, Olivia went over to Wesley, lightly touching his arm. "Can we leave now?" she mouthed.

"Society is no more inbred than at Hurstmere," he whispered, in return. "Pray make an effort—you're trained for this, my dear. Tomorrow we escape to Billidore."

Bracing shoulders, she left him and went to compliment an elderly woman on her choice of rich dress material. A chat on the want of goods ensued. With the topic exhausted, Olivia moved on to Mrs. Stuart and praised the few delicate pastries set out on the table. The widow lamented how difficult it was to keep a cook, and Olivia sympathized. As they prepared to leave, she thanked Major McTavish, assuring him, confidently, "I'm fit and fine, sir, and quite eager to set up a home for my Captain."

His eyebrow lifted. "Encouraging, indeed," he acknowledged, leaning back on his heels.

With a touch of her elbow, Wesley returned Olivia to again praise Mrs. Stuart for a delightful afternoon.

"Commendable application of your talents, Mrs. Bryson," he whispered as they stepped out onto the road.

"Tedious," she pronounced.

—17—

"An excellent choice, my love." Wesley acknowledged, pleased that she'd followed his advice. She wore sensible trousers, under her brown linen dress, and the boots he'd purchased in Lachine. His uniform was safely packed in her trunk, replaced by buckskin and a red woolen shirt. "Don't wish to be mistaken for a deer," he added, cheerily.

"Would someone shoot at us?" A line appeared between her eyes.

"I jest, Mrs. Bryson." He opened the courtyard door.

"A fair day for 'dee travel, Mrs. Bryson." Private Robbie Harris greeted Olivia with a courtly bow, then offered a brisk salute to Wesley.

"Private Harris!" Wesley accepted the private's salute. "You're prompt, as always. Your steady shot will soon fill my smokehouse with venison" He turned to Olivia, adding, "Deer are quite a nuisance at Billidore."

With Mrs. McGuire's blessing for "Safe travels", they followed a hired luggage cart. Mrs. George was waiting at the Cartwright wharf, along with four dour plaid-clad Scotsmen. Olivia acknowledged her companion with a curt nod. Mrs. George returned a brief smile. Wesley hoped this a sign of future camaraderie.

Once trunks and some supplies were secured between boxes of freight, Wesley guided Olivia and Mrs. George onto the mid-bench of the master canoe. He and Private Harris would travel alongside, in a small canoe packed to the gunwales with the remainder of their supplies.

Under a bright sun, the still waters of Cataraqui Bay allowed swift passage toward the portage at Kingston Mills. Shoulders touching, the women did not speak. Unlike voyageurs, the Scots tradesmen's only song was a rhythmic splashing of oars; they had little patience for frivolity.

Upstream of Kingston Mills dam, the river widened into Cataraqui Lake. Continuing north, the water's expanse gradually narrowed to a river, with shoreline forests thickening. Along the way, settlers waved. Clearings were now farther apart than the first stretch of their journey. Crude log cabins provided shelter, instead of the stone cottages of the Saint Lawrence River.

"Too expensive to haul up limestone," Wesley shouted from his canoe, noticing her looking about. "Trees are so plentiful we float them downstream for shipbuilding."

Gurgling waters could be heard around the river bent. A short while later they pulled to shore, below the shallow Jack's Rifts. Here, the Cataraqui River gently tumbled through a series of rapids for 500 feet. Though the water was less than two feet deep, Wesley carried Olivia and then Mrs. George ashore. The Scotsmen pulled their loaded canoe through a side channel. Wesley and Robbie Harris followed behind, towing their smaller craft.

Above the rifts, they paddled for over an hour. Grey cloud blanketed the sky when Wesley pointed out a forlorn shanty, high up the bank and surrounded by charred tree stumps. "Stephen Reed's clearing," he called up to her. "Billidore Rifts...just around the bend."

At the base of the rapids, a burly red-haired man waved from the landing.

"Hallo Ian!" Wesley hollered, casting a towing rope to him. Carefully the settler pulled both canoes to a cushioning mat of fir branches.

"Mrs. Douglas is above, bustling with excitement to have women nearby again," Ian Douglas announced, holding out steadying hands to help Olivia onto the wharf. Mrs. George gingerly stepped out from the canoe, unaided. "Go on ahead, Wesley," he encouraged. "Young Harris and I will bring up baggage and supplies."

Heaving his sack over his shoulder, Wesley grasped the handle of Mrs. George's canvas bag and led them up a stepped path. Wooden steps and hand rails, interspersed among boulders, eased the short climb. Though skies were overcast, the air buzzed with life.

Olivia stopped, midway up, at a narrow bridge that crossed the stream, running adjacent to the path.

"Ian built this bridge to make visiting easier." Wesley offered.

"Are we the only people here, aside from that family?" Olivia paused again, at the top of the path, this time to catch her breath.

"There are other settlers nearby, farther upriver or deeper in the bush. Pray, return a wave when they travel by. Come harvest's end, when the river freezes-up, there will be plenty of visiting." He noted her downcast expression. "Brewers is around the bend. It has a saw and a grist mill that adds to river traffic. That's where the Scot traders are going. I've been ordered to pay a visit there, in a few days."

Out from the woods dashed a large dog; Olivia screamed.

"Gizzy!" Wesley set down Mrs. George's bag and playfully tussled its massive head. "No need to fear this beast. Her heart is loyal, once she warms to you."

Mrs. George slowly extended her hand to the creature. The dog sniffed her fingers with an energetic tail wag. "I think we're going to be friends," she confirmed.

"And now to our home." Gently touching her arm, Wesley directed Olivia's attention to the log cabin. Thin smoky whiffs flowed up from a stone chimney, telling of activity within. Across the yard, in front of a crude cabin, an excited chicken clucked from its perch on the cedar rail fence. "That was my original shanty and now serves as our barn. The smaller wooden structure is a corn crib, and the stone outbuilding next to it, a smoke oven."

Olivia folded her arms.

"Water is only steps from your door." He set down both bags and lifted the wooden covering of the stone-walled well, hoping she'd look within. She didn't. Leaning on the roped lever over the well, he pulled up a bucket of water. Her attention shifted to a field behind the barn.

"Well placed, Captain Bryson," Mrs. George offered enthusiastically, untying the full bucket. "You've cleared away stumps, except for two overlooking the river. We can sit there, watch travelers, and listen to the soothing sound of rapids." Emitting a quiet whistle, she exclaimed, "And do I see a discreet privy, over by the gully?"

"You do indeed, Mrs. George."

Three fat squawking chickens, tumbled out from the shanty barn. "Awful birds," Olivia wrinkled her nose, pointing at a field of tangled vines and stalks, beyond the barn. "That muddle in the backfield needs clearing out to be a proper garden."

The cabin door opened and a voluptuous blond woman bounded forth. Purposeful brisk steps complemented her warm smile and rosy cheeks. Bouncing a curtsy, she wrapped ample arms about both Olivia and Mrs. George. "Within differences, strength abides—just like family. And that is why Native people call that tangled plot 'o squash, corn, and beans, the Three Sisters." With a firm grasp of both women's arms, she guided them toward the cabin.

"Mrs. Douglas, I presume," Olivia offered, shoulders stiff and shot Wesley a wide-eyed scowl. He bit his lip.

"Call me Sally." She bubbled, leading them into the cabin. "We'll not stand on formality. It'll be grand having women nearby."

A sweet aroma from the hearth fire filled the main room. Light poured through the river-facing window, over a stone sink. Another window overlooked the barnyard. More light trickled through doorways of two side bedrooms, each room having a window.

"It's not Hurstmere, but what do you think of the house I built?" Wesley's hand rested on Olivia's rigid shoulder. "The stone sink was made by a Kingston mason, and it drains outside and down the bank, to the river." He opened the river-facing door. "And this small foyer keeps out wind, insects, and, in winter, provides privacy for a commode."

"Smells like Granny Hoople's house," Olivia wrinkled her nose.

"Would you rather it smells like Mrs. Swallow's?" He suppressed an impatient groan. "Smouldering sage drives away mosquitos, mal-air, and hopefully the Ague."

Four place settings of workman's pottery waited on the table. A pot of stew sat at the center, wrapped in a tea towel.

"Is that chicken you've served, Mrs. Douglas," Olivia asked.

"Sally," she corrected, wiping hands on apron. "The girls and I enjoyed preparing your home. They're looking forward to coming to visit, tomorrow."

Olivia nodded serenely; Wesley touched her back. "Pray call me Olivia," she quickly supplied.

Smiling brightly, Mrs. George took Sally's hand. "It would please me to be known as Rosetta."

The door opened. Ian Douglas and Robert Harris carried in the largest of Olivia's trunks.

"Set it in my room—the one overlooking the river," Olivia directed. "The other will go against that wall, between the bedrooms."

"I'll bring up supplies," Wesley announced, following the men out.

"There's apple pie waiting in the larder." Sally opened a tin wall cupboard next to the stone sink. Inside was an assortment of covered pitchers, crockery, and the promised pie. "Mouse proof," she boasted, eyes twinkling.

The men continued to bring up supplies, piling them by the river side door.

"All accounted for—salt pork, flour, beans, lard, candles, soap," Wesley listed off, adding, "Hopefully everything you may need."

"Beautiful!" Rosetta George clasped her hands together.

"Will they stay there, piled on the floor?" Olivia asked.

"Oh no!" Sally laughed. "There's a trap door under the table, opening to a root cellar. Simply pull up the ring and step down the ladder."

Ian Douglas slid his arm around his wife's waist. "Outside this door hangs a bell, which can be heard over at our farm. Pray ring it, should you have need. Once you've settled, I'll bring Busy." Exchanging a nod with his wife, they left.

"Is Busy a servant?" Olivia's face lit up. Wesley shook his head.

"She's our milk cow." He shoved Olivia's smaller trunk against the wall, with more force than warranted. "Busy is short for *Bizhiki*, the Algonquin word for cow. She'll answer to both when ready to be milked."

"Quaint," Olivia lips turned up in attempt of smile.

Private Harris waited by the table, while Rosetta filled the bowls from the pot on the table.

"Where do we eat, Wesley?" Olivia asked, smile melting within pursed lips.

The young soldier pulled out a chair. "Your place, Mrs. Bryson."

—18—

Only a few mouthfuls of stew could cross Olivia's lips. She set her spoon down; churning belly and tightening temples foretold a massive headache.

She had considered Mrs. McGuire's accommodations meager; never had she anticipated living in such stark contrast to the opulence she'd fled.

The log cabin's cleanliness could not be faulted. It was neatly swept, with brightly coloured quilts and hooked rugs enhancing the sparse furnishing. Generous light flowed through white-curtained windows, overlooking both river and farm yard.

Yet, her bed was a mere bunk, hinged to a log wall. And the dried clay, lodged between spaces of that wall to keep out creatures and wind, would never keep out cold, nor those hideous insects buzzing about.

Wesley's pride that his stone sink drained to the outside did not acknowledge a need to draw water from the well and lug it inside, to fill a cistern. It could have been worse, she supposed, for she did not have to haul it up from the river.

An open hearth, equipped with cast iron skillets, stewing cauldron, and tea kettle, served as kitchen. About the fireplace were a rocking chair, woven willow settee, and blanketed daybed. These were at par with the poorest tenants of her family's estate. Wesley's shelf of well-worn books was a pathetic contrast to Charles' extensive collection, displayed in the Hurstmere library. Though rarely partaking of the many volumes, she took pride in their beautiful bindings.

Wesley's expectation for her to keep house in this hovel was impossible. She had no experience to draw from. She doubted if even the most experienced of Hurstmere servants would be capable of such a feat, under these rustic conditions.

Rising from the table, she declared exhaustion. As she turned to pull the bedroom curtain across the rope, her shin struck the trunk. A curtain and plank wall were all that separated her from Mrs. George's room and Private Harris out on the daybed. Privacy was no better than allowed a camp follower.

Pulling back the woolen blanket, her heart sank upon seeing the plain cotton sheets and the quilted mattress, beneath. Hurstmere's servants were served better with her family's cast-offs.

She'd expected some hardship, Canada being a colony, but not this poverty. Sitting on the bed, head buried in hands, she fought back tears.

Laughter travelled through the curtain, along with the sounds of shuffling, clanging, and splashing. They were putting away supplies, cleaning up and washing dishes. Nightfall had come.

Wiping her eyes, she recollected the sumptuous halls of her former childhood home, Albyne Abbey. She'd expended great effort there last December, eluding lecherous advances from Daniel Fremont, her assumed fiancé. The housemaids were not as fortunate, if rumours were true.

Then she recalled the blue morning room of Hurstmere. She'd passed the early part of most days, in that room, seated in a blue upholstered chair at a marble desk, tending to Charlotte's correspondence. A sob escaped at the memory of her lavish bedroom chamber. Then she remembered how quickly she'd leapt at the chance to escape that lonely luxury.

"Start a new fire," the Hoople Woman had said. She had no choice.

Curtains shifted and she looked up. Wesley came in with a lit candle and that frightening dog. He set the candle holder on the trunk, light filling the room.

"Informality is not impertinence, my dear." He coaxed, lifting her face, planting a soft kiss on her forehead. The creature brushed against her leg.

"I'm trying, Wesley," she looked up.

"I know." His thumb brushed a tear from her cheek and he helped her to stand. "Come join us for some pie."

She blew out the candle.

Private Harris welcomed her with an encouraging smile and steaming cup of tea. "I recall my first few weeks in Canada. 'Twas so cold—and so very strange."

Rosetta set a generous portion of pie, before her. "It was a fight to keep this for you."

She ate quietly, under Wesley's affirming smile.

"We'll be outside, preparing the smoke oven for a successful hunt," he announced when she set down her empty cup. The two men rose and went out.

"When is the birth expected?" Olivia asked, pushing her empty plate away.

"Christmas season." Rosetta put her dish in the sink and went over to the book shelf. Pulling out a volume, she sat on the settee and gave attention to perusing its pages.

"I thought you people couldn't read," Olivia quipped, opening her smaller trunk in search of the pew cover she'd begun before leaving England. Perhaps it could serve in their pew at the Kingston church, when in town. She sat on the rocking chair, sorting threads, ignored.

Rosetta only looked up when Robbie and Wesley's returned. "Smoke oven is ready to receive meat." Wesley pronounced. Olivia set down her handiwork and retired behind her bedchamber curtain. The cabin quieted, muffled conversation ceased. Wesley came in and lay beside her on their narrow bed.

"I pity Mrs. Reed," Olivia whispered, "It is any wonder—"

"I know this isn't the life you expected." His fingertip gently touched her lips. "Yet you've managed to both keep up with voyageurs and charm Kingston's matrons. Pray remain open to opportunity and continue to amaze me, Libby." His hand ran through her loosened hair.

"Sssshhh," she hushed, and drew him near.

—19—

Two days later, Olivia bid her husband, "Godspeed".

"Be assured that Robbie and I are experienced in the bush." He kissed her hand. "The Douglas family is a mere bell ring away and I leave you with plenty of firewood. May you ladies enjoy acquainting!"

Long after he'd disappeared upriver, her eyes remained on the portage path.

"You can't stay here." Stepping up from behind, Rosetta impatiently tapped her shoulder. "We have a tea to prepare. I need you to fetch a few eggs from those chickens." She nodded at the neat pile of wood stacked against the shanty. "After that, please bring in an armload of wood, while I search out our larder."

"*My* larder," Olivia corrected, marching by her.

With a head shake and a chuckle, Rosetta returned to the cabin.

Striding into the barn, Olivia's stout kick to the straw box sent chickens aflutter. Squatting, she gingerly flicked her hand into the box and found no eggs. Then, forced on hands and knees by her corset's restraint, she briskly tossed straw about and uncovered four eggs. She brought them inside and left them in a bowl on the table. Rosetta kept her head in the pantry larder, quietly humming.

Back out in the yard, Olivia squatted to gather wood. The corset pinched her belly. When attempting to stand, she stumbled off balance and dropped her armload.

"Where's my wood?" Rosetta called through the open cabin door.

Forced to her knees by the rigid corset stay, she regathered the logs. This time she tried to stand with legs spread apart. Again, she stumbled. She could only manage a log in each hand.

"We'll need more than that." Rosetta took the wood from her and bent to place them by the hearth.

"I'm quite aware," Olivia huffed. "What style of corset do you wear to move so freely?" She reached within the folds of Rosetta's dress; fingers pressed against a firm round belly. "You're un-corseted," she gasped, "a loose woman!"

Rosetta seized her wrist, fingernails threatening.

"How dare you touch me, Rosetta George!" Olivia yanked her hand free. Heart pounding, she retreated to her bedroom, more angry than afraid.

This was not a hair-pulling incident with her nieces. Nor was it a severe affront, as on the night Charles Eldenmont roughed her up over Wesley, and Charlotte intervened to prevent further harm. Rosetta was her inferior and the attack unprovoked. Now that they were alone in the clearing, who would subdue this surly woman should matters worsen?

Pressing cold hands against hot cheeks, she sat on the bed, indignant. The nail indentations were fading; her vexation was not.

Olivia removed her constraining garment and threw it against the wall. Inhaling deeply, she pulled in her abdomen and again rubbed her wrist. With dress back on, she stepped from her room, and noted the neat pile of fire wood had grown beside the hearth. Rosetta sat on the settee, seemingly contrite.

"I was unladylike," she sheepishly offered.

"You don't know your place," Olivia sniped with distain. "I'll not be ordered about in my own home. And I will definitely not tolerate—"

"My place?" Rosetta spat back. "You're like a child, Olivia Bryson, in attitude and ability! You're ignorant of even the basic skills to fend for yourself. How can I ever help you when you don't want to be told what to do?" She stood, arms folded. "I'm going out for some air. Ingredients are waiting to make scones. You need to bake them, too. Figure it out on your own."

On her own? A shiver ran up her spine. The insolent woman was astute. She was as ignorant as a child, but she wouldn't be treated as one.

"Please don't go." Clasping hands together, Olivia went to the cold hearth. "Please, respectfully, instruct me on building a fire, Mrs. George."

Rosetta pursed her lips in acknowledgement and handed her a basket from behind the wood pile. "Put a handful of this mix of straw and dried milkweed on a wood splint pile. Then fetch the flint box from the mantle." Pausing, with a tilt of her head, she asked, "Am I mindful enough of your feelings?"

Olivia nodded and did as bidden.

"Now get a piece of char cloth, from the flint box, and tuck it in a small space in the mix." She continued. "Then hold flint in your left hand and keep hitting it with the steel striker until you catch a spark to the cloth."

With her first strike, the wind from Olivia's hand scattered the milkweed.

"Rebuild the pile and start again," Rosetta leaned over, observing her closely.

Olivia's second try was no better. By the tenth attempt, patience depleted, she stood up and thrust the flint into Rosetta's hand. "I'm incompetent."

Rosetta repositioned the char cloth and rebuilt the straw pile. After three strikes, an ember appeared on the char cloth. With haste, she wrapped char cloth within the small pile of milkweed, straw, and shredded bark, and blew into the bundle. A wisp of smoke appeared, growing as she blew harder until a flame leapt up. Quickly, she set the bundle deeper in the hearth, adding larger kindling until the fire was sure enough to receive slower-burning logs.

Olivia washed her hands at the sink and went to the table to examine the assortment retrieved from the larder.

"Please instruct me," she invited, with mock contriteness.

Patiently, Rosetta guided her through blending flour, salt, and rising powder, with a combination of maple syrup, eggs, butter, and cream. Tossing in a handful of dried berries, Olivia pressed the thick batter into a larded skillet and cut it into wedges.

"These will be better than Old Pierre's biscuits," she boasted, chin lifting with pride.

"I should hope so," Rosetta mumbled, covering the pan with another skillet and burying it among the emerging coals. With a throat-clearing "Ahem", she asked, "Why do I offend you, Mrs. Bryson?"

Olivia's reply was cut off by Gizzy's bark and the sound of children's laughter coming from outside. She opened the door. A red-haired lad led a thick-limbed brown cow across the yard, a bell clanging from the beast's leather collar. Five children pranced behind followed by Sally Douglas with a plump baby in arms.

"Good Lord!" Olivia exclaimed. "Scottish clearances have their revenge."

"Pray remember, we must be polite," Rosetta muttered, walking by her and out the door.

"I'm Jamie, eldest of the Douglas clan," The boy announced, stroking the cow's thick flank. "Busy forages during the day—her bell lets us know where she be. She has to go in the barn at night, 'cause o' wolves. She is milked at dawn and before sunset. If you need help I can—"

"Mighty kind, Jamie," Rosetta interrupted, smiling warmly. "But I know my way around a farm, and soon, so will Mrs. Bryson. Please tie Busy in the stall." She looked back at Olivia. "Come, enjoy the scones Mrs. Bryson has made for a morning tea." With a beckoning sweep of her hand, she invited them into the cabin. Olivia's breath caught at Rosetta's presumption as hostess.

The children squealed with delight. A blond toddler held out her arms. Rosetta picked her up, the small hands clasping her face with a playfully giggle.

"She does that with Robbie Harris, too." Jamie shrugged, leading the cow into the shanty.

With children seated about the table, the women gathered by the hearth. Sally sat in the rocking chair, undid the buttons of her blouse, and began to suckle her baby. "Baby's almost weaned, but this is still the only way to get peace and quiet," she winked.

Olivia averted her eyes.

"This cabin is surprisingly well-appointed for a man," Rosetta offered, leading the conversation. "And the Captain has an excellent choice of reading."

"You ladies can read?" Sally's eyes lit up. "Ian is teaching the children, but I can't seem to learn. The older I get, the more ignorant I become."

"Pray have patience, you're never too old to learn," Rosetta encouraged. "These past few months my reading has greatly improved, and my script is getting easier to read."

Olivia glanced at the shelf behind her. Perhaps she should look over the collection, when she had time.

As the children finished their scones, Sally fastened her top button and pronounced, "Ian said not to tire you." With a firm hand, she directed the children toward the door. "I depart still welcome, before the rain comes." She offered a quick curtsy and led the children down the path.

Olivia rubbed her wrist, though it no longer hurt. The tumultuous day with Rosetta was nearing end and she was looking forward to doing some stitchery. Her desire was cut off by the basket thrust into her hands.

"Fetch some beans from the garden—'er please—a'fore the rain comes," Rosetta directed. "I'll tend to Busy."

Wind was picking up and sky darkening. A worse storm brewed within Olivia at Rosetta's ordering her about. Yet, she was not up to another fight. In the Sister Patch, knife in hand, the bean vines took the brunt of her frustration. "They can rot, for all I care," she snarled, snapping off pods.

Gizzy watched from a corner of the patch. With an excited yelp, the dog bolted to meet a woman and adolescent boy emerging from the bush. From their dark complexion, black hair, and clothing Olivia, recognized them as Native.

Shirtless, the boy wore deerskin trousers and carried a leather sack over his shoulder. The woman's short red dress revealed deerskin trousers; her bulky red shawl draped from shoulder to hip. About her neck she wore a beaded crucifix, similar to those worn by nuns at *Notre Dame de Vieux Moulin*. Had she stolen this off a nun in a massacre, Olivia wondered?

Clutching her knife, Olivia stepped forward and offered, "That dog won't hurt you."

The adolescent set his sack down, stepping back into the thick undergrowth, behind them. The woman's dark eyes remained on Olivia, ignoring Gizzy's excited prancing. A small head peeked out from the folds of her shawl.

"Your baby is charming," Olivia appeased.

"What is making that dog bark?" Rosetta demanded, rushing from the barn, shovel in hand.

The woman's gaze shifted, intently studying them both.

"Natives are allies of the British," Rosetta reassured Olivia. Then she uttered an indecipherable greeting to the woman.

The woman frowned. "Sounds like you're trying to speak Creek, but I am Anishinaabe, not Haudenosaunee."

The unanticipated fluent English prompted a giggle from Olivia. This was her chance to take charge. Stepping forward, she seized the moment. "I'm Mrs. Bryson and this is my companion, Mrs. George. Your English is excellent."

"My French is better." The woman reached out, touching Rosetta's belly. Olivia held her breath, expected Rosetta's nails to answer, but she merely smiled affirmation. "You have a baby coming this winter. May it go well."

The woman's attention shifted behind them, to the cabin. "Anwaatin Nyaweh is my name, and this is Eddie." Lifting the toddler from her shawl, she held him out to Olivia. "He has been walked out."

"He walks?" Olivia returned. "Good. I've never held a baby."

"He's no longer a baby," she corrected. "He has been introduced to the Creator's land through the Walking Out Ceremony of my people."

The child reached out to Olivia. She had no choice but to take him. He began to slip within her arms and she caught his bottom. Small arms wrapped about her neck.

Anwaatin looked up at the sky, a curious smirk filling her face. "Your husband needs two women to keep this place, eh?"

"I do my best," Olivia steadied the baby within her grasp. The child twisted around, reaching for his mother. She had already retreated into the bush, following the young warrior.

"You forgot your baby!" Olivia shouted after her, clutching the squirming child. High above, tree branches began to sway. Gizzy growled, tail between her legs.

Rosetta looked up. "Sky don't look good." She picked up Olivia's basket of beans and the sack left by the boy. "Best hurry inside."

A peculiar tingling danced about Olivia's scalp. "What about that woman?" She yelled, racing after Rosetta. The dog sprinted ahead of both women.

A brilliant flash coupled with a thunderous gut punch, answered. Branches burst from the tree under which they had just stood. The wind joined the fray, tearing branches off other trees, sending them falling in all directions. Olivia stumbled toward the cabin, dodging icy pellets, arms protectively covering the child's head.

Slamming the door behind, they shut out the tempest. Olivia collapsed in the rocking chair, the baby whimpering against her bosom. Beside her, Gizzy released a violent, muddy shake. Icy bullets angrily hammered the windows. Rosetta knelt at the hearth, stirring up and feeding the coals.

"What are we to do, Rosetta?" Olivia stroked the baby's thick thatch of black hair, as she used to cuddle the fat tabby cat that ruled Hurstmere's kitchen.

"We'll have us some tea and feed the boy a biscuit." She stood with a brisk sniff. "The cabin will keep us safe."

"What about his mama?"

"We care for him until she returns—she must have reasons for leaving." Rosetta pulled apart the slit at the back of the tot's woolen trousers, revealing his brown bottom. "She said he walks...that must mean he squats, so we need to watch out for his sprinklings and droppings. Maybe there's something in that sack for nighttime."

The toddler looked up at Olivia, sucking on his lower lip. She clasped his small body to her in response. Within her arms he fell into an exhausted sleep, his half-eaten biscuit falling to the floor. Gizzy leapt upon it.

"Wesley will perish out there," Olivia fretted, laying the child on the daybed.

"Your husband knows the bush, and he's not alone." Rosetta covered him with a quilt.

—20—

Rosetta shook Olivia awake with a firm squeeze to her shoulder.

"I need you to mind the baby while I milk," she whispered, and left Eddie on her bed.

Throwing a dress over her chemise, Olivia sauntered out to the shanty, Eddie in her arms. He squirmed so much during her unsuccessful egg search that she sat him on a stool, to watch Rosetta milk. A moment later he began to totter.

Rosetta leapt up, catching the child before he fell. "See if you can milk better that you can light a fire," she challenged. "Busy seems to like a gentle touch. Pet her flank, grasp a teat, and give a pull."

"Won't it hurt?" Olivia squared her shoulders and sat on the milk stool.

"Hurt's more if you don't."

Olivia set to work, imitating Rosetta, and a short stream of milk shot out. With an excited yelp, she pulled hand away, startling the cow.

"Watch those back legs. Don't want to be stepped on," she cautioned. "That stream was too weak—be firm, and no screaming. A good milking will keep her from drying up before her time."

Olivia began to massage the cow's udder with deep firm strokes. Her second pull prompted a stronger stream.

"That's good." Rosetta set Eddie down, holding tight to his hand.

"I used to massage my sister's shoulders to stop her grumpiness." she jutted her chin. "Thought it might relax Busy."

"Then keep going, until that udder is flabby. After that, wash her up and set her free to forage." Rosetta patted the cow's haunch and returned to the cabin, Eddie in tow.

Ian Douglas was at the top of the path when Olivia came out with her pail full.

"I've come to ensure no harm befell you from the storm." He looked around. "We've a tree down, near the sheep pen." He looked up at the dreary sky, adding, "Today will be a hot one."

"We were safe and secure in Wesley's cabin," Olivia assured him, "but a peculiar visitor left a baby boy with us, before the storm. A Native woman, called Anwaatin."

"Annie." He rolled his eyes with a deep inhale.

"Do you know this woman?"

"Aye...I ken the lass." With a shake of his head, he returned down the path to his clearing, without uttering another word.

"Definitely peculiar," Olivia recounted, leaving the pail of milk with Rosetta.

She returned to the Sister Patch, with axe and basket. As Ian predicted, the day warmed, though the sky remained dull and dreary. Broken corn stalks drooped over a muddy entanglement of bean stems and thicker squash vines. She hacked off a few squashes, then gave up to scoop handfuls of mucky bean pods from the ground. "They'll get a good washing," she muttered.

Her hands itched, covered with small red blisters from vine prickles. Mosquitoes attacked her neck and face. She briefly thought of Granny Hopple's skunk ointment—only briefly. The itch of a few bites was better than the horrid, pungent stench.

"That Sister Field is an abomination." She dropped her half-filled basket on the cabin floor and collapsed in the rocking chair. On the floor, Eddie contentedly sucked on a slice of dried apple. "Mosquitoes are a torment!"

Looking up from churning butter, Rosetta wiped her brow with a corner of her apron. "Rescue what you can—'er—please. We'll need that food come late winter."

"My hands ache," Olivia defended.

"Not as much as your belly will." Rosetta shrugged. "And cut stalk vines this long for kindling." She held hands apart, to show the needed length.

With a haughty sniff, Olivia retrieved black kid leather gloves from her smaller trunk, and stormed back to the field.

She continued hacking squash from the vine until her arm grew stiff with ache. A gourd pile grew at the field's edge, beside the stack of severed vines, chopped in suitable lengths. Meanwhile, insects buzzed about her face and neck. She met them with her limited store of mild oaths. Then a warm rain began; a few drops at first, increasing until her dress stuck to her back and legs.

Rosetta came out to help her, Eddie on her hip. "Rain's not so bad," she remarked. Snapping off a handful of bean pods, she tossed them into her basket. "Best to sing to lighten the work," she declared, and began a strange lament.

"No more pain, Mother's there 'spectin' me, Father's waitin' too, I'm goin' home."

Their toil continued; Olivia's ache merged within Rosetta's song. Thoughts drifted to the mother she never knew and the father who had little desire to know her. Her palatial childhood home was now in the possession of her step-brother, Nicolas.

Looking back at the cabin, a spark of gratitude ignited. This was her home. Eventually she'd learn proper homemaking skills and would no longer need Rosetta. Until then, she must tolerate the woman and make the best of the situation.

"We've done what we can." Rosetta interrupted her musings. "Baby needs to eat, and I need to milk that cow."

Olivia took Eddie back to the cabin. He'd soiled himself and had nothing to change into. Pulling out a knitted cotton towel, she stripped and washed him down, leaving his clothes in the stone sink.

"What are you to wear, little one?" She wrapped him in a towel and remembered those two bolts of horrid red-striped, greenish fabric. Spreading the fabric on the floor, she began to piece out a simple shirt and two sets of trousers.

"My husband bought this for me and I'm making something for the baby to wear." She stated, showing Rosetta the unfinished trousers upon her return from the barn.

"Good Lord, that's ugly," she laughed. "Your man sure got taken!" Pushing the table to the side, she lifted the trap door to the root cellar. "I'll put the squash down in the cellar and, tomorrow, we'll dry beans in the outside oven." She brought up with a portion of salt pork, and began a supper of fried squash, onions, and pork, topped with apples.

Stitchery was intuitive to Olivia; her mind wandered and she began to worry. Wesley was out in this horrid weather. What would be her lot should anything befall him? Sewing a garment together with yellow embroidery thread, she attempted to prompt conversation to divert her growing fear.

"The young Stuart lads are in need of a mother. Is Reverend Stuart courting anyone?"

"We'll dry these out for spring-time planting," Rosetta answered, scooping squash seeds from a gourd. She spread them over a towel, on the table, and went to wash hands in the sink.

"Are there any Picardville women of particular beauty?" Olivia probed.

Rosetta's eyes briefly fluttered in subtle eyeroll. "Never feed a dog onion scraps," she offered, wiping the back of her hand across her nose, while slicing an onion.

"Did you make up the song you sang today?" Olivia asked, again attempting engagement. "It wasn't cheery, but it lightened our work."

Rosetta turned away, and gave attention to the griddle. A delicious smell of frying onions filled the air, blending with her quiet humming.

"What have I done to offend you?" Olivia finally asked.

"Do you ever think a'fore you speak?" Rosetta returned, keeping her back to her.

"In Canada, I intend to speak my mind," Olivia asserted.

"Then make it worth listening to," she sniped.

Silence smothered the cabin. Olivia inhaled deeply, indignation supplanting fear. Rosetta finished preparing the meal, and laid it on the table. Olivia dressed the sleepy baby in his new trousers and shirt, and joined Rosetta at the table.

"You're either an unpleasant woman, or you've suffered great unpleasantness," Olivia surmised. Eddie sat on her knee, leaning against her.

"Aye," Rosetta replied, their eyes meeting. "And I'll say no more on that."

—

Days passed in wet twilight. Wesley had failed in his assurance to return within three days. Mud deepened and the cabin began to reek of wet wool and fried bacon. Olivia enjoyed milking simply because it brought her outside. She also enjoyed playing with the child. With Rosetta, civil conversation was limited to discussing chores.

"I'm setting some beans for tonight," Rosetta declared, the afternoon of the fourth day. "Tired of eating pork, those chickens are meant for laying, so beans it is."

Olivia did not complain. She now appreciated that a chicken might feed for a few days but a laying chicken would feed for months.

Gizzy jumped up, sniffing the air, and excitedly ran about the room. Olivia opened the door, and the dog dashed across the yard to the landing path. Wesley and Robbie emerged, carrying a headless deer carcass, on a pole, between them.

"I'm finally home, Mrs. Bryson." Wesley greeted, his face lit with smile.

Heaving a relieved sigh, she picked up Eddie, and ran to meet them. With deer hung from a shanty rafter, the men washed at the well.

Wesley held out his arms to her. "Who have we here?" he stroked the baby's cheek.

"A mysterious guest," she answered. "A Native woman abandoned him just before the storm, and disappeared into the bush. She called herself Anwaatin—Ian knows her as Annie. She said her baby's name is Eddie and he's been 'walked out' in some ritual those savages have."

His face went ashen. Taking the baby from her, he went into the cabin. By the fire, he sat gently rocking the child in his arms, his eyes glistening.

"Are you feeling ill, Wesley?" Olivia knelt beside him.

Eddie reached up, fingers catching within his beard. Wesley kissed the pudgy hand. Olivia's stomach knotted at the tender gesture.

"Food's on the table, y'all," Rosetta invited. "A mess of egg and greens, along with some beans."

"Take him, Mrs. George." Wesley pressed the child to her. With a firm grasp of Olivia's hand, he led her outside.

Part III—Awakened

Cataraqui River, Upper Canada (early autumn, 1815)

—21—

"Anwaatin was my wife."

She looked across the yard to the cabin. "Surprisingly well-appointed for a man," Rosetta George had observed. His declaration slowly penetrated her understanding. Of course, this had been no work of Sally Douglas, but of a woman sharing his life.

"Am *I* not your wife?" She turned to him, searching his face. His chin raised.

"You most certainly are!" He pulled her into his arms, his grasp strangely rough. "We were never churched, Olivia. I married Annie in the 'Way of the Country'."

"Then that marriage was not valid," she asserted, seeking assurance, "a mere—"

"Such marriages are recognized in Canada," he defended.

With a violent thrash, she tore free of his embrace, stepping beyond his reach. "Much as marrying in a tavern," she accused, studying his face, meeting his firm nod. Yet again, he'd hidden the truth, making her a fool.

"By this 'Way of the Country' you are a bloody bigamist!" she blasted.

"Our arrangement ended. A man of her choosing paid an agreed price and they married last summer."

"You lied to me!" she spat. "Nothing was ever kept safe—you held no constancy of affection." Her eyes sank to the shanty's sandy floor, where blood dripped from the headless deer carcass.

"I was neither prepared for Canada, nor war, Libby. Please understand I needed Annie to get on with life."

She looked up, heart pounding. "You sired Eddie, and I presume Rosetta's bastard, while I pined for you. All I can understand is my idiocy for expecting honour from a ladybird's spawn."

"Enough!" His bellow sent a chicken squawking out the door. "My son is from an acknowledged union, and Mrs. George is an unfortunate victim of...war." Running a hand through his hair, he bit his lip. "Pray believe me that Annie never told me of our child."

"How could you not know?"

"Duty kept us apart near our end. I can only presume she hid her condition, fearing I would not release her."

"As now you presume that I will live in her home and care for your bastard?" Temples throbbing, she turned away. "You used me, Wesley, to extract a commission from Charles. Wasn't that enough? Did you have to disgrace me?"

"It was my intention to tell you—"

"Before or after you bedded me?" She picked up a clump of dung from Busy's stall and let it fly, aiming for his face. It fell at his feet.

He kicked it away, with a proud flex of shoulders. "You used me to escape your family, Olivia. Any intimacy between us came at your insistence."

Her breath caught.

He turned from her, to the door, where Rosetta stood with Eddie balanced on her hip. "Robbie Harris has gone to tell Ian we've venison to share," she offered. "I must tend Busy."

Taking the child in his arms, he strode away.

"Don't you dare leave!" Olivia shouted after him. The cabin door slammed in reply. For several minutes, she waited, unsure of what to do. Rosetta sat in the stool and began to milk.

"Couldn't you at least give us privacy?" she growled.

"I pay no mind to other people's business," Rosetta calmly returned. "Cow needs tending...deer carcass needs butchering." Reverting to silence, she finished up milking, and returned to the cabin.

Olivia sat on the milking stool, thoughts rushing as she searched for an escape. Yet she was bound to Wesley, stuck in this clearing.

The cabin door opened and Wesley emerged. Hope kindled in her heart as he crossed the yard. Perhaps this had all been simply a misunderstanding and he was returning to apologize. Their eyes met and she knew better.

He laid her brown cardigan across her shoulders, his hand lingering tentatively.

She shrugged him off. "How can you believe this acceptable?"

"How could I believe you could hold any regard beyond yourself?" He cleared his throat. "Eddie is my child. Robbie Harris waits for me at the landing. We're leaving for Kingston."

"Now?"

"I give you free rein, to do as you wish," he answered, and walked away from her.

The shadows lengthened. Night fell, cold and empty. She pulled the cardigan tightly about, remembering how she had knit it anticipating their shared life. A sob escaped, then another, until she surrendered in a torrent of acceptance. He was gone.

Gently, a hand shook her from sleep's mercy. Shivering, she rubbed her arms.

"Get into the house, girl." Rosetta whispered. Busy shifted in her stall; Gizzy's wet nose nuzzled her neck.

"I'll not stay under his roof." She swatted the dog.

"This is his barn, too," she shrugged, and returned to the cabin.

Everything was his. Her stomach lurched and she heaved onto the earth floor.

Wiping her mouth across her sleeve, she kicked dirt over her vomit and then kicked more to cover the bloody dirt. "Probably wouldn't kill the chickens if they ate it," she mustered.

The aroma of baking bread drew her across the yard. Stopping at the well, she rinsed her mouth and splashed water over her face. Though morning was hours away, Rosetta was baking.

"I always bake when I need to think." Rosetta looked up at her entrance, then nodded to the single loaf of bread cooling on the table. "It's late, so I only made one. Eddie's asleep on my bed."

"Keep him there!" she shot back, then began slathering butter on a thick chunk of bread. She turned to face the room they'd shared and her stomach roiled. There was more purging to do.

Pulling quilt and sheets from the bed, she dragged them across the room, to the hearth.

"What *are* you doing?" Rosetta snorted with a mix of shock and amusement.

She stormed back into the bedroom. The quilted mattress caught in the narrow doorway. Groaning in exasperation, she committed to hack it apart, come morning. Then, returning to hearth, she stirring the coals.

"I will not sleep on the bed they shared," she huffed. "I'm burning linens, pillows—everything."

"Don't you go burning our cabin down, girl. And..." Rosetta stood, arms folded. "What makes you think they had that bed or any bed?"

"Don't mock me!" she screamed from the depth of her soul. A howl erupted from Rosetta's room.

"You're frightening the child. He ain't to blame." She ran for Eddie and began rocking him in the chair. With a teary glance at Olivia, he fell back to sleep.

"He left his bastard with me," Olivia sobbed.

"Rubbish talk don't help, Olivia," Rosetta soothed. "You need to cry—"

"Don't tell me what I need!"

"Well, I need sleep," she retorted, and retreated with Eddie behind her bedroom curtain.

—22—

Olivia awoke in the rocking chair, neck and shoulders stiff. Daylight trickled into the silent cabin. She laid two logs within the coals, stirring them alight. Gizzy watched, head tilted, as she emptied the cistern into the tea kettle and set it to boil.

Buttering a thick slice of bread, she grunted, "Jam would be nice." Gizzy whined, and she patted her head. "What do you eat, doggie?" A tail wag replied. Cutting a large end-piece from the loaf, she tossed it to the dog. With a quick leap, the creature caught it before it touched the floor.

She searched the larder for milk to make tea. The crock held a few spoonfuls; Rosetta must have used it up making butter. Her stomach protested, voracious with hunger, so she buttered the remaining piece of bread.

"What's that poor child going to eat?" Rosetta snatched the bread from Olivia's hand. Wesley's trousers peeked from beneath her dress.

"You're wearing my husband's trousers," Olivia snapped.

"I'm about to do your husband's work. That deer needs tending and Busy needs milking." She swabbed the remnant of bread in the remaining milk, returning the crock to the larder. "I'll take Eddie with me and feed him later. I don't trust your care of him."

"I'm no milk maid." She tossed her head defiantly. "But I would never harm a child."

"You didn't think of him, either, woman." Rosetta threw a shawl about her shoulders, and scooped Eddie up. Pulling open the door, she exclaimed, "Oh Good Lord!"

Jamie and 10-year-old Sadie Douglas stood at the threshold. "'Da sent us to tell you that he'll come up, later, to butcher the deer," he declared.

"Praise be! I need you to mind the baby, Sadie, while I milk. There's a bowl in the larder, with his meal." She glanced back at Olivia. "We've little else."

"I can milk," Jamie offered, "and add to the wood pile."

"We can search for eggs," bubbled Sadie, "after I feed the baby."

"I will gratefully avail myself of your help, Jamie, and go harvest beans from the back field." Rosetta marched out the door.

"What are you going to do, Mrs. Bryson?" Sadie looked at her, wide-eyed.

Her innocent inquiry came as spark to tinder.

"I'm going to destroy my black kid gloves," Olivia stormed out, following Rosetta to the Sister Patch, gloves and knife in hand.

Rosetta grunted at her approach. "Gather beans. We'll dry them in the oven. Corn can stand 'til later."

An hour passed. An arrow of geese sailed through the grey sky, mocking her with their chorus of cold honks. Busy roamed the edge of the bush, nibbling at greenery. Sadie's laughter accompanied the sound of Jamie's chopping. Olivia's back began to ache.

She returned to the cabin and emptied her basket on the table. Sadie had restored the linens and made her bed.

"Child has better home-making skills than I," she grumped. Through the window, she noted movement in the yard. Ian Douglas must have come to butcher; she went out to thank him.

Anwaatin knelt before the smoke oven, building a fire. "I've come to butcher the deer," she announced, carefully adding kindling to the first flames.

"What about your child?" Olivia lunged, hands reaching for the woman's braid. Her feet flew out from under her and she landed on her back, gasping in disbelief. In scrag fights with her spiteful nieces, she'd never failed to hold the upper hand.

Anwaatin looked down at her, smirking. "Stupid woman. Don't even try to fight—you white women don't know how."

Scrambling to her feet, Olivia again grasped at the woman's thick black braid. With a hard yank she brought her to her knees. The woman's legs flew up, wrapping about Olivia, knocking them both off balance.

Rolling in the dirt, they shrieked with passionate dissonance, Annie pummeling Olivia's back, Olivia digging nails into whatever she could reach. Both tore at each other's clothes and hair. Gizzy excitedly joined the fray, barking and nipping any limb that came near her.

SPLASH! Cold water broke their hold of each other. Another bucketful swiftly followed, leaving both women breathless and wet on the ground.

"That's how I separate indecent cats and fighting bitches." Sally threw the bucket to the ground. Jamie looked down on them, axe in hand. Beside them, Rosetta gaped, wide-eyed, Eddie in her arms, with Sadie hugging her waist.

Wrestling off the ground, Olivia sputtered, "How dare you Sally Douglas! You dreg of society, camp follower scum!"

Cheeks flushed, Sally heaved back, "Never have I seen such shenanigans, even among garrison women!" Turning to Rosetta, she took Eddie in her arms, her voice softening. "A beautiful baby, Annie...but what folly are you up to?"

"I came to help while my husband is away on duty." She meekly answered and sat up.

"Take back your baby," Olivia rasped, her back stiff with pride.

"I'm here to help," she repeated, ignoring Olivia, "and will stay until my husband returns from Niagara."

"Don't you mean my husband?" Olivia hissed.

"My husband travels with Wesley, as translator."

Throwing hands in the air, Olivia groaned. Yet again, Wesley had kept the truth from her.

Sally huffed, cheeks crimson. "I see no need for Ian to come and butcher." She set Eddie on the ground and wagged her finger, first at Annie, then Olivia. "I trust there'll be no more nonsense between you women." With a firm grasp of Sadie's hand, she trooped down the path to her clearing. Jamie sliced the axe into a log, and followed closely behind.

"I'll skin and butcher, and you piss into this." Annie unsheathed a knife from her waist scabbard and thrust the bucket at Olivia. Eddie wrapped chubby arms around Gizzy's neck.

Olivia gasped; the woman was serious. She threw the bucket away.

"Gon'na damage that bucket," muttered Rosetta.

"I should have you—"

"Don't you dare threaten me, Olivia Bryson," Rosetta stepped forward, fists clenched. "I'm all you have." With a swift turn, she marched off to the Sister Patch.

"Pee loosens hair from skins," Annie shrugged. "Between us women, there should be plenty for this hide."

Looking up at the towering trees around her, Olivia accepted she was out-numbered, without escape. Retreating to the cabin, she rocked in the chair by the hearth, pondering her predicament. Never in her long campaign against Charlotte, or her two nieces, had her tenacity and perseverance failed. These Canadian women baffled her. Rosetta seemed impervious to insult. The camp follower took Annie's side. And, as for Annie?

Wesley said he had needed that beastly Native. Social skills and charms were irrelevant, when one didn't know how to cook or care for a home. Any usefulness she could claim involved harvesting squash, milking a cow, and, now, voiding into a bucket. Her heart numbed with acceptance—she also needed these boorish provincials. Yet she would not allow these women to get the better of her. Pride compelled her to return outside.

"Give me that bucket," she growled.

Annie was working a flat blade on the hide, now nailed to the side of the shanty. The smoke house had several smoking embers. Eddie was fast asleep, pillowed against Gizzy's furry body.

"Over in the outhouse," she replied without looking up. "I'll continue fleshing, to ready this hide."

Olivia left her contribution by the smoke house and trudged back to the Patch. Rosetta handed her an axe. "Time to start filling the corn crib. You can stack stalks over at the side." She leaned back, hands on hips. "I'm done, here. Baby's kicking. Don't forget to leave something in that bucket."

"I'll do my fair share, here and in the bucket," she snarled.

Hacking corn stalks was more demanding than picking beans or chopping squash off a vine. Every joint of her body seemed to ache. Refusing to give in, she managed to empty three baskets into the crib.

"We'll shuck corn later," Annie affirmed when Olivia finally returned from the outhouse. "Meat's smoking now."

Olivia set the bucket beside Annie, careful not to spill its loathsome contents. Her delicate kid leather gloves were ruined, just like her life. Dripping in sweat, she removed her cardigan, tying it about her waist. Though the air carried a slight chill, she did not feel it.

"Fried venison steak and baked squash wait on the table," Rosetta called from the open cabin door.

"We have done a good day's work," Annie stood up, stretching arms to the sky. "Eddie and I will sleep on the daybed, by that warm fire."

"I make those decisions in my home," Olivia coughed. Her throat was parched and burning, and her temples throbbed. "This heat makes my head swim," she complained, upon entering. "Pray bank that fire, Rosetta."

Behind her bedroom curtain, she collapsed on the bed, violently trembling.

—23—

Wesley's day had not gone well. The murky mix of guilt and anger brewing within rendered him surly and impatient.

Astutely, Stephen Reed invited him for an ale at Thibault's and offered a listening ear. Out poured Wesley's predicament.

"Quite a circumstance for Mrs. Bryson to accept," Stephen replied on conclusion, as they left the tavern.

"Yet the worst of it is I did not know I even had a son," Wesley defended. "Annie kept his existence from me." He paused, head shaking slowly. "And now I must work with John Oneida, should I have need of a translator."

The sun had already set and evening's chill was upon them.

"A dastardly way for your wife to learn of Annie," Stephen repeated, sitting beside him on the upper step of his courtyard door. Drawing deep from his pipe, he blew out a smoke ring. Quietly they watched it rise and slowly fade. Down the street, raucous shouts erupted from the tavern they'd just left.

"Ignore them, Wesley," Stephen urged, touching his arm. "A gentleman shouldn't come to the aid of rabble-rousers."

Mrs. Cowlie came out from the cottage and stood in the doorway behind them. "Commotion, down the road, Wesley. Boys having a go, aye?" she chuckled, with a reflective puff of her pipe.

"Captain Bryson's mind is weighed with greater matters, Mrs. Cowlie."

"I've met your missus, a'fore she went upriver," she continued. "Mrs. Bryson will do you fine, Wes. She's got spice in her soul." She pointed the stem of her pipe at Stephen. "Your wife's askin' for you, Lieutenant Reed. Best go inside, for I must away."

She stepped down the stairs, between the men, her hand briefly resting on Wesley's shoulder. "No need to see me 'ome, luv. 'Tis but a hop-skip down the road."

They waited until she was on Brewery Street before going in. Gentle light flickered from the bedside candle and hearth embers. Violet Reed lay under a thick quilt, clutching Olivia's handkerchief to her face.

"Are you comfortable, my dear?" Stephen sat on the floor beside her and took her hand. Wesley pulled up a chair across from them.

"Pray return this to your wife." She offered up the hankie. "Lavender scent carries me away to England...poor Mrs. Bryson. A steward's daughter living close to wealth, but never part of it."

Wesley sighed with relief. Olivia had, at least, respected his wish for discretion.

"She's willing to tolerate much to better her lot." She sank into her pillow, closing her eyes.

"We demand too much of our delicate ladies." Stephen adjusted the quilt about her neck. "That's where I am at fault. This hovel is no better than that wretched clearing."

"Perhaps not enough is demanded of our ladies," Wesley replied to the subtle rebuke. He rose from his chair; lavender irritated his senses, merging desire and regret. Perhaps unrequited agony was better than reality's disappointment.

With a throat clearing cough, he retrieved a coin from his pocket. "Pray purchase a packet of lavender seeds to send to my wife on the next trip inland. Mrs. Reed must keep my wife's handkerchief. Undoubtedly, she intended it as a gift."

"Despite her crudeness, Jenny Cowlie is a good judge of character," Stephen reflected. "I'm sure Mrs. Bryson will step in line." He sniffed. "She has little choice in these matters."

Wesley scratched the back of his head. He'd given Olivia free rein to do as she wished. He could not presume she'd stay with him, yet what choice had he left her?

With a curt farewell, he went out into a surprisingly cold July night. Barracks Road was now deserted. The brawl had not lasted. Supplies were already loaded aboard ship for tomorrow's departure. He made note to bring his winter coat to Niagara. One never knew how long these investigations would take.

Upon brisk salute to the garrison sentry, he was informed a gentleman waited in his quarters.

John Oneida rose from Wesley's coveted leather chair and met him with a polite bow. He was richly dressed, with cream cravat and grey woolen trousers complementing an expensive top coat. Chiselled Native features and long braid enhanced the European apparel.

"*Tu portes des vêtements Européens?*" Wesley remarked, pulling up a wooden chair across from him.

"It makes for better perception—at least until Six Nations." John sat, leaning forward. "We must speak honestly if we are to work together. I hold no animosity, old friend. Can we begin with a handshake of peace?"

"Annie never told me of our son." He pressed a clenched fist down on the chair arm.

"She trusts no one...and I believe you understand that." John paused as if considering his words. "We churched only after Edward's birth, to ensure your right to claim him as your son. Yet she refused to bring him to you, until word came of your marriage."

"She brought Eddie to my wife," Wesley corrected, voice sharp.

"Annie carries much hurt from her past."

"Don't we all, John?" He inhaled deeply.

"Mrs. Bryson must be both courageous and generous for Annie to trust Eddie to her care."

"I truly hope so," Wesley winced.

"Annie has decided to stay at Billidore until I return from Niagara. There was no changing her mind." He stood.

"Aye, and a fine mess is begotten of my son, when he should have brought joy." Wesley got up, opened his wardrobe and retrieved a flask he reserved for sleepless nights. "Annie most certainly has a home at Billidore—it is her right." He filled two pewter goblets, and gave one to John. "And she may trust me to fully embrace my son and give him my name." He lifted his goblet and drank deep.

"Have faith, my friend. I believe our women will become sisters, in their own way." John set down his empty goblet. "Shall we now exchange peace?"

Wesley grasped John's hand with a firm shake. "And let us pray for their peace." He refilled their glasses.

John lifted his goblet. "And to our adventure!"

"An adventure, indeed!" Wesley affirmed.

—24—

"Drink up, luv," coaxed a gentle voice.

Olivia opened her mouth. Bitter liquid touched her tongue, spilling over her chin, and trickling down her neck.

"Better this time," another hushed voice confirmed. "She's keeping some down."

Her core rocked with convulsive shuddering. Shards of ice tore into her flesh, piercing deep into bone.

"You're not alone." Someone stroked her hair. She felt the weight of another blanket laid on top of her, and a warming rock pressed against her feet.

Adrift in darkness, the sun rose, burning face and neck, her throat tightening.

A rustle of silk skirts swished by the bed. Olivia looked up, shocked to see her sister glaring down at her. Charlotte scowled, then tore the pillow from under her head.

"This is what comes of dreaming, you fool! You've made *this* your bed," she hissed, pushing the pillow into Olivia's face. "Now sleep in it until you die."

Olivia pushed off the pillow, then leapt from her bed, through the open bedroom window. Down the river bank she tumbled, colliding against the old oak tree of Albyne's Park. Jane Blythe knelt beside her and gathered her within her arms.

"*Les vagues s'apaisèrent,*" she encouraged, gently. "*Ils purent se réjouir du calme revenu, et le Seigneur les conduisit à bon port.*"

"He maketh the storm a calm...waves...still." Olivia repeated. "They are glad...they be quiet...the Lord bringeth them unto their desired haven."

Jane vanished and soothing cold pressed to Olivia's forehead.

—

Pale light poured onto her bed. She was wearing Wesley's cotton work shirt instead of a sleeping gown. Between her bed and trunk was a commode. Looking through her open doorway, she watched Rosetta and Annie at the table, laughing.

"That woman is still here," she groaned in defeat. "And I'm too weak to fight her."

Struggling to the edge of the bed, she slipped her legs over and tried to stand. The room spun, her legs folding. Rosetta rushed in.

"She needs to eat," Annie pronounced from the doorway.

"You need to leave." Olivia's retort prompted their laughter.

"She has her fight," Rosetta nodded to Annie.

"What day is this?"

"It's mid-September." Annie sat beside her, on the edge of the bed. "You went down two weeks ago."

"Where's Wesley?" she asked, leaning away from the woman.

Rosetta pressed the back of her hand against Olivia's forehead. "Fever's broke—no need to concern him."

"What struck me?"

"Swamp Fever—the Ague," Rosetta returned. "It hits most new settlers. Fortunately, the Captain had plenty of Jesuit's Bark in store."

Leo Voisin's wedding gift and Granny Hoople's inquiry for assurance of provision now made sense.

Olivia held out a hand. "Please...help me up." Rosetta's strong arms wrapped about her waist. Slowly they walked to the table.

Annie set down a bowl of broth. "I'll not poison you," she quietly offered. Sitting beside her, she raised a spoon to Olivia's lips. The broth sat well in her stomach.

"You're on the mends," Rosetta encouraged, returning her to bed, tucking the quilt about her neck. "You'll be weak for a while. Just close your eyes and sleep like a baby."

—25—

"They can't survive another winter in tents." Wesley stood on the beach of Lake Ontario. Waves splashed against the rocks, piling ice high on shore.

To the south, he could see American sentries at Fort Niagara, watching over the Niagara River between them. Across the great lake—invisible to the naked eye—lay the young city of York. Behind him were the ruins of Newark.

"Frost has come too damn early," he muttered, head shaking. "Three hundred Newark homes and businesses destroyed during the American occupation, still in ruins. With building materials diverted to York, these people are doomed to suffer yet another winter in tents, dependent on military handouts.

"York is an obvious choice for capital and better use of funds," John defended. "Newark is but a cannon shot from Fort Niagara. Now that Americans have begun digging a canal from Albany, this town will never again be safe."

"There were at least 10 stores here before the war—a church or tavern on every corner," Wesley continued his lament. "Every structure was burnt to the ground; women and children cast out in winter's cruelty. My report must detail the Crown's failure to compensate these loyal families."

Wesley trudged back to the road, his boots weighed down by frozen mud. They continued to Queen Street, where he paused before a blackened stone foundation. A dirty, grey canvas tent stretched from remnants of a stone chimney, covering what had once been a root cellar.

"This was a dry goods store rivaling any found in Montreal. Belonged to a widow—"

"You're from the War Loss Claims, aye?" A woman peered from under the tarp and scrambled through the rubble, adjusting cap over unruly hair. She pulled her knitted grey shawl about her, and continued without waiting for confirmation. "I'm Mrs. MacDonald. This was my haberdashery." She shoved a stained paper in Wesley's hand. "Been waiting a long time to tell my story."

He scanned her account of possessions looted, provisions stolen, and property burned. As with others, she'd been given no warning to salvage clothing or provisions. A daughter died from exposure in the brutal cold. Her remaining children were now scattered to inland settlements. In addition to business inventory, she listed furnishings, clothing, and provided an estimate for loss of home and livelihood. Unlike Mrs. Swallow, of the Upper Saint Lawrence reach, her claims stood up to witness.

His heart grew heavy. She would never receive enough compensation to rebuild her life. The province had neither funds nor ambition.

"Pray help me. It's humiliating living on handouts." She clung to his coat sleeve. "My eldest boys are up in Ancaster, working for board. I need them back with me, to help rebuild."

Wesley struggled to find reassuring words. Gently he offered, "I commend your forbearance, Mrs. MacDonald," and tucked her claim within his inner coat pocket. "You can count on me to personally bring this before the Lieutenant Governor."

Her hand dropped, with a wearily muttered "Godspeed," and she retreated within her hovel.

Could Olivia survive such hardship? He shook his head. Could he survive Olivia? At present, he was incapable of even writing her. He should have attempted reconciliation before leaving Billidore. His only consolation was that she was in good hands and would never have to face such trial.

Darkness drew near. They continued along the deeply rutted road to Fort George, a biting wind cutting through Wesley's garments.

"With war's end, Francis Gore has deemed it safe enough to return from England and finish out his term as Lieutenant Governor." John Oneida's comment pierced his thoughts.

Wesley snorted with amusement. "Provisional Governors—Murrey, Robinson, or whomever now is in charge—they've all served ample penance"

"Penance?" John's burst of hearty laughter drove away the cold. "Eight gentlemen constrained to govern Upper Canada over the past ten years. We have become a penal colony for aspiring Court favourites, aye."

Wispy smoke hovered over Fort George's barracks, a promise of warmth. Six soldiers, milled about outside, immediately leaping to attention at their approach.

"Beggin' your pardon, Captain!" An eager private stepped forward with a brisk salute. "Permission to speak, sir!"

Wesley nodded assent.

"General Gordon Drummond awaits you, inside, sir."

A lump rose in his throat. Drummond, the only Canadian-born Lieutenant Governor of Upper Canada, had recently been elevated to Governor General of British North America. With a quick check of his uniform, and a sharp nod at John, they stepped inside.

"At ease, Captain Bryson. No need to explain your mission." General Drummond motioned to chairs, across the table, from where he sat. "It was I who sent for you to assess the many requests for compensation. You have a reputation for being observant and fair."

Wesley's thumping heart steadied. "How might I serve you, sir?" he ventured as they sat. General Drummond poured him a steaming cup of coffee. He waited for John to be served before drinking.

"A fine stew is on route from the mess. Stay and partake with me, after we talk business," the General invited, then cleared his throat. Wesley shifted in his chair, covering his nervousness with a sip of the strong black brew.

"Lieutenant Governor Gore and I are impatient with the delay for war damage compensation, Captain Bryson." Drummond began. "We need to reward frontier loyalty, with haste, for that blasted American canal holds threat of more hostilities." His speech increased in pace. "And now the terms of Treaty of Ghent are being ignored with American raiders crossing the Niagara, claiming their 1793 Fugitive Slave Act still applies on British soil. The audacity of loyal British subjects being considered as fugitives from Republican law!" He slammed the table with his fist.

Wesley startled. John folded his arms.

"Who won the bloody war?" Drummond's hard stare remained on Wesley, his question rhetorical. Inhaling deeply, he continued.

"Earlier today, I received word that a veteran of Butler's Rangers—Frederick Stark—was abducted in a raid near Fort Erie. He's a mill owner, married to a Scotswoman. I want a full report on this, Bryson."

"An African man?" Wesley ventured.

"Why else would he be seized?" Drummond's attention shifted to John Oneida. "You're a Haudenosaunee," he asserted, as if in accusation. "What do you know of John Norton?"

"*Teyoninhokarawen*, the Open Door," John confirmed, stating Norton's Mohawk name. "He lives on the Six Nations—"

"That man is Native only when it suits him," Drummond sniped. "This week a Mohawk village was attacked near Forty Mile. Six women and children were killed, while that half-breed plays in England."

Half-breed. Wesley's eyes briefly engaged John. Norton was the son of a Scot and a Native woman—mixed race—just as his son.

"As for Phelps and his Native wife," Drummond continued, "that traitor fled to the Republic when he should have been hanged for treason, along with the others at Burlington. His woman—Esther Hill—still holds claim to his land." He cleared his throat. "You're to investigate those claims and justify the Crown's seizure of that land."

"Under Haudenosaunee law, property belongs to women and not their husbands." John unfolded his arms, fists clenched in his lap. "They are not viewed as chattel, General."

Wesley's breath caught. Favour with the Governor General needed to be nurtured. Drummond's hard gaze rested on John Oneida.

"Mrs. Phelps' land is a wedding gift from Chief Joseph Brant," John bravely pressed, "Her loyalty to the Crown is unquestionable."

"This is British land, Mr. Oneida," the General spat back, cheeks reddening. "The sooner you people accept this, the better off you'll be."

John's jaw flexed; a knock at the door diverted the General's attention.

A team of attending privates marched in and set a tureen of steaming stew before the Governor, along with freshly baked bread and a pewter jug of ale. With a dismissive wave of his hand, they were again alone. Lifting the lid of the elaborate dish, Drummond ladled out two bowls, passing them to Wesley and John, before he generously filled his own dish.

"Natives need to stay protected on reserved lands," he resumed, tearing off a chunk of bread and dunking it in his bowl. "After Fort Erie, I want you to look into that raid of the Mohawk village. I expect both reports before you continue on to Six Nations." He stuffed the bread in his mouth, a morsel escaping onto the table."

John shifted in his chair, spoon gingerly stirring his bowl. Wesley struggled to eat, stomach churning. Mrs. MacDonald's petition weighed, heavily, within his pocket.

"I have a request from a Newark shopkeeper," he ventured.

"Petitions are continually shoved in my face, Captain Bryson." Drummond waved his hand, as if shooing a fly. "I refuse to allow my dinner ruined. And I refuse to endure this blasted cold barrack. Tonight, I sail to York." He ladled another heaping portion into his bowl and urged, "Eat up, gentlemen. We will meet in York in the new year, before you return to Kingston. I want your findings to provide sound argument against Ester Hill and the Six Nations claim of Phelps' land. The sooner that matter is cleared up, the sooner the land will be awarded to loyal British subjects."

"As ordered, sir." Wesley spooned a portion of beef into his mouth. Though it appeared inviting, the texture was chewy with gristle.

Reconciliation with Olivia had to be delayed and Mrs. MacDonald's petition would not be heard. Observations, put to pen, were his sole weapon. Exchanging a mute nod with John, he forced himself to swallow.

—26—

From her seat on the stump, Olivia had a clear view of the river. Gurgles traveled up from Billidore Rifts, filling her ears. Flowing swiftly by, Cataraqui's waters smoothed out toward the river bend. Only a few hours of paddling separated her from Kingston.

Sharp winds whistled through surrounding pines. Above, geese flew in an ever-shifting V, honking in chorus. Buttery-yellow, fiery-orange, and crimson-red leaves contrasted with her memory of silent English trees, losing their brown shriveled leaves. Within her red-striped brown dress and Wesley's deerskin coat, she blended into this Canadian symphony.

Inhaling deep of the cold crisp air, she conceded Wesley's wisdom: The ugly housedress kept her warm. She pondered how to think of Wesley. To love an ideal was easy; to love the imperfect was the work of a saint. She was no saint, yet tolerance was possible. It might even be attainable now that her nausea had ceased.

She stretched arms to the sky, infused with gratitude. Health improving, she willingly shucked her daily allotment of corn, faithfully milked Busy, and kept the hearth woodpile supplied and fire stoked. Strangely, this was the most liberty she'd ever known. In Charlotte's home, she had been harnessed by her sister's will and her brother-in-law's expectation, both of which consumed her vitality.

Here, the surrounding pines were a strong fortress. Rosetta and Annie left her alone to heal and work, but they too were a fortress. Woven within feverish Ague nightmares, their words anchored her

124

to life. And Sally Douglas had been there, caring for her despite all. Sighing deeply, Olivia accepted that the woman deserved her heartfelt apology.

A gentle hand rested on her shoulder. Startled, she looked up into Rosetta's dark probing eyes.

"Do you get frightened by the isolation, Rosie?" she asked.

"I welcome sanctuary." She drew back her hand, and sat on the other stump. "You've put that woe-be-gone fabric to good use with Eddie's clothes, your dress, and my shawl."

Olivia fixed a studied gaze on her companion. The shawl complemented her dark skin and bright smile. She was attractive, Olivia had to admit, both in character and appearance.

"Mrs. McGuire showed foresight in arranging us as companions. You saved my life, Rosetta," she confessed.

"Your care was mostly the work of Annie and Sally." She patted her belly. "I'm moving slower these days. My little one bounces."

"I was insulted when Wesley purchased this plaid fabric," Olivia continued aloud, mindless of whether or not Rosetta deemed her chatter worth listening to. "Yet it warmly clothes us and there's no being mistaken for a deer."

She shifted her gaze upriver, to the Douglas clearing. Two children ran about in a game of chase and catch. In the month since her outburst, Rosetta and Annie had slipped away several times to visit Sally. Dreading the encounter, she had yet to take a first step of reconciliation.

"We make the most with what we are dealt," Rosetta interrupted her thoughts.

"Were you ever stricken with the Ague, Rosie?"

"Fortunately not. Bark tea can bring on monthly bleeding." She leaned back to stretch her back and glanced downriver towards the bend.

"I've had no monthly course in three months," Olivia volunteered.

Rosetta turned, her warm smile reaching out. "How do you feel about this, Olivia?"

"I'm frightened."

"You're not alone...I am, as well."

"It's not just about birthing," Olivia sighed. "Am I capable of caring for the life that has resulted from my brief marriage?"

"We just do our best, Libby, and look to the Lord." Glancing back at the river bend, she clasped her hands together. "I somehow knew we would have guests."

Looking downstream, Olivia recognized Private Harris, paddling lead in a canoe with a young companion. Both lads were dressed in civilian deerskin.

Running down to the landing, Olivia met Ian Douglas. He grunted curt acknowledgment at her, before throwing an armful of fir branches into the water to cushion the birch vessel.

"Supplies and mail for you folk," Private Harris announced, leaping to the dock with wiry energy. "I will linger for any letters you might have. We've been given strict orders to return today." His companion tied up the craft, greeting Ian Douglas with a familiar hug.

"That will leave you enough time to join us for the meal Mrs. George is preparing." Olivia accepted a small sack, from Robbie. Ian left with a packet of letters and a wooden crate, while the lads continued to unload kegs onto the shore.

"Are these all for us?" Olivia asked.

"Aye. The Captain wants you be well provisioned, should his return be delayed." Robbie threw a sack over his shoulder and picked up a keg.

Olivia's heart lightened at this implication of Wesley's return. Hastening up to the cabin, she threw open the cabin door, with a gleeful, "Supplies and mail!"

"And hopefully news of Kingston and beyond," Rosetta swept a generous hand over the table. A crock of venison stew and loaf of bread already waited.

The freckled soldier set two kegs on the cabin floor and tugged his red tuque in greeting.

Robbie Harris smiled broadly upon entry. "You are here, Annie Nyaweh!" He greeted her with a formal bow and gave her a packet of letters from his sack. "Post Master wasn't wrong when he sent 'dis."

"And for you, Mrs. George, I bring something from Mr. Gutches." He brought out a package wrapped up in colourful cotton.

Rosetta chuckled with delight, unfolding her package. "Mr. Gutches steals my heart, once again. Oil, a scarf, and...." She held up a polished flat piece of wood. It had a handle, at one end, and long tapered teeth on the other. "He's carved me a hair pick!"

"We shall eat when your comrade returns." Olivia smiled, with stoic graciousness, honed from years of disappointment.

"I have a gift for you, Mrs. Bryson, from Lieutenant Reed." He retrieved a small paper box from the sack. "With 'de sorrow of his wife, 'dis was forgot."

Olivia lifted the lid. It was filled with small brown seeds.

"Lavender seeds," Rosetta identified. "Difficult to grow, but if they take hold, will be with you always." Suddenly frowning, she covered her mouth. "Did you say sorrow, Private Harris?"

Inhaling deeply, his eyes briefly closed. "Mrs. Reed did not survive 'de ordeal of birth. Lieutenant Reed is grieving."

"And the child?" Annie rested a hand on Rosetta's shoulder.

The door opened, chilling the room and interrupting his answer. The freckled soldier set a keg on the floor and tore off his tuque, revealing an unruly thatch of red hair. Rosetta wiped the corner of her eye with a corner of her apron and invited them to the table.

"Your letter, Mrs. Bryson." Robbie Harris handed her a thick letter with a prominent **WB** imbedded in the wax seal.

Olivia's breath caught. "Pray excuse me." She clutched the letter tightly, adding. "and do not stand on formality. Eat without me, for I must write a quick reply."

Wesley's letter was short, for it enveloped a second letter from Jane Blythe. She set it aside, for later reading.

> *Dear brave Olivia,*
> *I earnestly ask forgiveness for my unreasonable expectation of you. My return to Billidore will be delayed. Governor General Drummond has ordered that I report to him in York before traveling back to Kingston.*
> *Loyally yours, Wesley.*

A disappointed sigh escaped, then she noticed the postscript scrawled at the bottom of the page, noting that he'd sent a notarized copy of the marriage certificate to the solicitors of Charles Eldenmont at the time of their marriage. By this, Wesley exercised marital authority over Olivia, under the *Coverture* condition of law, removing any influence her brother-in law had in her life. Had he done this as an expression of protection? Or was it a declaration of triumph over her family?

"Oh Wes! What am I to make of you?" she moaned.

Animated conversation at the table drew her attention. She needed to join her guests, at least for appearances' sake.

Returning attention to the letter, her eyes rested on his use of "Loyally yours". He'd given her "free rein" to do as she pleased, yet he was choosing to declare loyalty. And so, she would freely choose to assume the best of his commitment.

Slipping Wesley's note beneath her pillow, she retrieved pen and paper from her writing box.

> *My dear husband,*
> *Over the past months, I've grown to appreciate your*
> *intentions for me to prosper in this new life. If you*
> *have patience with my struggle, I will endeavour to*
> *forgive your misguided efforts.*
> *Tenderly yours, Mrs. Bryson.*

She pressed her thumb to the wax rather than using her family seal to secure the note.

"Pray put this in the military post," she directed Private Harris, handing him her letter. She looked about the table, her heart light. "I hope you've saved me some food."

"Another joins our rousing religious discussion," Annie proclaimed, setting a steaming bowl of stew before her. "We have a Roman Catholic, a Methodist, a Presbyterian, and now Private Harris has a fellow Church of Englander to assist his defence. "

"I do not give much thought to these matters," Olivia sniffed. Sharing her table made egalitarian presumption inevitable. Yet, she remembered Wesley's insistence that she stand with his men at the chapel in Kingston. He did not consider this an abasement, but an expression of loyalty to those under his command. She must make effort with these young privates. They'd brought the post, for that she was appreciative.

Then she remembered the young African's reverence and supplied, "I have observed faith is of importance to Private Harris."

"We are not arguing faith, but participation in a church where not all are viewed as equal before God?" Rosetta tore off a chunk of bread. "Robbie's Reverend has enslaved servants, and allots pews according to wealth."

"Reverend Stuart must answer for his choices, Mrs. George," Robbie's dark eyes flashed, "as we all must. But I will not let his choices keep me from my momma."

The red-haired Presbyterian refilled his bowl. Annie dunked a morsel of bread into hers, and tucked it into Eddie's mouth.

"Does your mother reside in Kingston, Private Harris?" Olivia asked, attempting to shift to a lighter topic.

"She's with 'de Lord, in 'de company of heaven...and what we now discuss." Robbie held his hands open, with dramatic flourish. "When we stand before 'de Lord's altar for communion, heaven opens, with angels, and archangels and all company of heaven, lauding and magnifying His Holy name. I know my momma is standing with us, because she's in 'de company of Heaven."

"*Mon Dieu*! You're more Catholic than I," Annie laughed.

Rosetta turned to Olivia, eyes widening. "Do you believe this, as well?"

Olivia inhaled deeply. Religion was a social obligation. She'd retained little from Charles Eldenmont's sermon reading, Sunday evenings in the drawing room. As for church attendance, her thoughts were constantly adrift. "Those are mere words, to which I've given no thought."

The young Presbyterian's spoon dropped into his empty bowl with a pronounced clank. Fixing brilliant blue eyes on her, he asked, "D'ye ken, Mrs. Bryson, that our God hears words when spoken with faith?"

His brogue unnerved her. Likely a Highland crofter, like one of the many such tenant farmers evicted from her family's Scottish holdings to improve its profitability. Their plight had not been her concern. Yet in church, she had weekly offered, "Forgive me for what I have done or left undone," with no thought that it might be acknowledgement of her contribution to injustice.

Her heart stirred. She'd never eaten with a crofter, nor had she ever engaged in such forthright converse.

"I suppose I should 'ken,'" she conceded. "I truly should."

—27—

Wesley peered over the rocky edge, transfixed by careening waters less than 10 feet below. The water's potency mesmerised him with tempting savagery. If not careful, he could easily succumb to her pulverizing, thunderous beauty. Seemingly only a boot in depth, those falls drew in anything within half a league upstream. Closing his eyes, he allowed his senses to be overcome.

This was not his first encounter with Niagara Falls. During the war, he'd resisted her billowing, beckoning vapours; duty prevented his paying homage.

Eighteen months ago, and a mile inland, one of the bloodiest battles of the war had taken place. The American line had broken, and they'd withdrawn from the Niagara Frontier, defeated. Summer's heat had forced a quick burial of Canadian and British dead on the battle field. They had cremated American remains on a huge funeral pier that must have been visible to their retreating compatriots, across the river.

John gingerly crawled over beside him. "Have the Falls drawn you under her spell?" he shouted over the falling water's deafening din.

"I could stay here forever." Wesley eased away from the edge. Icy rime from the falls' chilling mist coated his deerskin jacket and the rock ledge where he lay.

"There's an Indian ladder, to the east, that will take us down into the gorge," John stretched out a hand to steady Wesley's last steps.

Walking east along the cliff edge, they found an opening in the brush. A slender cedar trunk, its branches cut off to about 3 inches in length, served as ladder. Propped against the rocky cliff, it extended to a ledge below, where another cedar trunk led deeper within the gorge. Every surface was glacial.

"Peculiar, cold and icy so early..." John waved him forward. "Shall we give it a go?"

Wesley looked down and shivered. "I've survived war. I have no need to prove my bravery."

John burst into jovial laughter. "Neither have I, my friend."

They returned to their horses, securely picketed among sheltering trees, inland of the river path. With brand and tack clearly identifying military issue, no one would dare touch the mounts for fear of severe penalty. Westward, they continued, to Macklan's Tavern, in Chippewa.

The innkeeper's gaze travelled from Wesley to John, before looking through the open door to their horses.

"We're on the Governor General's business and require accommodation," Wesley pushed by him. "Pray attend our horses, then serve up what's in the kitchen."

Heaping portions of chicken, with roasted potatoes were set before them, along with mugs of ale. "This should keep you gentlemen while your room is prepared," the innkeeper's lusty wife sniped.

Wesley's generous coin elicited her appreciative smile, and a second glass of ale. The common room was warm and the food tasty. John Oneida seemed preoccupied while they ate, their earlier camaraderie gone.

With a second mug, John emerged from his reflection. "Do you know that in 1764, 2,000 of the Haudenosaunee Nations gathered, near here, to negotiate with the British, nation to nation?"

"Wasn't sovereignty granted to them at that time?" Wesley asked in confirmation.

"Aye. From Lake Erie to Lake Ontario, where American Loyalists are now planted." He set his empty mug on the smooth wooden table. "When you write to the Governor about Newark settlers living like rats, don't forget to remind him that our hunting and fishing rights were bartered away for useless trinkets and dull plows."

"You're an American refugee, John, much as those Loyalists."

"Aye. I am an Oneida Haudenosaunee, taken as a child to the *Deux-Montagnes* Montreal mission, when my village was massacred by Americans. But understand that borders are of your making. My people eat from the same dish, with one spoon. And in 1764 we negotiated, in good faith, to share our dish with the British."

John leaned forward. "Butler's Rangers settled at Fort Erie, after the Revolution. Some were Black, others Mohawk, but all were armed and ready to defend this land for Britain." He drew a deep breath. "Now I hear that African shield settlements are planned for north of Lake Erie, south of Georgian Bay and east of Lake Huron."

"Blacks will get the same rights and land apportioning as Europeans," Wesley defended.

"What of our rights, Wesley? This was negotiated to be sovereign Indian land. You British have taken dish, spoon, and eat everything."

Wesley folded his arms. "There are many conflicting demands in Canada."

"What you don't denounce, you condone by your silence," John asserted. "A difficult task you will face with that Phelps situation."

"The Newark report is almost complete. I plead for resources to rebuild, yet I know Britain's treasury is depleted after years of war," Wesley defended. "All the government can offer in compensation is land."

"Whose land?" John challenged.

The door flew open, flooding the tavern with cold. Recognizing the British Lieutenant from the Kingston Garrison, Wesley motioned him to join them at the table. The innkeeper's wife brought over another tankard of ale.

"I've paused, only to warm up, while my horse is tended to." The lieutenant smiled with deference and sat. "I must not linger, for I'm longing to be with my family. Enough light remains that I might make it to Selkirk Point tonight."

"What news have you of Kingston?" Wesley invited. "I've been away over a month and, aside from orders, I've heard little of life?"

The officer drank deep of his ale. "A visit from the Governor General is anticipated, come spring. The ladies are all atwitter. Old Cartwright has finally passed on. And sadly..." He paused. "Lieutenant Reed's wife succumbed to childbirth."

Wesley's breath caught. The soldier finished his ale, wished them "God Speed" and left.

The shock of Violet Reed's death settled on Wesley. He turned to John and broached, "How did it fare when Annie birthed Eddie?"

"Our women helped her, as is our custom."

Wesley nodded in appreciation. The impregnable walls of an indigenous female community were seldom breached. They took care of each other. The same could be said of European women. He had never been able to confirm rumor of wanton outrage during the American occupation. Lips stayed tightly closed, much as they had with Mrs. George. He'd no choice but allow them a dignity of denial and omit these implications from his reports.

Was Olivia capable of such forbearance? She'd had difficulty enough shucking her privileged prejudice.

—28—

Olivia tucked Jane Blythe's letter within her dress pocket. She'd read it several times.

Though horrified to learn of Jane's expulsion from Charles' house, she was relieved to learn she now resided at the Haynes' residence, in London. Regret remained for implying Jane's assistance, in her flight to Canada. The poor woman had simply passed on a message, ignorant of its meaning.

Yet, Jane Blythe did not write in accusation, but to encourage her to seize opportunity. "Unforgiveness will mire you," she warned. "A new world opens for you. I pray you humbly open heart and mind to embrace the opportunity that is yours."

Across from her, Annie reclined on the settee, with Eddie napping within her arms. Jane's prayer was being answered.

He maketh the storm a calm. Who else but Annie could have prayed those words to break the Ague's hold? Words uttered in faith.

"You are a gifted healer, Annie Nyaweh," Olivia affirmed honestly. Her dull back ache still plagued, but she refrained from asking for an easing tincture. Mustn't build her up too much, she resolved.

Annie's eyes fluttered open. "I have much to learn," she yawned. "My father sent me to the *Deux-Montagnes* convent to learn European healing—he thought it was superior to our knowledge." Eddie stirred, looked around at Olivia, sucking his lower lip. "Our healing feeds a body when it ails. You Europeans fight the body, much as you fight anything you don't understand."

"I don't wish to fight, Annie, though I have yet to like you."

"Of that we are in agreement." She kissed the top of Eddie's head.

Olivia rose from the rocker, reached down to her toes, stretching out her back, and declared, "It is time I visit Sally." Playfully she tousled Eddie's head as she passed by. Her impulsive caress came as surprise—she had not been accustomed to sharing affection in England. Wesley's tenderness, in those first naïve days of marriage, had introduced her to this foreign language.

From her trunk, she retrieved a favourite cream silk scarf. Wrapping it about her bottle of lavender fragrance, she set off to the Douglas clearing.

Three pigs grunted from their pen at her approach. Ian Douglas paused his work of pulling out a stump, and scowled over his oxen pair. In the cabin's gable window, she caught a glimpse of small faces. The door opened, and she met the hard set of Sally Douglas's face.

"I'm here to seek your forgiveness," Olivia declared firmly, "and I've wish to also apologize to Jamie and Sadie, for my inexcusable insult to their mother."

"It's about time," Sally returned.

Olivia had anticipated some form of encouragement to her humble apology. But then, this woman had followed a husband to war, and twice doused her with cold water. She would tolerate no artifice.

"You cared generously for me, when I was struck down with the Ague," Olivia further ventured.

"It were my Christian duty." She folded her arms.

"But I was undeserving—"

"Our Good Lord commands us to 'Do unto others as you would have them do unto you.'" Sally's chin lifted in subtle challenge. "I didn't do it because you were deserving."

"Christian duty, that I have yet to learn."

"What you do shows your faith."

"Then I am arrogant sinner," Olivia conceded.

"You're a hoity-toity bitch." She tossed her head back. "And now that I have that out of the way, I feel better." A smile crept across her face. "If those are gifts of 'tonement, I'll consider your apology."

"It's my only bottle of lavender scent."

"Even better," Sally accepted the glass vessel.

"And this is my favourite scarf." Olivia draped the silk fabric about her ample neck.

"Come on in," Sally beckoned. A warm fire glowed on the hearth of her tidy cottage. Something delicious simmered in a cauldron. Overhead, at the top of narrow stairs, two heads peered down.

Pouring from a brown crockery teapot, Sally invited her to the table for a cup of tea.

Olivia sniffed the dark beverage in her cup.

"I'm no *voyageur*—there's no tobacco in it." Sally chuckled, across from her. "My herbs draw out the tea's flavour and life. And I certainly don't abide with sugar, though my Ian can afford it. It's a cruel luxury of the rich."

"You were in Jamaica?" Olivia sat up.

"No. I spent two years, in Iberia, with Wellesley's forces. But some 'o the wives come from the Islands and told tales."

"Jenny Cowlie said you were widowed."

Sally sipped from her cup. "You want my story, aye?"

The beverage must be safe, thought Olivia, and ventured a sip. Tangy peppery warmth flowed over her tongue. She sipped again.

"A tad of ginger—good for digestion." Sally nodded proudly. Drawing a deep breath, she cleared her throat. "To begin...Mill work was scarce to come by, in London, and my Da' earned too little to feed us all. So, when Pete asked for my hand—I were 14—we went off to war." She folded hands on the table, between them. "The forces treated us women well, but we earned our way laundryin', nursin', and fetchin'. From time to time, we even picked up a musket."

"Was your Pete good to you?"

"As good as 'e could be, I s'pose. We buried our first baby, with the soldiers, in Iberia." A gentle smile softened her face. "Aye...amid war, we loved as we could."

"And then you came to Canada?" Olivia prompted.

"We went back to England, soon after the baby died. But, a'fore I had time to launder our clothes, we shipped out to Canada." She studied the dregs of her cup, a frown darkening her face. "I later 'erd General Wellesley called us the scum of the earth." Flashing blue eyes surveyed Olivia. "We stood between England and that French horde, yet 'e called us scum!"

"It is I who am scum." Olivia reached for her hand. "Please forgive me Sally. While you fought for Britain, I entertained officers, and danced around marital entanglement." She didn't dare add that she had attended a *fête* in honour of General Wellesley, upon his return from the continent.

"Well, my children aren't 'appy with you, for sure." Sally withdrew her hand.

"You speak of them as your own?" Olivia probed. "My step-mother rid me from my father's life."

"When you love someone, you take their life as your own...and Ian's 'ad a share of life. When kicked off the land, 'e brought the family to Canada and wrestled out this farm. The first Mrs. Douglas lies up that rise." She nodded at the window. "I compete with a ghost, Olivia. I know what it is, movin' into 'er home, sleepin' in 'er bed and even bein' called by 'er name—when 'e forgets. Ian's a good man, and took my babe as 'is own. Your Wesley is a good man, too, and the partin', with Annie, was amicable."

"Amicable?"

"Annie's father wanted 'er to join the Church." She stroked her chin. "You must know by now, that girl is no nun. When Marie-Jeanne Voisin learned she'd run from the convent, she took 'er in and arranged the match with Wesley—"

"In this way of the country," Olivia sniffed, recalling the attractive Native wife of the Voyageur that sailed them to Lachine.

"People grab what they can in war. The convent wouldn't want 'er back if she 'ad a child. Wesley gained favour in Anishinaabe territory for trade in furs and prospectin', and 'er father soon came around."

"I do not know much of my husband's business endeavours."

"P'raps you should." Sally refilled their cups. "When Annie learned John had left *Deux-Montagnes*, no longer intendin' on the priesthood, she asked Wesley for freedom. Wesley set an 'igh bride price of furs and passed word among those 'e traded with that John Oneida agreed to pay it." She chuckled. "He 'adn't, but, bein' at seminary so long, 'e needed a bit 'o coaxin'."

"Wesley sold her?"

"A *Bride* price," Sally corrected, "in praise of 'er value as a wife, for the marriage arrangement—it's their custom." She nodded firmly. "Though John was surprised, 'e was more than agreeable. Seems 'is eye was on her all along. Wesley sold the furs to Leo Voisin, bought his Captaincy, and gave Annie a small dowry. Everything seemed nicely settled, 'cept Annie hadn't told your Captain she was carrying a child."

"Why didn't she?"

"My guess is Wesley is a good man and would insist on doin' right. That's why she never told him what that Frenchman did, either."

Looking down, running her finger along the edge of her teacup, Olivia impulsively confessed, "I forced Wesley to marry me."

A broad smile filled Sally's face. "We do what we must, aye?"

Olivia nodded. "But what do you mean about the Frenchman? It that Leo Voisin?"

"Never you mind about that—we woman watch out for each other," Sally answered, with a subtle swag. "When I first come, isolation frightened me more than those blasted Americans. That's what drove poor Violet Reed mad. But Annie helped me see different, and she'll help you, too." She stood up. "My soup smells done!" With a quick stir, she set the cauldron to cool on the hearth brick work.

"Your soup smells inviting."

With a wink, Sally retrieved a small cotton sack from her pantry drawer. "I'll spare you a bit 'o my secret mixture. Annie's been hankering for this blend for years." She placed the pouch in Olivia's hands, as if it was gold. "Enough magic to take you through winter— a pinch in the cauldron is enough." From a basket of windfall apples on the floor, she filled another sack. "Take some of these, too. Mind you, they're a mite fermented, so only good for cider. Can you carry them?"

Olivia nodded, tucking the spice bag into her pocket.

"It's up to you to live with consequence and settle your home. I 'erd Wesley flared up—but so did you. That man will come 'round," she confirmed, with a firm nod. "Do you knit?"

She pulled down a basket of wool balls, of cranberry, yellow and green shades. "These leftovers will keep your mind busy. Won't be long a'fore Rosetta needs to dress her baby."

"Do you know who the—"

"No talk!" Sally held up a hand. "Just support her."

"I may also be with child," Olivia further confided.

"Must be this durn cold weather." Sally's face lit up. "I'm expecting, come spring. Ian's well-experienced with lambing and farrowing— almost as good a midwife as Jenny Cowlie."

"Good Lord! Was he midwife for your last birth?"

A blast of cold air announced Ian's entrance. Directing a stern eye at Olivia, he announced, "You've a sack of oats set aside, in the Reed shanty. Best to winnow on a windy day, where chickens can clean up afterward."

"Thank you, Mr. Douglas, for your advice." Olivia planted a kiss on Sally's rosy cheek. "And thank you for time with your forgiving wife."

With that, she hoisted the booty over her shoulder and trudged up to her cabin. A wisp of smoke was visible from the chimney. Her heart warmed, remembering the delicious scent of Sally's cauldron.

"It's high time I prove myself Mistress of my home. There's plenty of squash in my root cellar." She optimistically plotted. "I shall make soup."

"How did you convince her to part with some of her precious spices?" exclaimed an amused Annie. "I've been trying for years."

"I humbled myself and paid dearly, with a favourite scarf and my only bottle of lavender water." Olivia knelt before her open trunk, in search of knitting needles. "She gave me some wool, so I guess I wasn't totally out-bargained."

"Tomorrow, we'll fetch that bag of oats from the Reed clearing, and collect leeks to add to your soup," Annie added. "I also need some sawed planks, to make a cradle board."

Rosetta nodded silent concession. A simple meal of fried eggs, salt pork, and boiled carrots waited on the table.

"When were you at the Reed's shanty?" Olivia asked.

"That's where I stayed, after leaving Eddie, so to keep an eye on you." Annie paused. "Rosetta will soon need a board, as will I, come Spring."

Folding her arms, Olivia raised her jaw. "And so will I."

"*Bien fait, ma sœur!*" Annie chortled.

"I am *not* your sister," Olivia retorted, noting Rosetta seemed distracted. She had to do her best to maintain peace in the cabin. "Are you ailing, Rosetta?" she asked.

"Just tired." She returned a weak smile and they finished the meal in silence.

Wind began to pick up, whistling through cracks in the chinking. Gizzy stirred, barking to be let out the door.

"Wolves must be around," Annie began to gather dishes from the table. "Busy and the chickens are safe in the barn, but Gizzy better stay in."

"Shouldn't we load the musket?" Olivia grasped Rosetta's hand.

"They're not interested in us." Annie turned to her with a smirk. "They're stalking those deer that nibble at our crib corn."

Night drew out, cold and fierce. Wind howled through the trees, rattling windows panes; Sally's insult rattled Olivia. Hoity-toity; mere words, like *Le Saut du Plat* on the Saint Lawrence River. Smooth waters that hid sharp piercing rocks.

"May my mind open to opportunity," she offered, drifting into sleep.

—29—

"Too damn close." Wesley reined his horse away from the bank. Even with an overcast sky, smoke from the American camp was visible across the river. "This border presents a complicated situation. With that Albany canal complete, we'll soon be overrun by Americans."

"*Les femmes sont compliquées*," John countered, with a quick tug of his reins. "Never lie to them, my friend. You'll only get caught."

"Pardon?" Wesley shot back in surprise. "Do you speak as soldier, priest, or husband?"

John snorted with laughter. "I speak of Mrs. MacDonald, in Newark. She knows your promise will return empty. And as for Mrs. Stark— she's no fool expecting the Council's help. She knows most of them are slave owners. These African shield colonies will only incite more raiding parties. All Americans need do is paddle across the Niagara, claim Canadian Black people are fugitives from their law, and no one will stop them."

Wesley couldn't contest John's assertion. Though Canadian restrictions had been imposed by the Legislative Council, limiting importation and resale of humanity, slavery remained legal in Canada. Mrs. Stark's husband could not look to his government for help.

John and Wesley had just left Frederick Stark's grist mill. Having completed their interview of his wife, they were returning east, toward Fort Erie. The missing man was a veteran of the disbanded Butler's Rangers. A number of African Loyalists served in this regiment 30 years ago, during the American Revolutionary War.

Both Stark's mill and sturdy stone cottage were situated by a fast rushing stream, feeding into Lake Erie. The man's prosperity evidenced good business sense and his wife reminded Wesley of Sally Douglas. Pleasant and shrewd, she had registered their five sons as white in the recent census.

"If I were a Native, you'd see them as Native," she huffed, in response to Wesley's challenge. "I'm a free-born Scot, and so are they."

Frederick Stark had left to open his mill early on a June morning. He never arrived, though it was a mere walk of 500 feet. A few hours later, an irritated farmer knocked at their door, demanding the mill open to grind his first crop of wheat.

Mrs. Stark provided a sketch and testimony from a military surveyor, evidencing a struggle outside the mill. She also had a separate witness account of a boat, crossing over to Buffalo with a Black man, gagged and tied. Four months had passed, without further news. Wesley assumed the man was either dead or irretrievable lost to enslavement.

"You gave false assurance to Mrs. Stark that her government would work with the New York officials to find her husband. You know as well as she, our government has abandoned that loyal British veteran. The most she can hope for is to be declared a widow in seven years." John looked up at the grey sky. "People need the truth to move forward."

"You don't make my job easy." Wesley noted a shifting V of noisy geese fleeing to the south. Snow flurries filled the air and his heart turned to Olivia. If he could offer false hope to Mrs. Stark, he could provide a few sincere words to his wife. "We'll spend a few days at

Queenston. The Secord house is still livable and I've heard they're amenable to paid borders. I'll complete the Stark report and dispatch it before we continue on to Six Nations."

John nodded and rode ahead.

Too many conflicting demands, Wesley mused. His investigations were challenging enough without adding the complication of a need to reconcile with Olivia Fairworth and his son.

He was no longer indebted to Charles Eldenmont. His present commission had come through his performance on the field of battle, bought with his trading profits. Yet he'd dealt foolishly in his marital situation.

Olivia was no army recruit, to be taught through hardship; she was a woman of entitlement. To her credit, she had complied with his terms to live on the clearing with Mrs. George. In their few shared days, his hope had grown for mutual contentment until her blasted temper had matched his. Skirting the truth had been a poor attempt at lessening hurt. Instead he had destroyed her trust. Facing unjust accusation, he had yet again walked away, history repeated. Fortunately, they'd had so little intimacy during that brief harmony, life-giving was hardly possible.

She was his for life; she had nowhere else to go. Somehow, he must correct his blundering efforts, and attempt reparation of the marriage.

—30—

"Have patience, Olivia." Rosetta poured the cauldron's contents into the slop bucket. "Simmering brings out the flavour. No amount of spice will cover up burnt food."

"I'll go serve it up to the Douglas pigs," Olivia offered, with humiliating dejection.

As Olivia walked by, Annie looked up from harvesting turnips and potatoes in the kitchen garden. "Gone to slop, eh?" she remarked.

"Well...I'll get the musket and have the toboggan ready for when you get back. We'll go the Reed clearing and dig up wild leeks. Maybe they will help."

A musket? Olivia fought a rush of panic. Did they need it for protection against wolves?

Ian accepted the bucket with a compassionate grin and emptied it into the trough. The pigs snorted their joy and raced over to consume.

"They're not particular," she mumbled.

"It will only get better," he consoled.

Upon her return, she dug out a small sheathed knife she'd found in Wesley's tool box. Though the blade was dull, it seeded courage.

Annie briskly led on the leaf-strewn river path, pulling the toboggan. Gizzy dove after a squirrel, into the woods. Olivia struggled behind, trying to keep up. Her back ache had returned.

Breathless, she arrived at the Reed's log shanty. Viewed from the river, she'd thought the simple structure forlorn. Yet, close-up, the well-kept building had a four-paned window and sturdy door, with a strong wooden latch. Olivia stared at the peculiar latch; it fastened from the outside.

"That won't keep people out," she remarked.

"It's to keep animals out." Annie dealt her a quick frown. "People are welcome to take shelter. There's another latch inside."

Olivia opened the door, surprised by the interior's tidiness. In the corner there was a roped bed with a rolled-up quilt mattress. Mid-room, a bare wooden table and two chairs waited for a meal to be prepared from the small kettle, hung over a neatly swept hearth. The sack of oats Ian had harvested waited behind the door.

"This cabin is quite agreeable," Olivia remarked.

"That's why I stayed here when I left Eddie with you."

"Why didn't you tell Wesley of his son?" Olivia confronted her confession. "Why wait until he had gone and leave him with me?" She attempted to lift the sack of oats; it was too heavy.

"Perhaps I wanted to cause problems." Annie sighed deeply, as if divesting a load.

"You most certainly succeeded."

"We both know the sorrow of wanting someone you can't have, Olivia." Annie hoisted the sack of oats on her shoulder with a grunt. "Love is work, both to get it and to give it. Wesley will come around, just like John."

Olivia followed her out to the toboggan. Annie set the sack on the toboggan and turned to face her.

"I entered the convent from the *Deux-Montagnes* residential school. The mission thought me a good candidate for I was quick to learn and interested in healing arts. Instead, the Good Sisters made me scrub floors and do laundry." She looked to the sky, with a scornful chortle. "Being a nun was my father's hope for me. Poor man didn't know what happened behind those walls…" She waved her hand as if swatting away a memory. "I ran away and accepted a marriage *du façon de la pays* to end the mission's claim on me. Wesley gained trading connections and I found refuge."

"Marriage for that reason is wrong."

"Is my reason any different than marrying to bring wealth or power into your family?" Annie shrugged. "John was also at the residential school, in the upper level. He began studies for priesthood and I assumed he'd chosen the Church over me. But he left the mission to become a British interpreter. And when he showed up with Wesley," she clasped her hands together, "buried embers flared, Olivia. I told Wesley everything, insisting he release me from our arrangement. He understood, and we lived as brother and sister until John paid my bride price."

Olivia drew a deep breath. "If you think Wesley so understanding, why did you not tell him about—"

"Would he abandon the mother of his child?" Brown eyes pierced Olivia's fear. "You know he would have insisted on marriage. John waited until after Eddie's birth for us to be churched, so Wesley would be recognized as my son's father. I did not want to lose John, so..." Annie nodded soberly. "I selfishly grieved Wesley."

"You were thorough," Olivia confirmed.

"He'll not stay away when he learns you are with child."

"I won't have him under those terms."

"And neither would I. So now you understand why I hid carrying his child?" Proudly lifting her chin, she loaded the musket with practiced efficiency. Snow flurries fluttered around them.

"Wolves?" Olivia's heart began to race.

"Goose for dinner—I'm tired of beans and pork. Your leeks are beyond those grazing geese." Annie marched briskly into the field. Mukluks, short tunic, and deerskin leggings, allowed her unimpeded movement through the underbrush. Gizzy leapt ahead, madly barking and chasing geese into flight.

Olivia's skirt snagged a branch. Yanking it free, she knotted it about her waist.

BOOM. With a sure shot, Annie brought a goose down. She turned, smirking, "They'll remember me and not come back next year."

Where will any of us be, next year, Olivia wondered as she fetched the bird and brought it back to the toboggan.

Slinging the musket over her shoulder, Annie unsheathed her knife and walked ahead. "And now we dig." She invited, and knelt to loosen the roots. Olivia pulled out her small blade and began the same. "Where did you find my old knife?" she asked, tossing a leek into the basket.

"In the box of chisels and hammers." Olivia pried up a root, holding it up proudly.

"Aye," Annie affirmed. "I'll hone your blade when we get back."

Soon, Olivia carried the full basket of leeks to the toboggan. Annie went into the shanty cabin, emerging with two boards and a handsaw.

"Are you stealing?"

"This is your clearing, Mrs. Bryson." With a firm shove, she wedged the boards next to the leek basket and wrapped the toboggan rein about her waist and Olivia's. "Stephen Reed sold it to your husband."

"Good Lord, I've become a beast of burden", Olivia huffed, remembering her disgust at Wesley pulling a canoe through the rapids. Life seemed to have a way of returning judgement.

Though they laboured with the load, the return trip along the river path passed surprisingly quickly. Pausing by the river bank, Annie cut a few willow branches and added them to the load. Olivia bent over, seeking to relieve her backache. Billidore's rumbling, tumbling waters encouraged; they were near home. The flurries were thickening to snowfall, yet she was wet with sweat.

Under a darkening sky, they stumbled up the path, deposited the lumber and branches in the shanty barn, and hung the goose from a rafter. Annie dragged the grain sack into the cabin.

149

"Busy's been milked, beans and biscuits are on the table," Rosetta greeted.

"Praise be," Olivia muttered, exhausted.

After dinner she bathed the scratches on her legs with salt water. In the evening's quiet, she shortened her red-striped brownish dress to just below the knee. With trousers beneath, she would be decent, protected, and free to move—like Annie.

Sleep did not come easily. Her back gnawed and she shifted frequently, trying to find comfort. Finally, she hobbled through the dark cabin, to the cistern, to make a cup of tea. Reaching for the kettle, her breath caught. A deep cramp surged through her core, buckling her legs.

"Dear Lord!" she wailed, huddling on the floor.

—31—

"You bring good news, Captain Bryson?" James Secord limped over to the hearth, pulled out a glowing twig, and lit his pipe. "I've heard nothing from the government regarding my request for a position." He handed Wesley a thin letter from the mantle, sealed with a thumb print. "Perhaps this brings good news—'tis addressed to you."

Wesley slipped the letter into his inner pocket. "Yours is one of the few houses that survived the occupation. It was presumed you'd no need of assistance." He looked about.

Greased paper filled many of the window panes allowing only diffuse light in. Sparse furnishings of a sturdy table, plain wooden chairs, and cradle contrasted with the sumptuous Kingston home of Secord's brother-in-law, Richard Cartwright, where he and other privileged officers enjoyed a few evenings of brandy and cards. Before Cartwright had declined in health, he had courted the good opinion of Kingston's military to ensure continued support of his business and political endeavours.

"Most of our glass panes were shattered or stolen," James Secord acknowledged. "As for our store...what couldn't be carried off, was rendered unusable." The baby stirred in the cradle. "She'll not stay quiet for long," he noted, distracted. Drawing from his pipe, he continued, "Captain Bryson, I'm not asking for charity. I'm requesting a government position or, at least, compensation for war damages. I want the dignity to rebuild my life and support my family."

"A hope we all share," John confirmed. "You've six children?"

"Aye. We've been blessed with five healthy daughters and an equally robust son," Mrs. Secord answered, entering the kitchen. "Our oldest, Mary, is out in service."

"In Kingston, with your sister, Mrs. Cartwright?" Wesley asked.

"She has my deepest sympathy for her husband's passing, but no," James Secord returned curtly.

Wealthy family dynamics are peculiar, Wesley mused to himself. Richard Cartwright's niece had been put out in service and her family left to live in poverty. His heart went out to Olivia and how her family had used her as barter for social promotion.

"I've set up your room, gentlemen." Mrs. Secord interrupted his reflection. Her smile warmed her delicate features. Tenderly cooing, she lifted the baby from the cradle, threw a towel over her shoulder, and sat to nurse.

"Mrs. Secord is my guardian angel," James drew from his pipe, emitting a short, harsh cough. "She pulled me from the Queenston battlefield."

"Now James...I wasn't the only wife there." She peeked discreetly, under the baby's covering, her gaze returning to her husband. "Mrs.

Hill, of the 100th Regiment, stopped those renegades from bayonetting you. She's your true guardian."

"Pardon?" Wesley sat up, with interest.

"Aye." A brown curl escaped from beneath her cap. "She fired a fallen soldier's musket, chasing them off, and helped me bring James home. Our girls cared for her baby, allowing her to return to the field and search for survivors."

"Lieutenant Fitzgibbon made no mention of women on the field," Wesley challenged.

"Nor did he make mention of Mrs. Secord in his report on the battle of Beaver Dams." James Secord spit into the hearth. "During my convalescence, while serving supper to the occupiers, my wife overheard their plans of surprise attack. She then walked 17 miles to Fitzgibbons' camp to warn him."

"Seventeen miles, through enemy lines?" John slapped a hand across his knee. "How is that possible?"

Graceful laughter flowed from her. "Who is to challenge a frantic woman, in search of her milk cow?" Fair complexion complemented her mischievous smile. "Your people, Mr. Oneida, accompanied me to DeCew House, on the last part of my journey, else I would have succumbed to exhaustion."

"I will draw your petition to the Governor General's attention," Wesley committed. "I meet with him in York in the new year."

"You must not have a family, Captain Bryson, to be so long away," Mrs. Secord's tender eyes rested on him.

"I'm married." Wesley exchanged a glance with John Oneida. "And I have a son." Acknowledging this filled his heart with warmth.

"Then your wife must be Canadian bred, to be understanding of such separation," she ventured.

"Though English-born, Mrs. Bryson is, indeed, a woman of understanding." He patted his coat where his letter was stowed, half in hope, half in dread.

"Have you a family, Mr. Oneida?" She shifted attention to John.

"Indeed, I do," he affirmed enthusiastically. My wife is expecting our first child, come spring. And I do hope, if a girl, she'll bear a noble strength like you, Mrs. Secord."

"May it be so," James Secord endorsed. "Much was expected of our women in the war, and they did not falter."

Outside, a howling wind rattled the paper windows. Mrs. Secord laid her sleeping baby in the cradle and went over to the bottom of the stair. "Come down children," she invited pleasingly. "It's time to supper with our guests."

Four children, ranging in ages from about 5 to 14 years, poured down the stair and helped set out the simple fare of beans, potatoes, and onions.

"We are blessed with children who willingly pull a heavy load." James' eyes lit with pride. "With my injury, I can't help much."

Wesley offered an affirming nod, but the family's state pierced him. Would they ever recover from war? James Secord was crippled, their livelihood destroyed. His gracious, delicate wife now bore a great load.

"Tomorrow, we face a long ride to The Forty," Wesley concluded at the end of the meal. "I insist that Mr. Oneida and I sleep in your warm kitchen, to allow us to leave quietly, come early morn."

James conceded, with an understanding nod.

Only after the family had retired upstairs did Wesley break the seal and read Olivia's note. "Bah!" He declared with a loud chortle.

"*Mon Dieu*, what's up?" John sat up on his bed roll.

"I am married to a spirited woman." Wesley tucked the note back in his pocket. She was willing to work with him; that's all he could hope for.

—32—

Olivia lay on her bed. Laughter flowed on a cold wind through the cabin's open door.

Outside, Annie began a song and Olivia recognized the words from her voyage inland.

"I met three girls, and all of them were pretty!"

With a girlish giggle, Rosetta echoed, "And all of *us* are pretty!"

Pretty? She wiped away a tear, calloused hand brushing dry skin. Perhaps she had been, but no longer.

"Handsomeness is a gift of birth; attractiveness a work of character," Jane Blythe had once encouraged, while they watched ladies flaunting their beauty in her step-brother's salon.

The promise of life was over; she was no longer with child.

"You'll pass more blood over the next while," Annie had warned, swaddling her in flannel before slipping Wesley's nightshirt over her shoulders. Crushed castor stones and herbal tea brought on merciful sleep.

Each course of blood was a reminder of her failure, both as wife and mother. For two days, she had cried. The red, pulpy mass remained tightly rolled within a blood-soaked towel in the bucket by her bed. She could not bring herself to part with it. No one forced her, though a rancid odour was beginning to seep out.

Powerless, she had roiled in waves of contraction, enduring the travail that killed her mother. The Billidore women held her, pressing her on, refusing to let her go until the final bloody expulsion.

"*Grace à Dieu*, I think she's passed it," Annie declared with relief.

"It's over, girl," Sally whispered, "You can rest."

"Let me hold him." Olivia sobbed.

"Whatever there was is with the Lord." Rosetta wiped Olivia's brow. "There's nothing to hold."

"I should have taken more care." Olivia grasped her hand.

Sally gently lifted her face. "Look at me, luv. 'Appens to many a woman."

Their camaraderie of acceptance softened the blow.

She caught another whiff from the bucket. A proper farewell was needed to honour her loss. Burning the bucket's contents in the hearth would respect neither grief, nor hope unfulfilled.

Olivia rose, changed her swaddling, and washed in the basin. Her red-striped dress still hung on the hook, from when she'd hemmed it. Pulling it over her trousers, she fetched her Book of Common Prayer and opened it to the Service for the Burial of the Dead.

Hand resting over the stained bundle, she read:

> *O Heavenly Father, give us the grace to entrust the soul of this child to thy unfailing care and love, and bring us all to thy heavenly kingdom.*

Sinking to her knees, she closed her eyes, fighting to retain composure. She craved a sign, something from God to show she'd been heard.

"Please," she looked up, waiting. A thin ray of sun briefly pierced grey skies. It was enough.

"Somehow I see you as a boy, little one, and will give you my name."
Exhaling deeply, she pronounced, "I commit you to God, Oliver
Bryson." Named, their time of shared body would never be forgotten.

From her trunk, she retrieved the jewellery casket. A sob escaped. "I
never thought this would hold my first born," she whispered,
emptying jewels and silk underclothes onto the bed. She would
secure the jewels under a bedroom floor board later.

Stuffing the bundle into the box, she fastened the hinge. Then she
filled a bucket with coals, and went out into the yard, casket clasped
under her arm.

Annie and Rosetta stopped singing as she walked by.

"Keep dancing, ladies." She held up her free hand, wanting privacy.
"I'll join you, once my task is done." From the barn she retrieved a
spade and continued beyond the Sister Patch and the lightning-
scorched pine. Stopping at the base of a large oak tree, she set the
casket down, spread coals on the ground and began digging.

Annie came over to watch. Rosetta followed with Eddie and began to
clap an upbeat rhythm. Then she added words, to the song:

> *Fare thee well...Fare thee well...I will meet you on*
> *the other shore.*

Other verses followed, Annie's voice echoing choruses of, "*In that
great gettin' up morning.*"

When the hole reached two-feet deep, Olivia stopped. The task took
all her strength, causing both her arms and heart to ache. Kneeling,
she gently set the casket into the grave.

"Merciful God, please take care of Oliver until I get to that other
shore," she prayed.

Annie shoveled the earth back into the hole, securing the grave with three large rocks. Olivia kept back a shovelful of dirt in the bucket. Come spring, she would plant her lavender seeds there.

Eddie reached up. She took him in her arms and joined in Rosetta's song.

Fare thee well...Fare thee well.

The song ended and quiet settled on them. Annie returned to the oats they had been threshing over a tarp. Olivia joined her. Together they picked up its edges, tossing the contents into the wind. Straw blew away; the heavier groats returned.

"I'll sweep it into the sack and store it in the root cellar until we bring up the grindstone." Annie offered, wrapping her arm about Olivia's shoulder.

"I'll milk Busy," Rosetta announced.

"And I'll go inside and make us a soup," Olivia declared, returning to her cabin.

—33—

Onions and leeks simmered in the cauldron. Olivia added chopped carrots, turnips, and squash along with a pinch of Sally's spice. The aroma was promising and she was hopeful of a fine meal; more so when her soda biscuits came out of the skillet oven unburnt.

They sat at the table. Annie took Rosetta and Olivia's hands and bowed her head, reciting a brief prayer in indecipherable murmur. Eddie snuggled in his mother's lap, eyes closed, worn out by his threshing dance.

"Are you thanking the Lord?" Rosetta's lips turned up with amusement.

"*Oui*, but not for her soup." Annie looked up, face aglow. "We're at peace at our table."

Olivia's breath caught. If her soup was to be fed to the Douglas pigs, it did not matter. This camaraderie nurtured her soul.

"*Pas mal de tout*," Annie pronounced upon her first spoonful. "And your biscuits hold well, too."

"Not bad at all?" Olivia sniffed with feigned insult.

"They dunk well," Rosetta confirmed. "Anything with biscuits tastes good." Gizzy lay at the door, whining.

"Deer must be at the corn crib," Annie rose from the table and laid Eddie on the daybed. With a brief touch, she acknowledged her Rosary, on the wall hook, above the pillow.

Olivia strode to the window to look out. An opaque white curtain of snow raced across the yard. Wind whistled through the surrounding pine trees.

"My scalp tingles," she remarked, "as if something is brew—"

CRACK-BOOM!

She fell to the floor, blueish light shattering the dark with an explosive roar. Eddie leapt up, his scream merging with Gizzy's frantic barking.

"*Mon Seigneur!*" Annie clutched Eddie to her bosom.

Rosetta clutched her belly. "Baby jumped!"

Scrambling up, panting, Olivia rubbed her eyes. "Never been so close," she heaved, daring to look out the window. Flickering clouds cast the pines in ghostly silhouette. In the distance, the heavens continued to flash and growl.

"We must prepare," Annie grimaced, handing Eddie to Rosetta. "Thunder in the snow brings a blizzard." She squared her shoulders. "Put a bit of oats in a sack, Rosie; Olivia and I will dress."

Olivia slipped on Wesley's deerskin jacket, tuque, and mitts, then pulled mukluks on her feet. Annie dressed with similar care. From the rafter storage she fetched a long rope, a few ragged quilts and four slender pointed meshes, she called "*Raquettes*".

"Tennis rackets?" Olivia giggled nervously.

"Snowshoes," Rosetta corrected. "Haudenosaunee ones have rounded frames."

"They walk on lakes, Anishinaabe walk through thick bush." Annie's lips pursed. "Carry these, Olivia. We'll need them to get back." Rope and blankets in hand, she asked Rosetta to light a lamp and leave it in the window facing the yard.

Knotting one end of the rope about her waist, Annie tied a mid-rope section about Olivia's wrist, directing her, "Follow by my side and hold tightly to my waist rope." With a sharp command for Gizzy to stay inside, she pulled open the door.

Cold wind flooded into the cabin along with billowing snow. The snow was already ankle deep on the cabin threshold. Annie tied the rope's free end to the bell hook ring and they trudged forward, into the howling maelstrom.

Olivia glanced back at the flickering window light and thought of the Longships Lighthouse of Land's End that guided ships safely back to England.

Untying the rope at the well, Annie looped it taunt around the pulley rest. Retying it about her waist, they trudged in the direction of the shanty.

Disoriented, within an increasingly turbulent sea of white, they crossed the yard, found the shanty's side wall and felt their way around, to the door. Annie untied the rope, attaching it through the iron ring, and they pushed inside.

Out of the gale force, Olivia's watery eyes adjusted to the dark. Busy lowed mournfully from her stall. "Poor cow," she shivered.

"With good feed, she can weather this," Annie rubbed down the cow's legs, fastened a blanket about her girth and fed her oats mixed with the clean hay cut from a beaver meadow. "Fill her stall with straw and spread it generously under her."

Olivia obeyed. Under Annie's soothing touch, Busy lay down.

"Tomorrow when you come to milk, you'll see she's fine."

"I'll milk?"

"That's winter life, *ma sœur*. And cover the chickens' straw box with the other quilt," Annie directed. "We don't want to eat chicken and dumplings, yet." She retrieved the shovel from the back of the shanty, "We'll need this to dig out of the cabin, come morning."

She lashed the *raquettes* on both their feet, then gripped Olivia's shoulder with her mittened hand. "Have no fear!"

Firmly barring the barn door, they faced a storm of dizzily whirling white. The cabin was no longer visible, the window's light drowned out.

Leading Olivia's hand to the rope she'd attached to the iron ring, Annie shouted, "Don't let go of this rope. It will lead us back." Olivia's instinctive nod went unseen.

Hunching into the wind, they laboured back toward the well. Olivia dared look up only briefly, for icy shards stung her eyes. Every lift of the *raquettes* burned, as she forced her legs onward. Her face was numb and heart pounding as they reached the well pulley. Despite the icy chill, sweat trickled down her back. Squinting in the direction of the cabin, a faint glow was visible in the window, beckoning them home.

Through the door they stumbled several minutes later, tossing off snow-crusted mittens. Olivia freed her burning legs of the *raquettes* and fell back on the floor.

"Never have I felt more alive in all my life," she howled, laughter infusing her spirit.

—34—

"Captain Bryson! I've yet to receive compensation for my horse," Robert Nelles interrupted from the upholstered settee that he shared with his 20-year-old daughter, Margaret. She looked up from sock-darning with an affirming nod.

Father and daughter worked united, as yoked oxen. Across the room, by the hearth, his youthful wife paused knitting to rock the cradle. Nelles had married this widow at the close of the war, and was now a proud father of the stirring infant.

Wesley cast about the comfortably furnished room, eyes briefly meeting John Oneida, seated in the corner with the lap desk. Comparison of the Nelles home with that of James Secord was inevitable. The two-storey stone residence reflected Robert Nelles' status as Justice of the Peace and Lieutenant Colonel of the 4th Regiment militia. He was also the representative in the Legislative Assembly of Upper Canada, replacing the fugitive Willcocks who had ordered Newark's destruction.

"Many conflicting demands await to be addressed, sir." Wesley returned. "Be assured, yours will be presented to the Governor when we meet in the new year."

"Harrumph!" Nelles snorted. "Needless delay."

"Perhaps we can adjourn to the privacy of your office, sir, to properly record the details," Wesley proposed. "Mr. Oneida will transcribe your presentation."

"Absolutely not," he snapped. "My daughter was left in charge, here, while my sons and I fought at Lundy's. She tended to her younger siblings and was forced to serve occupying Americans. She will attest to any details."

Mrs. Nelles quietly rose, gathered the baby from the cradle, and left the room. John Oneida opened his lap desk, retrieved paper, and dipped quill in ink.

"You were occupied by the Americans in 1812," prompted Wesley.

"My property was twice occupied, Captain," Robert Nelles amended, "while I was on campaign in Niagara."

Wesley exchanged a nod with John. "My condolences, sir, for your great loss."

"My brother, a son and my dear wife, gone within a year," Nelles affirmed soberly.

"Pay allowances have already been duly processed for your son's service and his time as prisoner-of-war," Wesley returned.

"When compensation is finally secured, I will hold a victory ball and rename The Forty to Grimsby in celebration," he declared. Margaret quietly smiled. "The Forty was simply a milestone, Grimsby will be a community."

"Returning to your details, sir," Wesley steered. Through the window, he caught a glimpse of billowing snow. He needed to finish this interview before the weather worsened. "Please describe the extent of property damage incurred during the occupation." His question was mere formality; he already knew the answer, for he'd been here during the aftermath.

"Understand, Captain," Nelles inhaled deeply. "Americans took over my home and ordered Margaret to care for a cartload of their wounded. She sought assistance from the mission—"

"George Blythe's daughter—Jane?" Wesley interrupted.

"Aye. The girl had stayed on at the mission, after her father was murdered, during the American occupation of York. She proved of use, for she'd been trained by Mohawks." Nelles coughed lightly. "Blythe's replacement, Reverend Cameron, was completely unfit for work on the frontier. He now serves in the Eastern Townships of Lower Canada. We still await a proper minister, for I can't keep up with legislative responsibilities, as well as perform weddings and—"

"War compensation, sir," Wesley prompted.

Nelles punched his fist into his hand. "My best horse and tack were commanded by British officers. It was never returned, and I demand 30 pounds in compensation."

Upon arrival, Wesley had noted that the windows and furniture of the Nelles estate were in good repair. The cattle and horses in the barn also appeared well-fed. Yet he recalled that two years previously, in the aftermath of battle, Margaret had refused to provide meat for his men. They'd no recourse but to slaughter Jane Blythe's milk cow.

"Noted," Wesley nodded at John.

Margaret Nelles sniffed sharply and supplied, "I was dreadfully frightened by those disrespectful red men. There were almost a thousand of them encamped on our land, claiming allegiance to the Crown."

"Might I be so delicate to ask of Miss Nelles, the nature of her concern with our Native allies?" Wesley ventured. "Did they—"

Robert Nelles bolted to his feet. "How dare you imply liberty! My daughter is a fine Christian and would never permit any misconduct."

Wesley immediately rose. "I ask for your forgiveness, sir." He bowed to Robert Nelles, then to his daughter. Tilting her head, she acknowledged the apology with a brief nod.

"Given," Nelles answered, sitting down. "I appreciate that you have a job to do." He motioned Wesley to again sit. "The Natives' request, for abandoned American arms and provisions was refused. They would not leave until Margaret paid them in flour and salted pork. Then they further demanded to be shod, clothed, and assured compensation for their wounded and dead."

"Clothed with what was left by the Americans?" Wesley surmised. John's pen scratched across the page.

"Aye," Nelles grunted. "Before his death, Joseph Brant and I laid out plans for a school, at Six Nations, to break Native dependency on the government."

"A school, sir?" John repeated, retrieving another page, dipping his quill in the ink pot. "Pray describe how such a venture would succeed." His dark eyes focused on Nelles.

"I thought an educated Indian, such as yourself, would be interested." He rubbed his hands together. "My proposal was that we settle Natives from their wandering ways by merging tutorial with spiritual."

"A religious boarding school?" Wesley restated.

"Exactly." Nelles' face lit up. "For it is only by setting them apart from their former way, in residence, that they will learn industry and ambition."

"How would they clothe and feed themselves, if not able to hunt or fish?" John probed.

"Farming!" he huffed, stabbing an index finger at John. "We will teach them civilized ways and proper faith so they settle down and no longer pose threat to our settlements. And they can purchase their needs with the fruit of their labour. Put that in your report, man."

John set down his pen. "Do you refer to settlements on the escarpment or, perhaps, further west, on the Six Nations tract?"

"I believe our investigation of your claim is complete, sir." Wesley interrupted, standing abruptly. "Tomorrow we're away to the Mohawk village, up the escarpment, to look into that renegade attack."

"Tragic event, indeed." Nelles nodded soberly. "Yet, to be expected when Natives stray from their protected land."

"Do you feel safe when you venture beyond your property, Lieutenant Colonel?" John again challenged, packing his lap desk.

Nelles returned a piercing glare and rang the bell pull. "My man will help see you out and help with your horses."

Wesley offered polite appreciation of the excellent dinner Nelles had provided. A grey-haired African appeared with their overcoats and led them out to the barn.

"It's a short walk to Joseph Green's Inn," he assured them. "If you take the path down by Forty Mile creek, you'll be sheltered from the wind."

"I've fought bile in my throat, all evening," John spat on the ground as they rode out of the yard.

"That man was elected to replace the traitor, Willcocks, his loyalty is viewed as unquestionable," Wesley lamented. "I fear his claims will take priority over most."

Rosetta slowly turned the coffee grinder wheel. "This oat bread is going to taste like coffee and the coffee will taste like oatmeal," she chuckled, feeding another handful of oat kernels into the opening beneath the crank.

"Then we'll have to brew our coffee strong, to go with the oat bread," Olivia lifted the lid of the butter churn. Yellowy curds floated in the buttermilk. "I've done what I can," she concluded. "A stronger arm is needed."

"I'll finish up." Annie took the churn paddle with a playful elbow to her ribs.

Olivia donned Wesley's coat over her trousers and red flannel shirt. She had stopped wearing a skirt with storm's onset. Now she was even considering cutting her hair.

For almost a week, the storm had held them in a frigid grip. Slowly it had abated, leaving snowdrifts that reached to the roof eaves. Wind had scoured the river down to a frozen surface. Upstream, Billidore's splashing waters remained open, coating the surrounding trees and rocks in ice.

They had kept active during their imposed confinement. Annie had finished Rosetta's cradle board and begun a second. Rosetta had read several books aloud, captivating them with her dramatic flair. Eddie had begun speaking a mixture of English and an Algonquin dialect, and gave Gizzy no peace. Olivia had completed knitting a few small articles of clothing, both for Eddie and Rosetta's expected child.

Repeated tramping between the cabin, well, and barn had packed down a path, so snowshoes were no longer needed to cross the yard. Busy continued providing milk, though less than before. Only Gizzy's prodding provoked the chickens to move within their straw refuge. Sadly, the fowl laid no eggs, though the squash seeds and skins disappeared between visits.

"Hope it's not mice," Olivia mused, fastening the barn door behind her.

With Busy fed, settled, and manure pitched, she carefully set the milk pail on the toboggan. From the side of the shanty, she dug out a load of wood, piling it next to the pail. Grey skies were rapidly darkening, warning of another storm. Carefully, she pulled the toboggan to the well and filled a second bucket with water. Clean snow was fine to wash in, but she preferred well water for cooking. Fortunately, deep within the earth, the well remained unfrozen.

Back in the cabin, she whipped off her tuque and announced, "I'm going to cut my hair."

"The only good reason to chop it off is to rid yourself of lice." Annie neatly arranged firewood beside the hearth. "That's what they did at the *Deux-Montagnes* school," she huffed, "whether you had them or not. And it stayed short once I became a postulate."

Olivia looked at Rosetta, bent over a cauldron, stirring root vegetable soup. Her brightly covered head wrap, the gift of Mr. Gutches, hid tightly braided hair. Only the beaded nape braid escaped. How fortunate she was to have orderly coif.

"Well..." she continued, "my hair is filthy, sticks to my scalp—"

"What would your Captain think?" Rosetta looked up.

"A few years back it was considered fashionable to cut one's hair short, in honour of guillotine victims." Olivia defended, unbraiding the first of her two messy side braids. "It was called a *Coiffure à la Titus*."

"Fashionable to look like you have lice?" Annie snorted.

"Using 'honour' of those victims to excuse ill-kept hair?" Rosetta shook her head. "Now *that* is putting on airs."

"I can no longer dress it properly." Olivia unraveled her second braid. Digging scissors from the sewing basket, she bent her head between her knees, and snipped. Her tresses fell at her feet.

"*Mon Dieu!*" Annie giggled. "You were serious."

"I guess I'll have to fix it up," Rosetta chided, with a roll of her eyes. "Hand me those scissors and sit at the table." Deftly, she evened out Olivia's hair, leaving a few short curls at the front, to frame her face.

"You have a gift for hair," Annie gasped.

"I've done this often," Rosetta acknowledged, curtly.

"When you were a slave?" Olivia prompted.

"When I was enslaved."

"Aren't they the same?" Olivia looked up at her, curious.

"One says who you are—the other says what was put on you." Rosetta handed the scissors back.

The scarred face of the Jamaican man shot through Olivia's mind. He had been branded for seeking freedom. Then another figure crept into her memory: a peculiar little brown boy, long absent from her childhood home, who had run errands for her father. Though richly dressed, he had worn a metal collar about his neck, like the estate dogs.

"Expressing it that way helps me," Olivia offered.

"Yet do you understand?" Rosetta challenged.

"My eyes are opening." She swept her hair from the floor, giving due consideration of her words. "The term 'slave' denies those who are enslaved their dignity as being made in God's image."

Annie gently covered Eddie with a quilt, briefly touching the Rosary hanging on the wall above the daybed.

"Aye...denial of dignity." Rosetta sat on the settee, eyes closed, hand resting on her belly. "I saw Native people hunted for sport...by bounty men. 'Riddin' the forest of vermin,' they bragged."

"Ah, yes, bounty hunters," Annie remarked, sitting beside her. "There have been raids near the Quinte, looking for African refugees."

"Aye," Rosetta confirmed. "There's a bounty on Negro fugitives fleeing to British territory—they make their living catching refugees...along with claiming scalps." She looked over at Eddie, soundly asleep. "They attacked the Creek refugees I was travelling with—killing children and old people who weren't fast enough to get away. I gave myself up, hoping they'd leave them be."

"Did they?" Olivia sat on the floor at her feet.

"I wear my braid to honour those killed." She looked intently at Olivia. "For two days I endured their filth."

"How did you escape?" Annie took her hand.

"They went out on foray, leaving only one to watch. I shoved a finger down my throat, forcing myself to vomit. The brute untied me to stop me from choking and I laid a rock to his head. Maybe I killed him— God knows." She paused to wipe something from the corner of her eye. "I tore into the bush and kept runnin' until I came across a kindly settler who took me to the British officer escorting Mohawk refugees up to Canada—Stephen Reed, before he was posted to Kingston." She looking up at the rafters and slowly shook her head. "I'll never understand why I survived...only know that my freedom come with consequence." Her hand flew back to her belly. "Baby's kicking."

"Can you ever love a child forced upon you?" Olivia probed.

"This little one ain't to blame for what happened," she calmly answered. "We'll make the most of being thrown together, and leave God to work life out."

"May I feel his quickening?" Olivia ventured.

"More than just quickening, these days," Rosetta smiled and pressed Olivia's hand into her belly. A soft poke greeted her. Gingerly, Olivia pushed back until a stout kick knocked her hand off.

"He's full of life!" she laughed, tossing her head back, enjoying the bounce of curls. "Curious how we three are runaways. And—"

A lone howl cut her off. It seemed close enough to be in the yard. Gizzy raced to the door. Lifting her head, she returned a spine-chilling reply.

"That's the bit of wolf in her." Annie went over and gently stroked the dog's chest.

"I secured the barn," Olivia immediately vouched, should there be a doubt.

A chorus of howls, yips, and yelps answered. Gizzy lay across the door, growling. The eerie chorus surrounded their cabin for several minutes, then moved down the embankment.

"They're chasing deer from our corn crib," Annie reassured her.

All went quiet.

"Quiet is worse," Rosetta shivered. "Conjures up all manner of dark thoughts."

"Tomorrow we search for deer remains," Annie concluded. "Gizzy will feast on bones, and, hopefully, I'll find enough pelt to make Eddie a coat."

—36—

Busy danced nervously, refusing to stand still for milking.

"You're safe, girl," Olivia pressed her forehead into her muzzle. "Wolves can't open the shanty latch." She fed her a handful of oats and corn, and firmly stroked Busy's flank until she settled. Pulling up a stool, Olivia began massaging her udder. "Good girl," she encouraged, and gave a firm pull. Milk squirted out.

Again, there were no eggs. Skittery chickens peeked their heads through the straw, ignoring corn kernels and squash skin. "Eat up," she encouraged, and went to load the toboggan with wood.

"What are you baking up?" Olivia asked, upon return. She filtered the bucket of milk, through a cheese cloth, into a crock urn.

"Corn pong," Rosetta replied curtly. "No eggs...tired of beans, just tired...I guess. This should hold us for a bit."

Adding water, lard, and salt to the freshly ground corn, she pummeled it into a thick batter. Dried apples and cider simmered in a larded pan. Once they became bloated and soft, she spooned generous portions of the batter on top, flattening each down until brown, before flipping.

"Mohawks call that griddle cake." Annie scooped the first pong into her mouth, washing it down with coffee. "But we don't make it with apples. Mmmmmm—this is good."

Eddie quietly ate, with Gizzy eagerly cleaning the floor under his chair."

"It is good," Olivia echoed. "And you've made enough for a week."

"Told you..." Rosetta muttered, "I'm tired of cooking."

"Ready to look for what's left of the deer?" Annie invited. "If nothing, we'll check snares I set up after the storm. A bit of rabbit stew would sit well with that pong, and rabbit fur is soft against a baby's skin."

"I can't bear to walk in *raquettes*," Olivia complained.

"We'll go slow," she acknowledged, with a reassuring smile at Rosetta. "And we'll be near enough to hear the bell."

Once in the yard, Annie leaned close to Olivia. "I think Rosie's time is near," she confided. "Her legs are swollen."

"What about you?" Olivia remarked. "Your back seems to be troubling you."

She shrugged, with a proud brace of shoulders. "My time is far off."

Near the corn crib, deer tracks, interspersed with paw prints, veered down the path to the river.

"This is where the deer alerted to those wolves." Annie pointed at the tracks. "See, from here they're spaced farther apart—they were running hard. My guess is three wolves and maybe five deer. Hopefully they were satisfied with the hunt and left my snares." Olivia studied the ground, envisioning Annie's description.

As they followed the tracks to the river, her thoughts turned to the day she first saw Annie. "Who was that boy with you, last summer?" she asked.

"Joseph—my brother. He's wintering at a hunting camp, north of Quinte. Do you have a brother?"

"I have three, by my father's second wife. My mother died with my birth."

Annie turned, dark eyes searching Olivia's face. "A terrible burden you carry," she offered.

Her observation was surprisingly accurate. Though never stated, Olivia had always sensed her father's resentment that her life had cost her mother's.

Passing the Douglas bridge, they continued to the landing. The snow was stained with splotches of blood; the wolves had wounded their quarry. Olivia followed the blood trail onto the windswept, frozen river. Deer remains were strewn about. Gizzy bounded forward, excitedly freeing a haunch, chewing off the bit of flesh still attached.

Annie continued on. Olivia held back; her eyes fixed on a gnawed skull in a patch of deep-red snow. Her stomach roiled.

Unsheathing her knife, Annie freed up a bloodied pelt fragment. "Enough for the cradleboard," she exclaimed excitedly, washing it with snow. "I hear something!" She looked up at the river bend, alarm filling her face.

Were the wolves returning? Heart pounding, Olivia turned, frozen with fear. A moment later, two sleds rounded the bend, each pulled by three dogs and carrying a rider and driver.

"We have visitors!" Olivia turned to Annie; she was nowhere to be seen. Gizzy pressed against her leg, body tense, growling.

Perhaps they brought supplies from Kingston. If not, they might have news of the outside. She must offer them refreshments, either way.

"Gentlemen!" Waving a mittened hand, she hailed their approach. "Wherever you are bound, pray stop in for refreshment." She hoped Wesley's coat was long enough to hide her trousered legs.

Gizzy burst into mad barking at the snarling sled dogs. Olivia grasped her collar to prevent a dog fight. One driver called something to the other, who laughed as they reined in their dogs.

"Have no fear, *Madame*," a woolly-bearded man leapt from his sled and dealt a strong boot to the nearest dog. Yelping, it cowered within the snarling pack. "We'll tie up our dogs down here."

Pierre Sabin stepped off the lead sled, whipping off his red tuque with a gracious bow. "Winter air has lent a charming glow to your countenance, *Madame* Bryson." He reached for her mittened hand. "How could your *Capitane* abandon you to this wilderness?"

"I will attend to arrangements, *Monsieur* Sabin." Pulling away, she led Gizzy up to the cabin. Whether overreacting or not, Pierre's familiarity unsettled her. Rosetta opened the door, Eddie at her side.

"Good Lord, Rosie! I've stupidly invited ruffians up for refreshments." She glanced about. "Where's Annie?" Her sharp inquiry met Rosetta's grimace, setting her heart racing. "It is just us?"

"Get something decent on," Rosetta ordered, grabbing the butcher knife, setting it between two squashes, on the table.

Olivia tied Gizzy to her bed post, threw off outer clothes and slipped the red-stripped dress over her trousers and Wesley's red shirt. Animated conversation approached, in the yard. They entered the cabin, slamming the door behind them.

A rancid odour of sweat, tobacco, and wet woolens filled her home. All four men had come up, leaving the dogs unattended. Somehow, Rosetta managed to have coffee brewing before sitting back at the table, Eddie in her arms. A plate of corn pong and applesauce waited before her as she slowly gouged out squash seeds with the knife.

"Mrs. George has brewed coffee," she glanced at Rosetta. Her face was taut, as if holding her breath.

Pierre Sabin pushed by the woolly-bearded man, with an approving smile. "*Enchantée!* Such a delightful cottage." His eyes lingered on her. "Are you not lonely without your *Capitane*?"

"I am quite content with my husband's provision," she tersely answered and poured out cups of black coffee. "I have my dear companion, and—" she exhaled boldly "—our neighbours are quite close...they will soon come up to hear of your news."

He took another step towards her. "I wish to ensure you are—"

The cabin door opened with a blast of frosty air.

Sally Douglas entered, one hand waving a small bloodied axe, the other, a freshly decapitated chicken. Blood oozed from its neck, onto the floor.

"Hallo gent'amen!" she greeted, holding the chicken high. "What news 'ave ye of Kingston and the garrison." Waving the axe, she tossed the bird on the table. "Bloody 'ell, Mrs. Bryson. Was in such 'urry so's not 'ta miss these gents, that I brought this bleedin' fella," she huffed, adding, "Ian and Jamie are on their way."

"*Désolée*! We have neither news, nor time to linger, for we must make White Fish Falls by dark." Sabin set his half-drunk mug beside the chicken, splashing the table. With a whistle and hand wave, he directed his men out. Grasping Olivia's hand, his lips crushed her palm. For that terrifying instant she felt as if he was pulling her out, but he let go. With a door slam, they were gone.

Sally heaved a deep sigh. Gizzy tore from her restraint, darted to the bloody puddle, lapping it up, tail-wagging. Rosetta set Eddie down, pushing chopped squash innards off the table, adding to Gizzy's feast.

Olivia's legs trembled and she sat, head within arms, at the table. The door flew open. Everyone startled.

Annie ran in. "They've gone upriver!"

"Damn blaggards—their stench lingers." Sally squeezed Olivia's shoulder.

Olivia chortled through teary eyes. "Sally, those blighters—"

"Are you laughin' or cryin'?" She chuckled, setting the axe on the table. "Cowards just take a bit 'o proddin' to move along—no need to bring in menfolk. Tonight, Ian can 'ave chicken stew—she wasn't a good layer, anyways."

"You ran off, Annie!" Olivia flared, awash with emotion. "You abandoned us to fend with those—"

"Go kindly, Olivia," Sally hushed, wrapping a protective arm about Annie's shoulders. "She was right to come to me for help. Pierre Sabin brutally attacked 'er when she was first carrying Eddie."

"I thought I might lose Eddie," Annie spat out, eyes flashing.

"Attacked? Do you mean..." Olivia's eyes shifted from Sally to Annie, grappling, "Does Wesley know?"

"Do you think us fools?" Sally huffed. "Someone would have died and Sabin's not worth it."

"Then I pray to God justice will find that man." Olivia quietly returned.

Rosetta stumbled to stand, grasping the table's edge. "I kept quiet as best I could." She moaned, skirt wet and clinging. "My time has come."

—37—

Wesley stood before charred remains of a longhouse. Beside him, a young Mohawk warrior recounted witness of the attack. John translated.

"The village was abandoned last spring, after our people moved to a settlement along the Grand. Clan Mother Soujeesh returned in autumn with some women and their children, to harvest crops left in the Sister Field. I often come here to hunt—game is scarce by the Grand—settlers scare them off. It was starting to rain, so I decided to spend the night with the Clan Mother's group. As I approached, I heard musket shot. Men were shooting at the camp," John translated. "They were white, wearing buckskin and fur hats, not tuques."

Looking ahead, across the snow-covered field, the warrior paused briefly. When he resumed, his voice was low and menacing. John fell silent.

"What did he say?" Wesley prompted.

"Five died here, Wesley—over in that ruined long house." He held his hand out, as if reaching. "One of them was his cousin. Soujeesh, stayed behind, to hold off the attackers, allowing the others to escape. He carried her body to Six Nations for burial." John knelt, hand digging into the earth. "Five killed—defenceless women and children harvesting their crops."

Wesley heaved with deep exhale. "Why?"

John stood to face him. "He believes this an act of retaliation for the War."

"On what basis would he say that?"

"Haudenosaunee were chased out of upper New York, after a long fight to preserve their hunting land. We allied with the British out of need." John's breathing grew heavy. "People do not forget the death of loved ones. Though I was a child, the attack on my village remains vivid." Eyes closed, the lines on his forehead deepened. "Tecumseh took Clan Mother Soujeesh to the Battle of the Thames, for she was a gifted healer. Many men of this village accompanied them."

"The attackers' attire is similar to that of the Fort Erie abductors," Wesley remarked. "Perhaps, assuming Upper Canada would soon be annexed, they were after African refugees?"

"Republicans claim them as fugitive," the warrior returned in fluent English. "Though we also have enslaved people, George Blythe refuged Africans among us." Pointing out a gully beyond the burned ruins, a smile crossed his face. "Life once filled this place. Reverend Blythe's daughter was apprenticed to Soujeesh and lived among us. We once caught her kissing Captain Cliveton, over there." His sneer returned. "You British have stolen our sovereignty, freedom, and land."

"When settlers come here, what will you do?" asked John.

"Farm, like a woman?" he scoffed. "Bah! I am a man. I will hunt in the High Country, marry into the Anishinaabe, and live free."

"North of the Great Lakes?" Wesley pressed.

"Aye! Source of the Grand Ottawa," John explained. Turning to the warrior, he volunteered, "I married an Anishinaabe."

"Yet you choose to be a servant of the British," the youth dismissed, and walked ahead into the bush.

"Insolence of youth!" Wesley huffed.

"Maybe it's discernment." John fastened his snowshoes and spat. "Their generation lives with the compromises we made to survive." He looked ahead to where the warrior had disappeared. "We have a long way to go before dark."

Wesley followed John at a respectful distance, allowing his companion privacy. The youth's insult had obviously stung.

He cast his eye about the village ruins, one final time, his heart reflecting on Eddie. How was he to raise his child of two worlds? In those few hours holding his son, warmth had filled his heart beyond what he'd thought possible. He now understood Mrs. Stark protectively registering her mixed-race children as Scots. Yet they bore two streams within their life river, as his son did. Both must be reconciled to flow aright.

The warrior's reference of George Blythe's daughter identified Jane Blythe as the woman Captain Cliveton had left behind. Providence had arranged his meeting her at Burlington Harbour. Her distress had returned Olivia to his life, bringing him much to resolve. Desperately, he prayed Olivia would love his son. He did not want to have to choose between the two.

Hastening after John, he declared, "My son is both Anishinaabe and European. I want him to be of both worlds."

"Of two minds and two masters?" John paused to face him. "Are you French or English, my friend?"

"My mother tongue is French, but I grew up in English, both in language and culture."

"You are European in both mind and flesh," John countered. "Eddie will be an apple, red on the outside and white within, fitting neither world."

"Good Lord, John! That's cruel. Somehow, reconciliation must be possible."

"I have struggled with this my whole life." John continued to the top of a ridge, then turned to look back, towards the village. "Aye...*Deux-Montagnes* tried to destroy my heritage until they saw it would serve their colonial purpose. For this I am fortunate. Yet, I had to fight to regain my language and culture. That young warrior was astute. I'm a terrible hunter—Annie's the one who keeps our table full." Shaking his head, hard laughter cut the air. "And the worst of it is I talk to my wife in French, a colonial language."

"Surely, I will find a solution for my son," Wesley asserted.

"Always an optimistic negotiator, my friend." John patted him on the back. "You should consider politics. Then you might influence what we do not yet see."

—38—

Rosetta gripped the hearth mantle, eyes squeezed shut. Garbed in Olivia's best silk night chemise and Annie's thick woolen socks, loosened hair tumbled over her face.

"The Mother must dress to celebrate and greet her child," Annie had insisted. "All knots must be unfastened and hair free flowing, for nothing on your body is to hinder the baby's arrival."

"We'll do whatever 'elps," Sally affirmed. "Water's broke; we need to move this along. Open up, Rosie," she ordered, spooning castor oil into her mouth.

Obediently swallowing, Rosetta moaned, "...so tired of this...hours of pacing...pain..."

Olivia firmly gripped her arm, leading her in another turn of the cabin's main room.

"You are washed, my knife flamed, and flannels wait." Annie laid Eddie on the daybed.

"Won't be long," Sally encouraged, spreading a bed of quilts in front of the fire. "Ian is just a bell ring away, should—"

"No!" Rosetta hissed through clenched teeth. "It's not proper."

"I'll brew you a special tea." Annie filled the kettle. "Can you sing for us, Sally? A calm song, to summon her child out."

"*My love is like a red, red rose...*" Sally slowly began. Her deep, rich voice surprised Olivia with its sensuality. Verse after verse, she filled the room with this ballad of sweet love. With Annie's tea ready, Sally's song ended with, "*...and I would love thee still my dear...though all the seas run dry.*"

"Drink up," Annie ordered, holding the tea cup to Rosetta's lips.

"Is such a love possible?" Olivia asked after Rosetta handed her the empty cup.

"If you choose to make it so," Sally nodded sagely. "It's Ian's favourite song."

"Please, sing us another," Olivia encouraged.

"There's this ballad I learned in France." A pleasant demeanor filled Sally's face. "It's seen me through many a dark time," Her hand rested on Rosetta's shoulder. "I'm sure it will liven you, luv."

Throwing head back, she began a jaunty army ditty, full of shady mischievous references. The women exploded with laughter and giggling.

"Salty lady!" Olivia yelped. "You're knocking the hoity-toity out of me."

"*Bon Dieu!*" Annie gasped between chortles. "I'm going to call Ian up to make you behave. That's so—"

"Not proper!" Rosetta howled. "Not proper at all!" Suddenly, wide-eyed, she dug fingernails into Olivia's arm. Screaming, legs buckling, she fell to her knees.

Gizzy barked frantically. Sally firmly grasped the dog's collar and threw her out the door. Anne pried Olivia's arm loose and sent her to comfort Eddie. Obediently, Olivia scooped him up, soothing him back to sleep on the day bed. The cabin quietened.

"Calm, we must have calm or the baby will scare and refuse to come out," Annie admonished, easing Rosetta onto the quilts, kneeling beside her. "Your time is near." She motioned Sally to join her. Olivia waited for direction. "When pain comes, don't cry out. Don't fight it. Push in and ride it."

Rosetta's features twisted in pain. Closing her eyes, she clasped Sally's arm. The moment soon passed, leaving her gasping for breath.

"Draw deep," Annie encouraged. "Another will soon follow."

"This will be mercifully fast," Sally affirmed, gently wiping her brow.

Crushing eyes shut, Rosetta embraced the wave of pain. At its passing, she looked frantically about the silent cabin, heaving with effort. Olivia laid fresh towels, under her.

"You son is eager to see the world," Annie rolled Rosetta onto her side. "Be ready," she coaxed.

An extended wave consumed Rosetta. Deeply growling, bearing down, a tiny purple body came out of her. It made no cry.

Annie cleared the small mouth, vigorously rubbing its limp body with a rough towel. The silence continued "She must pass the after birth," she whispered, passing the still form to Sally. "Keep rubbing the little one."

"What's wrong?" Rosetta cried.

Sally began to quietly sing a familiar hymn. "*What child is this, who lays to rest, on Mary's breast lay sleeping.*"

"My son?" Rosetta whispered. "Is he?"

"He's a girl." Annie began to knead her belly.

Rosetta whimpered; a tiny peep echoed her pain. Unwrapping the towel, Sally revealed a small hand reaching up. Olivia erupted with sobs of joy.

Annie firmly held Rosetta down, insisting, "The birth sac must pass." Sally guided the baby's open mouth to Rosetta's breast.

Upon first suckle, the purplish afterbirth passed. Tightly wrapping it within a towel, Annie beckoned Olivia over and entrusted it to her. Her hands free, Annie tied off the cord with a length of Olivia's embroidery thread, and cut it cleanly. "We'll bury this to honour its good work. I'll save a piece of cord to attach to the baby's cradle board."

"I'll melt the ground beneath the oak tree and bury this next to Oliver," Olivia confirmed.

"She is lively, like her mother." Annie praised, moving the infant to Rosetta's other breast. "Keep her warm and suckling." She shot an impatient glare at the door. Gizzy's barking had increased in frequency.

Olivia's joy held a taint of sadness, as she watched Rosetta tuck the tiny body beneath her silk gown. New life was not to be her lot.

"I'll warm up apple cider to celebrate," she proposed. "We've plenty of corn pong since those blighters didn't stay to eat." Kissing Rosetta's forehead, she added, "The gown is yours to keep, and there's nary a stain on it."

Rosetta nodded. "Was it only this morning they were here?"

"It's tomorrow." Sally corrected, picking up the last of the soiled towels. "Where did you learn to help in birth, Annie?"

Lying beside Rosetta, Annie covered a yawn with her hand. "My people invite young women to births, to prepare them for their own time."

"What will your daughter be named?" Sally brought over a basin of water and swaddling towels.

"I was going to call him Adam, for new beginnings." Kissing the baby's head, she passed her to Sally for washing.

Olivia returned with a tray with mugs of warm cider and bowls of corn pong. They ate, watching Sally's ministrations, ignoring the baby's whiny screams. Eddie remained fast asleep on the daybed.

"Cold water gets blood flowing and lungs opening," Sally stated, with a gaping yawn. "My family will awaken soon."

She tucked the baby back beneath Rosetta's gown. "Ian is leaving for Kingston tomorrow. He can take any letters and bring back what supplies you need." Wrestling to her feet, she threw her shawl about her shoulders. "I assume Wesley 'as credit at the military store."

"Ian will be away?" Olivia sat up, alert. "What if those—"

"Tosh!" Sally huffed. "Those blaggards won't be back anytime soon. And I definitely want my bit 'o calico to make a new dress for Hogmanay. Everything seems to be a mite tight, these days." She opened the door. Gizzy raced over to Rosetta's pallet, excitedly sniffing, tail wagging.

"You must sleep on my bed, Annie," Olivia insisted. Gently, she guided Rosetta and her baby, to her room. Placing a heated stone wrapped in toweling at her feet, she again kissed her forehead. "You did a good job, Rosie."

Whatever objections she had once held, were gone. Her duty was to care for those sheltering beneath her roof.

—39—

Olivia never returned to her bed; she didn't want to. Early each morning, Eddie crawled in with her for a brief snuggle. He seemed to consider the daybed his, with Olivia simply changing places with his mama. Annie's rosary now hung on a hook in the bedroom. Charlotte's linked heart medallion hung on a nail overhead.

Snow fell continuously for three days, delaying Ian in Kingston. He returned on the MacFie's dog sled, in good spirits, having sold his furs at a good price. Kingston was well stocked with supplies, and Ian brought the three women mail, along with a collection of books from Stephen Reed's shelf.

"Lieutenant Reed has moved to officer's quarters," he reported. Sheepishly holding out a package to Olivia, he smiled boyishly. "This for Sally." Olivia lifted a corner of the protective paper wrapping, revealing burgundy velvet. "The lass has never had a proper gown, and I would appreciate if—"

"Ian!" Olivia gushed. "There's plenty in this bolt—enough for both dress and short coat. I would be honoured to make Sally a gown for Hogmanay...yet...she's expecting calico."

"Aye. I bought some yardage for her and the girls." He winked. "But she deserves better."

"And she deserves the bit of muslin I've stored away. It'll make a fine chemise, so she can wear the dress many ways." She returned a wink. "This will be our secret."

Doffing his tuque at Rosetta, he sat in the rocking chair by the hearth. "How's your wee bairn?"

"Evie is eating well, and soiling even better," she glanced up at the cotton diapers, strung on a line between rafters.

"Eve, for new beginnings, aye?" He turned to Annie. "And you're getting on well?"

"Warm and well fed," she returned.

With curt bow to each of the three women, he left. Immediately, they tore open wax seals and devoured their letters.

Wesley's letter had been posted from Queenston, over a month ago. To Olivia's surprise he confided uncensored opinion of his investigations. She was particularly intrigued by his description of a courageous lady, Mrs. Secord, keeping home and family safe near a field of battle.

The name rang familiar. Last year, at her step-brother's hunting party, James Cliveton had offered a dinner toast to Mrs. Secord. He described her walk of almost 20 miles, through American-occupied territory, to warn the British army of an impending attack. He even credited her for saving Upper Canada, prompting a discussion where he disputed his fiancée's assertion of Mrs. Secord's impropriety.

Jane Blythe had said there was a certain madness in living so near a battlefield. Wesley confirmed such in his letter. He recounted Mrs. Secord running into a field of battle to bring her wounded husband home to die. Other women had also been on the field—military wives who took up fallen arms to continue the fight. Their bravery remained uncredited. Sally had said she'd done the same in France.

Would she have such courage, Olivia wondered?

Mrs. Secord had nursed her husband, James, back to life, Wesley continued. Yet James was now crippled, their family impoverished, and livelihood destroyed. The letter identified James Secord's sister as the late Richard Cartwright's wealthy widow.

"Good Lord!" Olivia muttered with shared frustration at that sharp-nosed woman. "True nobility is a sacrificial act of kindness, not a position of birth."

"Hah!" Annie loudly agreed, returning to her thick letter.

"Mrs. McGuire writes that Stephen Reed's baby girl is being cared for by a wet nurse in Picardville." Rosetta looked up. "I assumed she died at birth."

"He sends her away," Annie huffed, "as if she is at fault for her mother's death."

"A baby must be nursed," Olivia defended. "Yet, I do hope the child does not live under such a burden." She echoed Annie's earlier sympathetic observation of her own childhood.

Their eyes met. "We must make sure she doesn't," Annie affirmed.

Eddie reached up to Olivia. "Con," he uttered.

Ignoring his babble, she picked him up. He'd been making nonsensical noises throughout the past few days. She continued reading her letter.

Wesley reminded her that an officer's duty took precedence over personal desire. However, he confessed a longing to bridge the abyss between them, once his responsibilities were completed.

"Abyss?" she sniffed. "Quite apt."

A compromise might be obtained, he continued, for her to live in town, while he continued with duty. Her heart sank at his cold practicality. She had not communicated her enjoyment of independence at the clearing. He concluded with a hope that she'd acquired homemaking skills, reminding her again that he could not afford a servant.

Dare she tell him her homemaking skills had broadened beyond milking Busy, chopping kindling, and building a fire. In addition to squash soup, she now coaxed delicious gruel from dried apples, onions, and beans, to accompany soft biscuits. Would he appreciate that this came at a cost of calloused hands, dry skin, shorn hair, and abandonment of fashion? He would discover this, should he return home. Until then, she would live as she saw fit.

"Bah!" Folding his letter, she looked over at Annie. "This place is turning into a harem."

"Better that than a convent." Annie smiled, eyes twinkling. "Johnnie hopes to come for me, when Wesley goes on to York."

"Con," Eddie repeated, running sticky chubby fingers through Olivia's cropped hair.

"You must stay until Hogmanay," Rosetta asserted. "I need someone to dance with."

"I can dance with you." Olivia kissed Eddie's hand.

"Con," he persisted.

"Our son wants a scone," Annie translated, with an encouraging nod.

"Then we must make some, my child." Balancing Eddie on her hip, Olivia went over to the pantry.

—40—

For two days, Captain Wesley Bryson and John Oneida awaited summons to meet with Catharine Adonwentishon Brant, Clan Mother and third wife of War Chief Joseph Brant. Feared in earlier years for his many atrocities, her husband's latter life was spent in contemplative study of his new Christian faith, and settling his vast properties.

Eight years earlier, newly-widowed Mrs. Brant had moved from their Burlington manor to Mohawk Village, on the banks of the Grand River. As a Clan Mother of the Mohawk Nation, she now advocated for a return to traditional life to counter the encroachment of European settlement.

Snow continued to fall, temperatures tumbling into deep cold. Thickening ice on the Grand River opened travel between the various Six Nations villages of Mohawk, Cayuga, Onondaga, Oneida, Seneca, and Tuscarora, as well as indigenous nations from the Republic. They now dwelt in peace along the river, after generations of war among themselves and with European colonizers.

Chapel bells rang out from the Mohawk Church of England, infusing the wintry village with cheeriness. This deeply religious Mohawk community welcomed Advent as a period of both reflection and celebration. As the parishioners began the evening church service, melodic voices flowed across the snow, greeting Wesley where he sat in the village council house.

His accommodation was more than satisfactory. Beds, sheets, and English blankets were of the finest quality, with food savoury and bountiful. Wesley had had time to complete his report of the Elbema Creek massacre, prepare for meeting with Esther Hill Phelps, and even dispatch a letter to Olivia.

John knocked at the door of their shared room. "Put aside your work and come outside with me," he coaxed." You need to get some exercise—perhaps take in a spot of ice fishing."

With a brisk shake of his head, Wesley mumbled, "I've much to think about...no time..."

"I believe you would glean more information mingling with the people and listening to what is spoken of Epaphras Phelps," John challenged. "Treason is not easily hidden."

Wesley looked up. "Perhaps you're right. Why not hear it first hand?"

Outfitted with deerskin mukluks and mittens, a bearskin coat, and a knitted tuque, he followed John out onto the frozen river. Neither wore snowshoes. Icy wind numbed his nose, watering his eyes. His pace slowed as he laboured through snow drifts on the ice.

"There's shelter ahead," John urged, pointing out a wooden lean-to, mid-river.

"I'm impressed it stands in this gale." Wesley whipped off his mittens to blow his nose.

"Rocks help," John beckoned him onward with an energetic wave.

Within the shelter, a grizzly old Native huddled over a foot-size hole cut through the ice. From his bare hands, a fishing line reached into the dark waters. Glancing up at their approach, he chortled, "See if you can do better to bring up supper."

"Too cold for them to eat?" John asked.

"Too cold for me to fish," he flashed tobacco stained teeth and handed his fishing line to Wesley. "Try a jiggle or three."

Wrapping the line around his mittened hand, Wesley accepted the challenge. Squatting together, sheltered from the wind, the three men stared at the ice-hole.

"Old man...what do we hope to catch?" Wesley shivered.

"A bit of fresh air," he pulled out a pouch of tobacco and stuffed his pipe. "I've got a tomahawk—" he lifted a thick stick with a rock crudely roped at one end "—if you're lucky."

"You're a veteran of the war?" Wesley asked, attempting conversation. He pulled up the line, quickly releasing it several times, hoping to tempt a bite.

The old man replied in his native tongue and John burst into laughter.

"Which one?" he finally translated. "The French Indian, Revolutionary, or your latest? I fought alongside the British, on both our hunting grounds, the Mohawk Valley, and here in Canada. If you children-of-the-same-mother can't sit and smoke a pipe in peace, keep your next war in Europe."

A chuckle escaped from Wesley.

The old man passed his pipe to John. He drew deep, emitting a billowing cloud, then passed it on to Wesley with an elbow nudge.

A shared pipe was a significant gesture; to refuse would insult the old warrior. Wesley affirmed him with a patronizing nod, and drew deep. The sweet woody flavour surprised him. "Rich tobacco," he acknowledged with a surprised gasp.

John snickered. "You are fishing with a Sachem hereditary chief of the Mohawks. Thirty years ago, he travelled to England and met the King. He has more secret resources than your Leo Voisin."

The line tugged violently. "I've got something!" Wesley leapt up and began hauling hand-over-hand. The line resisted, taunt; he persevered, breathless with excitement and effort.

Minutes later, a fat golden-olive fish, with prominent brown blotches, flew from the hole. Flapping aggressively, it slid back towards the ice hole, its protruding mouth gasping frantically. Wesley grasped the tomahawk and, with a quick blow, stilled the fish.

"Well done." The elderly Sechem cut the hook from the creature's mouth, replacing it with a rope loop. Holding it high, he teased, "I presume this will be for Adonwentishon's table."

"By all means," Wesley cheerily agreed. "Pray take it to the honourable Mrs. Brant on my behalf, for I would not presume such liberty." John nodded with approval.

"And I will give the Clan Mother your greeting." The wise old man's face crinkled in smile.

"Well played," John affirmed, as the old man walked away.

"It would have gone better, had I known the significance of this encounter."

"He was looking for authentic humility, a rare trait among British," John explained. "You offered respect, soldier to soldier."

Late that evening, a white-haired African man delivered a written invitation for afternoon tea with Mrs. Brant, the following day.

"Tomorrow you serve as scribe," John advised. "More humility, for you to exhibit."

"Another test?" Wesley challenged his presumption.

"Think of the possibilities, my friend," John encouraged. "A reed that bends in the wind is stronger than a mighty oak."

"I won't argue," he conceded.

—41—

Catharine Adonwentishon Brant's spacious clapboard dwelling evidenced her substantial wealth as a leader of the Six Nations. Within matriarchal Haudenosaunee society, Clan Mothers were responsible for the welfare of the clan. They held final say over matters of leadership, property, and war, also served as Faithkeepers for all ceremonial services of life.

To investigate Esther Hill Phelps' challenge of the government's confiscation, Wesley's strategy was to understand and refute the Six

Nations' troublesome claim to the land. If sovereignty were at the core, then the issue would not easily be resolved. He would begin by interviewing Catharine Brant.

They walked past the white chapel. "Tonight, we attend Evensong," John commented. "It will be expected and respectful for us to attend."

"You're Roman Catholic, not Church of England." Wesley shifted the writing box to his other hip.

John shot him an impatient look. "Is God Roman?"

"Is he Haudenosaunee?" Wesley opened the picket gate with his free arm and looked beyond, to the frozen Grand.

"Joseph Brant's enslaved people built this house, most of the Mohawk village, and his Burlington manor, as well." John Oneida paused, looking down the Grand to the church steeple. "Upon his death, Brant granted land to those he freed. His widow carries his leadership mantle, yet she is not so gracious."

"There are still slaves here?" Wesley remembered the elderly servant that delivered Mrs. Brant's invitation.

"Mrs. Brant has her own...wealth," John rapped the bronze knocker.

An elderly African opened the door. With a genteel bow, he took their wraps and led them into the parlour. Overlooking the river, the lavish, well-positioned room had a generous fire in the hearth and handsome china decorating a table. Another elderly African stood in attendance by the table, dressed in scarlet, ruffles, and buckled shoes.

The door opened again and Mrs. Brant entered. Tall in stature, dark elegant features complemented her flashing eyes. Over her shoulders she wore a blanket of the finest red silk, bordered with cream lace. Her purple dress flowed to her knees, revealing close fitting scarlet leggings. Beads and silk ribbons ornamented her moccasins. Attractive, thought Wesley, but not practical.

She nodded a solemn greeting, gesturing for them to sit, and sat in the high-back chair across from them. Measured and firm, she addressed John Oneida in Mohawk.

Retrieving paper from his lap desk, Wesley dipped the pen nib in his inkwell and awaited translation. Unceded strength exuded from the tenor of her speech and mannerisms. He knew her father was Irish and that she'd been educated in English—at a missionary school, in New York State. Yet, he respected her use of Mohawk; an expression of sovereignty.

Mindfully waiting for translation, he recollected a wartime disagreement when a proud Mohawk Chief had refused to take orders from a Scots Officer of the British Military. Two translators had been required, for both had insisted on using their indigenous tongues of Mohawk and Gaelic. Yet the inconvenience helped reconcile by underscoring their shared position serving British occupiers.

"The Haldimand Tract was given to the Six Nations, by the King, for their alliance in the Revolutionary War." John began, pausing to assist Wesley's transcription. "It was for our sovereign use—six miles, both sides of the Grand River, from Lake Erie to its source, near Georgian Bay. In the eight years since my husband's death, settlers have become increasingly brazen at squatting on our tract. Now I learn that British surveyors have begun measuring northern reaches of the tract, forewarning further encroachment by settlers. Since they are military surveyors, I must assume your government dishonours our agreement of 1774."

She waited for Wesley to finish before continuing. John listened intently, nodding occasionally.

"She asserts that convicting Epaphras Phelps of treason, in absentia, is a ploy to grab more Six Nations land. Mr. Phelps loyally served Joseph Brant, both in the Mohawk Valley and here, in Canada, as his secretary and power-of-attorney. Never did Mr. Phelps raise an arm against the British. Nor did he fight the Americans, for they are his people. We, therefore, helped him escape to the Republic. Even if this false accusation of treason were true, the land is not his to confiscate."

"Phelps voluntarily left for the Republic," Wesley interrupted, impatiently. "Therefore, under law, he must forfeit his land. More importantly, he has been found guilty of treason in a court of law."

Eyes blazing, Catharine Brant replied in English. "Epaphras Phelps did not leave voluntarily. He was falsely accused of treason and my people helped him escape, to save his life. Does your government intend to accuse all Six Nations people with treason and confiscate the entire Haldimand Tract?"

Wesley set down his pen, ignoring John's concerned frown. "Why is the land not his? Did not Joseph Brant give it to him?"

"That land belongs to Esther Phelps. Under Haudenosaunee law, women control land, not their husbands, for we are not chattel," she declared with a proud set of her jaw. "But that is a mere ploy. Your executive council first argued Esther Phelps was an alien, and therefore unable to hold property." She paused, drawing a deep breath. "Mrs. Phelps is no more alien than Nelles, of Forty Mile. He also has property on the Grand—a gift of my husband, to which I did not agree."

"The late Richard Cartwright, of Kingston," John added, "was also born in the Republic."

"Both Nelles and Cartwright fought for the Crown," Wesley countered. "Epaphras Phelps did not."

"Borders are the making of your people, Captain—a European concept. We do not recognize them. Esther Phelps is an alien by only your definition." She adjusted the shawl about her shoulders, gesturing for the servant to add a log to the fire. "My husband gave the land to Esther Hill Phelps upon the birth of her son, Hiram. The land belongs to her."

"Under British common law, the land belongs to Epaphras Phelps," Wesley shot back, restoring the cover of his inkwell. "Esther Phelps is a '*feme covert*', a covered married woman, unable to hold property,"

"Let me remind you, we are a sovereign people. Our nationhood was acknowledged by our King." Catharine Brant folded her hands in her lap.

"This was revoked by the Quebec Act of 1774, some 40 years ago." Wesley set down his pen.

John leaned back, arms folded.

"And by that Act, you revoked our sovereignty and returned civil rights to the people of Quebec—a conquered people and your former enemies. Is this British justice, Captain?" Catharine defiantly lifted her chin. "Tell me why a loyal ally is sacrificed to appease a defeated enemy."

Wesley looked over at John. From the purse of his lips, he knew he would find no support.

"Speak up, sir," the Clan Mother pressed." Tell me why the married women of Quebec are not subject to the *Coverture* condition and, therefore, can own property, earn an income, and vote to elect government officials." She pointed an index finger at him in accusation. "Explain why these defeated enemies are awarded sovereign rights at the cost of loyal allies, who fought by your side through three wars."

Wesley cleared his throat. He knew the answer and so did Mrs. Brant. French Canadians vastly outnumbered the British in Canada. Only by ceding power to the Catholic Church, and allowing life to continue, as before their defeat, would French Canada live peaceably under British rule. By contrast, the Haudenosaunee were weakened from war and unable to resist. Denying their sovereignty would ensure they continued in this state. This was the truth, and it was not just.

Through his son, the fate of Indigenous peoples was now entwined with his own. His heart demanded that he defend his son's future. To make a difference with his life, he must take a stand. He cleared his throat, appreciating this first step.

"I acknowledge my impertinence, Mrs. Brant," he tendered.

She nodded, eyes questioning, waiting.

"Property passes through the Haudenosaunee female family line," he affirmed. "Therefore, I understand your position that the British *Coverture* condition does not apply to the sovereign people of Six Nations. Consequently, the property of Mrs. Phelps, a loyal ally of the British, cannot be confiscated for her husband's act of treason."

"That is how you must write it up," John rubbed his hands together.

Wesley leaned back in his chair and looked out upon the frozen Grand River. Six miles, both sides, was all the Haudenosaunee Confederacy had left to live off of. "This will not easily be resolved," he surmised. "Life will not be simple."

"Was is ever?" Catharine Brant sniffed. "Now, let us enjoy some tea." She motioned her scarlet-clad servant to pour and pass around a plate of maple cakes. "I wish to thank you, Captain Bryson, for the plump bass you sent to my table, yesterday. It was delicious."

"I'm pleased you enjoyed it," Wesley bowed.

"Tomorrow night, you gentlemen must come for dinner. Mrs. Phelps will join us."

—42—

"What do you think?" Olivia held up the burgundy gown for admiration. High in empire profile, she'd trimmed the low neckline with matching silk, snipped from a seldom-worn underskirt. The sleeves puffed at the shoulders, slimming to buttoned slender wrists. A short Spencer overcoat, lined with the underskirt, complemented the ensemble.

"Sally will be regal," Rosetta affirmed, gently tugging the hammock cord to keep Evie sleeping.

"I've also made a cream muslin under-chemise, to give variety of wear," Olivia added excitedly. Her favourite sleeping gown now belonged to Rosetta, her underskirt cut up into lining and trim, and her muslin dress remade into a chemise. She wouldn't miss them. Wesley's flannel shirts were far warmer and easier to launder.

"Hide that dress—quick!" Annie urged, dropping the window curtain. "Sally's coming across the yard. I'll put on the kettle."

Olivia buried the dress, under the quilts of Rosetta's bed.

With a brisk rap of the door, Sally strode in, boots stomping on the mat. Clearly frustrated, a scowl filled her face. In her arms she held folded yellow fabric, imprinted with small brown shapes.

"I 'ad enough fabric to make Sadie a dress." She heaved a deep sigh. "There's not e'nuf to even make me a skirt."

"Dear Sally," Rosetta offered sincerely. "You always care for others before yourself."

"*Ma chère amie.*" Annie reached a comforting arm about her waist. "Come have tea."

"Let me see what I can do." Olivia unfolded the bundle, holding it up. Sally was right. There was barely enough for a blouse, let alone a skirt. Matching this yellow to any of her dresses would be difficult. She never wore this shade; it would only be flattering against a darker complexion. "Ian's choice?" she asked.

Sally nodded sadly.

"Men should not buy for their wives," Olivia bemoaned. "I've managed to make use of fabric Wesley purchased, but Sally..." She leaned in, implying conspiracy. "I've a large piece of fabric in my trunk that would better suit you."

"Ah, luv..." Sally shook her head. "I wouldn't want to take any of your bridal clothes."

"You won't be." It wasn't a lie; she just couldn't think of anything at that moment. "There's enough here to make something else."

Sally hesitated. "Poor Ian. I don't want to 'urt—"

"He will be pleased you made Sadie a dress," Rosetta encouraged.

Sally's face brightened.

"Leave this with me," Olivia patted her shoulder, whispering, "I can make something for Rosetta with your leftover calico. And I have an idea for Annie."

"Come join us for tea and shortbread," Rosetta invited from the table, filling the cups and shifting the conversation. "I've noticed more dogsled traffic, with the river frozen."

"Winter is best for visiting," Annie affirmed. "No mosquitoes and not many chores." She turned to Sally. "Will we see the same people at your Hogmanay *fête* as last year?"

"Yes, and more!" Sally laughed. "An Irish family—the Cavanaughs—have settled upstream of the rifts. They've eight children and will bring a second fiddle."

"We'll have dancing, for sure!" Annie clasped hands together. "It's too bad Wesley is away, Olivia. He's such a good dancer."

Her remark struck Olivia like a blow. She'd never danced with Wesley. Anger welled up within the struggle to steady her breath. This was not Annie's fault, but because of restrictions she'd chosen to abide by in England.

"I've never danced with Wesley," she confessed. Eddie waddled over to her, lifting his arms. She picked him up and fed him a shortbread biscuit.

"*Quel dommage!*" Annie's eyes softened. "Please, forgive my insensitivity."

"You'll have your time, luv," Sally sympathized.

"Why didn't you dance with him?" Rosetta frowned. "Weren't you courting?"

"Wesley was my nieces' French tutor, and excluded from our family's social events," Olivia hesitated. She wanted to honour Wesley's desire for discretion. But she also wanted to be honest with these women. "My family forbade our courtship."

Putting down her cup, Annie folded her hands. "I fled the convent and Rosetta escaped enslavement. Tell us what you ran from, Olivia."

The invitation given, Olivia confided her tale of love thwarted and her arranged marriage to the estate heir. All spilled out: Wesley's acceptance of an officer's commission, her desperate misinterpretation of Jane Blythe's "kept safe" message, and the subsequent escape to Canada.

"I called upon my cousin—a merchant sea captain—crossed Atlantic, and thrust myself upon Wesley's mercy," she concluded. "Being who he is, he dutifully took me as wife." She looked around the table, stroking Eddie's head. "Since you respect the man, I trust you to keep his story here, never to leave."

"Wesley did care for you," Annie ventured. "He confided regret for accepting the commission. That is why he willingly released me to find happiness with John."

"Cor!" Sally huffed. "Your father was an earl? That makes you—"

"Privilege came at too great a price," Olivia interrupted, "I much prefer Mrs. Bryson—and Olivia to you dear women."

199

"At Hogmanay, I will dance with you," Rosetta shook her head merrily. "If only to say that I've danced with nobility."

"I will give you that honour, dear Rosie." She waved a hand in courtly gesture.

That evening, Olivia searched the contents of both her trunks. *Help me see opportunity,* she silently prayed.

Her eyes settled on a long-sleeved, green woolen gown, which she had frequently worn during the Atlantic crossing. The slightly faded garment needed laundering before lengthening. As a gown for Rosetta, it would match perfectly with a yellow calico chemise.

At the bottom, she found a light-blue cotton dress that would suit Sally's complexion. She'd worn this garment on the Jamaican excursion. The full skirt, with its creative paneling, could be altered to fit her abundant curves. "Ian will be pleased she'll have two new dresses," she confirmed with pleasure.

Then she thought of Annie, who did not wear European clothes. There was a navy-blue woolen riding jacket that would be suitable. When would she ever ride again, anyway? Wesley didn't even own a horse. Adding a rose silk scarf, Annie will be quite dashing, Olivia concluded.

The days ahead would be full and satisfying. She may not be able to carry a baby, but her stitchery was excellent.

—43—

Three weeks passed quickly for Wesley and John. Welcomed, they immersed within the Six Nations Grand community.

From north of Brant's Ford to near the mouth of the Great Erie Lake, they travelled by dog-sled. Days passed hunting, fishing, and skating on bones strapped to boots. In the evenings they visited and feasted. Embraced by winter's dormancy, the Grand River's homes welcomed them, both Indigenous and those granted by Joseph Brant to British settlers.

As a powerful self-made War Chief, Joseph Brant had dispersed Six Nations' land as his personal property, though it had been granted to the Six Nations. At Bunnell's Landing, he'd given land grants to his formerly enslaved. Yet, to the south, large holdings were sold to slave-owning American Loyalists. The allotment of these tracts demonstrated Joseph Brant's conflicting generosity and business acuity, and it had been done without the agreement of his wife.

West of Brant's Fort, they explored Phelps' disputed grant. Padlocked and boarded up, they were barred from entering the sturdy log house. From afar, Wesley noted the house, outbuildings, and fenced fields were untouched by war, unlike settlements further west, north of Lake Erie. The government's desire to reclaim this desirable property was understandable.

Corruption and nepotism had been rampant during the war's chaos. Mere accusation of treason was sufficient for a complicit Justice of the Peace, to seize the accused's land, selling it, below market price, and sometimes to the accuser. With Joseph Brant now deceased, allegations could easily be made against his secretary, Epaphras Phelps, to confiscate the property for British settlers. The unharmed condition of the Phelps tract only added to suspicion of his treason. Arguing for justice against the powerful executive council would also be a defence of Six Nations sovereignty.

Evening services at the chapel became Wesley's solace. Hymns— sung in the Mohawk tongue, their voices melodic and sincere— brought strength. Six Nations people were tired of war, and so was he. Peace must be protected.

Wesley dined twice with Esther Phelps at the home of Catharine Brant. Complimenting her impressive knowledge of North American politics, she acknowledged, "I've lived in both countries, Captain, it is my responsibility, both for myself and my children."

"Will you join your husband in America." John leaned forward in his chair.

She smiled, as if to a child. "My land is here, Mr. Oneida, or have you forgotten our ways?"

John nodded and turned to Wesley, "Unceded strength, aye?"

—

On the final evening of their stay at Mohawk Village, Catharine Brand hosted a *soirée* at the community hall. Everyone came out, bedecked in their finest, some in elaborate beaded buckskin, others in fine silk-laced gowns. Catharine Brant stood out regally, her traditional Mohawk ensemble of red tunic and purple trousers made of the finest silk.

Following a feast of roasted turkey, root vegetables, breads, and pickles, the Mohawks opened with a serpent dance.

Men and women formed a wide circle. Guided by a lead chanter, the circle slowly narrowed, coiling about him. Then, with raised hands, he reversed their steps to uncoil the circle.

"The dance is a symbol of a snake awakening and shedding its skin," John explained.

"Rather appropriate," Wesley nodded solemn agreement.

A fiddler came out and began a lively sequence of Scottish reels. Mohawk men were agile in dance, and their women good-humoured. Wesley gingerly approached Mrs. Brand and asked for the honour of a dance. With a graceful nod, she conceded.

Laughter filled the room, Mrs. Brant's face glowing with pleasure. John soon joined in with Mrs. Phelps as his partner. Wesley danced several jigs with Mrs. Brant until, breathless, she excused herself, freeing him to continue with maidens and matrons. He danced the whole night, for he loved dancing.

At the event's close, old women laid out a tea of sweets. They exchanged farewells and the guests went out to a cold dawn, John and Wesley returning to their room.

Coals glowed in the hearth. Mail waited on their shared night table.

"Fortunate it caught up with us before we were away," Wesley tore open Olivia's thumb-printed seal.

She'd written a pleasant account of clearing life, and river traffic. Her mention of Pierre Sabin stopping in on his way north, surprised him. Pierre was no longer his business associate, nor had he ever considered him a friend. Taking interest in his wife's well-being was inappropriate.

His heart lightened at her descriptions of Eddie chasing Gizzy, building towers with kindling, and asking for scones in English. She had closed her letter expressing anticipation for the Douglas Hogmanay gathering, followed by "tenderly yours, Mrs. Bryson".

Something had happened in the past four months to wrought her contentment—something good.

John folded his letter, setting it on the night table. "You have my deepest sympathy for your loss," he offered. "Mrs. Bryson survived and that's all that truly matters."

"Loss?" Wesley sat up, confused. "What loss?"

"*Mon Dieu,*" John inhaled sharply. "Perhaps I have misspoken."

"Perhaps you should speak," he returned. "Has something happened, of which I have no knowledge."

"Your wife's loss of the child she was carrying," John ventured.

"I knew nothing of a child."

"Probably from the effects of the Ague," John added, "where you almost lost your wife, as well."

"She only writes of good." Wesley picked up her letter, turning it over in his hands. A thumb print was her seal, not the Fairworth crest. "Why would she withhold this from me?"

"To not take you from duty," John offered in defence. "Is that not her duty?"

"But what of honesty!" Wesley's challenge fell flat. He had been equally guilty of withholding truth.

"Take good from this, Wesley," John held open his hands, in a priestly gesture of invitation. "The women have carried this burden together, as a three-strand cord." He lay back, pulling up his quilt. "Now allow me some sleep."

Wesley fetched the writing desk. He did not easily express vulnerability of sentiment, yet he knew only heartfelt words would do. Praise slowly flowed from his pen for Olivia's admirable courage and tenacity in choosing to be his wife. Gently, he urged that she no longer withhold fears and suffering from him, and committed to do the same. Their challenges were meant to be borne together, he reminded her, for all the years the Lord allowed.

A line from a Robbie Burns' poem came to him. In faith, he closed with these words:

I will love thee still, my dear,

While the sands o' life shall run.

Olivia was a mystery, a loyal mystery, and the woman he was choosing to love.

Woman's laughter travelled up to his window—young lovers in the night. Blowing out the candle, the evening flooded his thoughts. Drifting off, he remembered he had never had the good fortune to dance with his wife. Someday he must make amends.

In the light of a single candle and low fire, Olivia rocked in her chair, completing the final stitches to Rosetta's green dress. Eddie slept soundly on the daybed beside her.

Last year, at Stir-up Sunday, she'd thrown charms into the Christmas batter. Following tradition, she made a wish to accompany the charms; she'd wished that the love she'd forsaken, would return.

Then passed an unpleasant week at her step-brother's Advent shooting party, avoiding rakes and dandies. The worst of the lot was Daniel Fremont, her intended fiancé. Family pressure had been mounting for her to submit to their plans. At 28 years of age, she'd run out of time and excuses.

A rainy day's adventure with Jane Blythe had forged faith that escape was possible. After Jane innocently recounted Wesley's message, she had interpreted finding the coveted wishbone charm in her pudding portions as a sign her wish was granted. She merely had to act in faith and success would follow.

Had she known the cost of pursuing such hope, would she still have followed her heart?

When you love somebody, you take their life as your own. Sally's words flowed back to her from the day of their reconciliation. A flow of forgiveness, imparted by those who forgave, helped make reconciliation possible.

Blowing out her candle, she gathered Eddie in her arms and slipped under the quilt. No child should be held accountable for a parent's actions. Wesley trusted her to embrace his son. She'd grown to love Eddie and would savour whatever time she was allowed with the child.

She reflected on the collection of stuffed animals and dolls she had made for the Douglas children and those in her home. Even Evie would have a soft ball, made of burgundy velvet with an embroidered smiling face.

"All those years of embroidering decorative pew cushions are of benefit," she chuckled softly. "Yet, I probably would have had a better understanding of faith had I felt the hard floor beneath my knees." She stroked Eddie's thick thatch of hair. "I'll stand with Wesley, even if it is at the back of the church."

—

Christmas Eve was upon them. With Busy settled for the night, they gathered before the hearth to eat Annie's meat pies. "Poor man's *Tourières*", she called them, since they were made of venison, and not the traditional blend of veal, beef, and pork.

Forest greens and sage adorned the cabin, transforming it for celebration. Annie passed around heaping plates of meat pie, topped with fried apples, maple syrup, and beans. "Christmas *Tourtières* were the best part of convent life." She laid a hand on her belly, smiling. "Baby's bouncing with the maple syrup."

Evie began to whimper. Olivia gathered the emptied dishes and set them in the stone sink.

"Leave them!" Rosetta ordered from the rocker, opening her chemise to nurse. Annie sat before the fire, Eddie's head resting on her lap. Olivia sat on the willow settee, and picked up her knitting.

"*Ehstehn yayau dehtsaun we yisus ahattonnia...*" Annie began a haunting melody, singing in rhythmic half-chant.

A shiver ran up Olivia's spine. "What is that?"

"An old song, written by a Jesuit for a people no longer," Annie replied. "Singing it connects me with the past."

"It frightens me," Olivia confessed.

"Then I shall sing it in English, and you will not be frightened," Annie smiled and haltingly continued:

> *There are spirits, coming with a message for us, the*
> *sky people,*
> *They are coming to say,*
> *"Come on, be on top of life, rejoice!*
> *Mary has just given birth, come on rejoice!*
> *Three have left for such a place;*
> *They are men of great nature."*
> *I should make them part of my family.*

For several moments, they sat in reflection, listening to the crackling pop of hearth fire.

"From your perspective, our Christmas story sounds peculiar," Olivia finally ventured.

"*Your* Christmas story," Annie snickered. "You think God is European?"

"You probably think he's white, too," Rosetta sniffed. "Bible says I'm made in His image—so what does that say of God?" She patted Evie's back and was rewarded with a quiet belch.

"Religion is a work of man." Olivia shifted her gaze from Annie to Rosetta and inhaled deeply. "Faith is God's gift to mankind to feed hope."

"That don't answer my question." Rosetta wiped Evie's chin.

"Then I shall read the Christmas story." Olivia retrieved the Bible from the shelf and opened to a familiar passage:

> *And it came to pass in those days, there went out a*
> *decree from Caesar Augustus that the world should*
> *be taxed...*

She read on, concluding with:

> *For mine eyes have seen thy salvation: Which thou*
> *hast prepared before the face of all people; A light*
> *to lighten the Gentiles, and the glory of all people.*

Smiling broadly, she looked up, as if to the heavens. "Even people I find peculiar...for we are made in God's image. He is not made in ours."

"Well spoken, my sister," Annie affirmed.

Rosetta began to quietly sing.

> *Children, go where I send thee—How shall I send*
> *thee?*
> *I'm gonna send thee, one by one: One for the little*
> *bitty baby.*
> *Born by the virgin Mary. Born, Born, Born in*
> *Bethlehem.*

She continued on through twelve melodic verses, each expressing an aspect of Christian faith.

"This song is how we learned 'bout God," Rosetta offered, upon conclusion. "We weren't allowed to read."

"If you weren't allowed, how did you learn?" Annie asked.

"Planter's daughter thought it a joke, teaching a Black child to read— like a dog to do tricks." Rosetta laid Evie across her lap. "I got a sound cuffing, when her father found out. Wanted us kept ignorant, I s'pose."

"I chose to be ignorant," Olivia glanced at Wesley's bookshelf. A shiver crept up her spine. "To awaken was too painful."

"It's Christmas morning." Rosetta yawned with a robust stretch. "Do you know this is the best day to steal away?"

"Is that what you did?" Annie laid Eddie on the day bed, then filled the kettle.

"My time came in late summer, when I was hired out to a Richmond cotton mill. A massive storm came and I broke out of the barn where I'd been locked up. Figured the Lord would either take me or I'd get away, and I had made it as far as the Shenandoah Valley when I heard a hound bay."

"That's twice you've gotten away," Olivia exclaimed. "How?"

"I lifted my eyes up to the mountains..." Rosetta quoted, adding, "Those preacher words just popped into my head, probably since I was facing even more mountains."

"My help cometh from the Lord," Olivia completed her quote.

"Only, I didn't know that at the time," Rosetta winced. "Still, I tried my best to scramble up a mountain when that bounty hunter's dog caught up. Standing before a rocky crevasse I decided that I was going to die free."

"*Mon Dieu,*" Annie whispered.

"Just when I was about to jump, the hound let out an almighty yelp and ran back towards the woods. It only made it halfway, for it had an arrow juttin' from its neck, spurtin' blood all over. Then an Indian—a Creek warrior—came out of the bush." She cast a sympathetic look at Gizzy, asleep at Olivia's feet. "He took my hand, and told me his wife could make that dog taste like turkey."

"He lied," Annie laughed. "Tastes like bitter venison. Time for tea."

"Time for Christmas gifts." Olivia stood up, rubbing hands together. From her trunk, she gave Annie the navy riding coat with a brilliant scarf, and proudly presented Rosetta with the green dress and yellow under-chemise.

"This coat is so handsome!" Annie exclaimed. "And I have something to match your new dress, Rosie." Disappearing into her room, she returned with a lacy green necklace of glass beads. Woven to resemble a vine, it attached at the front with two leaves looping together.

"This is beautiful, Annie!" Rosetta held up the delicate jewellery, beads shimmering in the firelight.

"You're beautiful, Mrs. George," Olivia amended. "They were made to adorn you."

"I made one for you, too, Olivia." Annie produced an identical necklace from within the folds of her sleeve.

Olivia attached the beaded vine about her neck. Those jewels she'd hidden beneath the bedroom floorboard had cost her freedom. This adornment was a gift of love.

Rosetta set Evie on the daybed and went to her room. When she emerged, she set three sheets of paper on the table. "I wasn't always taking a snooze." With graphite, on paper, she'd captured Olivia's wit, Annie's mysterious smile, and Eddie's wide-eyed wonder.

"Do I truly look as that?" Olivia asked. Though her image pleasing, there was a hint of impatience in her features.

Rosetta laughed and Annie slipped an arm about Olivia's waist.

Part IV—Unceded Strength

York, Upper Canada (winter, 1816)

—45—

Midnight mass had left Wesley serene, at peace with himself, and a bit hungry.

"They've retired for the night," John whispered, carefully closing the back door of the house where they'd rented accommodations.

On the kitchen table waited two generous slices of pumpkin pie and a neatly scribed note:

> *There's cider in the pantry. Your shirts will be ready come morn.*

"A fine lady, indeed," Wesley affirmed. "I'm thankful we found this lodging."

Earlier that day, approaching York on Dundas Road, they met a sleigh loaded with freight, pulled by a lively team of horses.

"Oye!" Wesley reined his horse to a halt, waving his hand to catch the driver's attention. "Have you recommendation for lodging in York?"

"You're not wanting to stay at the Barracks, aye?" His face broke out in smile.

"I could do with some good food and a bit of quiet," Wesley returned.

"Well, for that there's none better than a yellow clapboard house, along this road, just north of the governor's manor. Can't miss it with that colour," he chuckled, amid a cloud of tobacco smoke. "The room is modest, clean and private, and cooking is the finest in Upper Canada."

"I assume they won't mind a Haudenosaunee Mohawk under their roof," John countered.

"You'll be most welcomed, sir. The landlady is a woman of grace." He tugged the brim of his hat. "Just knock at the rear kitchen door and tell the good lady that Joshua sent you. That's all the reference she needs." With a click of his tongue and snap of the reins he continued on his way.

They found the yellow house as described, surrounded by a white picket fence. Through the gate, they led their horses up a neatly shoveled path to the rear stable. John hitched the horses while Wesley stepped onto the porch and rapped on the door.

A well-dressed African woman, of middle age, opened. "Good afternoon, gentlemen. How may I be of help?" she offered, wiping hands on her apron.

"May I speak to your mistress?" Wesley politely inquired.

"I am Mistress," she returned, repeating firmly, "May I be of assistance?"

"Pray forgive," Wesley offered a polite head bow. "Joshua sent us."

Her face softened, lips turning up with welcome. "So, you've come seeking lodging." She beckoned them into a tidy kitchen, then opened a door by the hearth. "This room is available. It's warm and clean. Your horses will be stabled in the barn."

Wesley looked about. Between two quilt-covered beds, a linen-curtained window looked across a snowy yard to the stable. "Quite agreeable," he exchanged with John.

"I usually board students and include breakfast for 10 shillings a week, paid in advance," she stated. "And, for an extra 5 shillings, I'll arrange feed and care of your horses."

"This will give us breathing space from York society," John confirmed.

The woman nodded silent agreement. Wesley retrieved the required funds from his purse, while John brought in their scant baggage.

Soon they were out again, riding the snow-packed road to the York Garrison.

Lieutenant Maxwell greeted them cheerily. "Governor General Drummond wished to be informed of your arrival, but he will not be expected to attend to business on Christmas Eve."

"Then he is still in residence," Wesley pressed.

"Indeed." Maxwell hesitated. "He's residing at the governor's manor, a guest of Lieutenant Governor Gore. A Christmas feast is being held tomorrow evening for a select company of businessmen, members of the Council, and accompanying ladies." Frowning at a neat arrangement of papers on his desk, he mumbled, "Something rings familiar." Sifting through those papers, he looked up. "Pray accept my apologies, Captain Bryson. You are on the guest list."

"With a companion, I presume," Wesley returned.

"Certainly, sir. Dinner is at eight, after services."

"Inform him of my arrival, Lieutenant," Wesley ordered with formal salute, and left.

Outside the garrison's protective walls, a bitter lake wind catapulted icy pellets at them. Horses protested with halting steps. Church bells tolled in the distance, answered by a chorus of barking dogs. To the east, limestone edifices stood where once had been log cabins, pig sheds, and storage huts. The outward changes reflected ambitious growth and development. The Americans could be considered to have done York a favour by burning it to the ground. This former frontier settlement was developing into a suitable replacement for Newark.

"Why am I still here?" John shouted over the wind. "You've no need of a translator."

"I need a friend." Wesley tightened his scarf about his ears and ice-encrusted beard. "That invitation for tomorrow's soirée secures my suspicions that I am being courted. Else, why would someone of my rank be included at such an evening?" He heaved a throat clearing cough. "Until I learn more, a favourable impression must be maintained—church is in order."

"Not John Strachan's Church of England, if that's what you hope for me." John reined his horse onto Dundas street. "The Catholic mission near the wharf of the old town is my preference."

"We attend Strachan's," Wesley countered, breathless. "And I must prepare as best I can for tomorrow's event, for I've no suitable dress uniform."

"And I do?" John tittered. "My clothes are well-worn and in need of cleaning—perhaps I'll wear deer skin and mukluks."

With horses settled in the stable, a brisk snow-clearing stomp on the back porch announced their entrance. At the table, the grizzly cart driver looked up. Now dressed in a wool coat with silk cravat, he was clean-shaven with hair neatly combed.

"Good evening, gentlemen," he stood, grinning. "You're in time for dinner. Mrs. Carter always makes more than enough."

Mrs. Carter looked over from the cast-iron wood stove and curtsied. "I believe you've already met my husband, Mr. Joshua Carter," she greeted. "Pray let us eat, before we depart for Christmas Eve service."

She quickly arranged two more settings of fine china plate, silverware, and crystal glasses on the white linen cloth. Steaming mashed potatoes waited, along with carrots and sliced beef with seasoned gravy. An enticing aroma of baking pumpkin pie escaped the oven. Her husband brought over chairs to accommodate them and filled their glasses with wine.

A tall African youth bounded down the stairs and hastened through the parlour archway. Stopping before the table, he politely bowed, then sat.

"My son, Samuel," Joshua's face lit up. He reached for their hands and led them in appreciation for the Lord's provision.

"I told you this was the best house in York," he looked up, face wrinkled in smile. "Don't usually haul freight, these days, but I'd let my drivers off for Christmas feast, so had to deliver shipments, myself." He passed Wesley the bowl of mashed potatoes. "Mrs. Carter likes taking care of people."

The youth exchanged a warm glance with Joshua. "Don't we know!"

"Samuel is a private student of Reverend Strachan's. He's made fine progress since the war," Mrs. Carter declared proudly, passing the steaming bowl of gravy to John. "Are you of the Six Nations Grand, Mr. Oneida?"

"I'm a refugee from New York state," he curtly replied. "I was raised by Jesuit brothers, near Montreal."

"Then you'll want to attend midnight mass, at the Catholic mission," she supplied.

"Is there a barber you can suggest, Mr. Carter." Wesley took a sip from his glass. The red wine was surprisingly light, complementing the tender beef. "This is a good wine," he lifted the crystal goblet to Joshua.

"Had it shipped from Montreal." His eyes twinkled. "A barber, you say?"

"We're to attend the Governor's Christmas feast, tomorrow night," John explained. "I've no need with my braid, but Captain Bryson must make a favourable impression."

Samuel emitted a quiet whistle.

"Shush!" Mrs. Carter tittered with a quick tap of her son's hand. "I'll trim your beard and hair, sir. Joshua's barber is away, in Ancaster. Leave your shirts and I'll launder them, too—a gift for Christmas."

"I would not presume to—"

"I choose to do this, Captain." She lifted her chin with a gracious tilt of her head. "After all, doesn't our Lord choose to care for us."

Wesley nodded in appreciation.

"Will you be attending Reverend Strachan's church, Mr. Carter?" John asked.

"For now, we have a pew at St. James," he replied. "My wife hopes to build a church for the African community."

"And will you be part of that endeavour?" John pressed.

Joshua thoughtfully rubbed his chin. "The colour of skin has no part in my decision—I worship with those I cherish. Pew fees at St. James are expensive. Mrs. Carter wishes to abolish segregating believers based on wealth. I believe the Lord would agree."

"I would concur." Wesley sipped again of the excellent wine. "And with your gentle admonishment, Joshua, I choose to accompany Mr. Oneida to tonight's Catholic mass." He raised his glass to Mrs. Carter. "And I toast you, dear lady, for opening your home to us."

"Tomorrow, Reverend Strachan will have my attendance," John conceded, lifting his glass in toast.

—46—

Reverend John Strachan's bravery had saved St. James Church when the British military had retreated to Burlington, in 1813. York had twice been ransacked by the occupying Americans; Strachan had argued, both times, for the House of God to be respected. At the end of the war, he further persevered to negotiate a return of books, looted from his school library.

As a result, the tenacious Scot was firmly installed on the Executive Council of Upper Canada. His strong abolitionist sentiment was in stark contrast to this powerful community of slave owners, yet his religious ideals were respected and influenced both social and political life in Upper Canada.

Seated in the Carters' pew, halfway down the aisle, Wesley had a good view of Strachan's congregation. Few of African descent were in attendance, and John Oneida was the only one of indigenous heritage. Most were well-dressed—York's influential elite.

During the hymns, Wesley discreetly looked about, identifying a few businessmen and military officers he knew from his Montreal Christmases. His stomach sank.

A few pew rows ahead, he recognized Catherine, daughter of the Loyalist Entrepreneur Arthur Bayard. Last Christmas, in Montreal, they had shared company on sleigh rides, skating events, and at garrison dances. He had been contemplating an attachment when allegations of abuses had arisen regarding the American war-time occupation of Cornwall. He had been called away to investigate before he could express interest.

Wesley returned his attention as Reverend Strachan rose for the scripture reading and homily. This canny, influential man would have something to impart.

Standing at the pulpit, he began, "Every child, whatever his colour and language, is a child of Adam. As Christians, we must therefore recognize the copper-coloured Indian and the sable Negro as our brethren. Their support of the Crown in this recent war serves as testimony. They now share, with you, an exile wrought by great disrespect and deceit from our southern neighbours." A single cough at the rear of the chapel dared break the silence of his pause.

Strachan inhaled; shoulders broadening in challenge. "Our Lord was born under a godless tyranny. He, too, was a refugee, forced into exile. Peace will only be obtained among us when we deal in equitable terms with our friends' shared respect of the Gospel—our brethren of all colours, our brethren who share our faith. May peace be upon you this Christmas Day and continue into the future." He silently stepped down.

The Reverend's words revealed his unique opinion that aboriginal sovereignty, under the Crown, would block American expansion. Indigenous education was the best means, he felt, to ensure this sovereignty.

A complex man—much like Joseph Brant, mused Wesley.

John shifted in the pew, lips pursed. As they made their way towards the door, Wesley briefly met Catherine's gaze. He returned her raised eyebrow with a polite nod.

Within the tight church vestibule, Reverend Strachan greeted departing congregants with a cheery "Happy Christmas!" To John Oneida, he added an exuberant, "Wonderful to have a 'Son of Nature' in attendance."

"*Mon Seigneur!*" John muttered as they walked to the waiting sleigh. "That man just referred to me as fauna in the woods."

"Glean from his audacity," Wesley challenged. "Make it work for you,"

Tossing horse blankets to the back of the sleigh, Joshua helped his wife board. "Must make haste," he chortled, with a click of the reins. "Mrs. Carter has yet to cook two geese. We've a full house tonight."

Over the icy road they sped to the yellow house, harness bells ringing brightly in the cold air.

Several hours later, Samuel Carter raced the spirited team up to the governor's mansion. Flaming torches lit their approach. Every window sparkled with festive spirit.

"*Joyeux Noël!*" John exclaimed.

"I certainly hope it be a joyous Christmas," Wesley declared, stepping up to the manor's large oak door.

"Whom shall I announce, sir?" asked a footman, taking their coats and wraps.

Wesley supplied their names.

"Must remember what all the ladies are wearing," John murmured, following the footman inside.

"Why?" Wesley asked, bemused.

John shrugged. "Mrs. Carter requested a full description."

Faces turned as they entered the large foyer. Many had been at church earlier that day. Wesley recognized some members of the legislative council. To his discomfort, Catherine Bayard approached, lips turned up in shallow smile. He bowed in acknowledgement.

"You left church early, before I had opportunity to speak with you, Wesley." She curtsied. "Shall I have the pleasure of meeting your wife this evening." Acknowledging John Oneida with a glance, a small line briefly creased her delicate brows.

"Mrs. Bryson remains at our Cataraqui farm," Wesley returned. John walked away.

"Ah...a country girl." She tilted her head, playfully. "Perhaps, come spring, when the Lieutenant Governor is *fêted* in Kingston, I shall meet your shy lady."

"What takes you from Montreal, Miss Bayard?" he diverted.

"Papa is stirring up business here—too much competition with Montreal's old guard." A fashionably dressed young lady stepped up. Slipping an arm within Catherine's, she greeted Wesley with a quick bob and swish of her silken-rose garment.

His memory tingled, yet he could not place this woman. Surely, he would not forget such a fair maiden. "My dear companion 'Miss Maxwell', Catherine introduced.

"Enchanted," Miss Maxwell supplied.

The edge in her voice stirred his memory. *My brother, the lieutenant, will take a switch to you for such insolence,* he recalled from *Coteau-du-Lac.* Olivia would have enjoyed such an amusing coincidence. He cast about the room almost hoping she would appear. By the far wall, he noted John in conversation with Mrs. Strachan and the Reverend.

"Is your brother, Lieutenant Maxwell, in attendance tonight?" Wesley returned attention to her.

Miss Maxwell laughed with breezy amusement. "He is at the garrison tonight, so others can feast." With a head tilt, she asked, "Have we met, sir?"

"We have not," he supplied. A dance once shared at a military assembly hardly mattered, and he'd remained out of sight at *Coteau-du-Lac.* "However, I believe my wife would be delighted to make your acquaintance." He again bowed." Alas, you must excuse me, for I have yet to greet our host."

The dinner gong sounded, preventing escape. Arthur Bayard, Catherine's father, hastily appeared to accompany his daughter to the dining room.

"Captain Bryson, indeed, a pleasure to again meet." The rotund, moustached older gentleman extended a hand in hearty American greeting. Wesley had no choice but to join their group and offer Miss Maxwell his arm.

Two halls had been opened to accommodate the long dining table. Elegance suitable of a king's representative was limited due to American war-time looting. Candlelight danced over an arrangement of simple greenery, colourful red ribbons, and glassware. A tantalizing aroma of roasted meats travelled up from the kitchen, blending with the aromatic fir branches. From the foyer behind them came a dissonant melange of tuning instruments.

Wesley recognised Samuel Jarvis, having served with him in Niagara. He motioned him to the vacant chair across the table. From a prominent family, Jarvis had studied law before the war.

"Congratulations on your recent call to the bar," he greeted, then introduced the fiery young man to Catherine and Miss Maxwell.

The two ladies lit up with interest, and each sat at Wesley's side. With Arthur Bayard next to Jarvis, prattling ladies on each arm, and an elderly member of the council across from Miss Maxwell, Wesley anticipated an uncomfortable dinner. Written word was his forte, not conversation.

Olivia would carry this social challenge with ease. He inhaled the savoury fragrance of the festive table greenery. Closing his eyes, he remembered that first glimpse of her at *Vieux Moulin,* dress clinging to slender legs, walking barefoot ahead of him in the water. As prickly as a porcupine, she could effortlessly transform and emit a skylark's graceful song, when she chose to. Shining, without eclipsing, she wielded her wit as either a weapon or welcoming embrace.

"Pete Sabin gets out and about," Bayard interrupted his thoughts. "Saw him at the tables in Montreal. Gave him my ear, since he spoke quite optimistically about iron ore up the Gananoque."

"Did you give him your pocket book?" Wesley volleyed.

"Bah!" Bayard snorted in amusement. "Took his."

"Reed and I have ceased investing in his exploration." Wesley returned. "The man was more boast than action."

A bell rang, ending their exchange. Reverend Strachan stood, invited heads to bow, then gave a blessing of gratitude for the restored peace in Upper Canada. With the first note of his 'Amen', the room filled with chatter. Service men marched out platters of roast beef, venison, and grilled fish. Roasted potatoes, squash, carrots, baskets of breads and bowls of stewed cranberries followed.

"I've been looking into lumber," Bayard forked a mouthful of beef under his moustache. Samuel Jarvis sat back in his chair, clearly interested.

"Lumber in York?" Wesley set down his fork, to give attention.

"The Don Valley provides only paper-quality lumber. I need to explore further north." He cleared his throat with a phlegmy cough and spat under the table. "I predict this town will grow over the next few years, with war over and the government needing to rebuild edifices suitable for its legislative importance—limestone, of course." Bayard nodded confidently. "Queenston already has a quarry and there's tremendous potential in the Northern Grand."

"Hear, hear!" echoed young Jarvis.

"That's Native land," Wesley challenged.

"There's no Indian towns up by the Gorge," Bayard chuckled. "And upper Grand lumber is close enough for Lake Erie shipbuilding."

"It won't remain Native much longer," Jarvis supplemented. "The Phelps tract will be regained and others will follow."

Wesley gave heed. His Phelps report had been dispatched to Governor General Drummond. Had his recommendation for indigenous sovereignty been rejected, or was it temporarily withheld from the Council's consideration? Uncertainty compounded his present awkwardness. Halfway down the table, he observed Reverend Strachan, Mrs. Strachan, and John Oneida in discussion with Sir Drummond. Enviously, he strained to catch any of their conversation over the table chatter. It was of no use.

Discreetly, he watched Mrs. Strachan. Modestly dressed in light blue, her husband's admiration magnified her radiant beauty. When they'd married, she'd been widowed two years and was 10 years younger than he, with inherited wealth. Few knew of that noble woman's suffering.

During the war, after the American sacking of York, Strachan had sent his pregnant wife to Cornwall, believing it a refuge. His hope had been misplaced. The military and militia had abandoned the town to fight upriver, at Chrysler's Farm. American forces had quickly invaded, ravishing the town for three days.

Cornwall had been Wesley's first war compensation investigation. His interviews had revealed a conflicting blend of testimonies, causing him a good deal of frustration. Though he had pressed, he could gain no clear report of what atrocities had transpired during the occupation. The women had stuck together, staunchly denying any implication of indignity, with terse, stoic reply. Yet a village laundress had confided caring for Reverend Strachan's pregnant wife. Her physical and emotional wounds had been so great that the Reverend had despaired for her life.

Mrs. Strachan had safely delivered a healthy daughter later that year, and had since added a healthy son to their family. The Reverend's abhorrence for any tinge of Republicanism became deeply entrenched after Cornwall. In his report, Wesley cloaked Cornwall's ladies with a dignity through denial.

A Scottish reel rang out from the foyer. Dancing would soon to begin. Catherine Bayard slipped her hand under Wesley's arm. Miss Maxwell slipped a hand around his other. Wesley looked across at Samuel Jarvis, with a feigned look of helplessness.

"Jarvis, choose which one of these lovely ladies you will dance with first," he invited.

"With pleasure," Samuel Jarvis extended his hand to Catherine Bayard, with a polite bow.

"Miss. Maxwell, I will endeavour to introduce you to some fine gentleman, once I have the pleasure of this first dance." Wesley led her to the floor, next to Reverend Strachan and his wife. Mrs. Strachan recognized him with a subtle nod. He touched his forelock in discreet salute.

The music began, and the partners exchanged bows as the weaving steps of a reel began, aided by a caller. John Oneida was at the far end of the dancers, partnered with a russet-gowned matron. Her face flushed with enjoyment; his steps high and lively.

Laughter permeated the air, missteps punctuated by chatter. Another reel followed and Wesley remained with Miss Maxwell, rather than abandon her. He scanned the room for an acquaintance to pass her off to. Finally, he saw the son of a lumberman, and completed a satisfactory exchange before the third dance.

Nearby, Sir Drummond engaged in intense exchange with three gentlemen. Wesley stood to their side, waiting for an opportunity to converse with him. He did not wait long. Glancing back, the General immediately waved for him to join their group.

"Captain Bryson, I'm pleased you could make this evening." Wesley offered a formal bow as Sir Drummond introduced him to Lieutenant Governor Gore and two men of the executive council. "This is the man who has been investigating many of the compensation requests. A gentleman of promise, to be watched."

"A difficult job," affirmed Lieutenant Governor Gore. "Much to consider."

The conversation weaved between them, jumping from American encroachment on lumbering to refugee settlement, military allotments to compensation claims, and land seizures to canal building. Much was occurring of which he was ignorant. To his relief, they posed no questions, nor invited his opinion.

The evening had grown tiresome. He felt a strange envy watching Reverend Strachan dance with his wife. Their partnership was apparent. Yet, in maintaining her dignity, her husband forged protective politics. Republican ideals of equality would never be welcome in Upper Canada. Would many suffer as a result?

John Oneida continued to dance with several matrons, clearly enjoying their attention. Wesley retreated to the refreshment table for a cup of black coffee. Jarvis stood by him, watching Catherine dance with her father.

As the song came to a close, Jarvis squared his shoulders. "I believe I shall travel to Kingston in spring, and partake of the fair ladies of that city," he tendered and approached Catherine to offer her another dance.

The evening wore on and the *soirée* concluded. Down the driveway Wesley walked with John Oneida. "You abandoned me for York's influential matriarchy," Wesley yawned.

John smirked. "I've been gleaning—ladies like to talk. Rumour is the Council has a position in mind for you, and Jarvis was assigned to check you out."

Wesley snorted. "I paired him off with a belle I used to squire about." He picked up the pace, eager to return to the yellow house. "The chap has now committed to coming in spring to partake of Kingston's ladies."

John was quiet for a moment, then looked at Wesley. "I hope our women have had a Christmas feast, or at least a bit of dancing and feasting while they await our return."

"Olivia must be at my side for this Kingston event. She deserves some frivolity, though I find these events more work than pleasure."

"Soon I must return to Annie," John asserted, "to await the birth."

"There's no one more deserving of Annie than you, dear friend," Wesley acknowledged with a warm grip of his shoulder.

"I heartily agree." Looking up at the stars, he emitted a heart-felt laugh.

Midnight had come. Burning pinecone torches, planted in the snowbanks about the Douglas clearing, lit up the night. Sparks billowed up from a large, crackling fire in the yard's center, watched by pipe-smoking tale-bearing men.

More than 50 people had gathered to celebrate Hogmanay. They'd come on snowshoes or by dogsled throughout the evening. Patiently, they waited for the "First Footer" to pronounce a blessing over the Douglas household. Among them was young Robert Harris and his red-haired Presbyterian companion. They had arrived as darkness fell, bringing letters and packages from the outside world.

Olivia had not felt this buoyant since her "coming out" dance, nine years previous. Her entry into society had been a mere façade, delayed to the advanced age of 19, when plans were in place for marriage to the appointed heir of Charles Eldenmont's estate. Her older sister, Charlotte, had failed to produce a son. War, Olivia's tenacity, and the heir's gadding about had enabled her remaining "out" to the embarrassing, overripe age of 28. Tonight, she felt truly "out". Free of expectation, with mukluks on her feet and her cream dress over trousers, she was ready to dance.

Sally emerged from the house regally robed in burgundy velvet. She stood next to Ian, kilted in his clan's green and navy-blue tartan.

The crowd hushed and Olivia's heart beat excitedly as they waited for the First Footer begin the ritual. Suddenly, from within the gathering, a gravelly voice broke the silence.

"Fellow Scots, 33 years back, the British repealed the law which forbade wearing our clan's tartans and playing of the pipes. May it bring joy to our hearts that we have prevailed. Prosperity and good health to the Douglas Household, and all gathered!"

Joyous cheer erupted with shouts of "Long may your chimney smoke!" punctuating the merriment. An old man stepped forward holding high a loaf of bread, and entered the house. Proudly Ian invited everyone to follow him inside. "Women and children first," he beckoned, motioning Johnnie Elliot to pipe them in. "The bairns can sleep in our room, off the kitchen. Ye men will have to take turns coming in the cabin...and mind your swally!"

"Swally?" Olivia turned to Rosetta. Rosetta shrugged.

"Yer' drink," translated the red-haired Presbyterian.

From the background rose the humming of drones, building to the powerful outburst of a piped march. Evie awoke, screaming. Rosetta freed the baby from the cradle board and tied her within her shawl, on her hip. Eddie covered his ears, tucking face in the crook of Olivia's neck, as she and her companions squeezed into the cabin. On the table against the wall, Annie set out platters of meat pastries and short bread they'd spent the afternoon labouring over.

In the corner, a skin-drum player waited while Robert Cameron and Cian Cavanaugh tuned their fiddles. Then, with a quickly downed dram of spirits and a toothless grin, Robert began a lively gig. Cian swiftly joined in, along with several clacking spoons and the drum. Olivia fed sleepy Eddie a shortbread biscuit before laying him on Sally and Ian's bed among the sleeping babies. Sadie Douglas sat at the bedroom threshold, dressed in yellow calico, watching over her charges.

"Whoop!" Olivia yelped, pulling Annie to the floor. Round and round they twirled, prancing and clapping, as others joined in. A reel followed and Annie bowed out breathless, clutching her belly.

Rosetta stepped forward, sweeping wide the skirt of her green dress. Before Olivia could offer her hand, Jamie Douglas stepped forward and led Rosetta to the floor. Olivia felt a gentle touch of her elbow and turned to find the red-haired Presbyterian sheepishly standing beside her.

"Pardon me, milady. May I have the priv'ledge of escorting you to the floor?"

Her heart warmed at his daring presumption, "Only if you tell me your name," she answered. "Over these past months, your words on faith have brought me comfort."

"Ernest MacLaren," he supplied, offering his hand in escort. "And I am honoured, milady."

Clasping his hand, Olivia crammed between Rosetta and Sally. Dancing several reels, she continued gaily, ending with a lively jig and Robbie Harris as partner.

"I fancy a mug of cider," Cian Cavanaugh declared, setting his violin down and squeezing through the crowd to the food table. Robert Cameron joined him, while the First Footer gent produced a tin flute and began a melancholic tune.

"Your Irish dancing is impressive, Private Harris," Olivia complimented.

"Learned it from my momma," he proudly returned. "Some of her people were 'Red Legs'—Irish, that were sent to 'de Islands."

"White slaves?" she gasped.

"'Dey try to stay white, but suffer horribly when sun reddens, so were called Red Legs." His eyes lit up. "Och!" he exclaimed. "I near forgot, Mrs. Bryson." And he pulled a letter from his inner pocket.

"Thank you," she returned, tucking it within her sleeve, knowing it was from Wesley.

Banging two pewter mugs, Ian drew everyone's attention. With a nod to the tin flute player, he led Sally to the floor. Holding her hands, he began the ballad of devotion Sally had sung at Evie's birthing. His deep vibrant voice stirred sniffles throughout the cabin, with his concluding phrase,

And I will come again my love, though 'twere 10,000 miles.

Tears glistened on Sally's cheeks as Ian gently kissed her lips. The tin flute struck up to a jaunty tune and Ian led his wife in a promenade, arm about her waist.

Annie's hand rested on Olivia's shoulder. "Let's see what is left to eat on that table."

With meat pastries in hand, they sat on the stair. Annie seemed lost in thought, so Olivia pulled Wesley's letter from her sleeve. She could hear his voice in his descriptions of the Six Nations village, ice-fishing, smoking rich tobacco, eating equally rich food, and dancing until the early hours. Her eyes narrowed and she shook her head, but she read on.

> *It is to my tremendous regret that I have never danced with you, Mrs. Bryson. Though I must confess, six years ago I watched you from the shadows at Hurtsmere, greatly admiring the lightness of your step and the flush of joy upon your cheek. Perhaps, soon, I may have this pleasure.*

Features relaxing, Olivia tucked his letter back into her sleeve and wiped the corner of her eye. She rose and went outside for air, finding Private Harris warming at the bonfire.

"Thank you, again, Private Harris, for bringing my husband's letter," she offered.

"Good news, I trust," he smiled warmly.

"The very best," she returned, looking up at the sky. The fiddles again began to play, summoning the revellers to a last respite before returning to their clearings. "Might I have the privilege of a final dance before we must go our separate ways?"

"It would be a great honour, Mrs. Bryson." He held out his hand and they danced in the dawn of a new year.

With sincere wishes of "Health and prosperity," the Billidore women said their goodbyes and set out home, under a cold grey sky.

"This is the best fun I've ever had at a dance," Olivia yawned, pulling Eddie on the toboggan. "We celebrated with children and families, and there was nary a rake or a dandy among the lot."

—48—

By mid-January it was quite clear to Wesley the position he was being considered for had far greater responsibility than a grants and sales officer allocating land to settlers. Aside from indirect communication through Lieutenant Maxwell, he received little information. Lieutenant Governor Gore was to open Parliament in less than three weeks and insisted Wesley remain in York until then.

Governor General Drummond had not yet returned to Montreal, and on a snowy Monday morning he summoned Wesley to the garrison.

"You've managed to extract information that discredits many applicants for compensation," Sir Drummond snorted, scanning one of his reports. "I commend your skills, Captain, in acquiring this knowledge." He tossed the report on the desk between them. "Bryson. This lot in York will reject both your recommendations and you. Your laudable effort is a waste."

"I want to ensure Canadians are dealt with fairly."

Sir Drummond stuffed his pipe. "Then considerer law or run for legislative representative. You can make a way for yourself, there." He retrieved a sulphur stick from the box on his desk. Briskly swiping his boot sole, he lit his pipe. "Amazing innovation, these sticks," he commented with a quenching blow of air.

The lingering odour of sulphur triggered memories of cordite; war would always lurk within Wesley's mind.

"Soldiering has been my domain, sir. I'm new to political intrigue."

"You're a thinking man, Bryson." Sir Drummond leaned back in his chair, emitting a puff of smoke. "Your report on the Six Nations exhumes the issue of Native Sovereignty. This threatens lumbering, mining, and settlement expansion."

"I want truth revealed and justice awarded," Wesley rephrased. "Do you not desire this for Canada, sir?"

"I am Canadian-born, Bryson," he huffed. "It has been an honour to fight for my country and secure recognition of our Indigenous allies—men of undaunted courage. I've also fought to achieve respect for our military, their widows and orphans—and that involves generous land grants." He again drew from his pipe, emitting a tobacco cloud. Wesley's nose twinged with the sour odour. "I'm 44 years of age and you would think me an old man. My body bears wounds, my stomach ails me, and my 5-year-old daughter doesn't recognize me."

"You have served this country as few have," Wesley offered.

"My conscience is intact. Is yours?" Sir Drummond challenged.

Wesley chose to wait rather than parry.

Sir Drummond leaned forward. "The Council wishes to exploit your friendship with Mrs. Brant and your knowledge of the Mohawk argument for the Phelps tract. Their intent is to claim the Grand River lands."

"You've read my report, sir. I cannot disavow Six Nations sovereignty."

Sir Drummond sat back and set his pipe on the tray. "You maintain your conscience at the expense of career."

"I will not betray our Indigenous allies. We fought together on the Niagara and at Chrysler's farm." Wesley paused in appreciation of the man's influence. "Are you able to bury my reports along with your conscience, sir?"

Throwing his head back, Sir Drummond erupted in laughter. "You impertinent blaggard! I'm soon to England—you have no such escape and must live out your decision."

"Our allies have my loyalty," Wesley reaffirmed.

"Then you are an honourable man, Bryson." Still leaning back, he clasped his hands behind his neck. "And your soul will be at peace."

"Am I free to return to my family?"

"Take my advice: Don't squander what opportunity you have. Be honourable, but be shrewd."

Wesley nodded.

"Socialize with the leaders of Upper Canada and benefit from observing their positioning." He emptied his pipe in the spittoon by his feet. "While Gore was in England, he amassed considerable funds for the purpose of war recovery. Influential men now vie for a portion. Your investigations had been intended to aid in the dispersal."

Wesley whistled through his teeth. "They won't."

"Be discreet with that sentiment," Sir Drummond chuckled. "Stay another month as a resource for Gore, and learn to dance around their schemes. Get better at political intrigue, aye?" He stood, signally the end of their meeting. "Tomorrow I leave for Montreal."

Wesley's heart was heavy as he slowly rode back to the yellow house. Snow drifted across his path from the adjacent field, the icy wind numbing his face. His work would be corrupted and justice perverted. He had to steady his soul to withstand the assault.

Far off in the night, a lone wolf howled. In the flickering light of a crackling fire, Eddie whiffled a snore, nestled within Olivia's arms. She sank deeper under her thick quilt, savouring his sounds. Another day complete, her eyes closed in peace.

A moan stirred her. She listened, holding her breath. Annie was murmuring in her Native tongue. Securing Eddie in the daybed, between a pillow and the wall, she got up.

"Night terrors," Rosetta offered from Annie's doorway. "I'll settle her." She went in and knelt by the bed, resting her hand on Annie's head. "Peace, my sister. We're here with you." Olivia knelt beside her.

"*Ils viennent...*" Annie shoved the hand away. "*...on n'est pas assez fort.*"

"They are coming and we're not strong enough," Olivia translated.

"Who is coming?" Rosetta gingerly probed.

Annie sat up, gasping for breath. Rosetta embraced her, gently rocking. "Breathe girl," she coaxed. "They're gone now and will leave you alone."

"...help will not come..." she sobbed, her body shuddering.

Olivia took Annie's rosary from the wall hook and pressed the cross into the palm of her hand. Her body relaxed and she looked about the dark room, dazed.

"Who are they that torment you?" Rosetta ventured, wrapping a shawl about Annie's shoulders, helping her from the bed.

"We need some strong tea," Olivia suggested and hastened to put a kettle on the fire.

"I dreamt foolishness, yet it frightens me." Annie sat at the table, staring at her hands. "I saw a giant horse wading up the Ottawa Grand. It was formed of steel like a sword, and fire was its blood." She touched a hand to her heart. "Black smoke blew from the beast's nostrils and it ate trees as if they were grass."

Olivia set a steaming cup before Annie. Sipping slowly, hugging the cup, she continued, "What it didn't eat, it stomped on, crushing, destroying, and leaving the land desolate. It kicked up dirt, filling streams, and blocking rivers. Those forest creatures who could not run away were crushed under its hooves."

Her eyes met Olivia. "I tried to warn people of the beast, but they would not listen. Instead they chased me, yelling that there were too many trees and animals for the beast to destroy." She shivered. "They could not see as I did, this was only a lead horse; many more were soon to follow."

"It was only a dream," Rosetta soothed. "No horse could ever be that big."

But it could. Olivia had seen them in northern England; pit mines belching smoke from engine furnaces, pulling loads out of a land rendered waste by their work. Charles Eldenmont had invested in a network of these "Iron Horses", boasting someday they'd replace haulage by horse.

"You must miss your bush," Olivia offered as diversion.

"I do," Annie inhaled deeply. "I had terrible dreams, like this, before I left the convent." She looked intently at Olivia, pulling her shawl close "I miss John. Maybe we should flee to the northern High Country."

"You are free like the wind." Olivia took her hand. "Nothing can contain you, Annie."

Evie's cry drew Rosetta to her bedroom. She returned, babe in arms.

"Can one ever be truly free, Olivia?" Annie asked.

Olivia looked about her cabin and drew comfort. "I believe I am becoming free for I am growing in contentment with myself."

"I'm a bit more practical about all this freedom talk," Rosetta sniffed. "I need a house to raise Evie in, and a few acres to grow a garden. And I want to run a business—a store or perhaps a trading post—and give good value yet make money. Then I will sleep well for my needs will be met. That is freedom."

Annie laughed. "Do you have place for a man in that house?"

Rosetta kissed the top of Evie's head. "I ain't lookin', but if the Lord has someone in mind, then He'll just have to drop him in my garden."

—

Snow fell throughout the next few days, blending night and day. Once again, they relied on snowshoes to carry out chores in the yard.

Annie finished her cradle board and made a rabbit-pelt jacket for Eddie. Olivia tried to knit, but her hands kept cramping. "Must be the cold," she complained, craving diversion. "Maybe I'll read something—any suggestions?"

Rosetta looked up from her book. "Why don't you start at the top left shelf of the bookcase and work your way down to the bottom right?"

"At random?" Olivia's huff, met her withering look.

"Think of it as exploring—see what you discover. Persevere through confusion and boredom, and break open your mind."

Olivia sauntered to the shelf and retrieved the first book on the upper left: *A Theory of the Earth.*

"A tough one," Rosetta affirmed. "Anything, after that, will be an improvement."

"How does one keep attention through such drudgery?" Olivia asked.

Rosetta shrugged "Take notes and write questions of what confuses."

With a copy of *Johnson's: A Dictionary of the English Language*, and a pen and paper, Olivia plodded forward.

Occasionally she came across notes in the margin, written in Wesley's handwriting. She felt him near her, encouraging her to look for clues, study helpful illustrations and refer to other sections. Immersed in thought, her reading became a puzzle to be solved, much like a game of charades. To her surprise, Olivia found her mind refreshed.

—50—

At the back porch of the yellow house, Wesley brushed snow from his shoulders and beard. Having enthusiastically walked to his interview at the governor's manor, he had trudged back. Gore's skewed questions revealed that he had neither read Wesley's reports, nor even been briefed on them. Frustrated and cold, Wesley now accepted the proposed position would force him to allocate compensation funds to those predetermined by Gore and the Council.

With a stomp of his boots, he opened the kitchen door and his breath caught in surprise.

"My good man!" Stephen Reed exclaimed, extending his hand. They embraced with a good pounding of each other's back. "Came up today, by dog sled—the same one John Oneida just left on."

"He's gone?" Wesley's disappointment met Mrs. Carter's sombre nod. "I had much I needed to discuss with him."

"Obviously he felt it not of importance," Stephen replied.

"Mr. Oneida will be missed," she consoled. "He took the letter you'd written to Mrs. Bryson."

"You'll have to make do with me. John arranged my visit when he wrote me of your need of a friend." Stephen sat at the table. "Is York society getting the better of you?"

Wesley hung his coat on a hook and joined him at the table. "I was sorely grieved to learn of your wife," he offered earnestly.

"Thank you," Stephen stroked his chin. "I've needed to get out of Kingston and regroup—too many memories."

Mrs. Carter set a tea pot before them and poured three cups. "Beddings changed and there's a fresh towel for the lieutenant," she declared, sitting across from them. "How did it fare with Lieutenant Governor Gore, Wesley?"

"I've been put forward for the position of Treasury Assistant with the Council," Wesley volunteered. "The position involves divvying up the funds Gore raised in England, during the war."

Stephen emitted a low whistle under his breath. "You've grown in influence, my man."

"Well, they certainly could use an honest man," Mrs. Carter allowed. "Now, will you gentlemen take dinner here, or will you be going out?" She set down her cup, hands folded on the table. Stephen Reed dealt her a quick frown.

"Mrs. Carter has graciously opened her home to us because she likes taking care of people," Wesley quickly supplied.

"I see." He returned attention to Wesley. "What do you suggest?"

Fried eggs and bacon, with a good book by the fire, Wesley thought to himself, but he could see his friend was eager to get out. "We'll dine at the officer's mess, Mrs. Carter, and I'll introduce the Lieutenant to the York garrison."

"An excellent idea," she confirmed. Stephen smiled tersely.

"It'll be a cold ride," Wesley warned as they went out to saddle the horses.

"Your housekeeper presumes much of herself," Stephen commented, opening the stable door.

Wesley quietly saddled his horse. "Mrs. Carter is wife of Joshua Carter, proprietor of York's largest carting business," he corrected. "And you should know that her son, Samuel, is a private student of Reverend Strachan."

They rode out in silence. The wind had increased in both briskness and bite.

At the officer's mess, Wesley left their horses to the care of a young private. Entering the hall, the men rose to greet them and Wesley introduced Lieutenant Reed. The meal of beef stew had not yet been served. Seated mid-way down the common table, they accepting the tankard offered to each of them.

"Sabin told Bayard there are iron deposits, north of the Gananoque," Wesley began.

"Bayard is here?"

"With his daughter," Wesley shrugged. "He's looking into business opportunities."

"Is he aware we funded Sabin, and nothing was found?" Stephen's voice raised as he added, "despite his repeatedly returning to Bastard County?"

"Ah, yes...Benedict Arnold's land...a mystery indeed." Wesley tilted his head, attempting to ease the tension in his neck. "We'll not see a cent of return on our investment, even if ore is found. Bayard will claim it—he has the resources."

The hall door opened and the room filled with the sound of shifting chairs, as the officers again stood in acknowledgment of Miss

Maxwell's entrance on her brother's arm. Removing her hooded cape, she dealt Wesley a coy smile as they approached.

"Blessed is that man," Stephen whispered, "to have such a wife, willing to live in officer's quarters."

"The lady is his sister and lives in town," Wesley chuckled. "I believe she is acquainted with Catherine Bayard." He'd avoided Miss Maxwell over the past weeks. With Stephen as reinforcement, he invited them over.

"Lieutenant Maxwell, Miss Maxwell. Please grant us the pleasure of sitting with us and brightening our evening," Wesley supplied, hoping his insincerity was not obvious.

Maxwell tossed her blond curls with oblivious amusement.

"What do you think of our town," she gaily asked, accepting Stephen's hand in greeting.

"I find it a charming place," he surrendered fervently.

—51—

Olivia fastened the shanty door. There were no eggs to be found and Busy was producing half her previous quantity of milk. Extra portions of grain, corn, and coarse dried grass from beaver meadows were not helping. Olivia had tried gently massaging Busy's udder, but even pleading into the cow's soft brown eyes could not coax more milk.

Ian Douglas would know what to do; she turned from the shanty and headed down to his clearing.

"You'll have to dry her out to get her ready to calf, come next winter," he advised. "Johnnie Elliot has a fine bull you can breed her with."

"We shall have calf," she marvelled. "What fun!"

Ian laughed. "That's not how it works, lass. Elliot keeps the calf as payment."

"But it doesn't seem right to take a child from its mother, even for a cow."

He stroked his red beard. "That's his agreement."

Leaving the Douglas cabin, she thought she heard yelps down by the river. Gizzy paused at the bridge, head erect, tail wagging excitedly.

"Stay with me!" she hissed, grabbing the dog's collar, steering her up the path towards home. The sun had set, leaving a shadowy world. Clouds drifted across moon. Behind her a twig snapped. She raced across the yard, holding tight to the collar. Only at the cabin door did she turn to look.

A dark form entered the moonlight of the clearing, Native, with chiselled features.

"Wait, Mrs. Bryson!" He stepped towards her. "I am John Oneida."

"Annie's husband?" Her hand lingered on the door handle.

"*Oui,*" he affirmed, removing his tuque with a polite bow. "My dog team is secured at the landing."

"Pray bring them up and I will provide them with suet and scraps." She pulled Gizzy into the cabin.

"You bring in the dog? Who is out there?" Annie asked.

"Your husband," she answered, hands clasped together.

With an excited squeal, Annie flung on a shawl and ran out. Olivia assembled the dogs' food in a bucket, padding it out with cold oatmeal. Setting it just outside, she closed the door.

"I will give you a slice of salt pork, dear girl, for being my alert guardian," she assured Gizzy.

"We'll allow them some time," Rosetta softly suggested. "I assume they will take our little man back with them."

Picking Eddie up, Olivia kissed his chubby brown cheek and set him at the table while she served salt pork, fried apples with onions, beans, and cornbread. Rosetta set the table for four and they sat, Eddie content on Olivia's knee.

"We shan't wait; This isn't a time for etiquette." Olivia reached across the table for Rosetta's hand, and offered a simple thanksgiving for the food and for John's safe return.

The door opened. Annie glowed, arms about John. "We will leave early tomorrow," she announced.

John took Eddie from Olivia and swung him around. The little boy erupted in laughter.

Olivia rose to fill the kettle, trying to swallow the lump in her throat. John sat and began to feed Eddie from his plate. Her heart filled with a murky blend of warm pain. This man would love Wesley's son.

John looked up at her, softly smiling. He understood her struggle.

Annie cleared the table, John following her every move. Then, setting Eddie on the floor, he went out to check on the dogs. Rosetta nursed Evie by the fire, Olivia washed the dishes, and Annie settled her son to sleep. They'd endured together, through death, birth, fights, forgiveness, fear, and joy. Simple chores numbed the significance of this last night together.

"Your absence will be felt," Olivia breached the silence.

"You're going to miss me, aye?" Annie teased, eyes twinkling.

"Say it, Libby," Rosetta urged. "We won't hold it against you."

"Yes," she looked down into the sink and a sob escaped. "I will."

Annie's arms surrounded her. "Please fetch one of your silk handkerchiefs," she whispered.

When Olivia returned, Annie was kneeling by the hearth, running her knife blade through the flames. She stood up and nicked the palm of her left hand. Red drops seeped out, pooling.

Rosetta shifted Evie to the other arm and held out her left hand. Olivia hesitated, unsure of what to do.

"For a brief moment in time, our blood will flow together, as one," Annie explained.

"It's symbolic," Rosetta assured her.

Olivia presented her hand. With a deft touch, Annie nicked and tied their bloodied palms together, within the silk hankie. She looked at Rosetta, and then Olivia.

"We stand together, in this moment, our life forces mixing as one," she repeated. "This winter we have become sisters."

"Like squash, corn, and beans growing in the Sister Patch, our differences have made us strong," Olivia affirmed.

Opening the cabin door, John's eyes fixed on the bloody handkerchief tied about their hands. "*Mon Dieu*!" he exclaimed. "You women scare me sometimes."

Annie wiped their hands with the handkerchief and put it in the fire. "Good night," she concluded, stepping behind her bedroom curtain.

"I am to bed, as well," Rosetta yawned, carrying Evie off.

"Your husband speaks highly of you, Mrs. Bryson." John reached within his coat. "And I now understand his confidence in you." With a gracious nod, he handed her a letter and retreated behind the bedroom curtain.

Olivia tore open the seal. Wesley's descriptions of socials, Reverend Strachan's church, and Mrs. Carter's comfortable yellow house transported her to York. She read on, delighted by his openness in sharing his world:

I've encountered a lady who once held my interest, but be assured that she 'pales' in comparison with you. Even more intriguing, I have socialized with the mud-encased lady of Coteau-du-Lac. You'll be pleased to know that her feet have not rotted off.

Olivia chuckled, recalling the woman's arrogance.

Shifting topic, he wrote of a business venture in which he had sponsored Pierre Sabin to prospect for iron in the Upper Gananoque.

I suspect Pierre Sabin spent our investment at a gaming table. And now Sabin's fluid loyalty has shifted to a wealthy entrepreneur, and we will not see a cent in return. Pray take care with any dealing with the man. He is not to be trusted. Sadly, I learned this too late and have been gullible and irresponsible with our future. Please forgive me.
With deepest regard, Your Wesley"

"Forgiven," she quietly replied, tucking his letter under her pillow.

Alone on the daybed, she was comforted by his taking her into confidence. Eddie's departure would leave an emptiness in her heart. She had come to treasure the child's hugs, giggles, and even his sticky fingers. Dabbing her eyes with a corner of the quilt, she whispered, "Please Lord, may I someday have a house full of children."

Eddie woke her early the next morning wanting help on the chamber pot. Annie and John were already outside, loading the sled. Olivia tidied Eddie up and fed him a buttery slice of bread. John entered and gave the cabin one final look about, then picked Eddie up. Annie came in and stood beside him.

Rosetta retrieved two quilts from the rafters. "To keep you warm," she sniffed, giving them to Annie.

"I'll bundle Eddie in coat and tuque," Olivia offered.

"No." John carefully deposited Eddie in her arms. "Wesley desires to have him. Annie and I will entrust him to your care."

Olivia searched Annie's serene face.

"Yes," she confirmed. "His father must have his time." Gently stroking her child's cheek, she kissed his forehead and pronounced, "You will stay with your European mama."

—52—

Wesley turned away, stifling a yawn. This last week of January, another event had demanded his attention. Tonight, games of cards would fill the evening. Parliament's opening was a week away, after which he would be free to leave for Billidore.

Across the table, Stephen engaged in animated conversation with Miss Isabelle Maxwell. His grief seemed to have dissipated amid sleigh rides, skate parties, and evenings basking in her presence. It was good to see him smile again, but watching them Wesley's brow furrowed. He pondered when to brief his friend on this woman's true nature.

Later that evening, with Samuel Carter chauffeuring them back, he attempted the deed.

"My friend, I fear you are moving quickly in seeking companionship, so soon after your wife's passing," he began.

"Do you think me so unfeeling?" Stephen shot back. "My child needs a mother."

"Your child lives?" Wesley blurted out in surprise. This was not proceeding as he intended.

"Aye," he scowled. "I've placed her out to nurse with a woman in Picardville."

"Picardville? For Violet's child?"

"You dare to judge?" Stephen balked. "You foisted your Native baby on an English bride."

"Annie is staying with Mrs. George and my wife, at Billidore" Wesley curtly corrected.

"And that makes everything proper?" Stephen shook his head, with a pronounced guffaw.

Wesley studied his friend. He seemed a stranger.

"Will Miss Maxwell retain affection when she learns of your want of income?" Wesley calmly thrust.

"And who's to blame for that?" Stephen parried. "You invited me to invest in Sabin's schemes."

"Aye. I am at fault," he quietly owned, "and I will return the Billidore clearing to you." He extended his hand. "You deserve compensation for my drawing you into folly."

"These past months have not been easy." Stephen nodded, and accepted his hand. "I'll sell that land and get what I can. Miss Maxwell was left a small inheritance from her grandfather."

"You've proceeded that far in your friendship?" Wesley gulped.

"She is the kindest of ladies," Stephen returned.

Samuel pulled up to the back door. Stephen went into the house; Wesley stayed behind to help settle the team.

"What do you think, Sam?" he broached, once in the stable.

"My ma taught me to hold my opinion," he stroked the horse's neck.

"And?" Wesley pressed.

"She also told me to not listen in on conversations." He looked intently at Wesley. "Yet, when a door is left open at the Reverend's I do pay heed. Mr. Jarvis, the elder, asked the Reverend about your suitability as candidate for a treasury appointment."

Wesley's stomach tightened. "Where I would be both judge and prosecutor?"

"That's how it seems to be in York," he shrugged. "You'll be pleased to know the Reverend defended you as a man of moral fortitude—so it looks like you'll be deemed unsuitable."

Wesley laughed, with a friendly pat on the lad's back. "How long will you continue with Strachan?"

"Until I'm equipped to study law." He locked the stable door. "Then Joshua will send me to Montreal or France. He says they are more open to people of colour."

"Joshua is not your father?"

"Ma married Joshua last year, when we come to York. That's when he asked me to accept him as my Pa."

"Curious," Wesley noted, as they walked up to the back door.

"His son—only surviving child—died at Lundy's Lane. During the occupation, Joshua's home and most of his business were destroyed," Samuel supplied. "Ma found work cooking, at the inn where he was living while rebuilding his business. Her food lifted his spirits, so he started courting her. She thought he was only a driver." Quietly he opened the door. "Though Ma liked him, she didn't want to be poor, so she told him she would only marry someone who could give her a yellow house."

"Why that colour?"

"She always hankered for a yellow house—said it would be warm and bright inside, like sunlight. Of course, she never expected one." Samuel hung his coat and tuque on a hook by the door. "You can imagine how taken we were when Joshua took us on a Sunday drive and pulled into this yard. He told her he'd bought this house and had it painted 'specially for her. Goodnight." Samuel yawned and went up to bed. Wesley noted two letters waiting on the kitchen table: One had Olivia's flowing script and the other, unknown.

Wesley sat at the kitchen table and broke open the seal of Olivia's letter. His heart warmed with her descriptions of the Christmas dresses she had made and Evie's promise of curls.

> *Eddie's speech now includes 'Gi-Gi' for Gizzy, 'con' for when he wishes scones to be made, and addresses me as 'Ibb-Bee'. You'll be delighted to know that Eddie will be here upon your return. Annie wishes you to have time with your son. And I heartily agree.*

Wesley inhaled deeply; his heart warmed at the prospect, but it was her concluding salutation that affected him most.

May your time in York meet your desires.

Pray be shrewd, my husband.

I remain, your devoted wife, Olivia.

He turned the letter over in his hand, finger brushing her thumbprint seal. Closing his eyes, his breath deepened. Olivia was devoted to him, despite his misguided efforts.

What of the other letter? He tore open the plain wax seal, noting the signature of *Mrs. R. George*. He knew the woman was literate, but her clipped clean prose, augmented by sketches, brought Billidore to life.

He laughed, cried, and pondered as he read her perspective of life on the clearing. Vivid descriptions of Olivia's bout with the Ague, lightning strikes, wolves howling in the night, and milking Busy restored a world he'd left behind. And his eyes lightened reading of Olivia's courageous recovery from the miscarriage, Oliver's burial, and their Hogmanay celebration. Mrs. George's letter revealed little of her own experience, except her unique ability to portray astute observations.

He could see it was a different Olivia who lived on the clearing. Hair short, trousered, and laughing through farm chores; he must get to know more of this frontier woman.

—53—

"We flatter ourselves that York, recovering from a state of war during which she has been twice under the power of the enemy, will not only forget her disasters, but rise to greater prosperity under Your Excellency's auspicious administration."

"Bah!" Wesley tossed the salutation transcript back on the desk, biting his lower lip. "Auspicious administration? The blaggard spent the war in London and only came back once hostilities ended. The Executive Council's salutation to Gore is nothing more than a pathetic grovel for his favour in dispersing funds."

The library door opened; a footman entered. "Are you done, sir? Lieutenant Governor Gore is now available."

Wesley returned the document to its docket in the wooden drawer. He understood clearly the mandate he would be expected to apply for Gore. His reports were likely buried within some file. The Executive Council simply wanted his informed willingness to support their petitions to the Crown.

The Footman emitted a quiet cough and prompted him, "Sir!"

Wesley followed him out of the library then down the wide corridor. Only a few weeks ago he'd naively danced these halls, conversing politely with Gore. When they had met in Niagara, Governor General

Drummond had directed him to prepare for this day. Ready as could be, he raised his chin and quickened his pace.

Gore motioned to two leather chairs by a window, upon his entrance. They sat, overlooking a vast snow-blanketed field.

"I've finally perused some of your reports. Your thoroughness is quite impressive, Bryson." He drew a deep breath. "Your recommendations, however, are incongruous with the plans the Council intends to implement towards the future development of Upper Canada."

"Help me understand, sir?" Wesley invited, wanting to hear Gore's dismissive reasoning.

"You defend Haudenosaunee ownership of the Phelps' tract. Furthermore, you propose reinstatement of Six Nations sovereignty and suggest we have an Indian on the executive council?" Gore chuckled with disdain. "If I wasn't aware of your impressive war record, I would assume you a Republican. We've enough complication dealing with American entrepreneurs and African refugees, and now you want to give heed to the Natives?"

Wesley nodded, waiting for Gore to continue; instead, he met silence. Inhaling deeply, he had no choice but to attempt defence.

"You are Governor of Upper Canada, sir. I merely provide these suggestions based on my observations. For example, the loyal people of Newark are desperately in need of housing—"

"That was Simcoe's poor decision," Gore interrupted, leaning forward. "He set the provincial capital too close to a hostile border. And as for—"

A sharp rap at his office door interrupted. Wesley breathed a silent prayer for wisdom.

A footman entered and handed Gore a note. After a quick glance of it, Gore stood. "This requires my immediate attention, Bryson.

Consider what I have said. It would be a shame for you to lose out on opportunity. I'll see you at Parliament's opening celebration. You're on the list, as well as Lieutenant Reed."

Wesley left quickly. His relief was short lived—Reverend Strachan sent him an invitation for lunch the following day.

Mindful of the Reverend's influence, Wesley arrived promptly with the noon-time chime of church bells. Mrs. Strachan was away at a ladies' luncheon, allowing for open discussion over soup and rolls. Even the elderly African servant was dismissed for privacy.

Strachan wasted no time.

"As you are undoubtedly aware, Jarvis has put forward your name as treasury administrator for the executive council. His son believes you fit for the position."

"Over the past month the position has grown from a mere clerk to administrator," Wesley conveyed. "Although flattered, Reverend, my supposed 'fitness' grieves me. I cannot participate in a government that ignores loyal people who sacrificed much for this war."

Strachan's eyes pierced, as if in judgement. "Where is that Oneida chap? He would be of great value in dealing with the Six Nations people."

"He has returned to his wife. She is due to birth their first child."

"Commendable," he commented, pressing fingers together. "I understand you are fluent in the French language."

Wesley nodded, setting down his soup spoon. Strachan continued, "Command of the French language would be of great advantage in combatting the spread of French Catholic settlers into Upper Canada."

Wesley's stomach knotted. Cornwall's French, and those of the lower Ottawa Grand would live under the Executive Council's disregard.

"Gore proposes providing common schools, throughout the province, so that all have the right to be educated to read," Wesley diverted. "Would that replace your school, Reverend?

Strachan smiled, no offense taken. "There will be scholarships to my school, for those deemed worthy."

"Will Africans and Natives be eligible?" Wesley sat back in his chair.

"Sadly, no," he returned, honestly. "I must curtail my personal desire to placate those who provide funding." He rang the small dinner bell, summoning his servant. "I understand that you are staying at the Carter home."

"Mrs. Carter is a gracious hostess," Wesley answered.

"Her son is a fine example of promise—highly intelligent with an aptitude to learn. I wish he could attend my school. Alas, that would not be acceptable."

"A gifted lad," Wesley concurred. "He will withstand and thrive."

The servant brought in tea and biscuits and the conversation shifted to the new hospital Gore proposed in his speech at the Parliamentary Opening. They did not return to Wesley's potential with the Council Treasury, implying Reverend Strachan respected his position.

"May I break clean from this lot," Wesley murmured in half-hope and half-prayer as he trudged back to the yellow house.

—54—

Rosetta pummelled the washboard with Evie's cotton nappies. "Soon we'll be sitting in the dark and washing up with boiled water and sand. We've only a few slivers of lye soap left."

"Had I known candles and soap had to be made, I would have used them more sparingly." Olivia emitted a deep sign. "And Busy's milk has almost stopped, too."

"Perhaps Sally has soap to share," Rosetta grunted, wringing the stained nappy. "Eddie could use the outing and I need a load of firewood." She rubbed her hands together, plopping the wet nappy back in tub. "These will have to be boiled again."

With Eddie firmly tucked on the toboggan, Olivia raced down the icy path. Gizzy ran ahead, barking at anything that seemed to move.

The Douglas children excitedly welcomed Eddie and Gizzy, ushering them in to see their new puppy, a gift of the Elliot family.

"Sorry, luv," Sally greeted her request, filling the kettle. "I've no candles to spare and we've just enough soap to get through to late summer, when pigs are slaughtered. That's when I make mine. Been collecting ashes, for that day." She straightened her cap. "I believe Mary Cameron would be pleased to part with some soap. She always makes a bit extra for trade."

"Thank you, I shall purchase some from her," Olivia declared with relief.

"You can't eat money…if you understand my meaning." Sally's eyes warmed. "Mary would be appreciative to trade for some provisions." She filled their cups with tea. "Her husband is a sober, hard-working man, but the creek flowing through their allotment, turned out to be more of a swamp. A large portion of their grain rotted in the field last summer, but they've managing to keep pigs alive on wild grass from beaver meadows—goodness knows 'ow."

"I will gather ample provisions to trade," Olivia agreed. "Is it a far walk?"

"About two hours by snowshoe, across the river, following a path through the bush—if your legs can bear."

"My limbs are that of a soldier," Olivia smiled proudly.

"Osh! Now that is improper, milady." Sally dealt a teasing wink. "Tomorrow's weather looks fair and Jamie would be pleased to accompany you...always looking for excuse to visit young Bob, 'e is. Take Gizzy, too."

Wolves, thought Olivia, but instead supplied, "We'll have a fun adventure."

They chatted for over an hour, younger children playing at their feet. Olivia learned of women who were expecting, listened to conflicting rumors of the canal being built from the Ottawa Grand, and Sally shared that a British surveyor would pass through, come summer, to establish the best route.

"If it comes by way of the Cataraqui, a lock may be built at Billidore," Ian added, joining them for a cup of tea. "That's the talk up at Brewers Mills."

"That would certainly bring change," Olivia declared.

Pulling a tired Eddie up the path in the toboggan, Olivia smiled at the sight of wispy smoke rising over her cabin. Since the encounter with Pierre Sabin and his ruffians, she'd resolved to protect her home against any threat. That must now include the government's proposed canal.

"What quantity will be suitable for trade with Mrs. Cameron?" Rosetta asked, upon hearing Sally's proposal. Pushing aside the table, she lifted the trap door of the root cellar.

"No more that either I or Jamie can pull," Olivia proposed. "Make sure there's wheat and corn flour, oatmeal, a basket of squash, a sack of dried beans, and a slab of smoked venison." With firm practicality, she added, "I'll make some bannock with dried apples and cranberries to eat along the way."

Early the next morning, Jamie arrived to load the toboggan. Down the path they stomped to the landing, then laced on snowshoes. Gizzy ran ahead across the river, Jamie pulled the toboggan, with Olivia following. They entered the woods, following the narrow path.

Frosty vapor flowed with every breath. Gizzy's leaps eventually slowed and Jamie began to lag with the toboggan.

"I want my turn," she insisted from behind him.

He handed her the reins with a grateful smile and she leaned in, unsure of how long she would be able to pull. Her legs grew heavy and breathing laboured. Slowing pace, not wanting to waste endurance, she plodded on. Sweat trickled down her back.

The sky was now bluish grey and the wind picking up. Tree branches began to fall on the path. Stinging ice pellets bit exposed skin. Snow soon followed, light at first, but increasing.

She kept her head down, eyes on the path ahead. Cheeks numb and her eyes tearing, they plodded on, their pace ever slower. Gizzy trod at her feet, barely recognizable within ice-encrusted fur.

"Keep moving!" Jamie hollered over the howling wind. "We're almost there." With a forceful grab of the toboggan reins, he strode ahead.

Olivia followed, step by aching step. Squinting into the blowing snow, she saw a log structure. Jamie stumbled forward and banged on the cabin door.

—

"Good Lord!" Robert Cameron exclaimed, slamming the door behind them. "You're daft to be 'oot in this weather?"

"Weren't like this when we left," Jamie bent over, heaving. Shaking and shuddering, Gizzy scattered ice over the floor. Olivia collapsed beside them, hands rigid and unable to untie her snowshoes.

"Poor lass, you've been bitten by frost," Mary Cameron offered in sympathy. Peeling off wraps, she rubbed Olivia's hands, folding them within her arms. Swiftly she buried Olivia's feet within her own armpits. "You're cold as stone," she added, with a shiver. Behind her, children gathered, wide-eyed.

"We've-ve-ve come to tr-tr-trade for s-s-soap and c-candles," Olivia explained through chattering teeth. Life returned to her hands and feet with a torturous burning itch.

"Squeeze your hands to stop the burn," Mary directed. "I'll do your feet."

"You risked your life for soap?" Robert chortled.

Olivia glanced about the dim hearth-lit cabin. Laundry was strung in tidy array among the rafters, above a neatly swept floor. "With two babes, boiling nappies has become horrid," she winced as the pain spread from her toes to the soles of her feet.

"Don't talk, Mrs. Bryson," Mary encouraged, firmly squeezing her feet. "Pain is a good sign and won't last."

"Olivia," she whimpered, fighting back tears. "Pray call me Olivia."

A sandy haired Cameron lad of about 10 years sat beside her on the floor. "Mr. McGee froze his nose, last winter," he offered in consolation. "It turned black 'n fell off."

"Hush!" Mary Cameron shooed him away with a swat. "There's nae a mark of frost on your lovely skin...Olivia..." she whispered, adding, "I'll get you a dress."

"We've but potatoes to share," Robert Cameron offered, "but come and eat."

"We've ample to share on the toboggan—brought it to trade," Olivia wiggled fingers and toes, relieved that they obeyed through the tingling.

Robert and his oldest son, Rob, hauled in the toboggan.

"Oh darlin'!" A tear flowed down Mary's thin pale cheek. "It'll take me years to make enough soap to trade for this. And I've nae candles left, nor oil for a lamp."

Struggling to his feet, Jamie blurted out, "We can'na haul that—"

"Pray forgive my silliness," Olivia interrupted, deferring to their pride. "I do not understand how to do a proper trade, and now those provisions will spoil with this cold. Please help me not waste good food and keep them."

Mary slipped away, quickly returning with a faded woolen dress. "I insist you keep this dress. I dyed it in cranberry juice, but after so many washings it's become rose."

"This is a beautiful shade of rose, thank you for your thoughtfulness," Olivia sincerely supplied, appreciating this was likely her only other garment. She thought Mary's awkwardness at her trousers peculiar. Yet, even frontier women might consider them improper. "And I think we can live quite well by hearth light."

Mary nodded. "Days will soon lengthen."

"Aye. And, tonight, we have safe refuge in your home." Olivia slipped the rose dress over her clothes while Robert and his son transferred the provisions to the pantry and root cellar.

"I'll slice off some of that venison and quickly boil up a squash soup," Mary gaily proposed. "With spruce tea and your bannock, we'll have us a proper feast."

—55—

"Prosperity for this Province is utmost in my thoughts," Lieutenant Governor Francis Gore concluded in his Parliamentary opening speech. "This would be best accomplished by the passing of an act for the use of common schools throughout the Province of Upper Canada."

Wesley left the Parliamentary Hall pondering if he would ever return. Gore's vision dismissed his recommendation for Native sovereignty. With good conscience he could not execute the Council's mandate.

Indigenous languages and culture would be excluded from Gore's common schools. French Canadians had the right to language, religion, and culture in Lower Canada. What of the Haudenosaunee and Anishinaabe? If French-Canadians had their rights protected, why not Canada's Indigenous allies? Gore's vision cast a future Canada that left behind these First Nations.

Gore's promise of a hospital would anchor the provincial capital in York. Combined fields of education, medicine, and government would ensure the city's future. Newark would never regain her glory. Kingston would be relegated to being a military town. Those African refugees, the Indigenous, and war-weary settlers who had all fought to defend Canada would enjoy little of this prosperity.

Wesley must raise his son in this emerging Canada, but how could he blend his son's heritages of Anishinaabe, English, and French? In Lower Canada, a married woman retained personhood and held legal rights apart from her husband. The *Coverture* condition of British law prevented this in Upper Canada. To safeguard his family's future, he needed to consider life beyond the limitations Upper Canada presented.

Wesley turned up the driveway of the yellow house and walked in the back door. Mrs. Carter had a light tea waiting.

"Food is always served late at these affairs," she reminded him from across the table. Delicately clearing her throat, she asked, "How was your time with Gore?"

"Too many people seeking his ear." He bit into the meat pastry, washing it down with a sip of tea. "From what I've learned, I cannot accept the position. Yet to decline will destroy what influence I've built."

"Do you fear being passed over in life, Wesley? Are the schemes in this town truly what you want?" She refilled his cup. Not waiting for an answer, she soothed, "You face a long night. Your uniform is spot-washed, ironed, and waiting. Enjoy what you can, and—" She tilted her head, playfully. "—take note of what the ladies are wearing."

In his room, he reread Rosetta's letter, drawing comfort from the sketches and descriptions of Olivia's life on the clearing. One particular sketch stood out: Eddie seated on her lap, grasping her short hair as she beamed down at him. In all her prickly ways, Olivia loved his son.

This was not the Olivia he'd left screaming in the shanty barn. This woman had embraced frontier life and would walk by his side, wherever life took them.

Rubbing his eyes, he resolved in his decision. He longed to escape back to Billidore, but duty required that he remain to officially decline the position.

—

Oil lanterns lit up the governor's manor in a jolly winter display. Samuel drove the sleigh to the front door. Military watches bolted to attention at their approach.

Not waiting for Wesley, Stephen Reed hastened inside.

"Pray go to bed, Samuel," Wesley encouraged, "We'll find our own way home."

"Don't forget, Ma likes to be up on what the ladies wear," Samuel reminded him.

"I'm renown for keen, accurate observations," Wesley returned, with a brisk salute. Steeling himself, he went inside.

Merry music greeted his entrance as a footman took his coat. Ahead stood Governor Gore, busily chatting with a group of gentlemen, cheeks rosy with excitement. Tonight was a triumphant celebration of his second administration. Already by Miss Maxwell's side, Stephen Reed would likely give her his full attention this evening.

Wesley resolved to make the most of the event. Lent would soon be upon them: the pious season of restraint. Declining the position would exclude him from future colonial society.

Making his way about the room, he joined in several conversations, observing more than speaking—everyone enjoys an affirming listener. He took note of the ladies' gowns, offering compliments to matrons, where appropriate.

At dinner he was fortunate to be seated mid-table, next to Mr. Levius Sherwood, the elected legislative representative for his own county of Johnstown District. On his other side, Catherine Bayard engaged in exclusive flirtation with Samuel Jarvis. At the far end of the table, Stephen Reed and Isabelle Maxwell had eyes only for each other. Arthur Bayard had shrewdly managed to sit next to Gore. Mineral rights were reserved by the Crown, with arrangements at the discretion of the Lieutenant Governor; no doubt Bayard would raise it as a topic of conversation.

Ignored by Catherine, Wesley freely indulged in a *tête-à-tête* with Levius Sherwood, learning more of the planned canal between the Grand Ottawa and Kingston.

"A summer survey will investigate a possible route through Cranberry Bog, connecting the Cataraqui to the Rideau Lakes," Sherwood divulged.

"Right through Billidore Rifts, where I have my clearing," Wesley noted. "The land will need to be flooded or a canal dug, for the Cataraqui runs shallow, there."

"We'll leave those details to His Majesty's Military Engineers," Sherwood deflected. "I only know that our district will greatly benefit from the influx of settlers and commerce."

Music summoned from the Foyer.

"I would like to learn more," Wesley persisted, as they made their way to the dance floor.

"And I will gladly supply what I know," Sherwood responded,

Wesley pivoted to look behind, distracted by Samuel Jarvis's heated argument with a gentleman. Catherine Bayard met Wesley's inquiring frown, a look of distress clouding her face. Excusing himself, he hastened to her assistance. She grasped his arm.

"I fear they may challenge," she whispered. "That gentleman has implied Samuel misappropriated funds from Six Nations."

"Don't rule that out," Wesley led her back into the empty dining hall. Servants were busy clearing the tables; he pulled two chairs to the window, overlooking the yard. A heavy snowfall had begun.

"Do you mean a duel or his thievery?" She looked intently at him, a tear slipping down her fair cheek. He retrieved his handkerchief from his inner pocket and passed it to her.

"Both are possible. The accusing gentleman is John Ridout, a clerk in the Jarvis law office. He's party to many family secrets."

"Then Samuel will not hesitate at stealing from Papa." She reached for his hand. "Thank you for rescuing me. You're a good man."

He gently eased away. She searched his face.

"Are you content?" she asked, tucking his handkerchief within her sleeve.

"Very," he replied, and stood. "Mrs. Bryson is willing to take me as I am, and not form me into another."

She rose beside him, restoring her hand within his arm. "Shall we dance and put that hot-headed Jarvis in his place."

"Only if you dance with your papa, after." He led her out of the room. "I have a selection of matrons to attend to, and I do not wish Jarvis to take issue and challenge me."

56

An angry wind battered the cabin's log walls. Yet, under thick quilts, Olivia felt safe and warm. The delicious aroma of fresh baking travelled up to the loft.

Gracie Cameron playfully tussled Olivia's hair.

"Osh!" Her older sister, 10-year-old Nessa, giggled. "You're gon'na wake Mrs. Bryson."

"Why is her 'air shorn?" Gracie whispered. "Does she 'ave lice?"

"Ewww," Nessa shuddered.

"I like short hair." Olivia opened her eyes. "It's easy to care for, Gracie."

"I want long hair like Ma's," Gracie giggled, her eyes lighting up. "You'll nae be going out today—storm's gotten worse."

Olivia slithered out from under the quilts. Slipping on the rose dress, she scraped ice from a corner of the single-window pane. Outside, snow whipped about in the wind. With Wesley's red flannel shirt as a jacket, she would be warm.

"You girls cozy up, and I'll go help your mother," she invited, climbing down the loft ladder.

Robert Cameron looked up from the table, Jamie and young Rob seated with him. Mary's back was to Oliva, as she hunched over the hearth griddle.

"How may I be of help, Mary?" Olivia asked.

"You've already been of help, Mrs. Bryson," Robert returned, as Mary set a cup of hot brew before her.

Olivia took a sip. Spruce tea flavoured with maple syrup carried many a settler through lean winter months. "Ahh...lovely," she praised, hugging the cup between her hands.

Returning a pleased smile, Mary set a generous piece of warm bannock and a bowl of beans before her.

"Your dog was put out last night, but has nae returned." Robert donned his outer clothes, preparing for barn chores. "The MacFie clearing is nearby. She may 'ave gone there." The older boys dressed warmly to accompany him.

Olivia looked about the tidy cabin. Noting a small shelf of books, she asked, "Shall I read to the children?"

"That would be a treat!" Mary's face lit up. "Only...wait until the men return. They won't be long with Jamie to help."

The men...childhood did not last long on the frontier, Olivia reflected. "What books have you?"

"We've a Bible," Mary returned a thin smile, "Robinson Crusoe, Gulliver's Travels, and a volume of Burns' poetry—but that's in Scot's English."

"I could give it a muster," Olivia laughed.

The other children gathered to the table and ate. Then, the younger boys cleared the dishes, while the girls washed and swept up.

With everyone inside, warming cups of tea in hand, Olivia opened the Burns volume and began:

> *Wee, sleet, cowran, tim'rous beastie,*
> *O, what a panic's in thy breastie!*

Encouraged by children's giggles, she pressed on. Mary's eyes sparkled and her husband punctuated Olivia's reading with slaps of the knee and loud guffaws. With a pronounced sigh, she concluded:

> *But Och! I backward cast my e'e,*
> *On prospects drear!*

An' forward tho' I canna see,
I guess an' fear!

Closing the book, she offered an embellished curtsy, smiling broadly. Jamie stood up, leading the children in applause.

"Completely charming." Mary clasped her hands together. "What say 'ye, Robert, a wee bit 'o fiddling?"

The children leapt to their feet. Nessa ran to her parent's bedroom, returning with their father's fiddle. Young Rob took a handful of spoons from the drawer and passed them around.

Robert broke out in lively tune, accompanied by the older children enthusiastically clanking spoons as the younger ones pranced about. Mary pulled Olivia to her feet and led her in a lively reel, until the baby erupted in a wail, demanding to nurse. Olivia sat down, breathless.

"Tell of your journey to Canada," Mary invited, unbuttoning her chemise for the baby.

What could she divulge? She would not lie to these honest people, but she must also be discreet about her heritage.

"I come from a family of privilege," she began. "But privilege does not bring happiness. My mother died, my father remarried and sent me to live with a much older sister, to be a companion for her children. Yet I was lonely until a young man came to tutor her children. My sister had already promised me to another—"

"You had nae choice in a husband?" gasped Nessa.

"Indeed, I did, but it demanded that I give up affluence to marry the man—"

"Captain Bryson?" Nessa sat forward.

"Aye," Olivia confirmed. "I was foolish and selfishly choose comfort over love. Captain Wesley Bryson went off to war and I had several years to reflect on my folly." She paused, no longer bound by regret.

"Until?" Nessa and Gracie prompted, in unison. Mary nodded in affirmation.

"Until a distant relative returned from Canada, with a secret message from the Captain."

Nessa bounced with excitement in her chair.

"So, I hopped on the ship and came hither." She raised hands with triumphant flourish. "For if that good man would have me back, after I spurned him, I would definitely accept his life and what came with it, here in Canada."

The children clapped.

"He is, indeed, a good man," Mary confirmed, sitting the baby up to burp. The younger children waited, the quiet only interrupted by the children's giggles upon the baby's relief.

Robert Cameron picked up his fiddle and began playing another tune. Jamie and young Rob got up and endeavoured to step-dance. The children laughed at their attempts at fancy foot work. After a while, they wearied and began a game of draughts. The cabin again fell quiet until a bark at the cabin door announced Gizzy's return from jaunting. Nessa allowed her in.

The storm was easing—tomorrow they would be able to set out for home—yet Olivia felt uneasy. Perhaps something was amiss with Wesley. Surely Ian would look in on Rosetta and the babies. Rubbing her temples, she struggled to clear her thoughts.

Glimpsing her concern, Mary rose. "You must be thinking of home. Don't worry, Olivia. It'll be clear tomorrow and you'll be able to set out early if you wish. I'll fetch your soap."

Welcoming the diversion, Olivia helped her with wrapping the few soap cakes. Yet her concerns lingered. After the sun set, nestled between Gracie and Nessa, she offered a silent prayer.

"Dear Lord, whoever or whatever has gone awry, please be there and help."

57

Snow had ceased, yet the sky remained grey. Musket on his back, Jamie pulled the toboggan, with Olivia and Gizzy following behind.

"With a lighter load, we can make it in a little more than an hour," he huffed. "Try to keep up."

Olivia accepted the challenge. Retracing the bush path, her laboured breath competed with the sounds of scraping branches against the toboggan and snowshoes swishing upon fresh snow. Just as she was about to ask for a rest, a man came around the bend ahead, hurrying towards them.

"Papa!" Jamie shouted.

"Good Lord!" Ian exclaimed, embracing his son and reaching a hand to Olivia. "You both are safe." His face was strangely grave.

"What is wrong, Ian?" Olivia asked, her stomach tightening in a knot.

Stepping forward, he gripped her shoulders. "Your cabin is destroyed, lass." He searched her face, ensuring her understanding, and repeated. "It's burnt to the ground. Rosetta and the wee bairns have disappeared."

Recalling her sense of dread, she murmured, "Rosetta was unarmed."

"Cian Cavanaugh hastened down to Kingston to have the garrison mount a proper search," Ian pledged. "Abduction of an officer's child and destruction of his property will be taken seriously."

"Do you dare imply Rosetta bears blame?" She gasped. "She would only go against her will."

"I make no accusation. We both know she is a fine woman—but snow has buried any evidence to confront evil talk."

She pushed on, forcing aching legs through the bush, Ian and Jamie following. The path opened up, crossing the river. She wrestled up the embankment to her home.

Three thick log walls remained. The wall and portions of roof, nearest the yard, had caved in, charred wood filling the cabin.

She stared at the ruins, her disbelief shattering into acceptance. Nothing was left; the fate of Rosetta and the babies a mystery.

Ian stood behind her in quiet support. "There are no bodies within," he quietly supplied.

Slowly she circled the cabin, peering through cracked window panes. Scorched remnants of her possessions lay scattered throughout the ruins. Behind her, Gizzy whined at the closed shanty barn door, tail raised excitedly.

"This was no accident," she surmised. "The fire started by the door. That is the area most charred, not the hearth. And the cabin appears ransacked." She searched Ian's face. "Why? What riches have I?" She glanced back at the barn. "And why is that dog behaving so. Could they be sheltering in the barn?"

"Nae, lass. No one's in the barn—I've searched," he declared.

She attempted to push away a blackened rafter, barring the threshold. Ian pulled her back, "The storm stopped the spread of the fire, but it's not safe to enter the cabin. It may collapse on you. Jamie and I must first clear away debris."

With a firm kick, he sent the beam back. Charred shingles and splintered cross timbers tumbled about. A scorched remnant of Rosetta's green dress lay beneath. Olivia pulled it out. Had the wind

266

blow it there or was it by a human hand? Deeper within, she could see Eddie's stuffed wolf. Ian helped her to her feet, leading her away.

Sally raced up the path, breathless.

"Our babies...Rosetta..." Olivia sobbed within her comforting arms. "They've been abducted."

"Never heard of raiders this far upriver." Ian scratched his beard, muttering, "Yet, with a strong sled team...through bush...it is only a matter of hours from the Republic."

Olivia's attention shifted to Gizzy, noticeably alert by the barn door. "What's in the shanty, Ian?" she challenged.

"The cow's dead, Olivia," he returned. "Best not go inside."

She pushed by him. A chicken darted out from the straw. She gasped, hand flying to her throat. Busy's carcass hung from the rafter.

"As much as you'd love to bury your beloved cow, we must butcher her," Sally stood by her side. Gizzy pressed against her leg.

She thought of Eddie, scared and hungry. And what of Rosetta and the baby? This was not a time to be weak.

"Sabin!" she spat out. "He knew we were here alone."

"Speculatin' helps no one," Sally cautioned. "Best leave this to God's judgement."

"I must do something!" she protested. Averting eyes from Busy, she retrieved baskets and a shovel. "I can search the debris for clues."

"Then learn what you can and save what is possible, luv. I'll go prepare a bed for you." With a firm shoulder squeeze, Sally returned to her clearing.

"Blizzard smothered the fire a'fore it went through the floor, lass. You might find something salvageable," Ian gruffly affirmed. "Only go where I deem safe."

She peered inside, waiting while Jamie and his father began clearing away the rafter and rubble barring the threshold.

A roof beam had collapsed Rosetta's room, fire consuming the bed, curtains, and inner wall. Olivia sifted through the first load of debris, loaded it on the toboggan, then pushed it down the privy gully. Come spring, melting snow would flush the acidic remnants into the river.

Evie's charred cradle board leaned against the wall, near the threshold. Rosetta's few clothes were scattered and scorched, nothing savable. Firmly kicking to the floorboards, she found the removable board and recovered Rosetta's crock of coin.

We've done enough for today, lass." Ian leaned back, hands on hips.

"Supports my assertion that Rosetta was taken by surprise," she held up the crock.

"Aye," Ian concurred. "If the woman was of sound mind, she would have taken her coin."

"You still think her responsible?"

"Nae, Olivia. I'm thinking the way others will," he softened. "Now, let's go down."

Olivia looked up at the darkening sky, remarking, "Another storm will soon be upon us." She stored Rosetta's coins, cradle board, and dress remnant in the barn. With a soulful tremble, she laid her hand on Busy's cold body and thanked God for the creature's life. "You will continue to give life, dear Busy, and I will miss you dearly."

Ian waited, outside. "Tell Sally we'll be late. We need to tend to the cow...er...Busy."

"Pray share Busy with the Cameron family, and others you know who are in need." She walked away, her mind alive with questions.

58

For several days Wesley's stomach gnawed at him. He presumed his malady a result of the stagnant society in which he waited. Kingston had the same effect on him, when he stayed too long in town. He'd not yet had opportunity to clearly refuse the Treasury position.

Mrs. Carter's ginger tea gave no relief. Neither did Stephen Reed, for he completely endorsed his acceptance of the position. "So you can pass some *largesse* on to me," he asserted. Wesley knew these words were more than jest.

Tonight, he was expected at cards. "Lent begins next week, after which we'll have no fun until mid-April," Miss Catherine Bayard pouted, insisting on his company to balance the gathering. Stephen Reed, Miss Isabelle Maxwell, her Lieutenant brother, and Miss Wainwright were also to attend

When he arrived, Wesley found Samuel Jarvis also in attendance with Miss Mary Powell, daughter of William Powell of the executive council. As the servants brought out wine, Jarvis made no effort to cloak his interest in Wesley's plans. "You've yet to accept the Treasury opportunity, Bryson." He cast a glance at Catherine. "If you remain elusive, you risk becoming a spinster."

Catherine flexed her lovely shoulders. Mary smiled at Wesley, with subtle raise of a delicate eyebrow.

"You're not yet on the Council, Samuel, and are not privy to my ambition," Wesley retorted.

"The Captain has much to consider," Stephen intervened.

Jarvis smirked. "Your crop of oats? How to spend your half-pension? Or maybe which tree to chop down for firewood?"

Stroking his beard, Wesley calmly studied the hard twist of his mouth. A man, much like Jarvis, had scarred his face; mockery is best ignored.

Catherine motioned an African servant to clear the table. "I shall let you form a foursome at cards, while Wesley and I have a go at two-handed whist." Grasping his hand, she led him to a corner table. "I want nothing of Samuel's hot-headedness," she whispered, shuffling the cards.

"And so, you invite Miss Powell?"

"Diversion is better than rejection." She smiled brightly. "I do look forward to meeting your shy Mrs. Bryson, come April."

"You must bring Miss Maxwell," Wesley returned. "My wife would enjoy her acquaintance."

"I suspect she'll come, even without my invitation. She seems quite fond of Lieutenant Reed."

Giddy laughter erupted at the other table. Samuel Jarvis was recounting a fishing trip he'd enjoyed last summer.

The salon door opened and a servant entered. "Pardon, Miss Bayard," he discreetly interrupted.

Setting down her cards, Catherine emitted a sharp sniff. "What is it?"

"Samuel Carter had come with a message for Captain Bryson," he bowed.

Wesley stood, the knot in his stomach tightening—it must be important to interrupt this gathering.

Samuel waited in the hallway, Wesley's coat and wrap already in hand. "A soldier arrived by dog sled to take you to Kingston. He would not divulge the reason."

"Please convey my apology to Miss Bayard," Wesley instructed the servant as he donned his outerwear. Samuel's sleigh and horses waited outside. With a flick of the reigns, they raced across the snow to the yellow house.

A young red-haired man bolted to his feet at Wesley's entrance. "Private MacLaren, Captain," he supplied.

"At ease, Private," Wesley returned. "Now tell me what this is about."

"Your house has been destroyed by fire, sir. Mrs. Bryson is safe, but your son, Mrs. George, and her wee babe are missing."

"Missing?" Wesley stepped forward, the Fort Erie abduction flooding his mind. Yet, if this were such a situation, the lives of Mrs. George and her child would be of value, but not that of his son.

"Major McTavish has dispatched a team to Billidore, to investigate," the Private continued, eyes straight ahead. "He's also sent an officer to Sackett's Harbour, to learn what he can. This matter has been given utmost priority, Captain, and I've come to fetch you back to Kingston."

"Pray have something to eat while I pack," Wesley invited, turning to Mrs. Carter to ensure her agreement. With an understanding nod, she prepared a plate of chicken and a buttery potato.

"I'll tend to his dogs," Samuel offered.

Wesley returned from packing and wrote a hasty note to Reverend Strachan, explaining that family matters required his urgent return to Kingston.

Looking across the table at the young private, he asked, "You're a friend of Private Harris?"

"Aye, sir," he returned. "With all respect, Captain, I'm acquainted with Mrs. Bryson and Mrs. George. This matter has stung my heart."

Settling up payment with Mrs. Carter, he took her hand and bowed. "Your home has been a refuge from folly, Ma'am. I came close to being seduced by power and authority—"

"You've held firm, Wesley," she interrupted. "That's what matters. May God continue to strengthen you."

Two hours later they were well beyond York, heading east on Kingston Road. Private MacLaren sat in the sled with Wesley driving the team. The dogs had ceased barking, their run beginning to slow. They needed rest and food to continue. Passing the ruins of an old trading post, they stopped at an inn.

"We're not open," barked the surly Loyalist innkeeper, angered at being awakened. Wesley tossed him a coin and the man opened the door, grumbling as he fetched a plate of beans and eggs, setting it at a table by the fire.

"What of my dogs?" Wesley challenged.

"That's all I'm serving," the man growled.

Private MacLaren ventured out with his bowl of beans, defending, "It won't kill them."

Before sunrise they were back on the trail, Wesley continuing to drive the team. They stopped just before dusk, at Grover's Tavern, in Alnwick. Many of the settlement's houses were still damaged from the War, but the inn was habitable. More importantly, John Grover was hospitable. He provided a room, a decent bowl of stew, and sent gristle, bones, and potatoes out to the dogs.

Rising again with the sun, they passed through Quinte and arrived at Kingston Garrison while it was still light. McTavish met with Wesley immediately and wasted no small talk.

"I understand you have a child by a Native woman," he asserted, hands clasped, seated by the fire.

"Edward Nyaweh Bryson is my son," Wesley affirmed. "He was left in the care of Mrs. Bryson while I was on duty."

"Harrumph!" McTavish snorted, with a brisk shake of his head. "I've dispatched an officer to Sackett's Harbour to make inquiries." He got up, retrieved a bulky fabric item from a cabinet and set it on the desk. "Your wife found these among the ruins of your cabin."

Wesley's heart sank as he recognized Olivia's cream silk dress. McTavish carefully unfolded the skirt to reveal the dried mud stain of a foot print embedded within its fine fibers. He then laid out broken pieces of a crock jug, carrying an odour of spirits. "She also provides this as proof that Mrs. George and the children were abducted."

Wesley muttered an oath under his breath. "That dress is my wife's, as Mrs. Cowlie can attest. But I have never seen that jug."

"I understand the fire's damage is quite extensive. Little is salvageable, save a few items stored under floor boards for safe keeping. Your milk cow was killed—shot at close range." He paused, eyes piercing. "It there anyone who would have reason to do this to you—perhaps your Indian woman?"

"Major..." Wesley clenched his fists, inhaling deeply and choosing his words carefully, "My former wife, now Mrs. John Oneida, and Mrs. Bryson are the best of companions. Mrs. George attested to that in a letter."

"John Oneida's wife?" McTavish snorted. "Quite convenient to pass your 'affair of the country' on to your—"

"My son has been abducted!" Wesley cut him off. "I must go comfort my wife. Private Harris will sled me up to Billidore tomorrow morning,"

"Do what you must," McTavish stood. Wesley saluted and left.

Before retiring to his officer's quarters, he trekked by Stephen Reed's cottage. The door was locked, windows tightly shuttered, never again to be revisited.

59

"We're done for today, lass. A strong cup of tea is in order," Ian Douglas coaxed. "Wind's picked up and we face more snow."

Olivia held Rosetta's sketch of Eddie in her hands. Somehow his parchment likeness had survived, yellowed by smoke. Her heart reached out in hope.

"Your lad's in the Lord's hands, lass." Ian gently touched her shoulder, steering her out of the charred ruins.

"I should have loved him better."

"God knows I've been down that path." He nodded, in shared understanding. "You did your best." His attention drew downriver, where a dog sled rounded the bend.

Barking madly, Gizzy raced down the river path.

"Now who would that be?" Ian strode after the dog; Olivia remained at the top.

Wesley stepped off the sled, handing the reins to Robbie Harris, and greeted Ian with a mittened slap on the back. Ian gestured back toward Olivia with a nod.

How could I believe you could hold any regard beyond yourself? Wesley's last words returned as she watched him approach. A wall of hurt remained between them.

"I'm home," he stood before her, face reddened from cold, eyes questioning.

"There's no home, Wesley," she answered in truth.

Taking the parchment from her, he studied the sketch. Then he looked up, eyes glistening, and carefully slipped it within his coat.

"We must find him," she committed. "One of my dresses had a footprint—"

"It wasn't a military boot print," he affirmed. "McTavish keeps the evidence, but it won't result in much. What I learned from my Niagara investigations is it's up to us to find those we love." They walked across the yard, toward the broken pieces of their home, his comforting arm about her shoulders.

Wesley peered within, surveying the destruction.

"The gully is filled with debris. Little was salvageable," Olivia supplied.

"What of your trunks with all your garments?"

"Contents were scattered about—everything ruined, either by fire or water. I have but one dress—a gift from Mrs. Cameron. And Mrs. Cavanaugh gave me a chemise, a frayed half-corset, and a quilt." She chuckled. "Your red flannel shirt, trousers and deerskin coat have served me well."

"We are paupers, Libby." They stepped over the charred oaken threshold. Biting his lip, he looked up through the gaping roof, at the greying sky.

"We are rich with fine neighbours who have shared what little they have." She lifted the trap door to the root cellar. "There is much here that is edible—enough to share. Sadly, that includes dear sweet Busy." She dropped the door with a slam.

"You'll have to live in the officer's quarters."

"You have the Reed clearing," she countered.

"No longer," he shook his head. "I've returned the property to Stephen."

"We can squat there until we rebuild," she pressed. "My jewellery was not found by whoever did this. Under marriage law, they are yours and, with your investments—"

"We have no investments," he interrupted, through gritted teeth. "I was a ruddy fool to sponsor Pierre Sabin. His findings will be sold to a higher bidder."

"Then you are rid of the man." She stood at the doorway to the bedroom they had shared. "Now we must find Eddie, dear Rosetta, and her sweet child."

"You know my son better than I," he conceded.

"And I know that if you accept the position in York, it would grieve us both."

"Then we shall beg lodging of the Douglas family." He tucked her hand in the crux of his arm. "And tomorrow, we visit the Reed clearing. For certain, Stephen Reed will tarry in York to enjoy the company of Miss Isabelle Maxwell."

"The woman whose boots I refused to remove?"

"Aye." He opened the door of the Douglas cottage. Olivia pulled off her tuque with a shake of her head. His mouth dropped.

"Much easier to care for," she supplied.

Sally Douglas had a generous meal of roasted fish and baked squash waiting on the table.

"Och!" Ian's hand flew to his forehead when he heard of their plans for the Reed property. "In all the excitement of the fire, I didn't see if that shanty was left untouched."

"It's not a shanty," Olivia asserted. "It's a cabin with a proper chimney."

—60—

Wesley's first encounter with Olivia Fairworth had been in the library, at Hurstmere. She'd come to observe his French lesson with her nieces, and had sat in a corner, busily stitching. The constant motion of her hands had attested to an inner restlessness, confirmed by her pursed lips. He had found her distracting.

He had been about to ask her to leave when her sharp gaze stilled his tongue. He had recognized a trapped soul—dependent on the whims of others. In that, they had been aligned; in that, they had drawn mutual comfort.

Now, Wesley savoured the ease with which Olivia moved, in a faded rose dress, clearing dishes from the Douglas table. Even with grief-clouded eyes, she possessed a calm he'd never seen before.

"Here's something for the dogs, Robbie." She filled a bucket with table scraps, cooking grease, and burnt squash from their root cellar, adding, "I'll have biscuits and hot tea, waiting for your return."

Ian and Wesley went out with Private Harris to feed the pigs and dogs. "The work of those women will not go to waste," Ian declared, emptying the bucket into the trough. "Pigs will be well-fed into summer."

"Olivia and Mrs. George harvested this?" Wesley shook his head in disbelief.

"Annie too," Ian rubbed his beard with a chuckle. "It was a bit 'o free-for-all, until Sally settled them with a few buckets of cold water." He shrugged, adding, "Mrs. Rosetta George is a fine woman."

"May the Good Lord keep them safe," Robbie Harris quietly affirmed, his eyes clouded with concern. Wesley's hand briefly rested on his shoulder.

Looking up from her knitting upon their return, Sally offered, "Olivia's up the stair, readin' to the children. She'll not be down until the 'morrow." Robbie collected his tea, sat down beside her, and began winding her wool.

Wesley nodded in appreciation. Perhaps it was best she retire early—a proper courting was due her. He chortled with amusement. Had they just met, he would have wanted to court her.

He awoke, Robbie snoring beside him on a mat by the hearth. Olivia deftly stepped over them, in trousers and his red shirt, a steely determined look on her face. Quietly, she stirred up coals in the hearth, set a kettle to boil, and began frying bacon on the spider griddle.

Ian came out from the bedroom. "Sally had a poor time last night, with her time so near," he confided to Olivia. "She needs to sleep a wee bit longer."

"Beans, biscuits, and bacon are already started," she nodded and set out plates and mugs.

Wesley folded up his bedroll and sat at the table. Robbie, Ian, and Jamie soon joined him. Gingerly, Wesley ate a spoonful of beans, determined to praise her however it tasted.

"This is good," he gulped with surprise, sopping up beans with a biscuit.

"Maple syrup," she mumbled, filling his cup with dark tea. Tossing rind scraps and grease in a bucket for the sled dogs, she set a ladleful in a chipped bowl on the floor and invited Gizzy over with a click of her tongue.

"When the children have eaten, we'll leave," she declared.

"Aye, ma'am." Wesley drank up his tea, amazed by her command of the kitchen.

With Robbie pulling tools on toboggan, they snowshoed downriver to the Reed clearing. Olivia kept pace with Wesley, for he travelled slowly so as not to tax her. Up the bank they climbed to the clearing.

The shanty door hung open, top hinge torn away. The small window was shattered, as if kicked in, and the mattress lay on the floor, shredded. Gnawed remnants of frozen meat were abandoned within the hearth's ashes.

Olivia briskly set a chair aright. Robbie went out for the tool box and Wesley picked up the largest piece of a shattered crock jug.

"Is this similar to the one found in our home?" he asked.

"Aye," she answered, and began sweeping glass shards from beneath the window.

He liked her acquisition of stoic speech. "We'll need a bedroll, greased window paper and a hinge for the door, to make this livable," he assessed.

"Two bedrolls—three if Robbie stays with us," she amended. He noted her blush as she looked away.

Robbie stomped in to report, "Plenty of firewood. Roof appears solid."

"We can salvage a few glass panes from our cabin," Olivia added.

"Livable," Wesley concluded, inviting Robbie to lift the door while he reattached the hinge.

Snow had begun to fall when they returned to the Douglas clearing, at mid-day.

"You have a visitor," Ian greeted, nodding to a Native youth seated at the table. His red blanket cape over buckskin, and thick braided hair set an imposing presence. He stood and turned.

"Joseph!" Wesley exclaimed, wrapping him in warm embrace. "Have you come to help us search for Eddie?"

"No, my brother. I've come to take you to Annie. My nephew is safe."

"Surely she had nothing to do with—"

Joseph's hand shot up to halt any assertion. "The African woman kept him safe during the raid, but she fears returning to Kingston."

279

"Rosetta's safe?" Olivia gasped with relief.

"You will hear the account from her," Joseph answered. "I am merely my sister's messenger."

"I'll return to Kingston with this good news," Robbie Harris beamed.

"Immediately," Wesley concurred.

—61—

Olivia stopped to catch her breath. Legs aching, she didn't want to hold them up, but she could not continue.

"A few hours of light remain, Mrs. Bryson," Joseph encouraged in accented English.

"Perhaps ride the toboggan?" Wesley coaxed.

Untying her snowshoes, she squeezed in among boxes of supplies. The pace picked up as Joseph led, Wesley pulling the toboggan, and Gizzy romping behind.

From the direction of the fading sun, she discerned they were travelling west. Stopping at the edge of a frozen lake, Joseph announced, "We camp for the night."

Olivia stepped forward. "If you have a flint box, I'll build a fire. Tell me where you want it."

"You know how to build a fire?" Wesley's eyes opened wide, and he went off to gather dead fall, grassy twigs, and dried reeds.

Joseph kicked snow away from near the base of a rock outcrop. "This is out of the wind."

Olivia stomped the snow down for their shelter, then looked up at the darkening sky. Snow flurries were growing heavier and denser. "We need to hurry, Wesley. Cut some cross pieces and I'll make a platform for the fire."

With thick branches laid side by side and cross pieces beneath, she stuffed smaller twigs and dried reeds into the centre gap. After several strikes of flint on char, she coaxed the grass to flame, feeding it twigs until it grew large enough to take branches and small split logs.

"Did my sister teach you that?" Joseph asked as he tied together a lean-to frame, behind her.

"Rosetta was my teacher." She filled a kettle loosely with clean snow, and set it on a cross log over the flames.

"Good Lord, woman!" Wesley returned with an armful of fir branches to roof the lean-to. "You are a wonder."

Tossing leaves into the kettle, she passed out blueberry scones. The tea took only a few minutes more. Sitting with the lean-to open to the fire, and fir branches scattered over the floor, they were warm and sheltered from both wind and snow.

"First watch," Wesley claimed, reaching into the sack for a third scone.

Olivia lay back on the fir branches, shifting to find a comfortable position on the fir needles. Gizzy lay between her and Joseph, with Wesley seated at her feet. A wolf howled in the distance. Gizzy's ears perked, but Olivia hugged her close.

"*Les loups chantent*," Joseph remarked.

"Wolves singing," Wesley echoed and Olivia drifted off to sleep.

—

By dawn's frosty light, they smothered the fire with snow and set off. Hilly terrain slowed their travel, yet Olivia chose to walk behind Joseph and the toboggan. She did not want to ride until absolutely necessary.

Wesley snowshoed up behind her. "Swallow your pride Libby, and get on that toboggan—we'll travel faster." He took the reins from Joseph, and waited until she obeyed.

They pressed on for several hours, until an aroma of smoke caught Olivia off guard. Her stomach tightened with stirred memory of her home, now in ruins. Wesley picked up the pace and they emerged from the woods.

Bark-covered dome huts filled a forest clearing. Olivia struggled off the toboggan to walk beside Wesley and Joseph as curious observers emerged. A woman peered out from under a skin-flap door. Behind her hut, two old women stopped work on a hide stretched over a frame, eyes following their transit. A girl picked up her puppy and ran behind them, giggling.

They continued through the camp to a large fire where a deer carcass roasted on a spit. Two old warriors rose in greeting and spoke to Joseph, pointing to a nearby hut. The door flap lifted and Annie stepped out.

"John's child sleeps, inside," she announced before Olivia asked. "A strong boy, you'll hear him when he awakens."

Eddie squeezed out from behind her and ran to Olivia, loudly squealing "Ibb-Bee! Ibb-Bee!" Burying him within her arms, she smothered his face with kisses.

"Please present him to his father," she urged Annie.

"We will do this, together," Annie insisted.

Each took a hand, walking the little boy to Wesley. He took the boy in his arms, a silent tear flowing down his cheek. Olivia stepped away.

"Your son, Edward Bryson," Annie declared, hand resting on Wesley's shoulder.

The door flap lifted again. Rosetta emerged; her face revealed weariness. She was dressed Anishinaabe style, in a short deerskin tunic over red woolen leggings, head uncovered with hair tightly braided. Evie nestled within a red blanket about her shoulders.

Olivia rushed to her, the women embracing. Annie remained at their side, clasping the cross about her neck, and uttered, "*Grace au Seigneur*," followed by a robust "Enough crying!"

John Oneida poked his head out from under the flap "inviting them within.

Savouring the hut's sparse simplicity, Olivia remarked, "Everything one needs to live is here." Fir branches surrounded a sunken fire pit, blanketing the floor, infusing the air with vibrant fragrance. Comfortably warm, a roof hole drew smoke out of the shelter, while the kettle and cauldron hung ready on hooks by the fire.

An old woman sat in the corner with Annie's sleeping infant swaddled within her arms. An empty cradle board leaned against a neat pile of furs and blankets.

"Cornbread and tea will soon be ready," she invited. "And there'll be a bit 'o venison once it's finished roastin'. Ya din'na want to eat it bloody."

Olivia stifled a nervous laugh at the woman's unanticipated Scottish accent.

Wesley sat with Eddie in his arms. John lit a pipe, passing it first to Wesley and then Joseph, seated by the door flap. Sweet tobacco filled the air while Annie served up tea and hot cornbread.

"Do we get to share the pipe?" Olivia asked, eyes briefly engaging with Wesley. Eddie snatched a piece of cornbread from his father's unwatched hand.

The old woman chuckled. "I din'na think English ladies smoked a pipe."

"I thought it customary to share a pipe among friends," she gracefully nodded to the peculiar hostess.

Joseph passed Olivia the pipe. Drawing deep, she erupted in a fit of choking. Wesley leaned forward in concern while John nodded firm approval.

"We need to bring back a bit of hoity-toity," Annie stroked her back, lifting a tea cup to her lips.

"I'll have a go." Rosetta took the pipe to her lips, drew deep and blew out a large smoke ring that rose up, escaping through the roof hole. "Wintering with Creek people taught me many skills." She passed the pipe to the old woman. "I introduce to you Mrs. Maggie Stewart, daughter of a Hudson's Bay Scot trader and an Anishinaabe maiden. She's a voyageur's widow and mother of eight children, some of whom live in Montreal, some in the High Country, and her youngest son camps here."

"They nae want my tale, Rosie," the old woman's face crinkled in smile. "Tell them how you come to be here, lass."

"Aye, my story," Rosetta nodded, her eyes meeting Olivia. Inhaling deep, she began.

"I had an uneasiness that gnawed at me, as soon as you left, Olivia. Skies had darkened and the wind was thickening with snow, so I bundled myself and the babies extra well to go out and milk Busy. I tried to assure myself it was just concern about the coming snow storm. Then, from downriver, I heard dogs barking and panicked at the thought of those blaggards who'd come the day of Evie's birth."

"Blaggards?" Wesley asked sharply. Rosetta held up her hand to continue uninterrupted.

"The heavy snowfall didn't let me see clearly. I was cut off from the Douglas clearing, so hid behind the barn and watched. I could make out the forms of men moving through the trees, making their way towards the cabin. It must have been Providence, but Evie was slumbering in my shawl and Eddie quietly held my hand." Her eyes widened. "I was about to go greet them when they kicked the door in! I pulled Eddie away and fled to the back bush, hoping they hadn't seen me."

Annie's baby began to whimper and she quickly took him to her breast. Olivia glanced at Wesley. His features had hardened, though Eddie still slept peacefully within his arms.

Gently stroking Evie's hair, Rosetta continued. "I stumbled down the ravine beyond the clearing and by God's mercy the babies didn't cry out—Eddie even laughed thinking it was a game. The snow was deep, but I struggled as best I could to put distance from the cabin. I hoped to find a path, through the bush, to the Douglas cabin. And I hoped snow would cover my tracks."

"She was following a stream, taking her deeper into the bush," Joseph supplemented.

"Wind grew strong and snow fell so thick that I could see no more than an arm's distance. I thought of wolves, and asked the Lord to forgive my foolishness for running off in panic."

"You weren't foolish, Rosetta," Wesley cut in. "Our home was ransacked and torched."

"That fear was given to guide you away from them," Olivia affirmed. "Yet how did you survive overnight in the blizzard?"

"I crawled under a thick spruce and dug out a snow cave—like a mama bear with her cubs. Wolves did howl, but far off. I stayed awake with the babies sleeping soundly against me, keeping a breathing hole open. I was able to nurse and, by Providence, even had a biscuit in my pocket for Eddie."

Olivia refilled Rosetta's cup. "How did you get out?"

"Late the next day, when the wind had died back, Evie started to whimper. Then I heard scratching and feared a wolf had found us."

Exhaling deeply, she looked at Joseph. "I screamed, Eddie screamed, poor Evie wailed—"

"And I wanted run away from their noise," Joseph laughed. "We were hunting in the lull of the storm and I saw vapour coming through the breathing hole. I thought it was a deer sheltering down there."

"He dug us out, and gave us something to eat," Rosetta supplemented. "Then he brought us here, on toboggan."

"The camp overlooked that I failed to bring back a deer," he shrugged. "They were happy to have Eddie again with us."

"Joseph sent word to Annie, down at Quinte," Rosetta concluded.

"Quinte?" Wesley exclaimed. "I sledded by there, two days ago. What where you doing there, John?" Eddie stirred within his arms and he returned a gentle "Hush". Olivia drew comfort observing his care; he would be a good father.

"Annie gave birth in Quinte and stayed on to learn Haudenosaunee remedies from a healer."

"It's a mercy of God that we sit together in this hut," Olivia concluded.

"Amen," Maggie Stewart declared with a deep puff of tobacco smoke.

—62—

Wesley savoured his environment. For the first merciful moment since hearing of the attack on his home, he was at rest. With his son's chubby body pressed against him, all things seemed possible.

"Ah, Rosie, I'm so grateful to have you safe," Olivia held up her thumb, thoughtfully inspecting it. "Last time we three were gathered, we joined our blood in union."

Annie chuckled, "*Mon Dieu!* We certainly didn't start that way."

286

Rosetta smiled softly. "We bore each other through much and have become truly united."

"Closer than sisters," Olivia supplemented, then lifted her tea cup to Maggie Stewart, declaring, "Long may your chimney smoke, Maggie Stewart!" The hut erupted in laughter at the traditional Hogmanay blessing.

"I'll take that, lass." Her face lit up. "And now, I'll go see if that venison is fit for eatin'." Inviting the others to join, she lifted up the deerskin flap and went out. Joseph followed, along with Annie, John, and their baby, snug in his cradleboard.

Olivia crawled over to Wesley's side for what he hoped would be words of affection. Instead, she winked with a whispered warning, "Eddie hasn't been relieved, so take care."

Crawling back to Rosetta, she offered, "I'll take Evie and change her swaddling so you can join them at the fire."

Rosetta passed her the baby, a basket of moss, and a cradle board, then went out. Olivia quietly hummed, as she set about the task. Wesley's heart ached. They'd never spoken of the child she had carried.

"Pray forgive me, Olivia, for not being with you, when you lost our child," he ventured.

She looked up, eyes soft. "There's naught to forgive, Wessie. I did my best carrying Oliver." She paused, swallowing hard. "The Ague did its worst. What remains lies buried under the oak tree."

"Perhaps..." He bit his lip. There would be no expectation of another. Childbirth was to be feared. She'd survived, and that was all that mattered.

"Perhaps?" she frowned, questioning.

"Perhaps you have never been as beautiful to me as you are tonight," he supplied sincerely.

She returned a coy smile. "Are you making sweet with me, Captain Bryson?"

"Perhaps I am."

The door flap lifted and Annie poked her head inside.

"Come," she urged. "Roast venison is ready at the communal fire." They followed her out and found the group passing around a pan of bread, while others cut portions from the meat on the spit.

Olivia held Evie on her lap, with Eddie seated by her side. Gizzy waited at her feet for any pieces that dropped to the ground. With his family safe, Wesley shifted his thoughts to those of an investigator.

"I must learn what I can of your observations, Mrs. George," he sat beside her on the bench. "Everyone is suspect."

Her lips pursed. "I fear blame will fall on me."

"It shouldn't. I left your letter with Major McTavish, to attest to your innocence and good faith with my wife." He supplied. "And we found a man's foot print on Olivia's dress." He paused in reflection. "Yet, I don't understand why the cabin was ransacked...Might it have been an intent of abduction?"

"This is not the first time I've been hunted." Her eyes flashed in the firelight.

"I recently investigated the abduction of an African mill owner, in Niagara." He took her hand. "We'll get to the bottom of this mystery."

"I fear returning to Kingston," she added, "should there be bounty on me."

"Understandable." He released her hand. "But I need your testimony. You are the only witness of the attack. I'm confident you'll be safe with the Nortons. They are well-respected Christian people. And Mrs. McGuire seeks only your best."

"Aye." She rose. "I must defend my name. Tomorrow I will return with you to Kingston." Taking her child from Olivia, she retreated to the hut.

"Annie and I will accompany you as far as the old Mississauga path to Kingston." John sat down where Rosetta had been. "We'll stay at Quinte until summer arrives."

"That may be forever, if this horrid weather persists."

"Strange, indeed." He affirmed.

—

Annie poked her head into the hut. "Good morning! Well, maybe not. Spring hides from us in this cold. Yet, even with a thick fog about us, we must away."

Wesley roused from where he had slept by the door, Eddie nestled in his arms. Olivia stirred next to Rosetta and Evie. Outside, Maggie Stewart helped load the toboggan. With a firm hug, she wished Olivia, "*Diadhachd!*"

"Godspeed!" Olivia translated. "I know this from the Scots, up the Cataraqui."

She laughed. "We will meet again, my daughter."

A few hours later, the woman shared a tearful embrace and promised to find each other again. Annie and John headed west to Quinte. Further beyond, at Kingston Mills, Wesley hired a farmer to sled them on to Kingston.

—63—

Mrs. McGuire opened the courtyard door with joyful cheer, welcoming them into her warm kitchen.

"Rosetta's little girl," she cooed, stroking Evie's sleeping cheek. She then knelt to coax Eddie from behind Olivia's trousered leg. "And who have we here?" She looked up at Wesley.

"This is Edward Nyaweh Bryson," Olivia answered for him. "Annie and Wesley's son, and loved by me."

"Off with your wraps and I'll prepare a little something to eat," Mrs. McGuire ordered, shooing her children upstairs with a promise they could play with the babies the following morning.

They convened at the kitchen table, and she filled their cups from her brown tea pot. "I've but one room available this week," she apologized, pushing a platter of buttered bread, cheese, and pickles to them. "The lot coming from York has claim on them all after that."

"York?" Olivia looked at Wesley.

"After Easter, officials of the executive council and their clingers are holding assembly here," he confirmed.

"I will return to the Norton household, tomorrow," Rosetta ventured.

"Rosetta, the babies, and I shall share the room tonight," Olivia settled. "Wesley will stay at his officer's quarters."

"Lovely!" Mrs. McGuire tapped her fingers on the table. "The Nortons will be so pleased to have a baby in their home." She turned to Wesley, face sombre. "Rumours abound this executive council holds out promises of position and prosperity."

Wesley folded his arms. "Along with corruption, continued enslavement, erosion of treaty promises—"

"We intend to live at the Reed shanty, come snow melt," Olivia interrupted, with a tight tenacious smile.

"As long as you are in town, there's also Stephen Reed's cottage," Mrs. McGuire sat forward, lifting the chatelaine from her waist. "He's left me his key, requesting that I find him a tenant. With all this business preparing for the parliamentary assembly, I've only had time to clean it out, so it's still empty."

"Then I shall move in this week." Olivia optimistically proposed. "A bit of whitewashing can make it a cheery home."

"Do you know what has become of Stephen's baby?" Wesley asked.

"Aye...the wee girl has been put out to Picardville." Mrs. McGuire shook her head, looking down. "The wet-nurse says the poor babe is failing."

"A pity," Rosetta hugged Evie to her bosom.

"Indeed, a pity. Life is so fragile," Wesley reflected, rising to his feet. "I must report in at the garrison." He turned to Olivia. "Might I ask for your company at church tomorrow, Mrs. Bryson?"

"I've but one faded dress," she replied.

"And I can only provide Anishinaabe clothes," Rosetta came to her defence, "for I will not part with my remaining dress."

"I have a cape and bonnet that you can have," Mrs. McGuire offered.

"Over your rose dress, that would be most suitable," Wesley's eyes remained on Olivia. "People will only notice the radiance of your smile."

"You again charm me, Captain." Olivia teased.

"I'm trying," he returned with boyish sincerity.

—

Early next morning Olivia proudly walked down Grave Street, Wesley, by her side, with Eddie in her arms. She looked ahead, smile fixed, ignoring the awkward stares of those they passed. She recognized ladies from Mrs. McTavish's garden tea, but they stepped to the side, eyebrows raised, as if her embrace of her husband's child polluted their sensibilities.

At the back of the church, she refused Wesley's help, and discreetly bounced Eddie within arms to keep him calm.

"Pardon me Ma'am," Private Harris ventured, mid-service. "I used to help my momma."

With a polite nod, she passed him Eddie and slipped her arm within Wesley's.

"We shan't eat at the tavern—the money is best spent furnishing our cottage if we are to stay in Kingston," she reminded him as they left the church. "Please feed Eddie at the officer's mess; I have an errand to complete."

Marching up Grave Street, she continued past the lower graveyard, toward the cluster of six cabins that made up Picardville.

At the first and largest cabin, she rapped at the door. A haggard pipe-smoking woman opened, brushing dishevelled hair from her eyes. "What can I do fer?" she growled, the metallic stench of old gin flowing on her breath.

A garishly dressed younger woman pushed the woman aside. "What do you want?" she echoed.

Olivia met the woman's hard stare, with a lift of her chin. "I seek the Reed baby, put out here to nurse."

"Poor thing 'asn't long." She looked down the road. "You'll find 'er at Dot's—last cabin."

Olivia strode on. Finding the cabin door ajar, she entered, noting a neglected hearth. On a filthy corner bed slept a young woman, each snore emitting gin's tangy odour. The cold cabin held no cradle. Marching to the bed, Olivia reached for the trollop to shake her into sobriety, but a glint caught her eye. Charlotte's heart medallion encircled the woman's neck.

Startled she leapt back, heel striking against a wooden crate. She heard a muffled whimper. Eyes darted the room, yet she saw nothing, save the box at her feet.

She lifted its stained covering, her breath catching at the reek of urine. Tiny glazed eyes peered up within a bundle of soiled towels. She would have thought it a corpse, but the eyelids fluttered.

Snatching up the rancid bundle, she tore from the cabin, and raced back to McGuire's Inn.

"I've stolen the Reed baby!" she heaved, rushing into the kitchen.

"What have you there?" Meg McGuire looked up from reading a newspaper with Jenny Cowlie.

Jenny bustled over and peeled back the baby's fetid wrappings. "Never seen a rash so 'orrid!" she gasped. The baby's swollen torso was covered with a deep red rash, yellow pus oozing from gaping sores. "Get the kettle, Meg, and fill a mixing bowl. I'll bathe her in warm water and apple cider."

Meg McGuire directed Olivia to gather an armload of clean towels from the scullery shelf.

"Wouldn't know she's almost 7 months," Jenny murmured, setting her in the prepared bath. The baby continued to whimper, thin limbs lifting, but she gave little struggle.

"Mix three spoonfuls of apple cider in a warm cup of butter, Mrs Bryson," Jenny ordered, while gently drying the baby. "And Meg, I'll need you to cook up a milky gruel."

The baby lay passive while Jenny applied the ointment. Then, bundled loosely in a clean towel, she passed her to Olivia.

"I'm surprised Dot allowed this." Jenny tossed the filthy wrappings in the fire, leaving the soiled towels in the scullery, and lit her pipe.

"How could you leave her in the care of such a woman?" Olivia challenged. "That wet-nurse was drunk—passed out—and the child left in a box on the floor, as if waiting to be buried."

"Mercy me!" Jenny inhaled deeply of her pipe and emitted a thoughtful puff. "There's no excuse for that...and she was paid well."

"Stephen was to look in on the babe," Mrs. McGuire defended.

"He's in York, courting a lady, his child forgotten," Olivia spat out. "And what do you know of this Dot?" she pressed, resolved to learn what she could before coming forth with accusation. "Does she have family...maybe a man?"

"Her own child died just before Mrs. Reed passed," Jenny supplied. "And I know one man frequents her—a bit 'o brute."

The baby's eyes fluttered open, mouth gaping. "The baby's hungry," Olivia interpreted.

"That baby is starving," Mrs. McGuire handed Olivia a cup of the warm milky oatmeal she'd just prepared. "Spoon in only a few drops at a time, luv. That's all she can bear for now."

Olivia touched the runny mixture to the babe's lips. A pink tongue peeked out, lapping it in. "She eating!"

"Not too much," Mrs. McGuire again cautioned, "or it will come back up."

The kitchen door opened. Wesley stepped in, Eddie on his shoulders. "What have we here?" he cheerfully asked, setting Eddie on the floor. The little boy ran over, pulling at the towel and exposing the infant's tiny feet.

"Our new daughter," Olivia declared, returning the spoon to the bowl. "You surprised me with our dear Eddie. I now present you with the Reed baby."

"Does Stephen Reed know of this?" he balked.

"Did the Lieutenant know his babe was kept in drunken squalor, in Picardville?" she retorted.

"The babe must be properly cared for until Lieutenant Reed returns," Jenny Cowlie defended. "Mrs. Bryson has made herself available."

"Pray call me Olivia," she corrected.

"What is the baby's name?" Wesley asked. Mrs. McGuire and Jenny Cowlie both shrugged.

"The baby is a girl." Olivia rubbed the small foot between her thumb and forefinger. Her eyes fluttered open and Eddie giggled. "I'll call her Stephanie, for now."

"Try another wee touch of oatmeal," Mrs. McGuire encouraged. "Follow with a few spoons of boiled water."

"Stephen will be here next week, for the assembly," Wesley reminded her. "We'll ask, then what care he desires for his child."

Olivia spooned cooled water on the babe's tiny tongue.

She slept little that night. In the morning Eddie's snuggles roused her. Yawning, she got up to change Stephanie's soiled swaddling. Though exhausted, she could not be happier.

—64—

"*Oye! Lève-tôt, mon amie!*" Leo Voisin shouted, rapping on the door at Wesley's officer quarters. "I've come to 'elp, so get up."

Wesley leapt from bed and slipped on trousers to greet his old friend. Leo's son, Jean-Leo, stood behind him holding a canvas sack.

"You travelled all night?" Wesley asked.

"We arrived late and took a room at Thibault's. They're boarding my dogs...*mais*..." Leo looked about Wesley's room. "Where is your Madame?"

"I'll dress and we can breakfast with her at Meg McGuire's."

Leo lifted an eyebrow.

"We are on good terms, Leo." Wesley supplied. "You can help us move in to Stephen Reed's cottage."

They walked up Barracks street, Wesley pausing to point out the Reed cottage on Brewery Road. Again, Leo raised an eyebrow.

With a firm knock at the McGuire kitchen door, they entered. Olivia looked up from helping Lizzie McGuire feed Stephanie. "*Monsieur* Voison." She stood with a curtsy. "And young *Monsieur* Voisin."

"Jean-Leo," the young man supplemented with a polite bow. His flashing eyes caught hold of Lizzie, as he set the canvas sack against the wall. Her cheeks flushed in response.

"Sit down, gentlemen. I shall fry you eggs and bacon." Olivia bustled to the warming oven, pulling out a tray of biscuits, then filled cups with strong tea. She soon had plates of crispy bacon, sweetened with maple syrup, and eggs delicately browned.

Wesley looked up at her, impressed. "How is the baby?" he asked, sitting Eddie on his lap.

"She's doing quite well and has already soiled twice," she returned absently, with a polite head dip to Leo. "Pray forgive, *Monsieur*. We are caring for Stephen Reed's child."

He smiled broadly. "I understand, for I have a seventh child, expected this summer."

"*Félicitations!*" Wesley offered.

"And this is your son, my friend?" Leo stroked Eddie's head.

"Edward Nyaweh Bryson," Wesley returned. Olivia gave Eddie a biscuit. Jean-Leo moved around the table to sit beside Lizzie, his attention remaining respectably on the baby.

"Madame Bryson..." Leo opened, turning his attention to Olivia. "Do you know 'ow the fire started?"

"It was deliberately set, near the door to the yard. The hearth was little damaged with the yard side of the cabin most burnt," she asserted firmly. "I don't know why our home was destroyed."

"What we do know is at least three men were seen," Wesley added. "They killed our cow and ransacked our home, before setting it ablaze. Nothing of value appears stolen, for we live simply." He nodded in confirmation at Olivia.

"Ransacked?" Leo rubbed his beard. "Maybe retaliation, you t'ink? Or were they searching for somet'ing?"

"Or somebody," Wesley added. "Mrs. George, an African lady, was living at the cabin. Fortunately, she was in the barn, and escaped into the bush with her baby and Eddie."

"If looking for 'er, why tear apart your cabin?" Leo frowned. "Makes no sense."

"We have nothing of great value," Wesley repeated. "Olivia's jewellery was left, untouched, under a floorboard. No one knew of her jewels, save Mrs. George—who is completely trustable."

"No, Wesley," Olivia corrected, mouth open as if in thought. "While waiting for you to come to Montreal I wrote five jewellers, for assessment, should I need to sell them." She wouldn't mention seeing the heart pennant about Dot's neck. Let the truth be exposed by other means.

"You write whom?" Leo leaned forward.

"I have a list—kept with my jewellery." She ran upstairs, quickly returning, and laid a pearl brooch, three heavy gold chains, and a ruby ring on the table.

"Family heirlooms?" Leo gingerly picked up a gold chain, whistling through his teeth. "A valuable ensemble you 'ave—a good weight."

"Those chains were my grandfather's," Olivia explained. "More an investment than adornment."

Leo scanned the list of jewellers. "Four establishments are 'onourable," he pronounced. "Only Duvernay is questionable and is known for *les manigances*...'er...schemes." He looked intently at Olivia. "Did you receive an estimate from anyone?"

"Not one," she replied. "Perhaps they believed my items were stolen." She folded her hands, as if in prayer. "May I prevail upon you, *Monsieur*, to sell them in Montreal for a 10 percent cut? Although they are now my husband's property, I believe in Montreal, under Quebec Law, I retain the right to dispense with them as I see fit."

"And you see fit to have my friend sell them for you?" Wesley challenged, irritated by her presumption.

"At a 10 percent cut, I'm quite sure *Monsieur* Voisin would ensure a good return for all of us," she defended curtly. "And I do not think this jewellery is suitable for a Captain's wife."

Leo Voisin slapped his knee, with a hearty laugh. He directed his son over with the sack. "Your Council's grand assembly is to be 'ere. My wife is desolated by the loss of your home and possessions, and selected materials for you...per'aps not suitable for a captain's wife, but beautiful, *en tous cas*."

From the sack he produced bolts of lavender silk, cream muslin, lace trimmings, and pearl buttons.

"*Monsieur*!" Olivia exclaimed, flinging arms about his neck. "Your wife must have heard my prayers. She is a saint!"

"*Vraiment!*" He took her hands and rose to his feet. "Now let us go to the cottage and see what work is needed."

With Lizzie minding the babies, Olivia began making the cottage a home.

"The white walls would, indeed, brighten the interior," Wesley stood back, confirming Olivia's proposal. "Do you think we can partition off a bedroom, Leo?"

"Is that possible?" Olivia gasped, looking first at Wesley and then Leo.

"It can be done," Leo nodded firmly to Wesley. "I t'ink you could also build out the courtyard stoop and make a scullery."

"Have we the funds, Wesley?" Olivia clutched Wesley's sleeve.

"Another year, Mrs. Bryson," Wesley lips pursed. "My first installment of back pay should be forthcoming, and we still have to furnish this place and farm the clearing."

She nodded, compliant, choosing not to push the matter of her jewellery's worth.

They discarded the stained settee—they would have to purchase a large mattress since only a bedstead remained. Mrs. McGuire offered the cradle for Stephanie, but Eddie needed a bed. There were some dishes in the cupboard, but they would have to purchase utensils, cooking vessels, linens, and curtains.

Leaving the men to begin work, Olivia reviewed her list, and headed for the Cartwright store.

"No mattress 'ere," the clerk snapped.

"Then where does one purchase furnishings?" she shot back, shoulders braced.

"You can make it yourself, order it from Montreal, or see what you can pick up at a sheriff's auction," he curtly replied, directing attention to an elderly couple entering the store.

Irritated, she turned to leave, but her eye caught a water-stained bolt of muslin behind the counter. Boiling it with tea bags would even out the discolouration and provide for a charming house dress, she thought.

"Surely a fine establishment, such as yours, does not condescend to selling damaged fabric." She interrupted, pointing at the bolt. "I have need of rags."

"That's all it's good fer," he grumped, accepting her small complementary payment.

Pulling her cape close, she walked a few streets over to the Norton's house. Mrs. Norton opened upon her first rap of the back door. Behind her, Rosetta was dancing with Evie on her hip.

"Baby's teething and gave Rosetta a bit of a rough night," Mrs. Norton explained, placing the kettle on the fire grill. "Please join us for a cup of tea."

"That would be lovely," Olivia returned, adding "And...'er...may I have the used tea leaves to dye some muslin?" She showed them the stained bolt and detailed her plans to make a dress.

"Certainly. I can also spare a spool of green embroidery thread that will give lovely contrast," Mrs Norton offered. "And perhaps you can help adjust my dress for Rosetta?" She collected a navy calico garment from the side table. Rosetta exchanged an amused look with the shorter and wider Mrs. Norton.

"Fetch me some scissors and a stitch ripper." Olivia quickly assessed the task. "I'll narrow the skirt to add length. And, while I work, we can chat."

As she teased apart a seam, separating the skirt from the bodice, she recounted, "I've assumed care of Lieutenant Reed's baby—poor child was put out to nurse at Picardville and horribly neglected, but is now recovering."

Slipping the bodice inside-out over Rosetta's shoulders, she continued, "There's much to be done in preparing the Reed cottage for our needs." Basting the skirt to the bodice, she ran the baste down the skirt length, while describing the work to be undertaken. "Do you have recommendation of a mattress maker and a carpenter to make Eddie a bed?"

"Mrs. Mink makes good quality mattresses from her sheep's wool," Mrs. Norton supplied, pouring Olivia and Rosetta another cup of the tea.

"Washed?" Olivia asked, sipping from her cup.

"You can depend on it!" She affirmed, offering them an accompanying biscuit. "Her husband will make the bed for your little boy. I can make arrangements, if you like."

"Please do, that would be of great help." Olivia basted the cut panel to the skirt bottom. "I'll leave you to stitch seams together and finish properly, Rosetta."

"Thank you, Mrs. Norton, for the biscuit," she offered with a curtsy. "Now I must press on for I have many errands. Rosie, would you accompany me to the gate?"

Out in the yard's privacy, she turned to Rosetta and quickly confided, "I saw my heart pendant about Dot's neck."

Rosetta hand flew to her mouth.

"Aye—the Picardville prostitute caring for Lieutenant Reed's baby," she confirmed. "You are the only person I have shared this with. And, until I learn enough to bring a proper charge, we must keep this between us."

"Why not tell Wesley?"

"For the same reason Annie kept silent. I know that Wesley will defend me. I want this resolved justly, with no violence."

"It grieves me that Dot would be involved. I've cared for her when…" Rosetta's voice broke. Hand resting on Olivia's arm, she inhaled deeply. "I'll have Jenny Cowlie discreetly inquire of Dot's bawd."

"And now, I return to feed little Stephanie."

"Pray guard your heart, Libby. The child must someday return to her father."

"I won't guard my heart against a child's affection, Rosie," she returned. "They are the innocents within our consequences."

Her work done, Olivia returned home and spent the following day arranging the cottage. By the week's end, their privacy wall was complete, the cottage interior whitewashed, and their furnishings installed.

Leo and his son left, assuring Olivia he would get the best deal for her jewellery. Mrs. McGuire provided some slightly worn linens at a good price. With donations from the garrison mess she outfitted the kitchen. Mattresses and furnishings arrived earlier than expected, and cottage was ready to receive them. Wesley was proud and Olivia's happiness overflowed, for Stephanie had begun eating carrots mashed in oatmeal.

Upon moving in, Mrs. Cowlie was Olivia's first guest.

"Do you think spring will ever come, Jenny?" she asked, pouring tea. At her feet, Eddie played with wood scraps, gifted by the garrison carpenter. Gizzy lounged by the fire, while Stephanie slept soundly in the cradle.

"Never seen the cold stay this long," Mrs. Cowlie mused, hugging her hot teacup. "My bones ache."

"This will warm you." Olivia draped a plaid about her shoulders. "Laundering takes a toll, aye?"

Jenny looked at the fire, distracted. "O've done a bit of chattin' up at Picardville. Dot should stand before a judge for neglectin' Lieutenant Reed's babe."

"She almost killed Stephanie," Olivia concurred. "But our little girl is a fighter. She eats well and looks about, taking in life."

"Stephanie, aye?" She looked up smiling.

"I don't know her name. It was either that or Violet."

Mrs. Cowlie's face darkened. "Dot is heading for deeper trouble. 'Er man goes by Tom and prospects for Pierre Sabin. The man's none too smart—a bad piece of work—drinks and knocks 'er about."

"I believe he came to our clearing, last autumn, with Sabin and two others. We were alone, Rosetta and I, and had Sally not..." Olivia paused, searching for words. "Before anything could happen, Sally appeared, wielding a bloody axe and threw a headless chicken on the table. They left as quick as lightening."

"That Sally's a clever one," Jenny snorted. "Upriver, news is she's been safely delivered of a boy."

"Ian's a good midwife." Olivia heaved a deep sigh of relief. Stephanie stirred. Picking up the baby, she began feeding her spoons of warmed milk.

"And you're a good Mam," Jenny affirmed.

"Someday again, I hope to be. I lost one last autumn. Never even felt quickening."

"It never gets easy, Olivia...best you pour love into those that need it."

"I will do what I can, as long as I'm allowed."

Jenny Cowlie set her unlit pipe in her teeth and stood. Olivia suddenly grasped the older woman's hand. If she was going investigate on her behalf, she must know everything.

"I saw a necklace of mine—just a trinket—about Dot's neck. I used to hang it at the head of my bed," she divulged. "She could only have gotten it from Tom. You *must* keep that between us. Only Rosetta knows, for I haven't yet told Wesley."

"Smart to keep that quiet until we learn, 'fer sure, who's behind this," she warned. "Tom's one to follow orders, not make 'em." Frowning, she scratched under her cap, then looked intently at Olivia. "Sabin's not to be taken lightly."

A shiver ran up her spine.

"Don't fret, luv. We'll watch out for each other." She squeezed Olivia's hand before releasing it.

"As camp followers must do," Olivia returned.

Jenny's face cracked with smile. "That we do, girl, that we do."

That evening, Wesley joined Olivia for a simple meal of fried bread, dipped in egg. Looking about the cabin, contentment filled his face.

"You've a way with style, Olivia," he ventured as he stood to leave.

"I do my best, Captain." She took his coat from the hook and handed it to him.

From his inner coat pocket, he produced a pair of black leather slippers. "I believe I owe you these." He placed them in her hands and went out into the night.

Olivia closed the door between them. Though people may talk, they had an unspoken understanding of the need to heal.

—66—

Restless, Wesley paced the foyer, his striding a distraction. The hotel concierge couldn't demand he leave. He'd come at the request of Lieutenant Governor Gore.

The wait was purposeful, a means to demean him. Pausing, he looked up the stairs, his nervous vitality threatening to dissipate. Movement caught his attention; Gore's assistant was descending, his tailored suit and cravat impeccable.

"Good to see you again, Bryson." James Macauley smiled pleasantly, hand extended. "You departed York without warning. I understand your farm was destroyed by fire."

Wesley gripped his hand, firmly. "I presume, since an aide is sent in his stead, Gore hasn't time to meet."

Macauley's smile vanished and he rubbed his shaken hand. "A better suited candidate has been chosen."

Wesley returned a curt nod. "I am relieved."

"Lieutenant Reed shows promise."

"Jolly good for him." Wesley forced a smile, stepping back.

"Governor Gore still wishes you and Mrs. Bryson attend tonight's festivities," Macauley placated.

"I will, if only to please my wife," Wesley returned. "You fought with me at Lundy's, James. Let us again shake in friendship, for I hold no ill feelings." He extended his hand.

James Macauley shook with shared relief.

Leaving the hotel, a brisk lake wind pounded his back as he strode Front Street to the garrison. A weight was gone, his decision made for him. It remained only to reassure Stephen Reed that he held no resentment; friendship forged on the battlefield ran deep.

"Captain Bryson. Major McTavish is waiting to see you," the garrison sergeant stated, with a salute.

"Thank you." Wesley returned the salute.

Closing his office door, the Major ordered him "At ease," opened his desk cabinet, and poured two glasses of port. "To your continued presence, in Kingston," he toasted.

"Word travels fast." Wesley drank deep, then set the empty glass on the desk. "I have nothing but sincere good wishes for Reed."

"Your investigative observations have been praised for their thoroughness."

"Yet my recommendations were cast—"

"Opinions," McTavish interrupted. "They were mere opinions that do not meet the Council's vision for Canada. I hope Mrs. Bryson will be satisfied, returning to your clearing."

"Will I be satisfied?" Wesley bit his lip, leaning forward. "Mrs. Bryson makes the most of any situation."

"Her embrace of your Native son is indeed commendable."

"With all due respect, sir," Wesley's shoulders stiffened, "there's nothing to be commended. Edward Nyaweh Bryson is a bright, affectionate child, whom we both cherish."

McTavish sat back in his chair, his smile rigid. "Reed has returned to the Fort, preparing to buy out. It would be in your interest to assure him of your support."

"That was my purpose in coming, sir." Wesley stood with formal salute. "Reed and I have served together for many years and I will continue to support the man, though our perspectives may differ."

Upstairs, Stephen Reed's attendant opened upon Wesley's firm rap, then returned to shaving Stephen. There was an awkward silence as Wesley waited for the ministrations to be complete.

"This is a personal visit," Wesley broached. "I've come to wish you nothing but the best in your opportunity with the Council."

"Thank you," Stephen returned, dismissing his attendant. "I thought you might have complaint of my Brewery Street cottage. I understand you've let it?" He stood to wipe his hands on a towel. "I no longer have need of the clearing, so will return it under your name."

Wesley ignored the condescension. "I've come to talk of your daughter."

Stephen's eyes flashed, "I've been woefully negligent of the child." Then his face softened. "To be honest, I hadn't expected her to survive this long."

"Neither had her wet nurse." Wesley remained seated, eyes fixed on Stephen. "Mrs. Bryson has taken charge of her."

"I was not told this." His chin lifted. "Of course, I shall reimburse you for any expenses incurred."

"We want no payment," Wesley spat out. "We wish to know your intensions for Stephanie."

"Stephanie?" He repeated quietly. "Is that what you call her? Violet and I spoke of many names, but could not settle."

"We found no record of a baptism or christening."

"I have yet to..." Running a hand through his hair, he gazed out the small window. "It was enough to bury Violet."

"You did your best as a husband," Wesley ventured.

"I expected too much of my wife—she was ill-fitted for this country."

"A blameless child exists, the fruit of your union."

Stephen looked at him, eyes questioning.

Wesley nodded affirmation. "She is at your cottage. Pray come and see your little girl," he invited.

—

307

Hesitating before the cottage door, Wesley pondered how Olivia would respond to an unexpected meeting with Stephen Reed. They had never even been introduced.

Eddie bolted at the sound of the door, arms extended, Gizzy in his wake. Wesley picked up his son. Olivia looked up, surprised as Stephen entered. Quickly, she put down the spoon with which she had been feeding Stephanie, and wiped the babe's carrot-coated chin. A delicious aroma of stew, sage, and baking bread warmed Wesley's senses.

"I've brought Lieutenant Reed," he announced.

"We finally meet, sir," Olivia curtsied, her smile warm. "Stephanie is having a good feed of carrots. Would you care to feed her, while I serve up lunch? We've plenty to share."

Stephen stepped forward, eyes glistening. "I've never held a baby," he confessed.

"Neither had I until I met Eddie. Pray, sit." She threw a towel over his shoulder and arranged his hands to support Stephanie's small body. "See if you can get a few more spoonfuls into that mouth. She loves mashed carrots so much that she is turning orange. Squash gives her gas." A smile crossed her face and she covered it with her hand. "Pray forgive," she offered. "Little humans are quite uncensored but such a delight."

"Stephanie is a good name," he returned a polite smile, aiming the spoon's tip at her lips. She leapt towards it, tiny hands reaching. "Good girl!" he praised, excitedly.

He offered several more spoonfuls until she began to spit the food back. Gently wiping her face, Stephen looked about. "You've made commendable enhancements to the cottage. I would not know it as same place."

"I only wish I could have been more of comfort to Mrs. Reed," Olivia replied. "Canada is a difficult change for English ladies."

"In your brief acquaintance, I believe you did bring her comfort." Tenderly he touched his daughter's small nose.

She set out the meal and they enjoyed a leisurely lunch and afternoon of pleasant conversation.

"It is with regret that I must leave to ready for this evening," Stephen eventually declared, passing Stephanie back to Olivia.

"I'll accompany you back to the garrison," Wesley looked at Olivia with an understanding nod. "My dress uniform is there."

—67—

Jenny Cowlie looked up from her comfortable chair, empty pipe upside down in her mouth. "Yer lady is primping," she greeted Wesley, her hand gently rocking the cradle beside her. "She will be so luv'ly on your arm."

Assuming a wait, Wesley removed his coat, hanging it on a hook, beside his deerskin jacket. A moment later a rustle of silk announced Olivia's emergence from the cottage bedroom, Eddie in her arms.

His breath caught. The high-waisted lavender bodice perfectly framed a beaded-green vine about her slim neck, enhancing her pale complexion. Long thin sleeves complemented a full skirt, lengthened at the back with a slight train. Through her short hair, she had woven lavender and green ribbon, reminding him of a wood elf.

"Lavender becomes you," he pronounced, his eyes briefly revisiting the beaded vines about her neck.

She set Eddie down and curtsied. "I've done what I can—even made a bag for my new slippers." She lifted her skirt, revealing mukluks beneath.

"You're a vision," he whispered. With a wink at Jenny, he draped a cape over her shoulders.

"Mind 'yer manners," Jenny chortled, rising to close the door behind them.

Arm in arm, they walked from Quarry to Clarence Street, Olivia gathering up her skirt to protect it from the snow. Many people waited outside the hotel, hoping for a glimpse of the finely dressed people stepping out of carriages.

"I need not remind you of your previous acquaintance with Miss Maxwell," he frowned. "I had thought it amusing, only Stephen is smitten with the woman and to discourage him, now, would only deepen his affection."

"Would she be a good mother to Stephanie?" Olivia pursed her lips.

"Will she be the wife Stephen needs?" Wesley returned. "I don't know if she is even aware of his child."

A footman opened the door and they entered the grand foyer. Candlelight and greenery had transformed it from the barren space he'd paced only hours earlier.

Leaving their wraps with another footman, they entered the gaily-lit assembly hall. From across the room, Stephen dealt Wesley a firm nod. Catherine Bayard was by his side, bedecked in pale blue. She turned, displaying her elegant profile and glittering silver necklace.

"Is *that* Miss Maxwell? I hardly recall her." Olivia's voice bore a slight edge.

"No." Wesley cleared his throat. Searching for words, he settled on honesty. "That is the lady I once courted, in Montreal."

"And also, last month, in York?"

"Nay, my love. In York, I deepened in appreciation of the treasure you are." He lifted her ungloved hand to his lips, noting the slight roughness.

Catherine strode over on Stephen's arm. "So, this is your little lady, Wesley." She curtsied with lips curled in half smile.

"From your accent, I judge you hail from America." Olivia returned the curtsy.

"Indeed, I do." Catherine tilted her head. "Have you been welcomed into Canadian Society?"

Olivia exchanged a warm glance with Wesley. "I've spent little time in Kingston, but am acquainted with many fine settlers, up at my husband's clearing." Her humble posturing surprised him.

"Poor dear!" Catherine's attention shifted to Wesley. "I must assist your dear, deprived wife."

"That would be most generous, Miss Bayard." Olivia replied, stroking Wesley's sleeve.

Just then, the gathering hushed as the Lieutenant Governor entered the Hall. The crowd parted as Gore crossed the room, returning gregarious greetings to the many bows and curtsies. He glanced at Wesley, then his gaze fixed on Olivia and he stepped back with obvious surprise.

"Lady Olivia Fairworth!" He bowed gallantly. "I heard that you were in Canada."

"Major—er—Lieutenant Governor Gore," Olivia returned a curtsy and offered her hand. "Is Arabella here with you?"

The gathering milled nearby, ears opening to hear what had captured the Lieutenant Governor's regard.

"Alas, she remains in England." His fat lips pressed to her hand. "Your sister-in-law, the Countess Fairworth, was in good health when I was last at Albyne Abbey, this past summer. Her family has been most benevolent in contributing to my rebuilding fund."

"Aye...the Pinney's are indeed generous," she laughed lightly, eyes warmly fixed on Gore.

"I was not aware that Captain Bryson is your husband?" he briefly scanned Wesley, head tilted.

Olivia's light laughter answered. "Alas, I am at fault for this confusion. I have been rather discreet in my life in Canada, as an officer's wife." Instruments began to tune up in the background.

"Delightful!" His smile returned. "Lady Olivia, I insist on the privilege of a first dance."

"It would be my pleasure, sir." She glanced at Wesley. "My dear husband will most definitely be in agreement." She leaned in, whispering something with implied intimacy, causing Gore to break out in hearty laughter.

"Good man," he proclaimed, and continued his journey across the room.

"What did you say to him?" Stephen asked.

"My truth: I prefer to be known, simply, as Mrs. Bryson." She smiled at Catherine. "With my husband's support, I choose to live anonymously among settlers, and journal of life as an officer's wife on the Canadian frontier."

Catherine turned to Wesley, wide eyed. He smiled in return.

Fiddles, flutes, and drums began to play quietly, inviting dancers to assemble. Francis Gore returned to lead Olivia to the floor. Wesley had no choice but to accompany Catherine Bayard. Further down the line, he noted Stephen had found Miss Isabelle Maxwell.

A graceful polonaise followed. Amid the movements of the dance, Wesley watched Olivia, envious of her ease with the Lieutenant Governor. Gore's afternoon rejection became a fading memory.

"You didn't tell me she was titled," Catherine hissed as they promenaded the length of the dance floor. "You made me a fool," she added on their second promenade encounter.

"Take care with presumptions," he concluded at their final bow.

Lieutenant Governor Gore returned Olivia to Wesley with an appreciative bow. "Thank you, Captain, for this respite. And now I must attend to colonial business."

Immediately, Stephen Reed came over with Miss Maxwell's arm possessively entwined within his.

"Ah!" Olivia initiated a curtsy and extended her hand. Wesley held his breath—the evening was not playing out as he'd envisioned. "My husband said we are already acquainted." She turned to him, eyes twinkling. "I believe he is mistaken."

"A Scottish reel." The dance caller drew attention from the platform. "Please assemble."

"Shall we dance, Captain?" Olivia coyly tilted her head.

"I shall savour our first dance, Lady Olivia," he whispered, slipping his hand about her waist, leading her to the floor.

Around they pranced, circling, and promenading to the cheery fiddle music. Several more dances were called, ending with another sedate polonaise, to which they gracefully sauntered. Briefly allowing his eyes to drift from her, Wesley noted the envious looks of ladies who'd previously shunned Olivia at church. Word had travelled the room, yet her eyes remained on him.

The music paused and a dinner bell summoned the guests to a light repast of cheeses, pastries, and wine. Wesley and Olivia meandered to the adjacent room where decorated tables were beautifully arranged for the gathering.

Miss Maxwell and Stephen were already seated and invited them to join their group.

"It's quite intriguing that you wear Indian beads, Lady Olivia," Isabelle Maxwell offered. "How did you acquire such rustic handiwork?"

"This was a gift from a very dear friend, a world away from here," Olivia replied, lips turned up in smile. "I much prefer their simplicity over jewels."

Isabelle's forehead daintily creased. "You *do* seem familiar to me, Mrs. Bryson," she challenged. "Perhaps you are the one confused?"

"I think not," Olivia's eyes flashed, chin lifting. Wesley recognized his wife's ire, and held his breath. "My husband recalls a woman coated in mud, caterwauling by the *Coteau-du-Lac* canal, demanding I remove her boots." She paused with a playful head shake. "The besom even threatened to have a switch taken to me."

Isabelle Maxwell's hands flew up, covering flushed cheeks. "Your husband is indeed mistaken!"

"Ladies!" Pierre Sabin suddenly loomed over them. Bowing with flourish, his boot heels clicked.

"Who allowed you in?" Stephen Reed objected.

Pierre looked past him, eyes resting on Olivia's necklace. "Quaint," he murmured.

"Again, we meet, *Monsieur* Sabin!" Isabelle marvelled. "Have you just arrived from Montreal?"

"Indeed." Sabin pulled up the chair and sat on Isabelle's other side. Stephen drummed fingers on the table, unable to contain his irritation.

"I 'eard the bush had its way with you, Madame Bryson. *Quel dommage*...everything destroyed by fire."

"Not everything, *Monsieur* Sabin," Olivia deflected, hand sliding about Wesley's arm. "We have friendships, fine music, and good food."

"And wisdom." Stephen Reed leaned forward, clasping hands together. Wesley's stomach churned with the rising tension.

"Alas, I must leave this fine group," Olivia touched her lips, stifling a dainty yawn. "No longer can I dance the night through, with babies to attend to." She stood, and Wesley followed, relieved.

Slowly they sauntered back to the cottage, the moonless night dark and crisp. "I would have liked to stay, Wessie, but the cost of the company was not worth enduring."

"I fear Miss Maxwell may have felt the same of Lady Olivia Fairworth Bryson," he laughed. Stopping before the cottage door, he released her arm.

"And what of you?" she reached out, retaking his hand.

He swallowed hard; any lingering uncertainty vanquished. Tentatively he leaned forward, his lips brushing against her cheek. "Libby," he whispered, "please believe me when I declare my love for you has been..."

"Kept safe?" She looked up at him, studying his face.

He nodded. "Always."

"Then hurry back to me." She opened the door.

Jenny Cowlie was fast asleep on the settee. Olivia gently touched her shoulder and she sat up with a snort.

"I shall ensure you safely home, Jenny," Wesley offered, wrapping a plaid about her shoulders.

"Always the gentleman," she grunted.

"Shan't be long, Lady Olivia," Wesley promised with a courtly bow.

—68—

Jarred awake by a sharp pounding on the cottage door, Olivia grasped her husband's shoulder with a firm shake.

"Wake up, Wessie!" Wrapping her quilt about her, she leapt up, peering through the window curtains—it was Stephen Reed. Quickly, she donned her rose dress.

"What's his bother?" Wesley groaned, pulling on trousers before opening the cottage door.

Stephen stumbled in. "Pierre Sabin and I are to duel at dawn."

Olivia lit a candle. Stephanie stirred, and she picked her up with a quiet, "Shush."

"Surely you didn't challenge him over his sham ventures?" Wesley pulled up a chair, inviting him to sit. "Blame me for that folly."

"He took liberties with Isabelle—attempted to kiss her." Stephen remained standing, legs apart, hands on his hips. "Then he called me a fool for coming to her defence. One affront led to another. When I challenged him about our investment, he dared call me a liar."

"Call it off!" Wesley heaved deeply and began pacing the floor. "Blame it on the wine or some other excuse, Stephen."

"I'm no coward!"

"You're a ruddy fool!" Wesley bellowed and threw his hands in air. "Isabelle Maxwell is not worth it."

Eddie sat up in his bed, rubbing his eyes, looking about.

316

"Please! You're waking the babies," Olivia pleaded, kneeling by Eddie's bed to stroke his head.

"I'll not concede honour, Wesley." Stephen stepped back, towards the door. "I have not come to seek permission, but to ask you to stand with me." He opened the door and turned. "Sabin accepted my challenge. I have written my will and we meet, at dawn, at the Upper Burial Grounds. William Jarvis will arbitrate."

Wesley threw on his old deerskin coat.

"Don't let him duel!" Olivia cried out.

"My life is not worth it if I don't." Stephen interjected, his eyes intent, yet sorrowful.

She watched from the window as they disappeared around the corner of Thibault's Inn. Behind her hung the lavender dress, lifeless on a bedroom hook. How quickly life could deteriorate!

We women take care of each other. She'd kept from Wesley seeing her pendant about Dot's neck. And she'd not given air to its connection with Sabin's employee, Tom, and the fire. Annie had also withheld Pierre's act of debauchery from Wesley. They had presumed keeping these offences would protect him from rash chivalry, yet pride is a fragile master. This night she had failed. Teasing Isabelle Maxwell had caused insult and pride to flare. Now, someone would die. She must stand with Wesley, and accept responsibility for this death challenge.

Wrapping Stephanie in a shawl, she gathered Eddie in her other arm and hastened to McGuire Inn. Mrs. McGuire was in the kitchen, planning the day's meals.

"Oh, dear Lord!" Meg exclaimed, upon hearing the news. "I'll care for the babes, but don't go alone. Fetch Rosetta—it's almost sunrise!"

—

Rosetta was already dressed and tending to Evie when Olivia knocked at the door. Without hesitation, Mrs. Norton offered to care for the baby, entreating them to pray for peace.

Hand-in-hand they raced up Rear Street, continuing on to the Upper Burial Grounds.

Six men stood in a group. Olivia recognized all but two: a well-dressed gentleman and a soldier who held open the dueling pistol box. Pierre Sabin and Stephen watched the gentleman—the arbitrator—as he primed both guns and restored them to the box. Wesley and Major McTavish stood off to the side. Focused on the proceeding, no one turned, at the women's approach.

"I give you one final opportunity to resolve." The arbitrator looked at Stephen and then Pierre Sabin.

Both men returned a grave nod. Stephen squared his shoulders and Pierre lifted his chin.

"Very well, gentlemen. Stephen, you've issued challenge and Pierre, you accepted. Since neither of you wish to reconcile, we shall proceed," the arbitrator declared. "You each will have only one shot and there is to be no dumb shooting. I'll permit no firing into the air, to add further insult by implying the other unworthy of the challenge." Then he gestured for them to step forward and select a weapon. "May the judgement of God determine the outcome."

Olivia held her breath, tightening her hold of Rosetta's hand.

Stephen Reed and Pierre Sabin stood back to back and cocked the pistols. They began their walk, the arbiter counting out their paces.

"...eight, nine, ten!"

The men whirled. A single shot rang out.

Stephen's hand jerked, pistol dropping beside him. Eyes wide with shock, he collapsed. Wesley rushed to his side and knelt, holding an ear to his mouth. A deep red stain slowly spread across Stephen's chest.

"His pistol did not fire," Olivia gasped. Darting over, she picked up the weapon and repeated to Wesley. "It did not fire!"

"Put it down, Libby!" Wesley shouted, bolting to his feet. "Judgement has been decided."

"There was no judgement—Stephen had a faulty pistol." She turned to face Pierre Sabin. "You have escaped judgement."

"Libby!" Wesley implored. "Put it down."

"I charge you to defend your man, Pierre Sabin. Tell me how his woman wears my necklace, taken just before my house was torched."

Sabin stepped towards her. "Tom's a cursed fool—that proves nothing!"

"But I know what you did to Anwaatin Nyaweh, Wesley's first wife. I have people who can confirm her testimony."

Sabin took another step towards her. "*Le mot d'une Sauvagesse?*"

"Who's the savage?" she hurled back. "You raped a pregnant woman!" The pistol trembled in her hand. "And what would you have done to my son, had your henchmen caught him?"

Sabin's face reddened as he threw his empty pistol to the ground.

"I hold you to account for your many abuses. Arson, attempted abduction, theft, rape, fraud..." Heart racing, her fingers tightly gripped the pistol handle. "What say you, Pierre Sabin?"

With a ferocious growl, he leapt at her, seizing her throat. Stumbling back, she raised her hands, desperate to pull him loose. Her vision blurred amid a clamour of fists and shouts. Then a thunderclap shattered with blinding fury and she fell into blackness.

Wesley pressed her hand to his lips and breathed a quiet prayer. Her future grim, every breath mattered.

Three days had passed. Concussed and still unconscious, her condition was unknown.

"May the Judgement of God determine the outcome," the arbiter had invoked.

Stephen had fallen. Snatching up his unfired pistol, Olivia had lambasted Sabin with accusations. Arson and attempted abduction he already suspected, but rape? How could he have let this happen?

He had frozen with a mix of confusion and rage when Sabin had rushed forward, seizing her throat. As her hands flew up in protection, Stephen's pistol had fired. All present had attested she had merely held the weapon's handle, struggling within his tightening grip. At such close quarters, half of Sabin's head had blasted away, covering Olivia in his blood.

Hang fire had done the deed—the judgement of God.

Lingering in this unconscious state, Olivia risked dying of thirst. Yet Wesley refused to entrust her to a military medic. Death would only be hastened by their blood-letting.

Mrs. Cowlie took over her care until Annie and John arrived from Quinte, bringing Meena, an aged healer. Maggie Stewart accompanied them and took charge of the babies at McGuire Inn.

"Wesley, you need to rest." Annie interrupted his thoughts. She stood at the cottage's bedroom door.

Releasing Olivia's hand, he looked up. "Outrage for Cornwall's women infuriated me, yet I was so oblivious to the suffering of those I care about..." his voice caught. "I did not prevent the same from happening under my roof. Can you ever forgive me Annie?"

"You need not ask, my brother." Her dark eyes met him. "I could not tell you, for fear you would try to exact justice and end up planted in the Upper Ground.

"Must Olivia pay?" He looked back at his wife's bandaged face.

"She is yet with us," Annie supplied. "And Rosetta needs something of you."

Wesley quietly rose, leaving her to tend his wife. Rosetta sat by the hearth, in Wesley's leather chair.

"How is she?"

"Still with us," he supplied. "And how are you, Mrs. George?"

"Would you accompany me to the garrison, Captain? Major McTavish requests my presence and I wish to have a witness."

Wesley glanced back at the room where Olivia lay. Annie nodded encouragement.

"Aye," he confirmed. "I must talk to him, as well."

"Olivia and I have shared many challenges Captain," Rosetta offered as they stepped out. "She's a woman that don't quit."

A half chuckle escaped, and he tucked her arm within his. "You've been a friend to both of us, Mrs. George."

"I'll allow you the privilege of addressing me as Rosetta," she returned, as they turned down Barracks Road. "You can trust that if there is any way back, Olivia will fight to take it."

"How can we guide her back, Rosetta?"

"We talk as if she's with us, and we pray, Wesley."

They stepped inside the barracks. The Major expected them and they were ushered into his office. Wesley pulled up a chair for Rosetta, then remained standing at attention.

"At ease, Captain, and take a seat," McTavish ordered. "How is Mrs. Bryson?"

"No change, sir," he pulled up a chair beside Rosetta.

"I presume Mrs. George is in your confidence," McTavish asked.

"Mrs. George is," he replied, exchanging a quick nod with her.

"We have much to discuss," McTavish cleared his throat. "Regarding Mr. Sabin, I've agreed with William Jarvis's witness that a hang fire of Lieutenant Reed's pistol ended his life. There will be no mention of Mrs. Bryson."

"What of the accusations Mrs. Bryson made, sir?" Rosetta asked.

He shot her a hard look, firmly repeating, "There will be no mention of Mrs. Bryson. The matter is closed." Again, he cleared his throat. "I must also inform you, Captain, that Lieutenant Reed left a witnessed will in his quarters."

"He mentioned he had written a will," Wesley concurred.

"He left you his property and all possessions, to dispense towards the care of his daughter, Stephanie Violet Reed. And he named you as the child's guardian." McTavish sniffed.

"Mrs. Bryson and I will care for the child as our own," Wesley returned.

"And now to Mrs. George." Looking intently at her, McTavish retrieved a letter from his drawer.

Wesley recognized the letter Rosetta had written to him at Six Nations. So did Rosetta.

"That was private correspondence with Captain Bryson!" She sat forward.

"Correspondence substantiating your loyalty to the Brysons," McTavish answered, with a polite nod. "I wish to acknowledge that the many contributions made by your people, are greatly appreciated, Mrs. George."

"What do mean by 'your people', Major?" Her voice took on a sharp edge.

He inhaled deeply, clearly vexed. "Mrs. George, I—"

"Are you talkin' about *we* woman who give birth, alone in shanties, deep in the frontier?"

His face reddened. "I simply mean—"

"We Loyalists, p'raps?" she again interrupted. "*We* who come to this land of our own choosing, to live freely under rule of law and not rule of might?" She sat back with a defiant thrust of her jaw and a finger wag. "I'll not have you drive an axe between loyal British subjects, whatever our origin."

"I did not mean to offend, Mrs. George," he interjected, far too harshly, trying to gain control.

"Don't you dare use that tone on me!" she retorted. "Irish, Scot, Negro, Native, or English, we are one under God."

Wesley sat back in his chair, enjoying Rosetta's advantage.

"Mrs. George, pray listen to me." The Major folded his arms; she returned a firm nod. "I had been directed to secure your assistance on the frontier. Your ability to transcribe observations to page is remarkable."

"That was private correspondence." She dealt a side glare at Wesley.

"Captain Bryson submitted this letter as testimony of your loyalty to both Crown and life under it." McTavish repeated, inhaling deeply. "I have been requested, by the Council, to set up a mutually favourable arrangement with you." He rose to his feet, hand offered. "Pray accept my apology for any implied condescension."

"It wasn't implied...it *was* condescending," she corrected, rising to accept his hand. "Now stop these useless pleasantries, and describe what you require of me." She sat down.

He returned his chair; hands folded on the desk. "There has been an influx of American lumbermen and their retainers within the Grand Ottawa River basin—a motley mix of rebels, rogues, and lumbermen. We need discreet observation of their activities, for our military presence is limited there, at present." He paused to ensure her engagement.

"Go on," she prompted.

"Soon, military settlements will be established, as a buffer to the south. And a canal is proposed to open up and fill the region with loyal British subjects. Until that day, being alerted to suspicious activity will be of obvious value."

"It will be years before order is firmly established there," Wesley remarked.

"Aye," McTavish confirmed. "That is why we need someone there immediately, to provide observation."

"Which am I? Rogue, rebel or lumberman?" Rosetta challenged.

"You are a Loyal British subject," McTavish returned, "both trustworthy and capable."

"Thank you," she tilted her head, with a gracious nod. "We *can* have a mutually advantageous relationship. You need a spy. I need to start a business. These are my terms." It was her turn to pause, ensuring his engagement.

"I am a God-loving Christian mother, and expect to be treated as such. I require a suitable companion to maintain my reputation. We must have a proper cottage, with a few acres for gardening. I'm sure you can release a few acres of clerical reserve into my possession, and provide the necessary structure for both residence and business."

"How would you accomplish espionage work, under such idyllic circumstances?" McTavish's voice lifted, tainted with amusement.

Rosetta's lips softened in smile. "In running a dry goods store or trading post I will hear much of the comings and goings of the Ottawa Valley. I will also gain access to certain homes through my excellent cooking. My companion would add to knowledge of the area as an experienced midwife and laundress."

"Mrs. Cowlie?" Wesley asked.

"Exactly. We would be observing in plain sight. Thus, we both need compensation for our good work."

"I'm impressed." Major McTavish leaned back, clasping hands behind his neck. "You have thought this through."

"I have prayed this through," she corrected.

—70—

Light trickled deep into the dry well, pale shades of grey swirling around her.

Ears ringing, head throbbing, she looked up. Faint voices travelled within the light, over the rim, to where she lay at the bottom of the shaft. She tried to reach up but her arms were tied down, unable to move. Did they know she was there?

"Help me!" she cried out. "Pour down some water! If I could lick moisture from the cold stone floor, it would relieve my tormenting thirst."

Instead, they threw down brimstone, robbing her of breath as if to scare her away. The light pulled away, leaving her behind and forgotten. She could still hear them, farther off now.

"You can't leave!" she pleaded, trembling with cold. "I'm still here."

"He bringeth them out of their distresses. He bringeth them unto their desired haven."

The voices seemed closer, almost discernible this time. Had they heard her?

Tongue thick, hands flailing, her fingers dug into cloth. Clutching tightly, desperate to keep them near, she groaned.

"A cup of water, quick, Jenny!" Annie's voice penetrated her darkness.

Drops touched her tongue, creeping down her throat. Swallowing hungrily, she begged for more, like Stephanie clinging to life. Reaching up, she grasped a woman's braid. Arms drew her within a woodsy-smoky scent.

"Rest, sister," Annie soothed, trying to pry her fingers loose from her hair.

Fearing a return to darkness, Olivia held fast. Cold water splashed over her face and neck.

"Mercy woman," she rasped, "White woman can't fight."

"Olivia Bryson can," Annie chuckled. "But relax your grip so you don't spill the cup again, sister."

Head throbbing, she ran her hands over the thick bandages covering her face. Again, the cup touched her lips and water trickled into her mouth, as a rough towel gently dried her off.

"Drink slow, luv. So's you don't choke."

"Jenny?" Her hand found the space, in her teeth, where the pipe usually rested.

"Aye. You're remembering."

"What happened?" she gasped, throat aching.

"You were injured at the duel."

"Pierre Sabin and Stephen Reed?"

"Rest, luv. Answers will find you. You've returned, and that's all that matters."

Olivia lay back on soft pillows. An aroma of tangy sage comforted her senses. Her thoughts drifted in muted tones, then sharpened again: something terrible had happened. Dread filled her, unleashed in hazy memory. Reaching out she touched Wesley's beard.

"I'm here Libby," he whispered, lips caressing her fingers.

"My head is bandaged." She pulled his hand to her breast. "What happened?"

"What do you remember?" he gently invited.

"Running up Battery Street, babies in my arms."

"The babes are safe in the care of Maggie Steward, at McGuire Inn. She came up from Quinte with a healer, Meena."

"For Pierre Sabin and Stephen Reed?"

"Both succumbed at the duel," he quietly supplied, "a shot through Stephen's heart, another through Sabin's head."

"Horrid." Her hands returned to the bandaging. Cloth wrapped around her forehead, covering her eyes. "How was I injured?" she asked. "Give me the truth."

"Stephen's pistol did not fire. You lifted his weapon from the ground. It fired when Sabin leapt at you."

"I...I...killed him?" she faltered, heart racing.
He gripped her hand. "You merely held the pistol. Both Major McTavish and William Jarvis, the arbitrator, attest that it was the hang fire of Stephen's weapon that killed Sabin. Had he not attacked you, he would be alive."

"Had I not picked up the gun, he would be alive." She clutched his hand. "God has judged me."

"Had he not attacked you, he would still be alive." Wesley repeated, his voice strong with authority. "Do not presume to speak for God, Libby. Before the duel, William Jarvis pronounced, 'May the judgment of God determine the outcome.' We must, therefore, trust in Sovereign Providence and live with the consequences of our part in it."

She struggled to understand his narrative. "Why did he attack me?"

"You held him accountable for many misdeeds."

"Oh, Good Lord!" Her chest tightened. "I spoke of things not mine to share...they'll not forgive me."

"They love you, Libby, as do I." His beard brushed against her cheek. "Rest. Tomorrow, Meena will remove your bandaging."

—

She heard footsteps approaching her bed. "Who's there?" she cried.

"I'm looking in on you," Rosetta answered. "Making sure you're still awake. Annie's beside me."

Olivia reached out. Annie took one hand, Rosetta the other. "How are the babies?" she asked.

"Maggie Steward is doing a fine job," Rosetta answered. "She's taking care of Evie and little Johnnie, too."

"Annie?" A firm squeeze of her hand replied. "Pray forgive me for disclosing Sabin's offenses."

"Let's only talk of us, Olivia," Annie diverted. "I came here, from Quinte, by steam boat—a swimming Iron Horse. I had to fight panic remembering my nightmare."

"Iron horses will open up this country," Olivia sighed. "I have seen them in England. You had to see their great strength for yourself."

"We'll have to learn to rein these iron horses to do good," Annie returned. "I am going with John to Six Nations and will live among the Haudenosaunee."

"We each have our battles ahead," Rosetta stated flatly. "Jenny Cowlie and I are locating up north, to the Grand Ottawa River, and will serve as British spies. "

"Of my people?" Annie asked.

"Never," Rosetta laughed, yet her tone bore a hard edge. "American lumbermen, opening up the country, chopping down forests—"

"Destroying our hunting grounds, ruining fishing streams, and chasing us off as if we are vermin," Annie softly accused.

"I've been promised a small cottage and a few acres. And I will have a business."

"Does that make it right?" she countered.

"It is not right," Olivia soothed, addressing the hurt in Annie's voice. "It's what Rosetta must do to survive." She hugged both their hands to her breast. "Promise me that we will remain sisters, whatever path we must take."

Their arms surrounded her. Her eyes burned with the tears that could not flow.

"Tomorrow I travel by dog sled to the Grand Ottawa," Rosetta quietly offered, her hand slipping from Olivia's. "With the lingering cold it is still possible to use the road from Elizabethtown."

"That's the Smuggler's Road," Annie chuckled. "A good start for spying on Americans." Her hand slid from Olivia's grip. "John and I leave by steamer for Niagara, tonight. Yes! Again, we will use an Iron Horse engine. Meena will stay until she has done what is possible for you, and Maggie Stewart declares she will stay on to help with the children."

"Why would she?" Olivia's curiosity piqued. "I hardly know her."

"Because she likes a warm house, wearing nice dresses, and sleeping on a bed." Annie stepped away. "She has lived both the Anishinaabe and European ways, so will be of great help to you."

Their footsteps retreated from her room. "You leave without a goodbye or Godspeed?"

"I never say goodbye," Annie answered.

"Nor will I," Rosetta promised.

—71—

"Are you ready, dear wife?" Wesley's stomach knotted with anticipation.

"Will it matter if I am marked horribly?" her voice trembled.

"We would then be a well-matched couple," he answered with an ill-attempted jest.

"You can grow a beard, but what am I to do?" she whimpered.

"Perhaps grow your hair and surround your face with curls," he quickly supplied. Encouraged by her spunk, he gently outlined the edge of her chin with his fingertip. "I am grateful you are alive, that's all that matters."

They would live for tomorrow, not for what yesterday had taken.

"This will hurt," Meena warned. "Skin will peel off where it is dead." Gingerly, she began unraveling the bandaging, then paused. "What is underneath should continue to heal but it will be sensitive."

Olivia grasped hold of Wesley's hands.

"You're strong, my child," Meena affirmed, gently teasing away bandaging. Bits of skin clung to the wrap, exposing pink beneath. "No weeping sores are visible." She nodded at Wesley. "Looks clean, so no need to use maggots."

Olivia gasped. Wesley was relieved.

"Keep your eyes closed," Meena ordered. With a soft clean flannel, she washed Olivia's forehead with boiled water. Olivia winced, sucking air between her teeth.

"Every breeze, every touch will be painful. But this will not last long," Meena explained, turning to Wesley, "Ah...the joyous pain of life." She smiled, and began tenderly washing Olivia's eyelids, repeatedly murmuring, "Promising...promising." Then she motioned him to lift a candle to Olivia's face.

Though the forehead was discoloured, her skin had not puckered. "The burn did not go deep," Meena pronounced.

"Open your eyes, Libby, and tell us what you see," Wesley coaxed.

Olivia's eyelids fluttered and she quickly turned away from the flame.

"Does it hurt?" Meena asked.

"It's too bright—can't look at it," she whispered.

Setting the candle on the side table, Wesley gently squeezed her hand. "Can you see me?"

Teary eyes looked at him. "I can, Wessie, though my right eye blurs." Biting her lip, she asked. "What do you see?"

"I see the beautiful, courageous woman that I will spend my life with," he answered honestly.

"Scarring may remain on your forehead." Meena peered at her face. "A few tresses of hair should cover it."

"We will have tales to tell our grandchildren," he encouraged. "How three women spent a winter in a cabin, strengthening each other, as corn, beans, and squash planted together."

"Which am I?"

Meena snorted. "What is your wife, Captain? Corn, beans, or squash?"

"Her spirit is too full to be limited to a single vegetable, Meena." He answered, cautiously.

"You should go into politics," she chuckled. "Now let your woman rest. Tomorrow will be difficult for her."

Wesley kissed Olivia's hand. "I received a note from Leo Voisin. Your jewellery will fetch a tidy sum, enough to purchase a small farm at the foot of *Mont Royal*, in Montreal, should you decide."

"Why Montreal?" Meena asked.

"Because the *Coverture* condition of married women does not apply in the Lower Canada. And, as a married woman, Olivia Bryson can retain property, conduct business, and even vote for me, should I enter politics, as you have just suggested."

"Just as the Haudenosaunee." Meera affirmed.

"Montreal?" Olivia protested. "Weren't we to stay in Kingston, and farm Billidore?"

"There will be talk regarding the duel," Wesley calmly supplied. "To stay in Kingston is not wise."

"Then you've requested transfer to Montreal?"

"I intend to pension out and sell any land grant I receive." He paused. "Pray forgive me, Olivia...I've spoken more than you are ready for. Try to rest."

"How can I rest? You've made plans without my knowledge," she groaned, attempting to sit up. "Why can't we live in the Reed shanty?"

Sauntering into the bedroom, Gizzy collapsed on the rug beside the bed, her girth noticeably larger. "My word, Wessie! What have you been feeding that dog? She's gotten so fat!"

"We may have puppies. I only hope it's not by a wolf." He pressed his lips to her hand again. "Pray understand, dear woman, until today I was unsure if you were blind. The extent of your concussion is still unknown. Please accept that I have had to make plans to accommodate you."

"You're not letting your wife rest, Captain," Meena urged. "Tomorrow we will try to get her walking."

Olivia sank into the pillows.

"Slowly, Libby," Wesley soothed. "I want you strong and by my side." He left with Gizzy, entrusting her to Meena's care.

—72—

Ridiculous—to be expected to sleep? She'd missed so much entrapped in darkness.

And to Montreal? She had longed to return to the city for her wedding day, her desire set on shopping, dancing, and promenading about the city. None of that mattered now. She missed the peace of the woods, the soothing gurgle of Billidore Rifts, and the scamper of Eddie's feet, playing as she rocked Stephanie to sleep.

Drawing back her quilts, she shifted her legs to the edge of the bed. Ears ringing, a tight band encircled her head. With a strong push, she touched her feet to the floor and tried to stand. The room swayed as though she were back on a ship in the mid-Atlantic. Her stomach lurched, propelling its contents onto the floor, her legs buckling beneath her.

"What are you doing?" Meena raced in.

"I tried to stand," she sobbed, "I want to get on with life."

"You are concussed, woman." Meena scolded. Helping her rise, she guided her into the main room. "Lay on the floor while I clean you and the room."

"What's wrong with me?" Olivia cowered, covering her eyes, from the room's light. "Everything is swirling about. My head throbs terribly and ringing of my ears won't stop."

"It is to be expected." Meena's voice softened. Washing her face, she replaced the soiled night gown with one of Wesley's night shirts.

Back in bed, tears slipped down Olivia's cheeks. "Everyone is so kind to me."

"Enjoy their gift—someday you will do the same for others," Meena encouraged. "Now, I'll go make you toast and tea."

Returning with a tray, she sat on the edge of the bed while Olivia ate. "I saw many soldiers in the war concussed from cannon fire and gun shots," she explained. "You must not be hard on yourself for it takes time to heal."

"You were on the field of battle?"

"As you are, now," Meena smiled firmly. "So be patient with the journey back to life."

Already, Olivia felt her head lightening.

"Your husband is a good man," Meena continued. "He needs a strong woman to stand with him; a woman who takes care of herself and her family."

"Will my right eye continue to weep?"

"You will get used to it. And if that eye still troubles, an eye lens may help." Meena set the tray on a nearby chair. "Enough effort for today. Tomorrow, you will stand and take a few steps, with my help." Straightening the bed quilt, she tucked a pillow behind Olivia's head. "No more questions. Let your mind be still."

"Is my dog to bear pups?"

Meena laughed. "Most definitely."

"Someday I hope to bear a child," Olivia confided.

"Hope is a gift of the Creator," Meena answered, picking up the tray. "Now, try to rest."

Olivia closed her eyes, her heart content.

—73—

(Montreal—Autumn, 1817)

Leo Voison leap out of the way of a fast-approaching *calèche,*

"*Mon Dieu*! Such 'urry 'des days in Montreal." He turned to Wesley with a smile. "My son is 'de worst…intends to marry 'dat eldest McGuire girl."

Wesley pulled shut the large wooden door of the *Hervieux et fils* law office. With a firm twist and shake of the knob, he ensured the door locked and returned the key to the safety of his coat's inner-pocket

"Lizzie is but a child," he acknowledged, adjusting the shoulder strap on his satchel of work papers.

"No younger than Marie-Jeanne, when she married me."

"But he has no means—" Wesley swallowed his words. Olivia's family had accused him of same, years ago. "The lad's smitten, aye?" He instead offered, with sympathy. "She's a fine young lady. Shall I enquire about work, on his behalf, or write a letter of commendation to Meg McGuire?"

"Meg saw the wisdom in 'dis union, before I." Swiping a sulphur stick against the wall, Leo lit his pipe with a punctuating flare. "She's business woman." Blowing out the flame, he smothered the stick under his boot. "Love 'as motivated my son to train Gizzy's puppies for sled work, and win a contract to carry winter post between *Montréal* and York. And..." Leo chuckled. "...'e arranged, with Quinte Haudenosaunee, to carry fur down to St. Regis, for American trade. Someday my boy will be richer than me!"

"Resourceful," Wesley laughed. They set out west, along *Rue Notre Dame*.

"*Bien oui*! They'll wed come spring, *mon ami*." Leo looked up at the darkening sky. "Hervieux must trust you, to let you lock up."

"I'm always last to leave." They turned north, onto the road up Beaver Hall Hill. "Hervieux counts my years at Cambridge and military investigations as qualification toward barrister. Instead of the usual 7 years to read law, I shall be qualified in two."

"Much to learn in two years." Leo paused at the rise, looking back toward the city. "Good 'ting they tore down 'de old walls. *Montréal* pours out, and will soon reach *Mont Royal*."

Torches moved about at *Place D'Armes*, soldiers beginning their night watch. In the dark, faint light escaped through the windows of houses lining Beaver Hall Road. Church bells rang, gathering families for their evening meal. Above, his family awaited his return.

"There are not enough English civil law lawyers, to meet Montreal's needs," he continued, "hence Hervieux's desire to hasten my training."

Leo emitted a low whistle. "Right place; right time, eh?"

"Better than expected," he affirmed. Continuing on, they crossed St. Catherine Road. "Last year, everyone was selling off property because of failed crops. This year, the city reaches north, and property is in great demand. Thank you for advising Olivia to buy land with the sale of her jewellery. She's made a fine profit selling a few acres. I never thought her a woman-of-business—she's surprised me."

"Ah, yes," Leo emitted a loud guffaw. "I bring a letter for Olivia, from Marie-Jeanne—some'ting to do with women's fine undergarments. *Mon Dieu!*" His voice fell to a whisper. "I never t'ought I would talk about such matters as a business venture."

"Well there's money to be made. Montreal's growing population of merchants and tradespeople have gracious, ambitious wives. Olivia teaches seamstress skills at the Grey Nuns orphanage, to provide those girls a means to earn a living. A harvest awaits...but we'll leave that to our ladies, aye?"

Entering the open reach, near the foot of the mountain, a blustery autumn wind assailed them. Wesley glanced to the east, where the Native village of Hochelaga had been, 300 years ago. Then he looked west, towards the St. Sulpice monastery and the ruins of a French "mountain fort" that once repelled Iroquois raids. Tonight, no cart traffic traversed this upper road across Montreal Island.

Crossing the road, Wesley savoured the glow of moonlight on his large slope-roofed stone cottage. He opened the wooden gate at the back of the property.

"I thought I could train her, like a recruit, to be my wife," Wesley confided. "I did a poor job, Leo." He clicked the latch back into place. "*Grace à Dieu!* She stuck by me through my bumbling attempts."

Leo's hand rested on his shoulder. "Best to merge with strength, my friend, and not fight it."

"A lesson I continue to learn," Wesley supplemented.

Leo patted his back. "Much better than giving orders, eh?"

"Aye. Olivia manages our home and farm, for I've enough burden with my law studies."

"She keeps a cow and pigs?" They passed two out-buildings bordering the small farmyard.

"That's Olivia's hennery," Wesley explained. "She's hired two Garrison children—a lass and her younger brother—to help with chickens and house chores." He stomped on the backdoor stone step then thrust his boots through the door scraper, to rid them of mud.

A freckled girl opened the door, with a quick curtsy and twinkling blue eyes. Gentle light drew them into the cottage, along with the delicious aroma of chicken stew and baked apples.

"Hallo, Captain," she greeted. "I 'ope yer day went well, sir."

"Thank you, Elsie. It did, indeed," he returned. "Please take *Monsieur* Voisin's wraps and place them in the guest room."

Bolting across the room, Eddie leapt into his arms, with an exuberant "Papa!"

Olivia stood at the settee, where she'd been reading a picture book with Stephanie. Repositioning the baby to her hip, she whipped off her house cap, and quickly drew curls over her forehead. Her face brightened with smile; Wesley's heart warmed with sympathy. It was over a year now, and the scarring faded, but she was still self-conscious.

"*Monsieur* Voisin!" She strode over, hand extended. "Welcome to our home."

"*Madame.*" Leo kissed her hand, with a polite bow. "This is your little boy?" He caressed the tiny cheek. "Marie-Jeanne said it went well for you."

"With the help of her midwife," Olivia supplemented. "Meet our little George; Eddie and Stephanie's brother."

"You named him after the King?" Leo broke into a grin, his hands held out to take the baby.

"He's named after our dear friend Mrs. George," Wesley laughed.

"Ah, *Madame* George," Leo nodded. "She 'as a strong business sense and sends me many fine furs." Gingerly balancing the baby, he drew out a letter from his pocket, and gave it to Olivia. "My wife sends you a business proposition."

"I will study this letter with great interest," she committed, pocketing it within her skirt. "We had great fun tossing around ideas when last together, birthing George." Hand tucked within his elbow, she led Leo to an inviting table.

Maggie Stewart came out from the kitchen, bearing a platter of freshly baked bread rolls and set them next to a steaming tureen of stew. "Come, children, it's time to eat," she bid in Algonquin.

Eddie helped Stephanie down from the settee and brought her to the table.

"Is that Algonquin, I 'ear?" Leo turned to Wesley, with a raised eyebrow.

"*Oui, Monsieur.*" Olivia proudly lifted her chin. "I intend to surprise Annie when next we meet." Taking George from Leo, she laid the baby in the cradle, covering him with a quilt. "Now let us eat, and you can tell us all your news," she invited.

They sat around the large wooden table, Wesley at the head, and Leo at the honoured seat opposite him. Elsie and her younger brother perched on a bench with the children, while Maggie and Olivia sat on the other side.

"Please do the honours, Mrs. Bryson," Wesley took Olivia's hand.

"It will be my pleasure, dear husband," she returned. And in halting Algonquin, she thanked the Creator for their bounty.

Book Four— Rebels, Rogues, & Lumbermen

Chaudière, Upper Canada (July 1819)

—1—

"That fool's been sitting on our bench for near an hour." Rosetta George lifted the corner of her kitchen window curtain for another glimpse. "I believe he's yet to sleep off his effects from last night. I suppose drunks are to be expected, living near Mary's Tavern."

"Mary should 'ave ferried the blighter back to Wrightsville. Folks might get a wrong impression if you let him sit there," protested Jenny Cowlie, her protective companion and business partner. Returning her unlit clay pipe to the space between her teeth, she muttered, "I'll take the broom and move 'im on."

"By the cut of his coat and thigh boots, I'd say he's an English dandy on an adventure," Rosetta hesitated. "Lost his hat, too."

"Doesn't look that worse for wear," Jenny grunted. "Probably 'asn't been at it long enough."

"What you lookin' at Mama?" Four-year-old Evie held up her arms. Rosetta picked her up, allowing her daughter to see what had drawn their attention. "Poor man needs bed, Mama," she innocently pronounced with a bob of her thick brown curls.

The man turned to the window, as if he had heard, his expression dazed. Thin and clean-shaven, sharp features complemented unruly black hair in need of a comb. Rosetta dropped the curtain, tittering with embarrassment. "Oh dear, Jenny! I've been seen. Now we must deal with him."

"Shall I set the dogs on 'im?"

"Keep the dogs inside," Rosetta countered. "He does look like he could use a meal—if only to sober up. I'll put him to work, a'fore I feed him, and teach him to earn his way." She set Evie down, grabbed the axe, and ventured out the front door.

At her approach, the man rose on unsteady feet and attempted to doff his missing hat. "A colleen of colour," he greeted.

"A drunken Irishman," she returned with a curt nod. "Either get out of my garden or make yourself useful! I have a load of firewood that needs to be chopped into kindling and you look like you could use a meal. Split me a good measure of kindling and I'll provide a plate of beans and biscuit with a hot cup of sobering coffee."

He frowned, one side of his mouth turning up in apparent confusion.

"You'll have to get used to hard work if you intend to survive in this country," she provoked, handing him the axe.

"Aye," he winced, accepted the implement, and tottering to the woodpile. Removing his jacket, he undid the cravat of his expensively tailored shirt, and gingerly set up a log for splitting.

Inside again, Rosetta sat at her corner desk, intent on finishing up her weekly report. Evie took out her brightly painted wooden farm animals and began lining them up on the floor.

Chop. Chop. The axe haltingly began its work, then stopped abruptly.

Jenny opened the back door to holler at him to get back to work. "Rosie, come quick!" The man was outstretched, face down on the ground, his long thin body still.

"Mercy, Lord!" Rosetta marched across the yard, Evie in her wake. The dogs leapt out, barking excitedly. "Wasted and passed out!" she stormed. "I won't have that in my garden."

Kneeling beside the still body, Jenny rolled him over and rested a hand on his forehead. Shivering, with teeth chattering, he moaned in pain. "Poor fella is burning up!" She leaned down to smell his breath, then looked up face somber.

"Lord have mercy on us, Rosetta! The poor blighter's not drunk—he's got the Ague."

Printed in the USA
CPSIA information can be obtained
at www.ICGtesting.com
JSHW052314071023
49554JS00002B/6

9 781999 239343